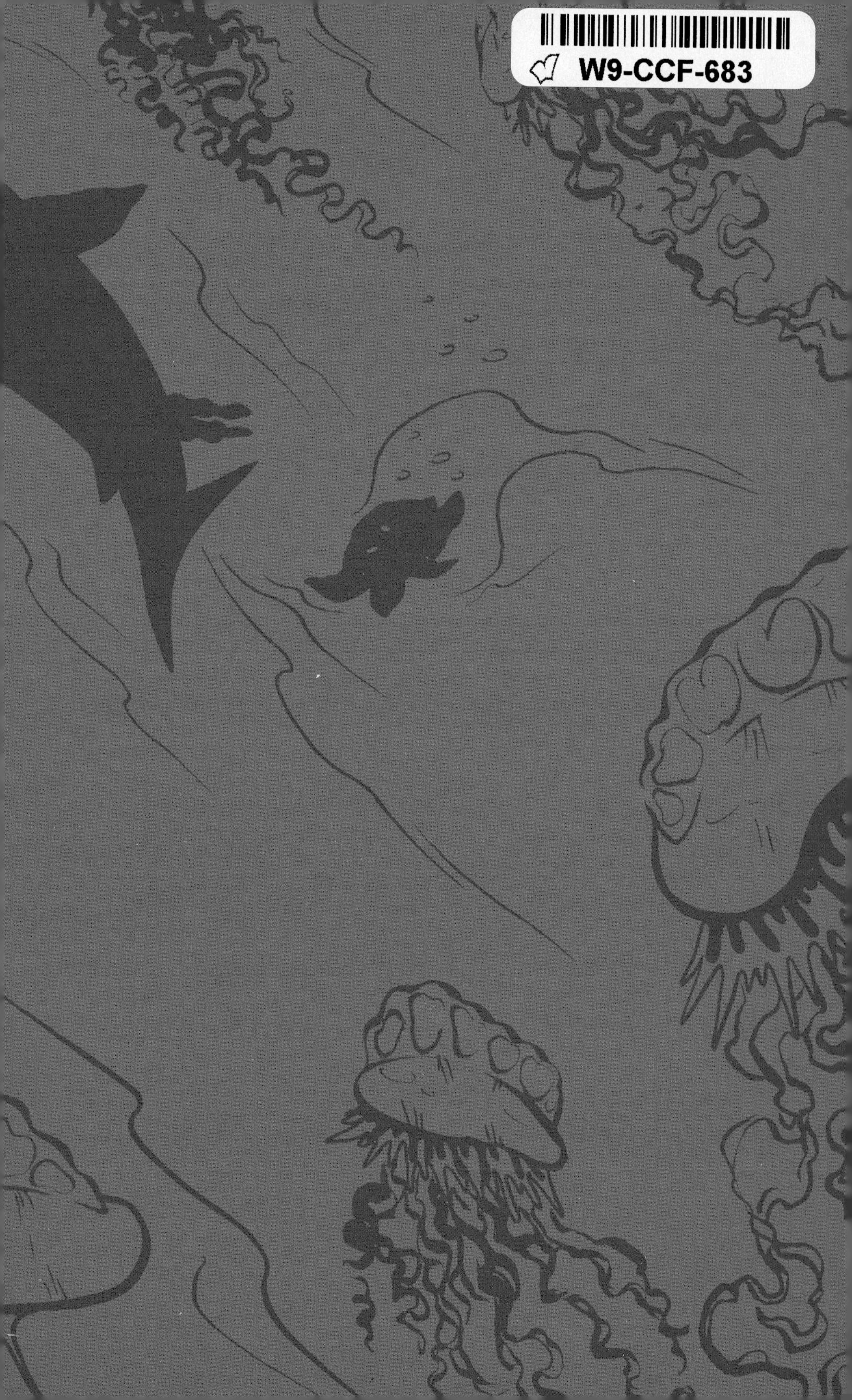

XOC

THE JOURNEY OF
A GREAT WHITE

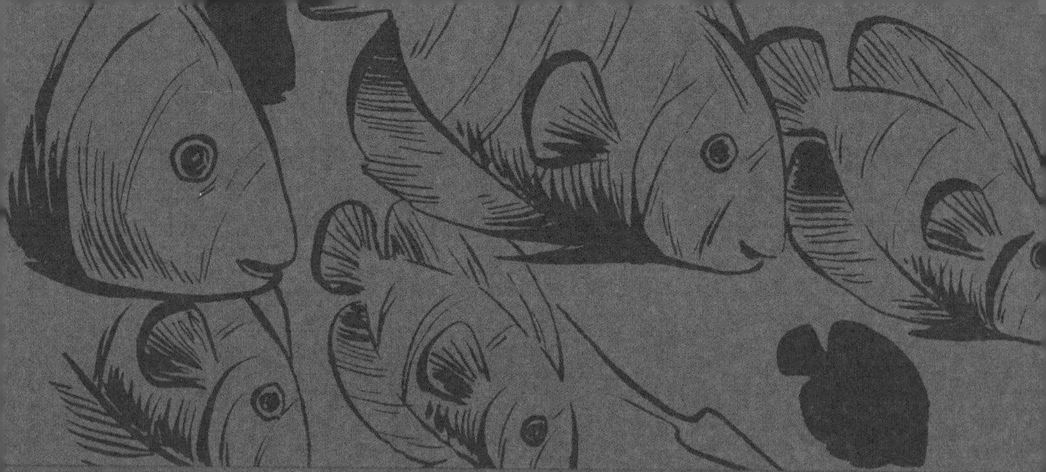

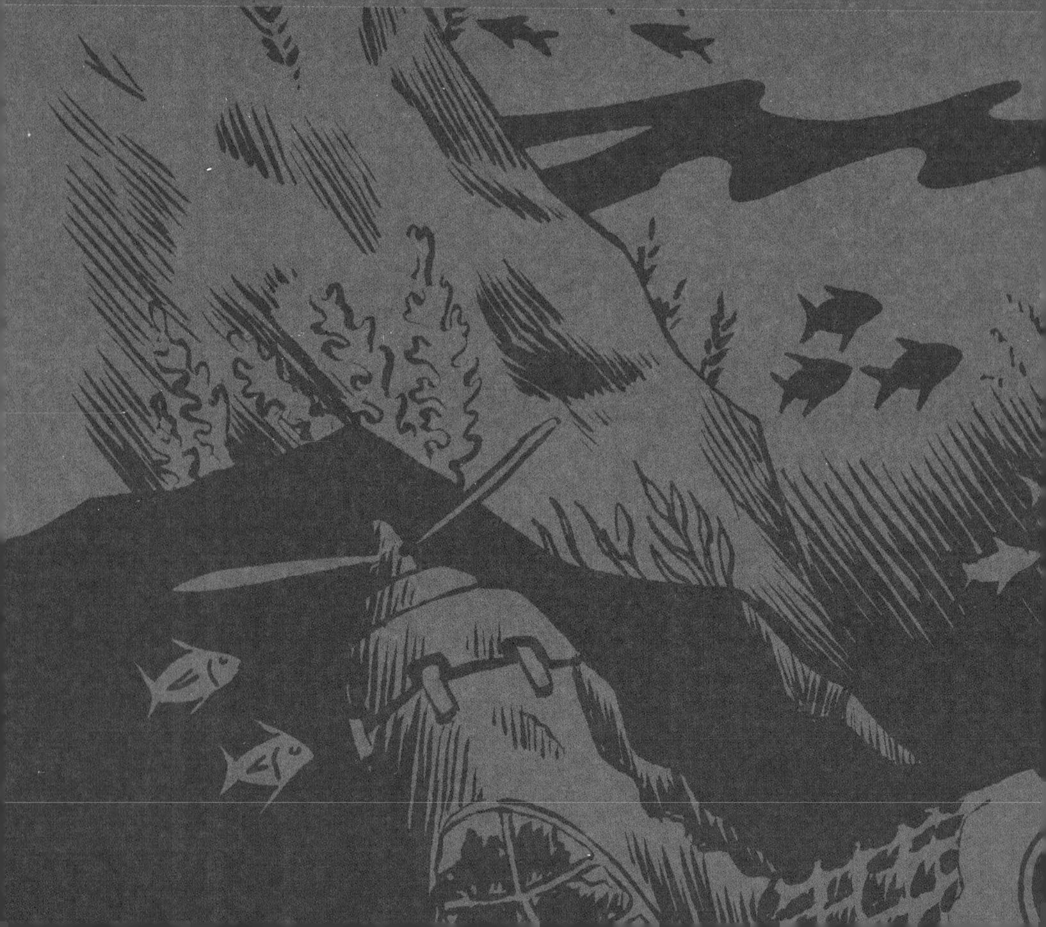

XOC

THE JOURNEY OF
A GREAT WHITE

by MATT DEMBICKI

Colored by
EVAN KEELING

Lettered by
ED BRISSON

Book designed by
JOSH ELLIOTT

Edited by
JILL BEATON

AN ONI PRESS PUBLICATION

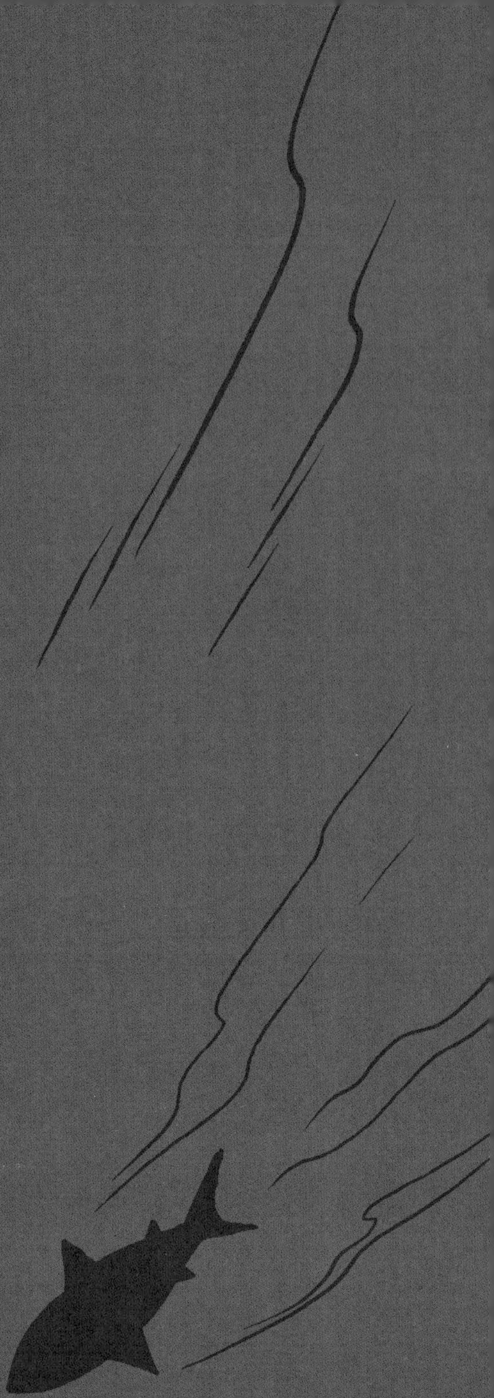

Published by Oni Press, Inc.
Joe Nozemack, publisher
James Lucas Jones, editor in chief
Cory Casoni, marketing director
Keith Wood, art director
George Rohac, operations director
Jill Beaton, editor
Charlie Chu, editor
Troy Look, digital prepress lead

XOC: The Journey of a Great White, July 2012. Published by Oni Press, Inc. 1305 SE Martin Luther King Jr. Blvd., Suite A, Portland, OR 97214.

ONI PRESS, INC.
1305 SE Martin Luther King Jr. Blvd.
Suite A
Portland, OR 97214
USA

www.onipress.com
http://xocing.blogspot.com/

First Edition: July 2012
978-1-934964-85-9

Library of Congress Control Number 2012930401

10 9 8 7 6 5 4 3 2

Printed in China.

XOC (pronounced "shock") is an ancient Mayan word for demon fish (though there are other translations) and likely the origin of the English word shark. The story behind how it entered the English language is rather interesting. Capt. John Hawkins was said to have brought a carcass of a beast that killed some of his crew while they were pirating off the coast of Mexico. He heard some of the local people call it "xoc" and he apparently brought that term back to the Old World with him. The specimen was exhibited in London in 1569 right outside a shop. According to Languagehat.com, a broadsheet post about the fish read:

"There is no proper name for it that I knowe but that sertayne men of Captayne Haukinses doth call it a sharke. And it is to bee seene in London, at the Red Lyon, in Fletestreete."

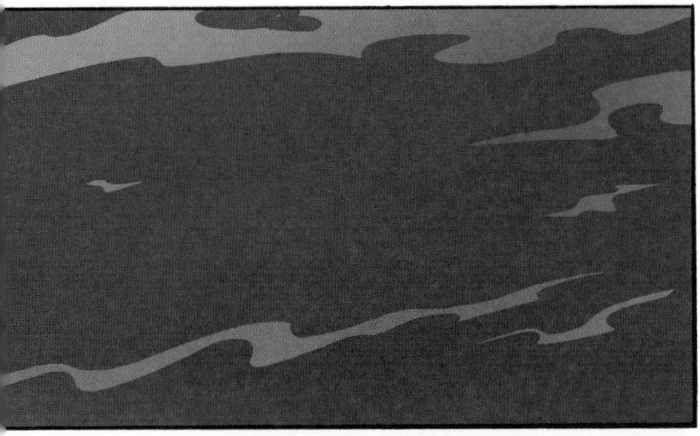

It is dawn. Light cracks the cold, dark waters of the Pacific.

As the sun rises, its eams wedge leeper and wider into the ocean.

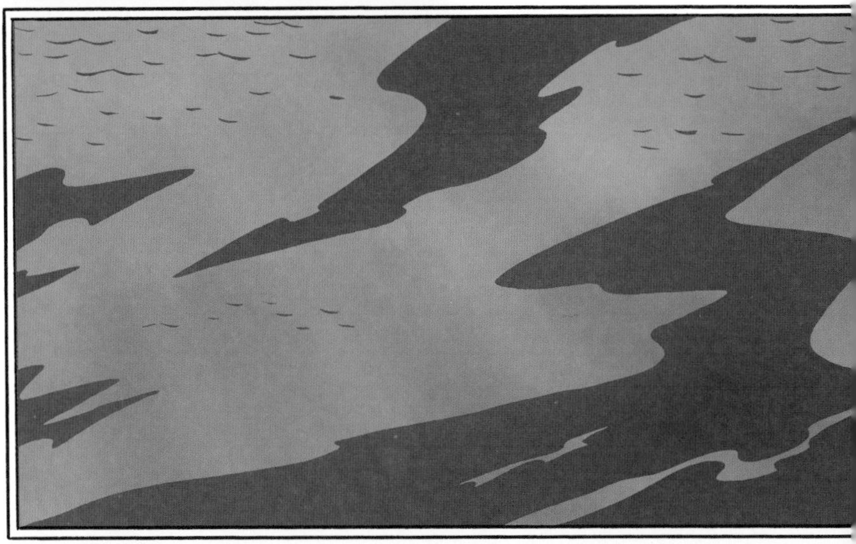

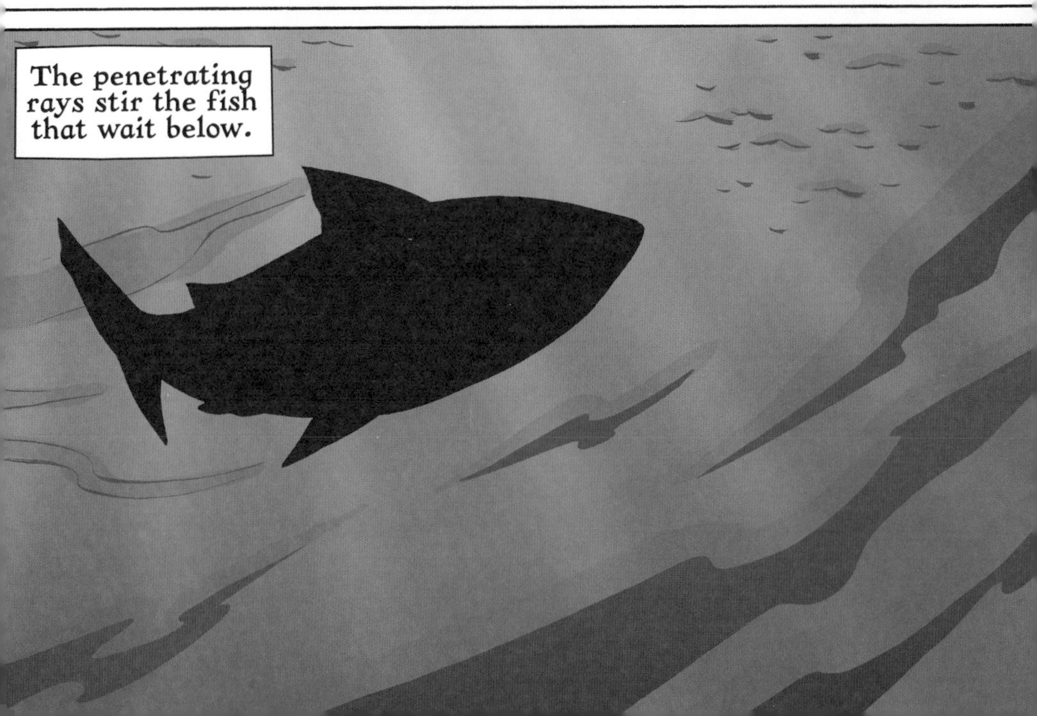
The penetrating rays stir the fish that wait below.

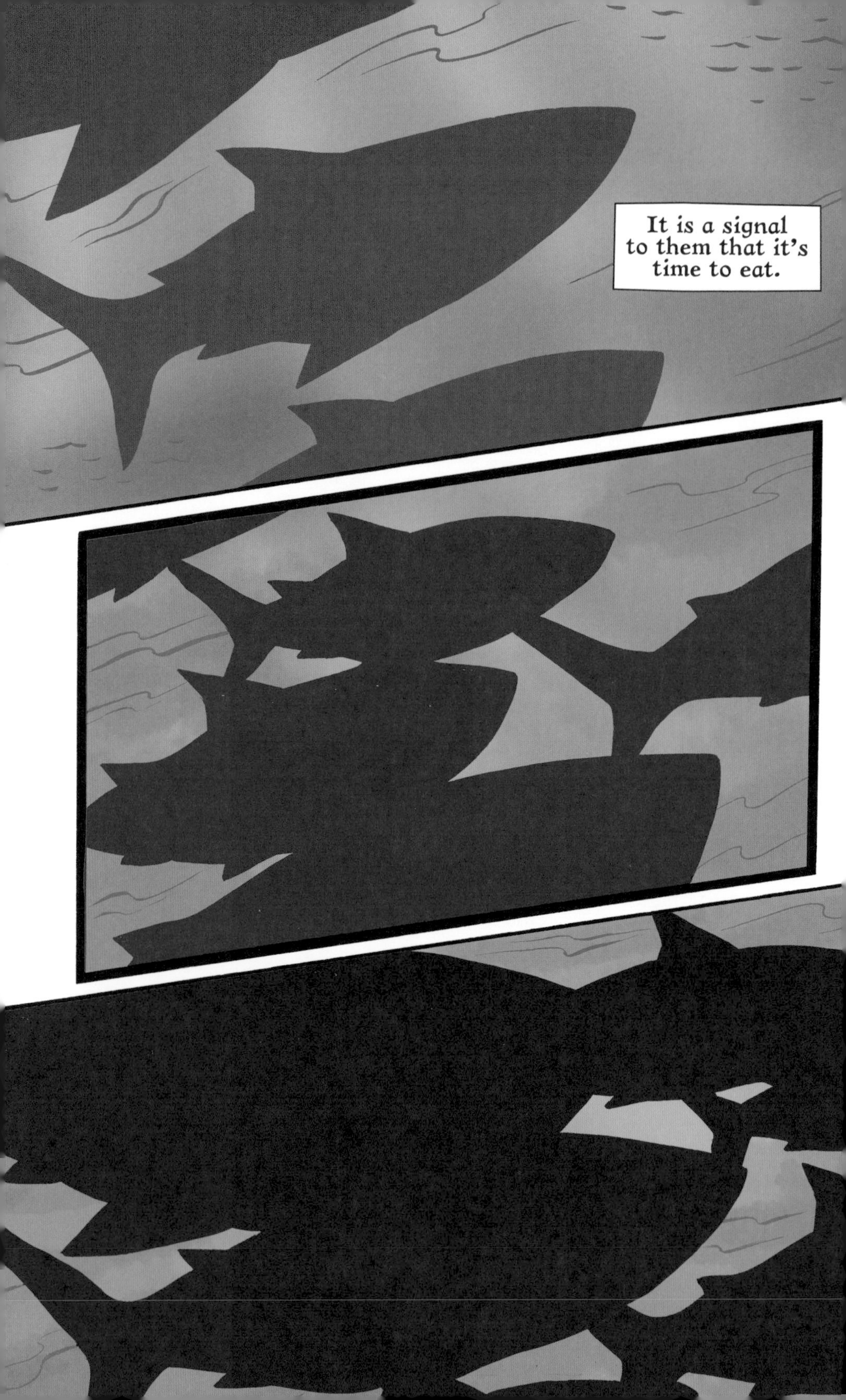
It is a signal to them that it's time to eat.

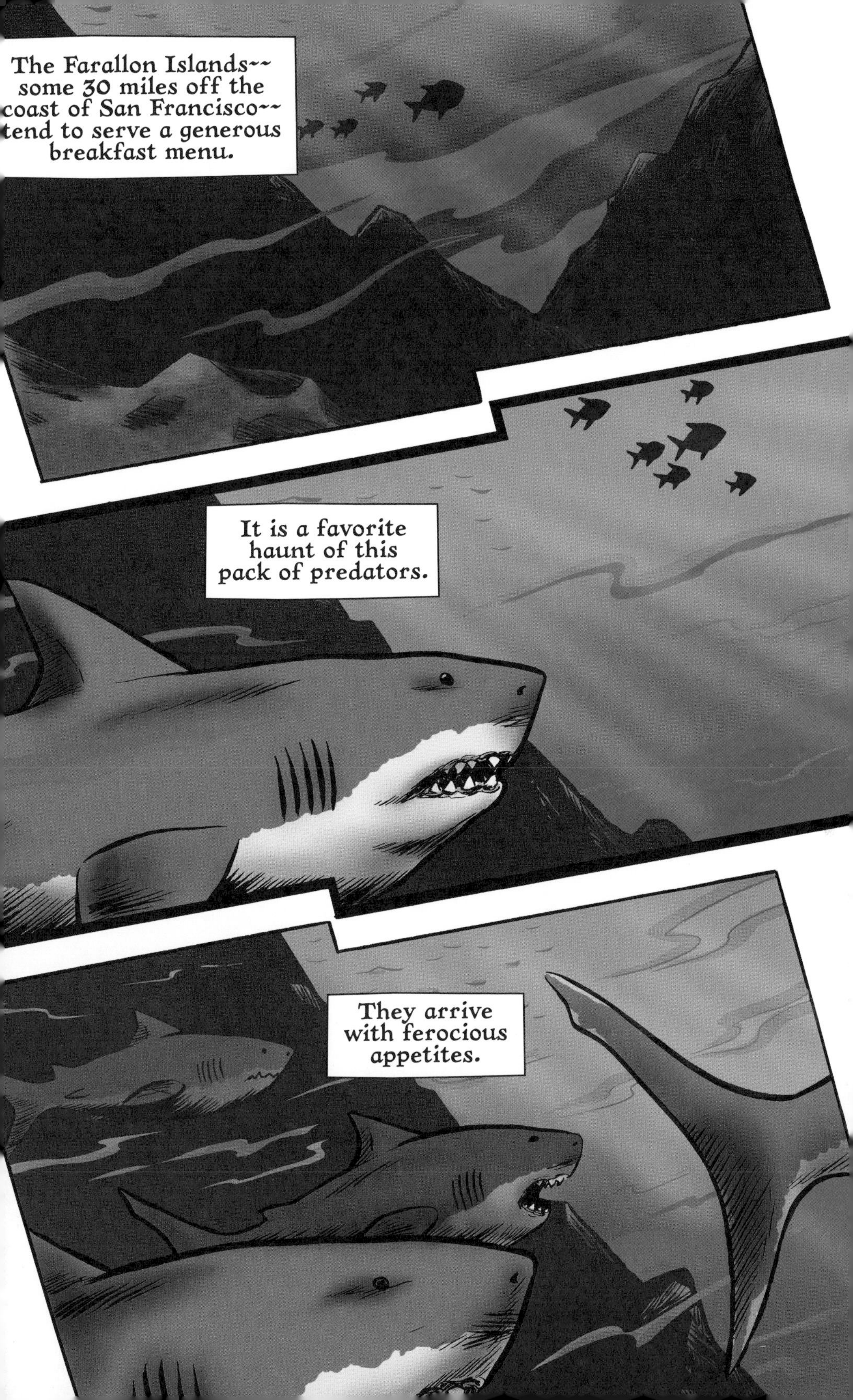
The Farallon Islands--some 30 miles off the coast of San Francisco--tend to serve a generous breakfast menu.
It is a favorite haunt of this pack of predators.
They arrive with ferocious appetites.

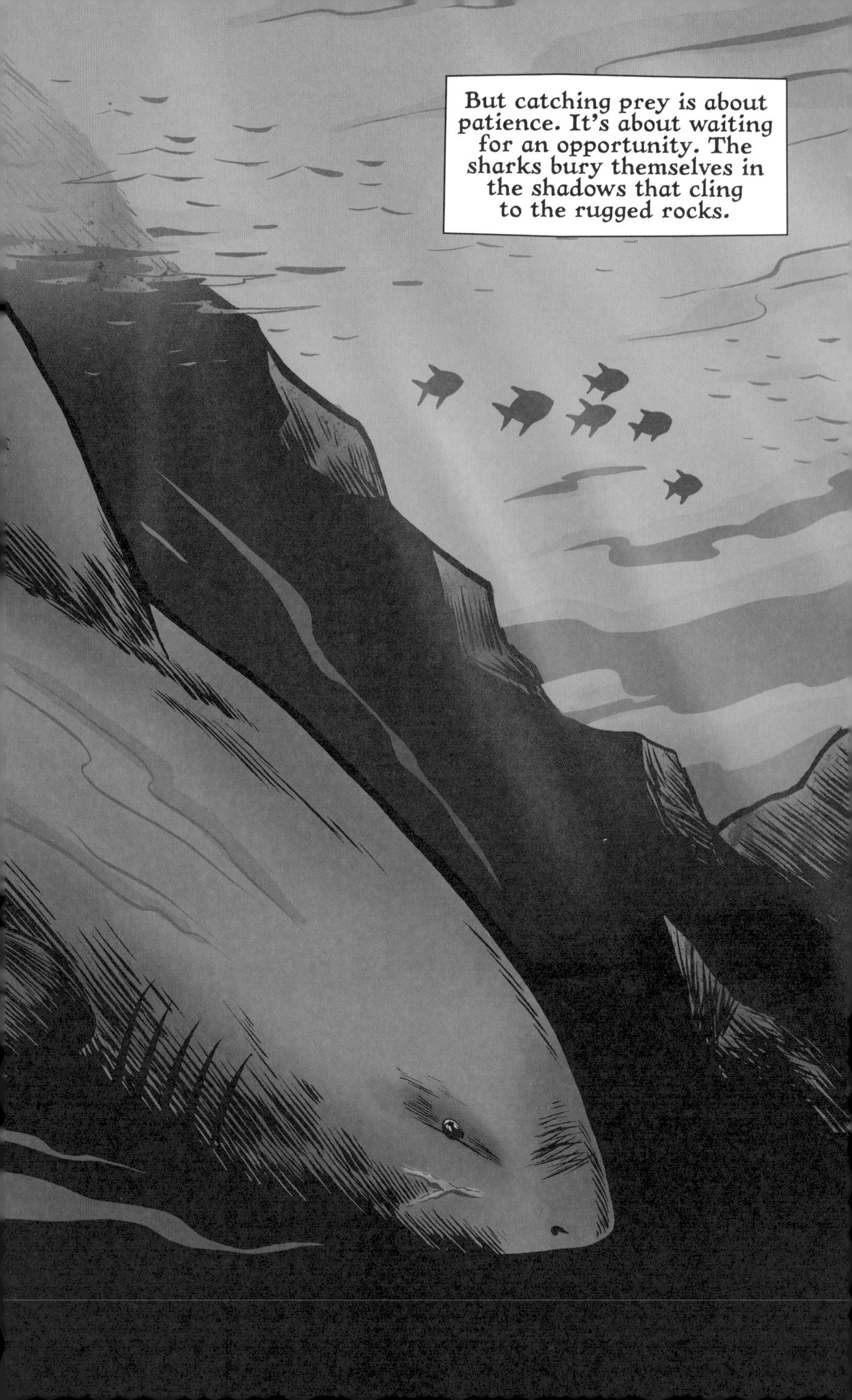
But catching prey is about patience. It's about waiting for an opportunity. The sharks bury themselves in the shadows that cling to the rugged rocks.

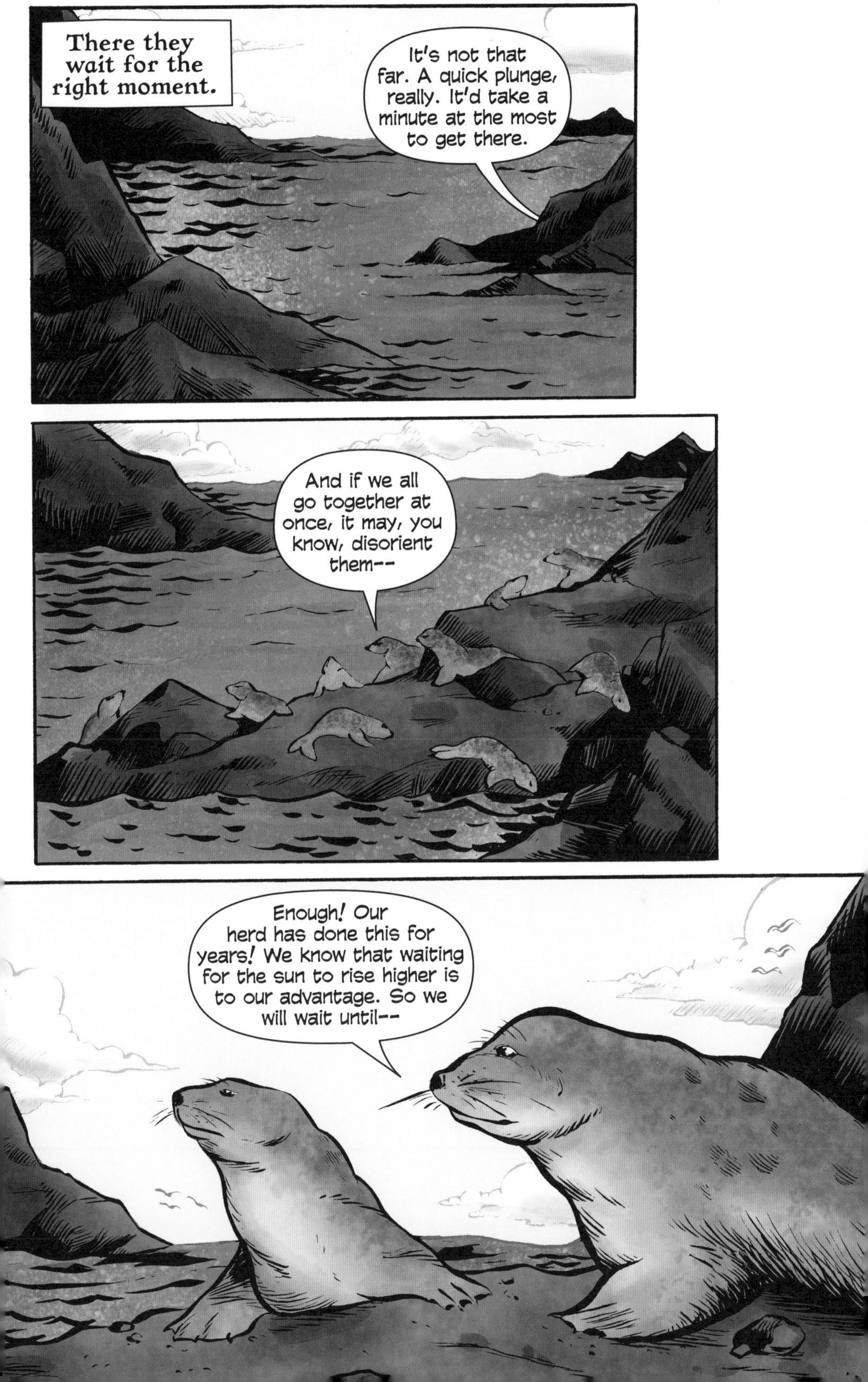
There they wait for the right moment.
It's not that far. A quick plunge, really. It'd take a minute at the most to get there.
And if we all go together at once, it may, you know, disorient them--
Enough! Our herd has done this for years! We know that waiting for the sun to rise higher is to our advantage. So we will wait until--

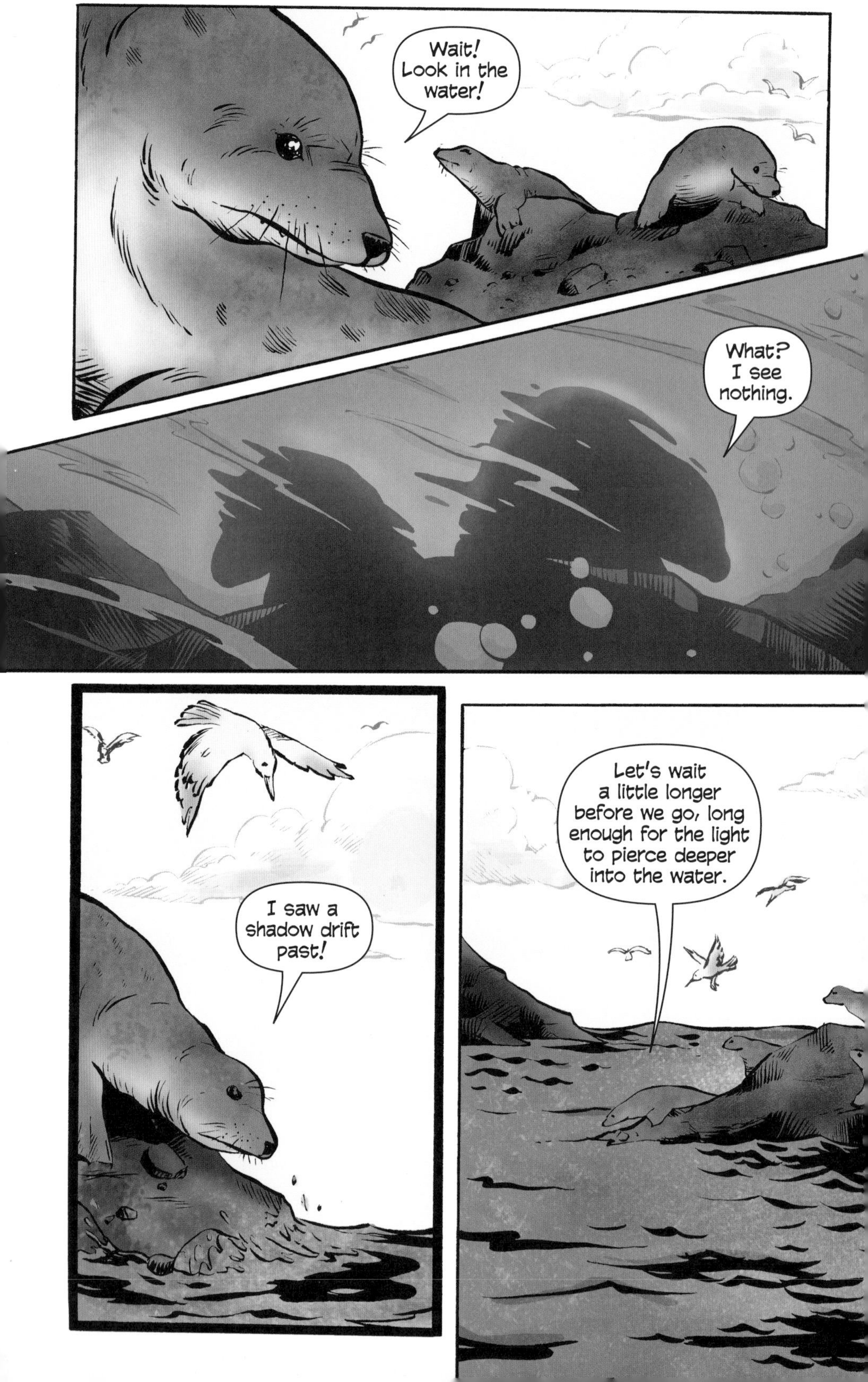
Wait! Look in the water!
What? I see nothing.
I saw a shadow drift past!
Let's wait a little longer before we go, long enough for the light to pierce deeper into the water.

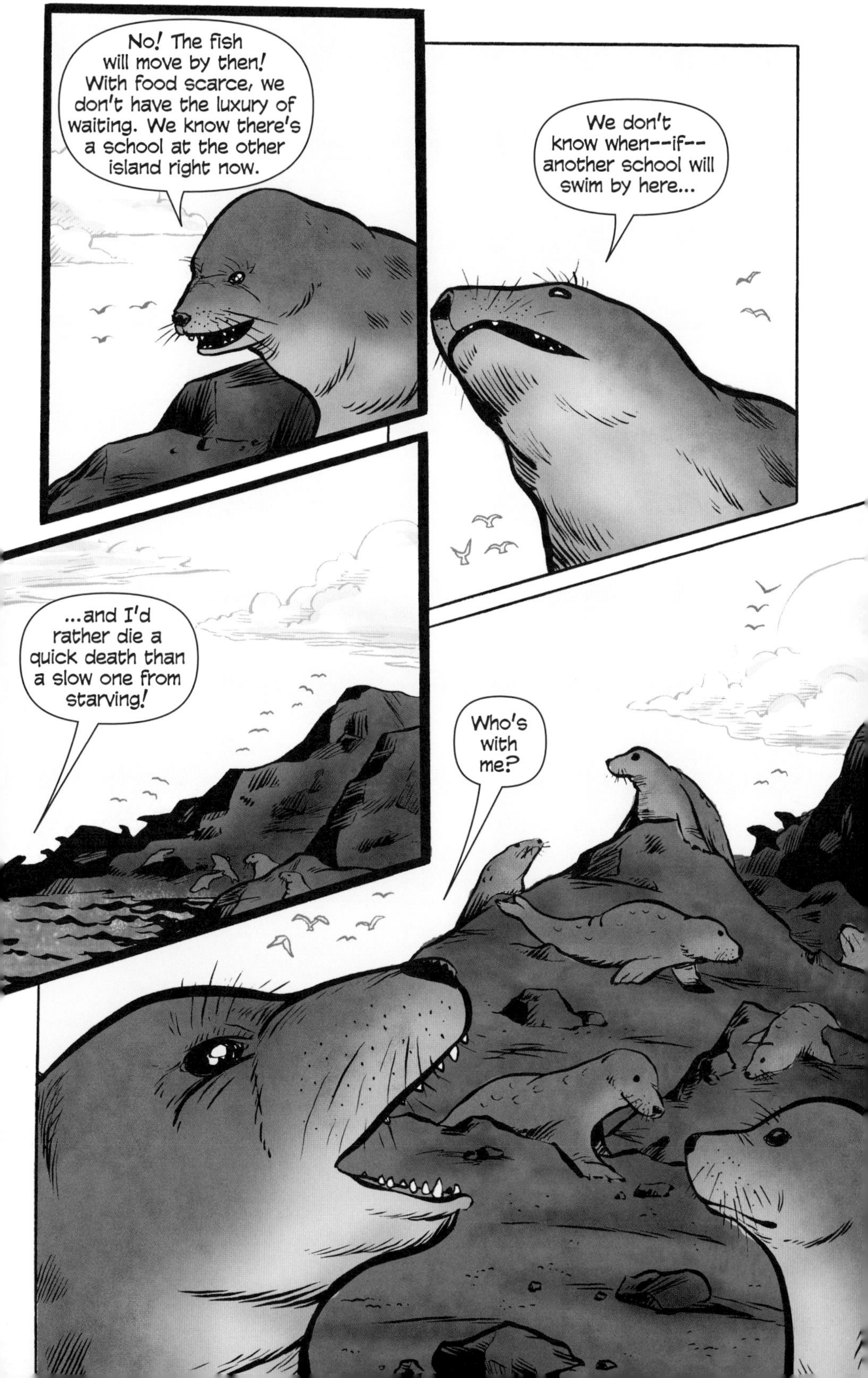
No! The fish will move by then! With food scarce, we don't have the luxury of waiting. We know there's a school at the other island right now.
We don't know when--if--another school will swim by here...
...and I'd rather die a quick death than a slow one from starving!
Who's with me?

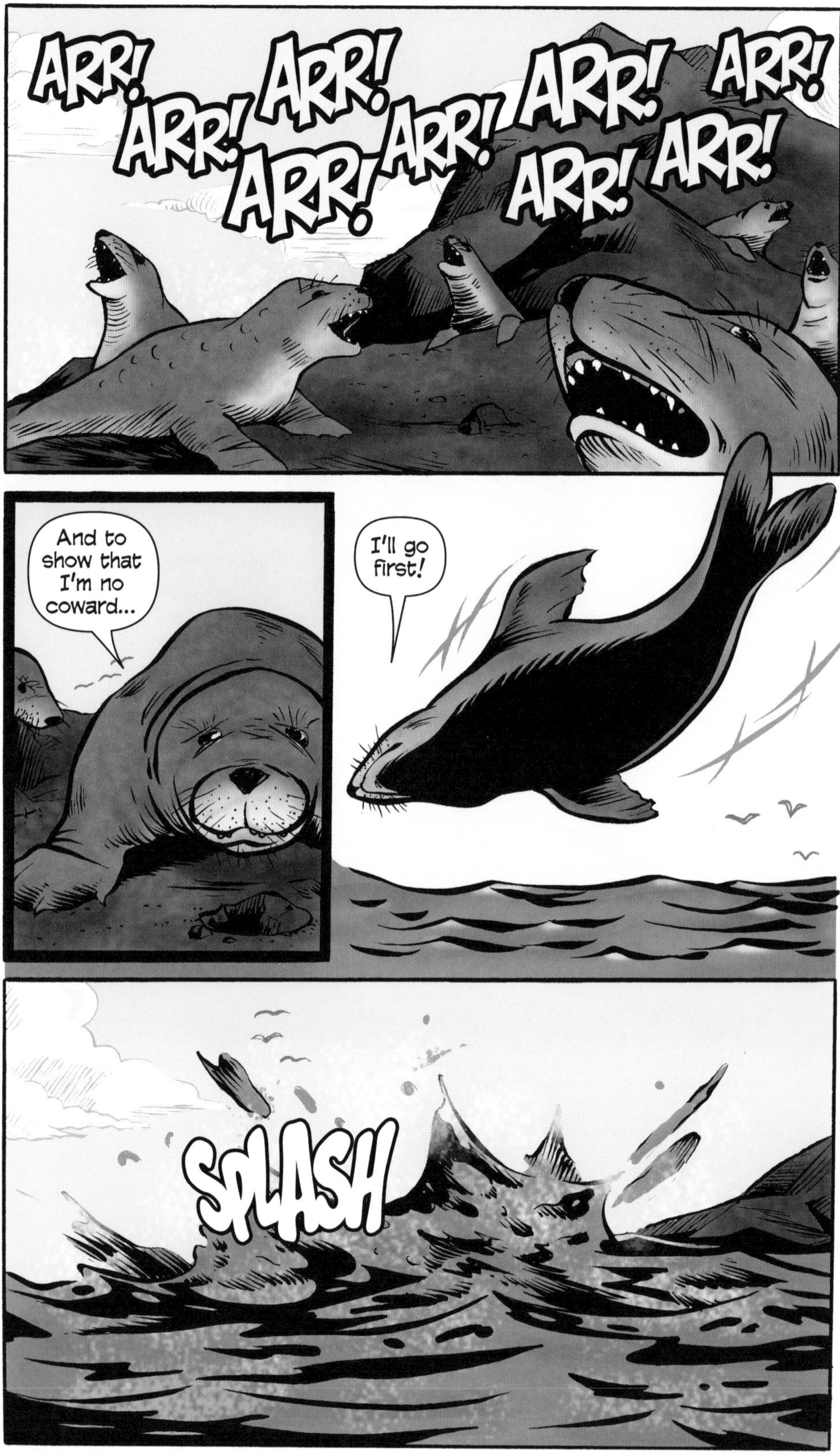
ARR! ARR! ARR! ARR! ARR! ARR! ARR! ARR! ARR!
And to show that I'm no coward...
I'll go first!
SPLASH

The water is murky and cold. Even the phocid's thick layer of blubber cannot blanket it from the initial shock.

Yet he moves quickly.

There's no time to look around to see if it's safe. The less movement, the better. A straight path is the fastest one.

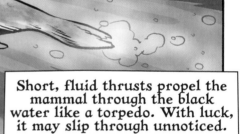

Short, fluid thrusts propel the mammal through the black water like a torpedo. With luck, it may slip through unnoticed.

There! I can see the foam from the waves crashing on the rocks!

But that's unlikely.

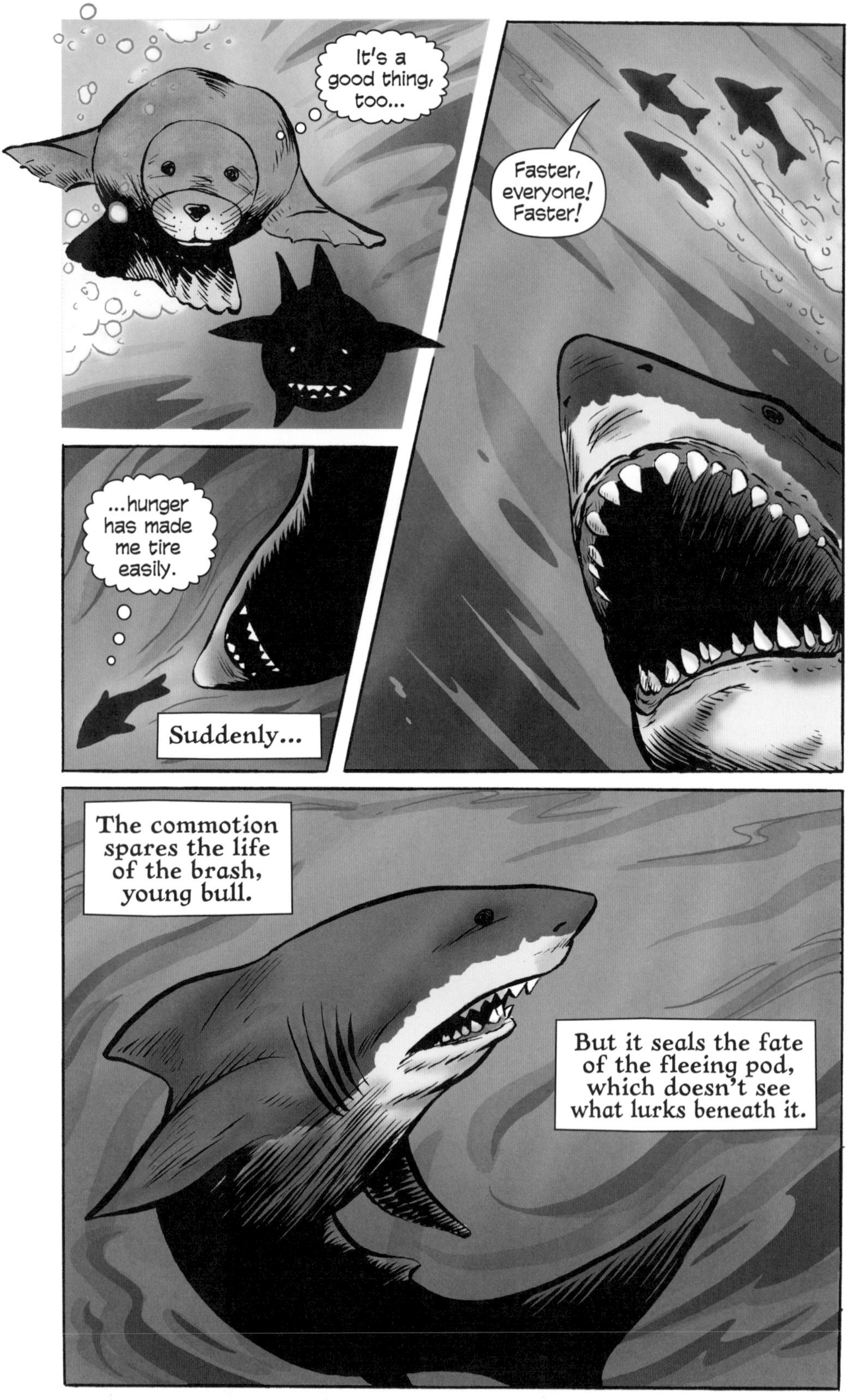
It's a good thing, too...
Faster, everyone! Faster!
...hunger has made me tire easily.
Suddenly...
The commotion spares the life of the brash, young bull.
But it seals the fate of the fleeing pod, which doesn't see what lurks beneath it.

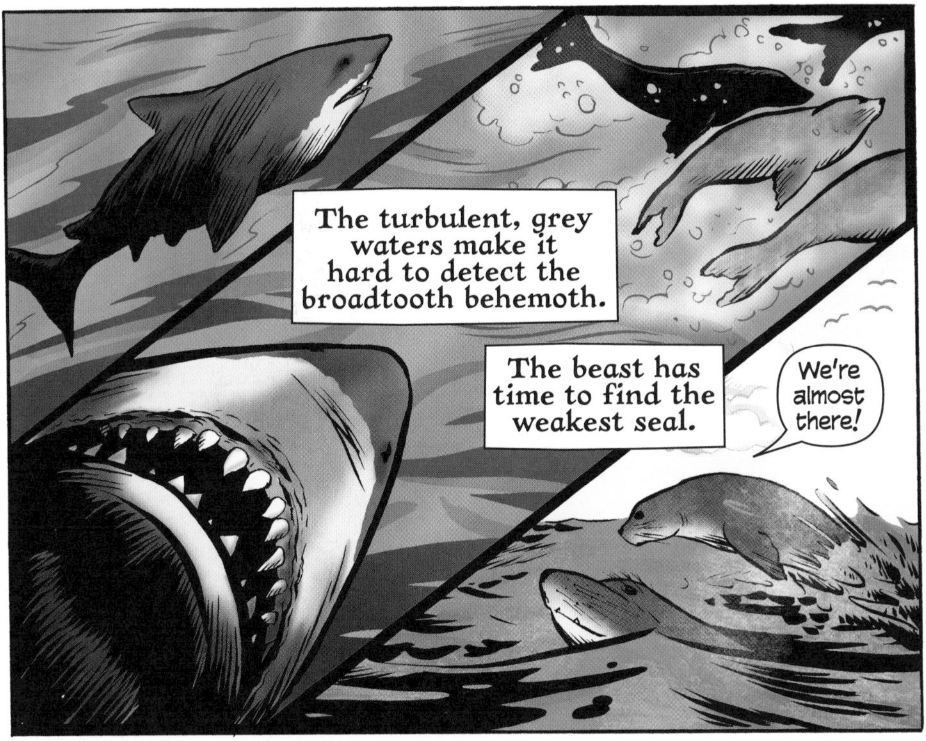
The turbulent, grey waters make it hard to detect the broadtooth behemoth.
The beast has time to find the weakest seal.
We're almost there!

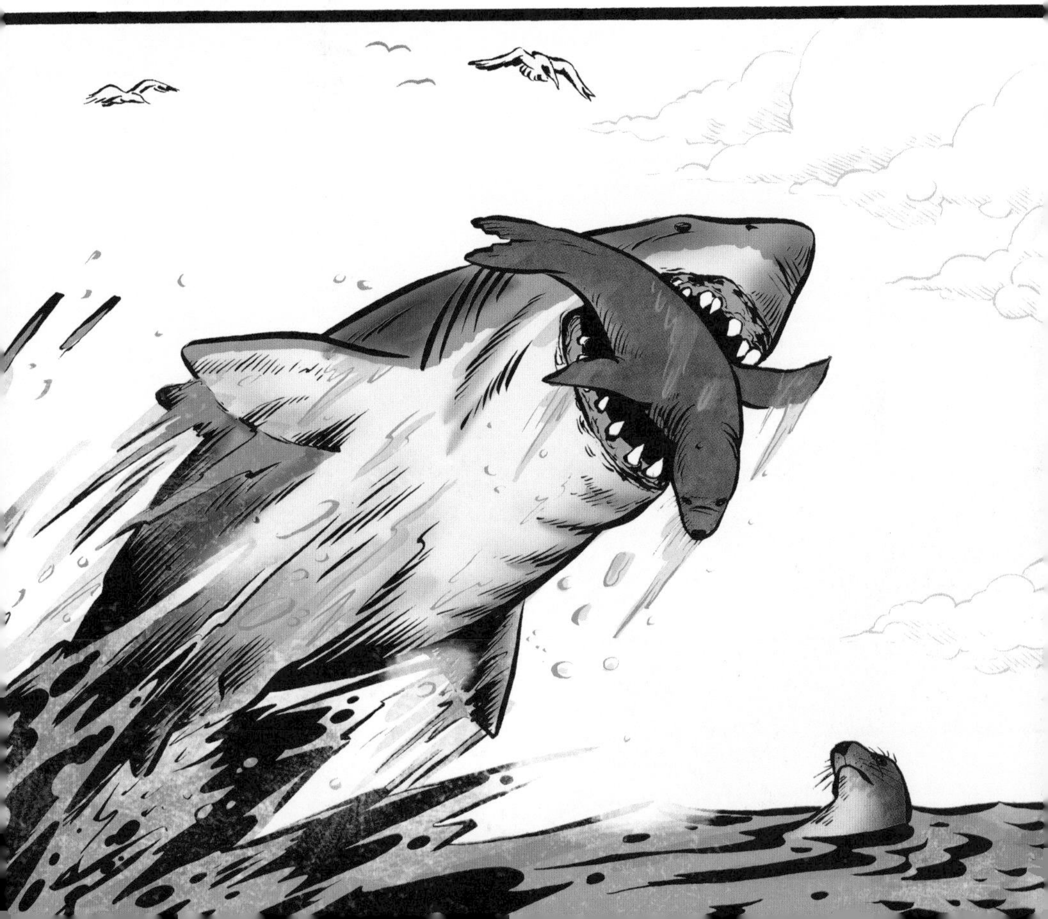

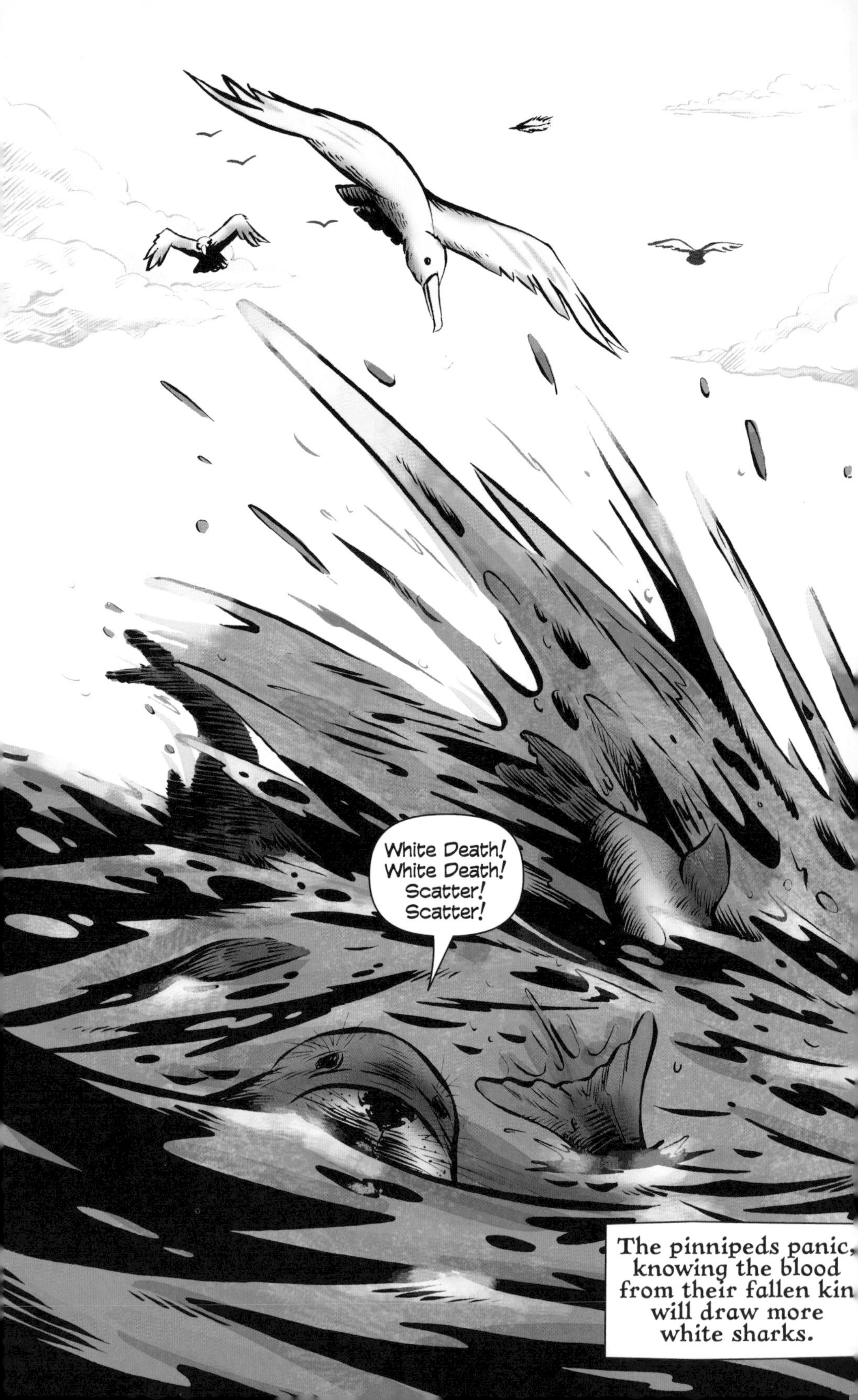
White Death! White Death! Scatter! Scatter!
The pinnipeds panic, knowing the blood from their fallen kin will draw more white sharks.

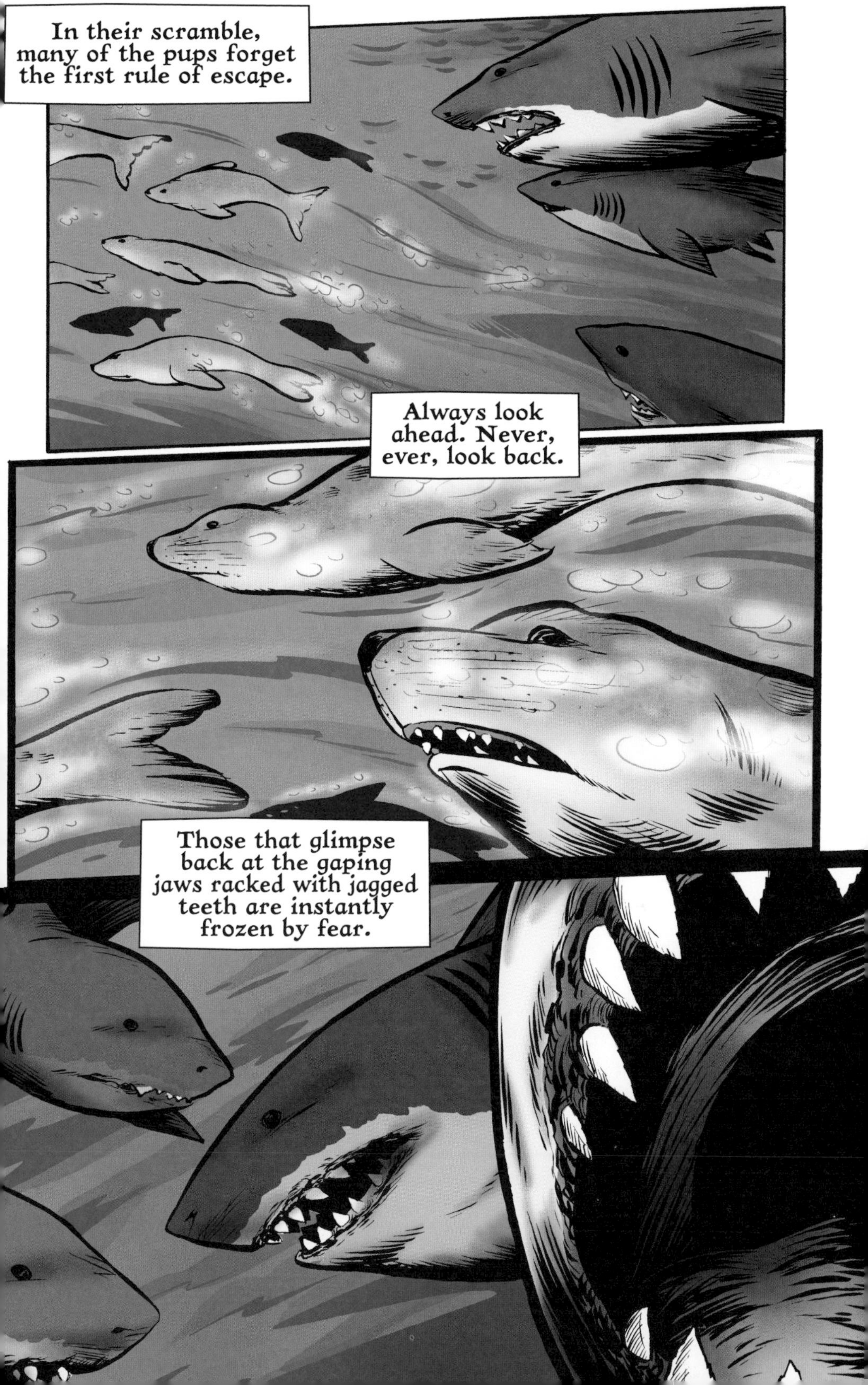
In their scramble, many of the pups forget the first rule of escape.
Always look ahead. Never, ever, look back.
Those that glimpse back at the gaping jaws racked with jagged teeth are instantly frozen by fear.

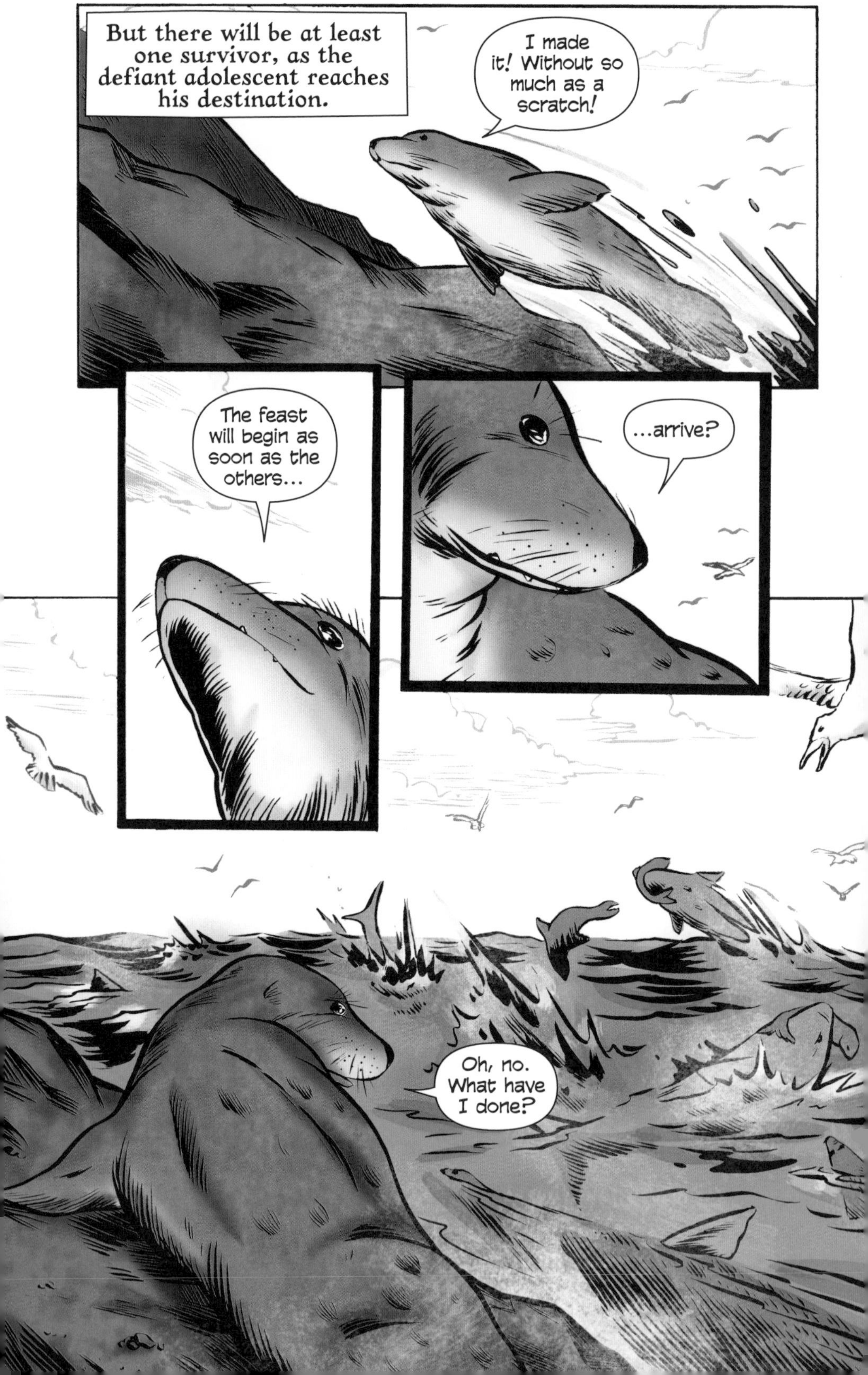
But there will be at least one survivor, as the defiant adolescent reaches his destination.
I made it! Without so much as a scratch!
The feast will begin as soon as the others...
...arrive?
Oh, no. What have I done?

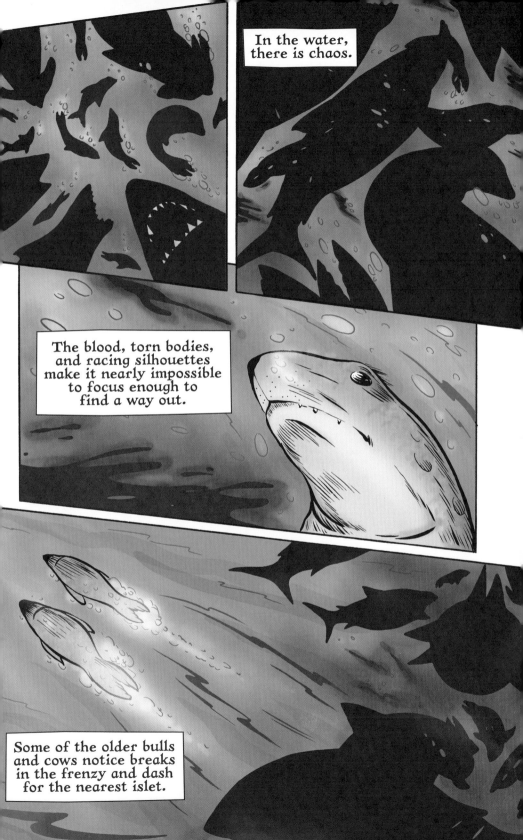

In the water, there is chaos.

The blood, torn bodies, and racing silhouettes make it nearly impossible to focus enough to find a way out.

Some of the older bulls and cows notice breaks in the frenzy and dash for the nearest islet.

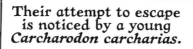

Their attempt to escape
is noticed by a young
Carcharodon carcharias.

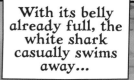

But with daylight
spreading, the duo sees
the pursuing predator
and use their experience
to outmaneuver it.

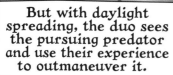

With its belly
already full, the
white shark
casually swims
away...

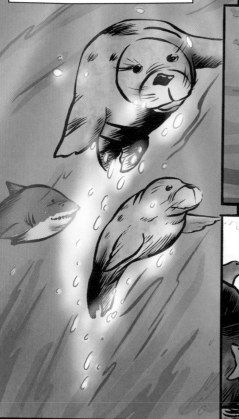

...and the two
seals reach
land with a
handful of
others.

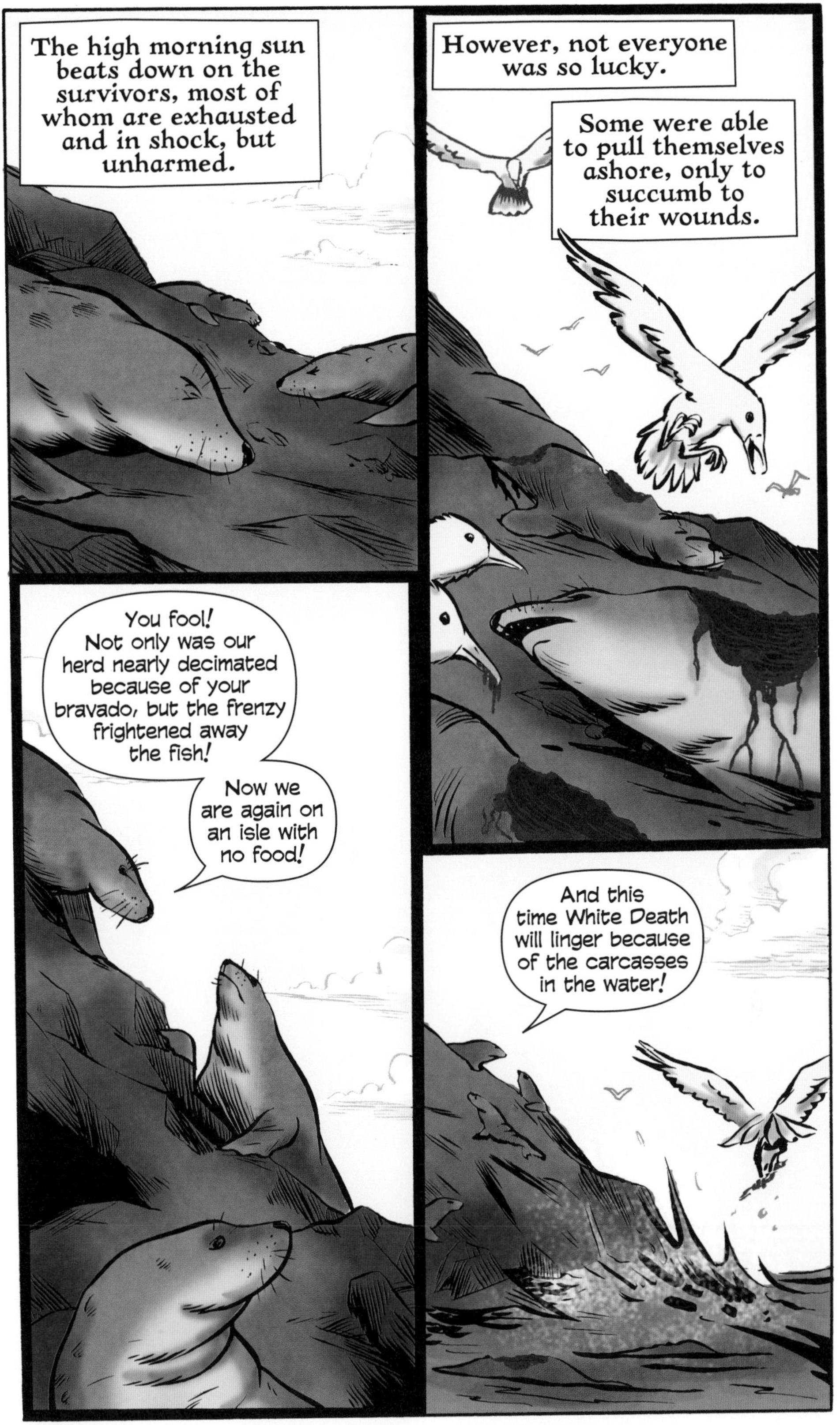
The high morning sun beats down on the survivors, most of whom are exhausted and in shock, but unharmed.
However, not everyone was so lucky.
Some were able to pull themselves ashore, only to succumb to their wounds.
You fool! Not only was our herd nearly decimated because of your bravado, but the frenzy frightened away the fish!
Now we are again on an isle with no food!
And this time White Death will linger because of the carcasses in the water!

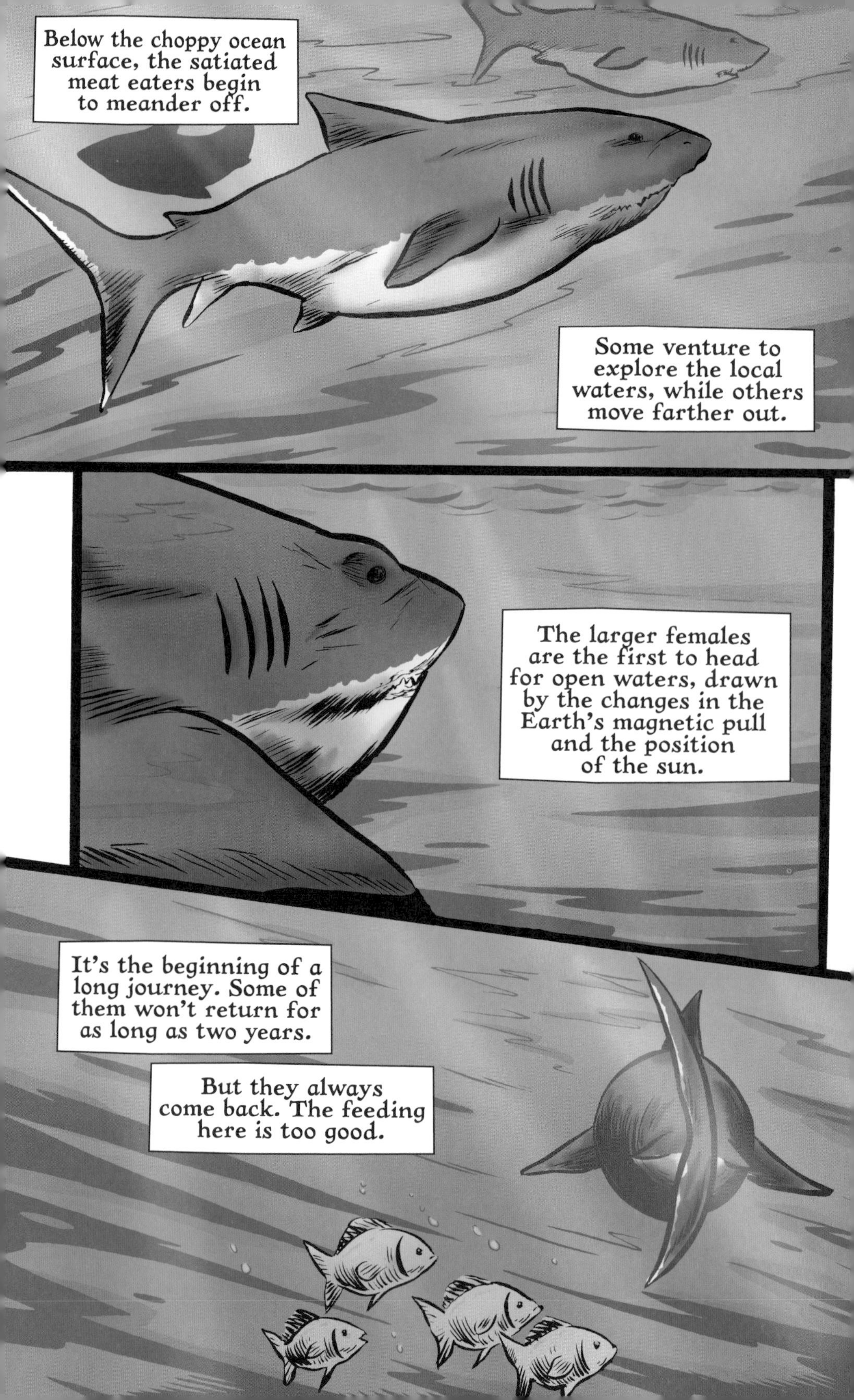
Below the choppy ocean surface, the satiated meat eaters begin to meander off.
Some venture to explore the local waters, while others move farther out.
The larger females are the first to head for open waters, drawn by the changes in the Earth's magnetic pull and the position of the sun.
It's the beginning of a long journey. Some of them won't return for as long as two years.
But they always come back. The feeding here is too good.

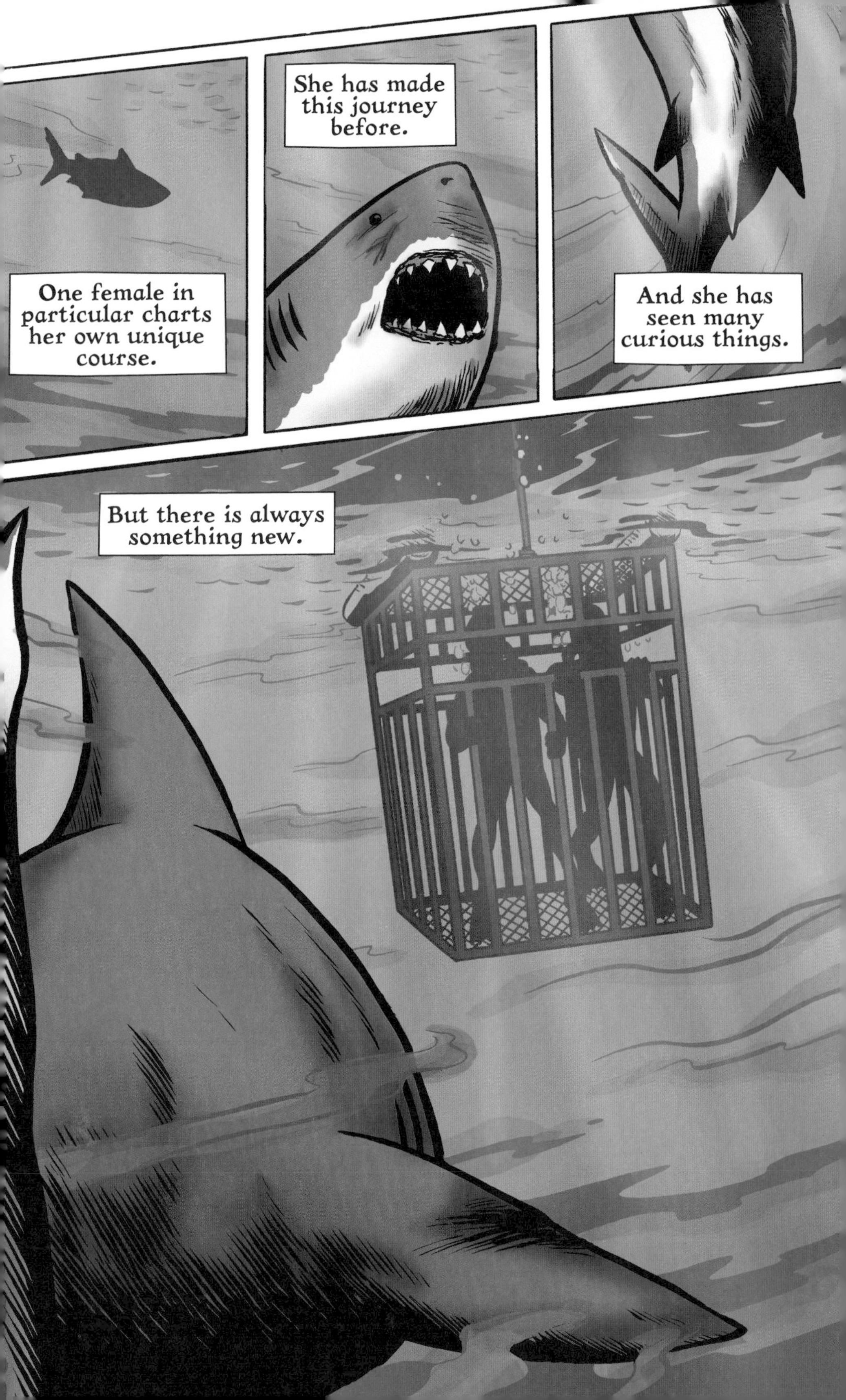
One female in particular charts her own unique course.
She has made this journey before.
And she has seen many curious things.
But there is always something new.

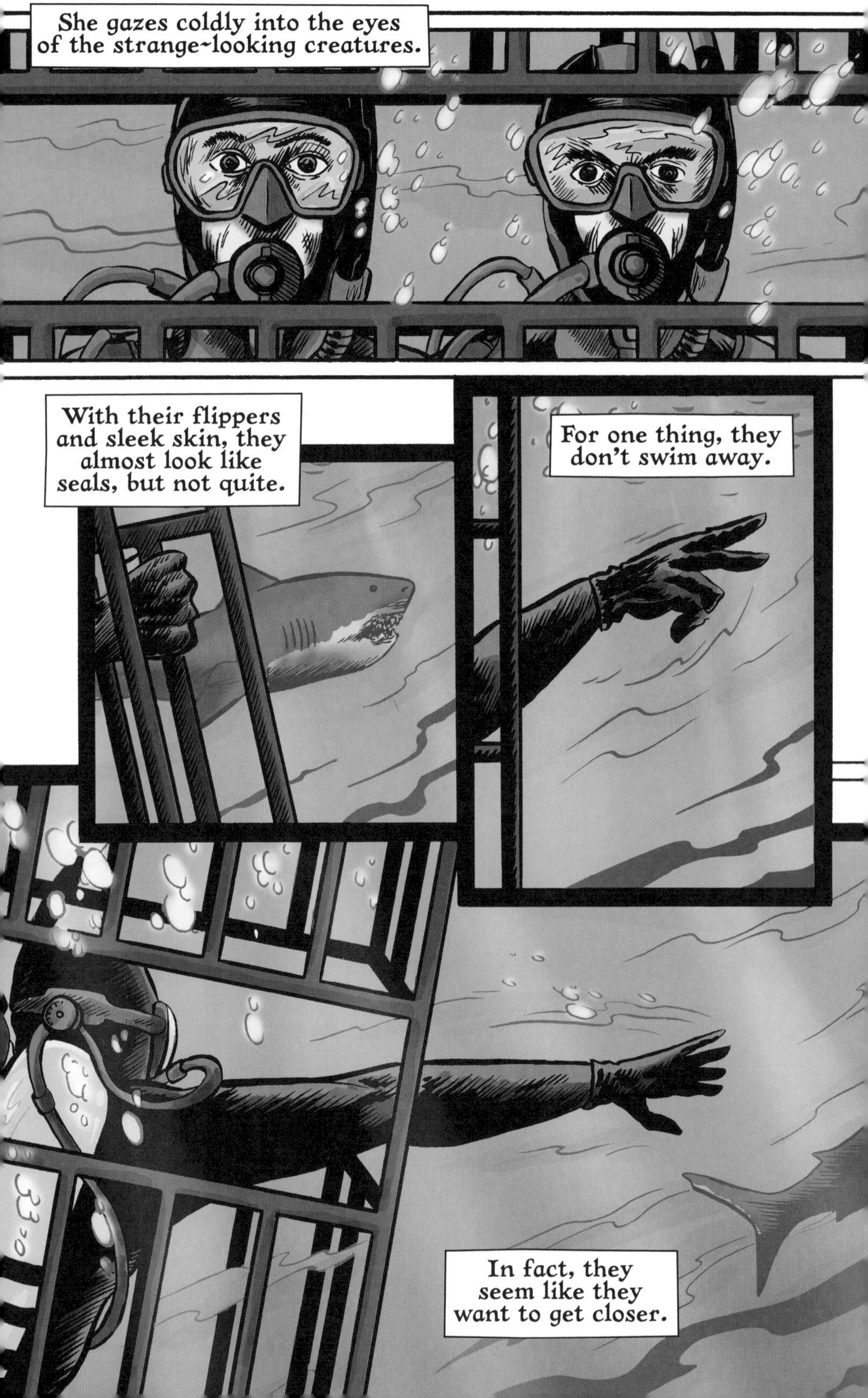
She gazes coldly into the eyes of the strange~looking creatures.
With their flippers and sleek skin, they almost look like seals, but not quite.
For one thing, they don't swim away.
In fact, they seem like they want to get closer.

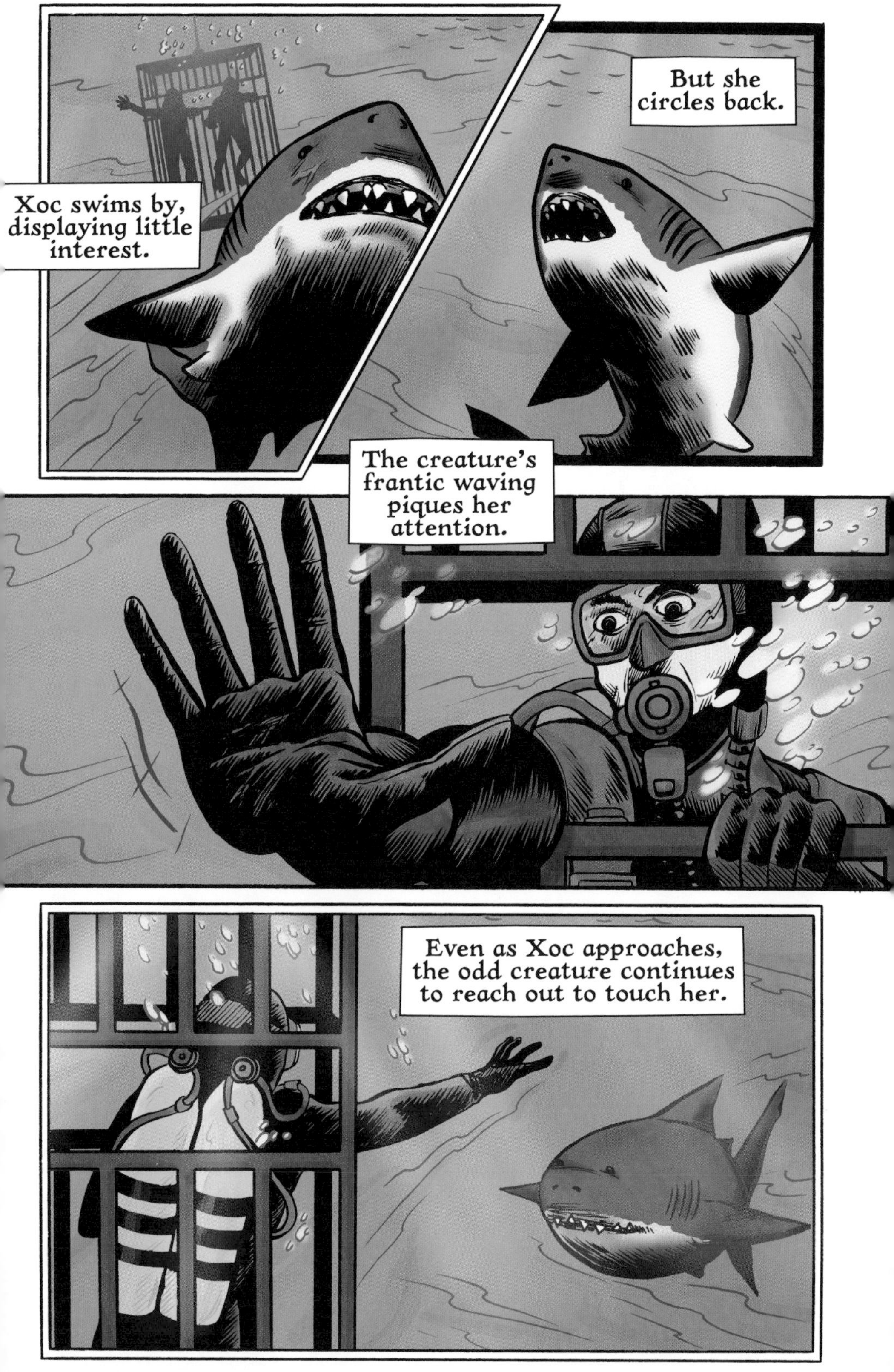
Xoc swims by, displaying little interest.
But she circles back.
The creature's frantic waving piques her attention.
Even as Xoc approaches, the odd creature continues to reach out to touch her.

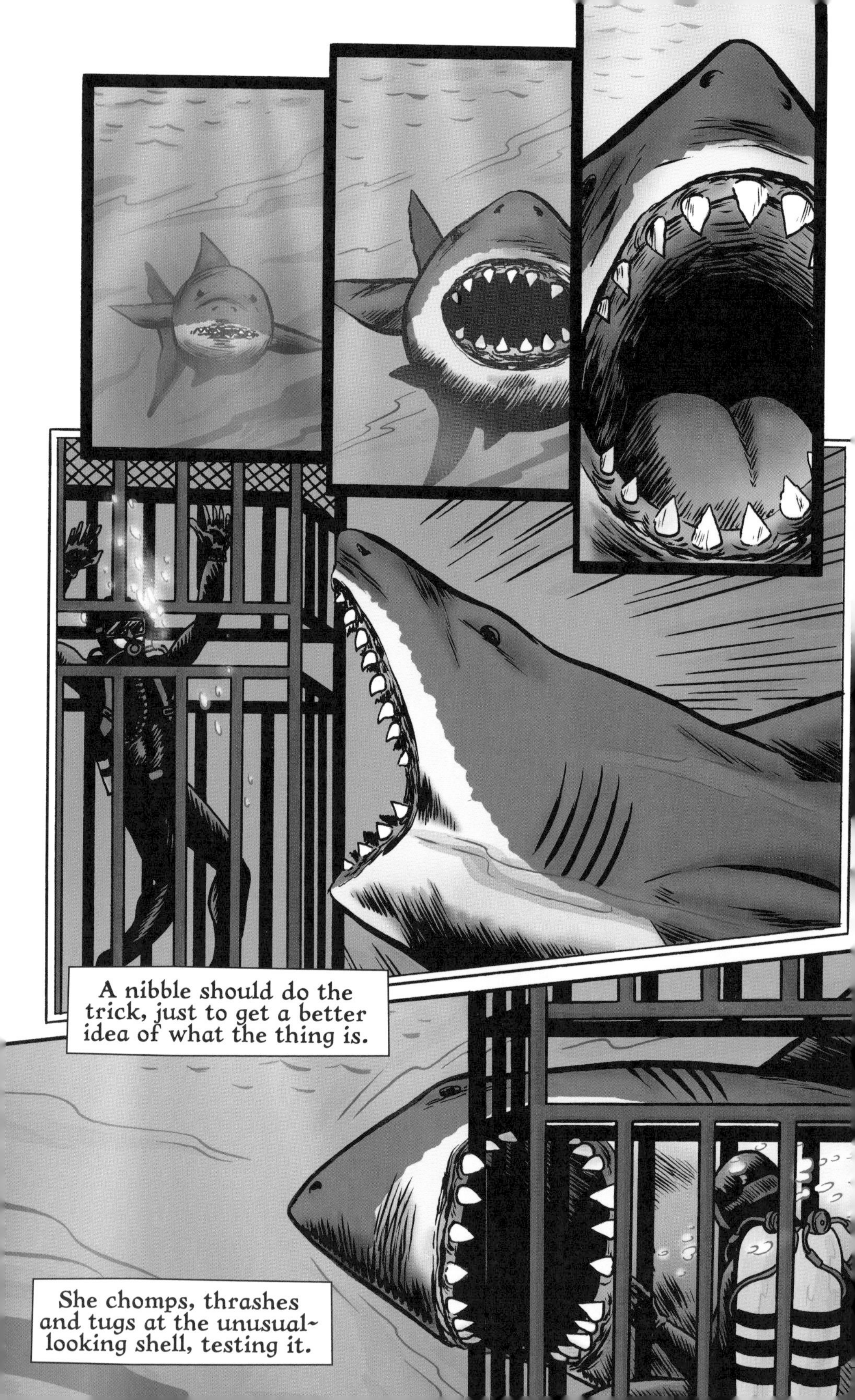
A nibble should do the trick, just to get a better idea of what the thing is.
She chomps, thrashes and tugs at the unusual-looking shell, testing it.

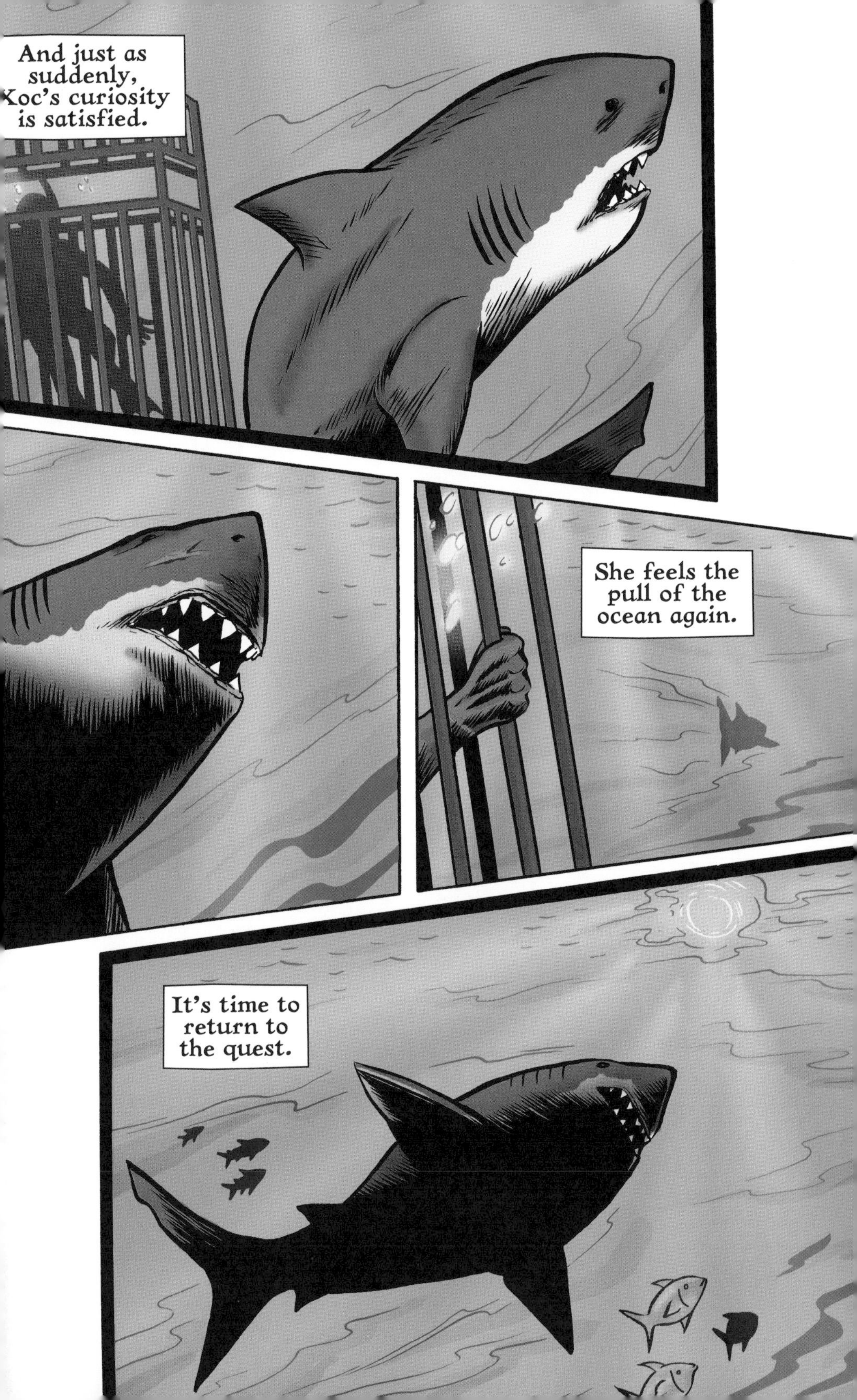
And just as suddenly, Koc's curiosity is satisfied.
She feels the pull of the ocean again.
It's time to return to the quest.

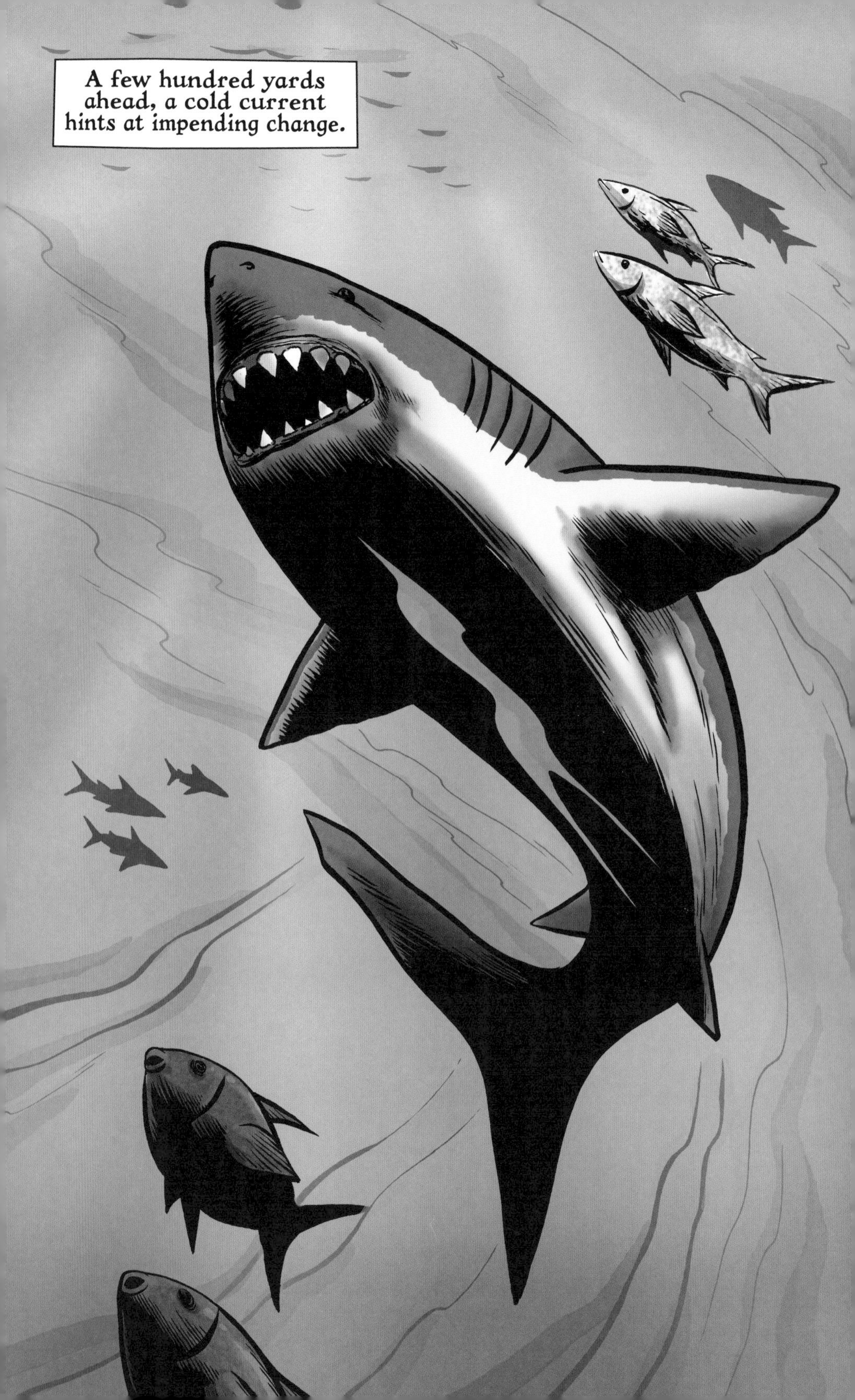
A few hundred yards ahead, a cold current hints at impending change.

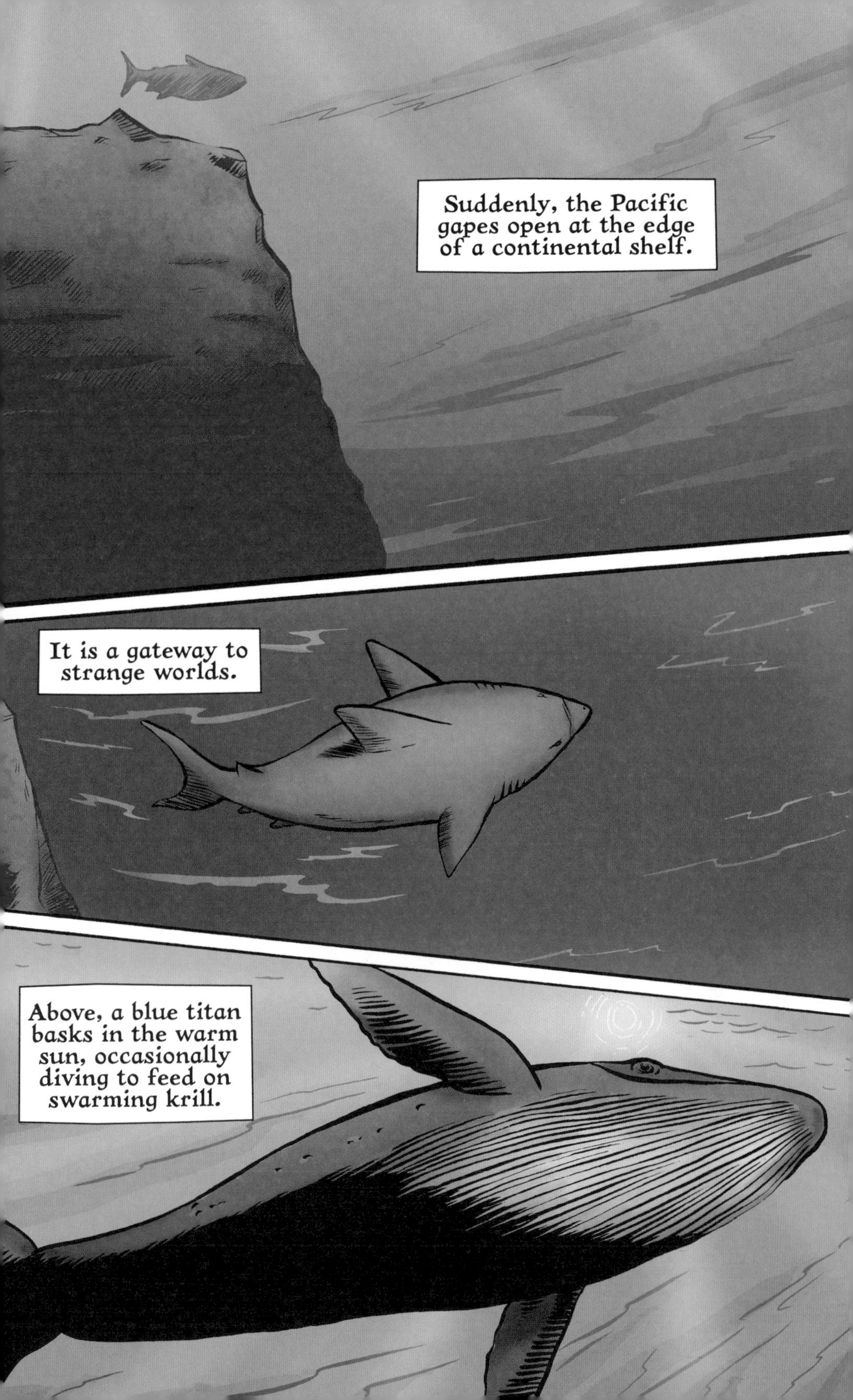
Suddenly, the Pacific gapes open at the edge of a continental shelf.
It is a gateway to strange worlds.
Above, a blue titan basks in the warm sun, occasionally diving to feed on swarming krill.

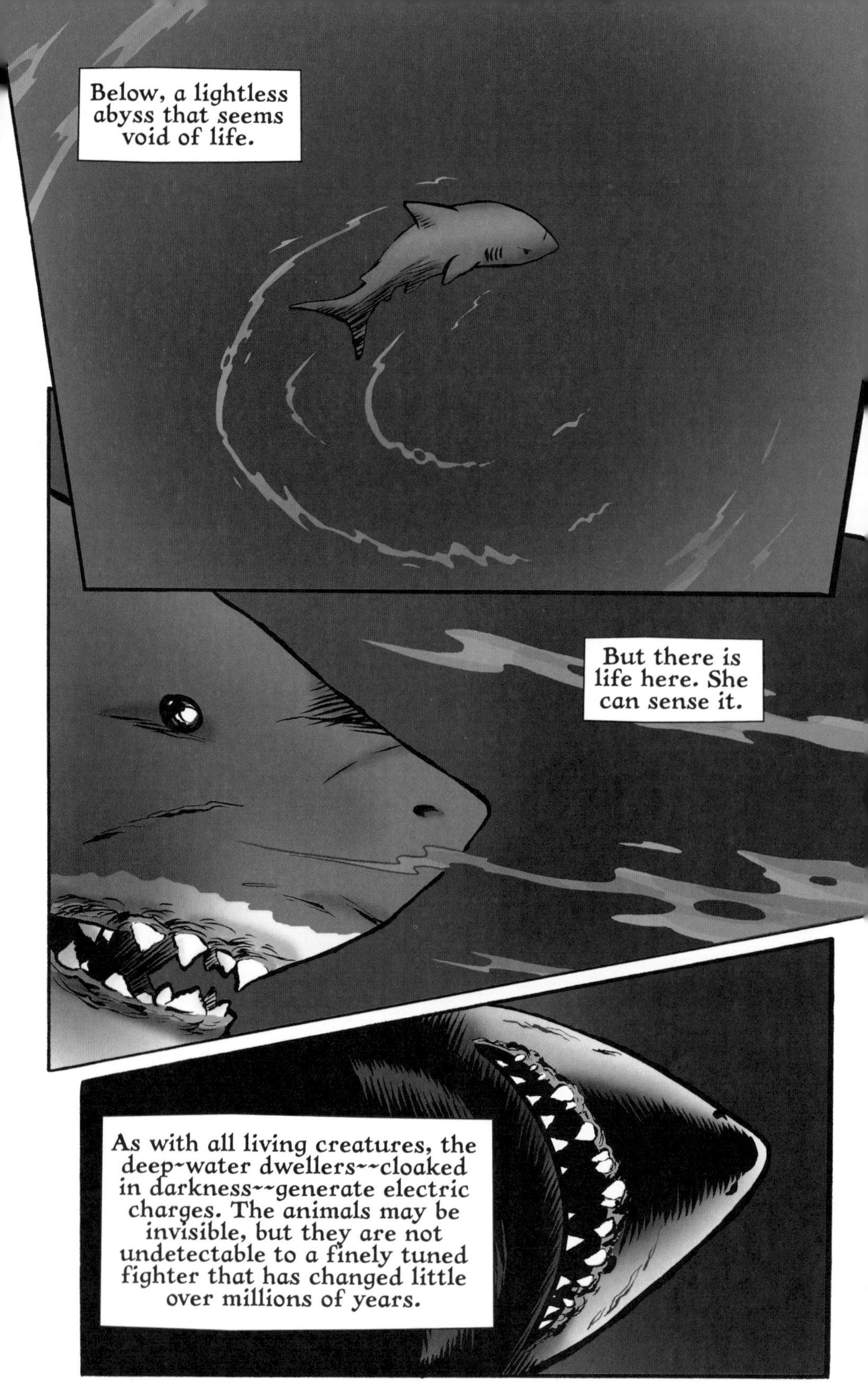
Below, a lightless abyss that seems void of life.
But there is life here. She can sense it.
As with all living creatures, the deep-water dwellers--cloaked in darkness--generate electric charges. The animals may be invisible, but they are not undetectable to a finely tuned fighter that has changed little over millions of years.

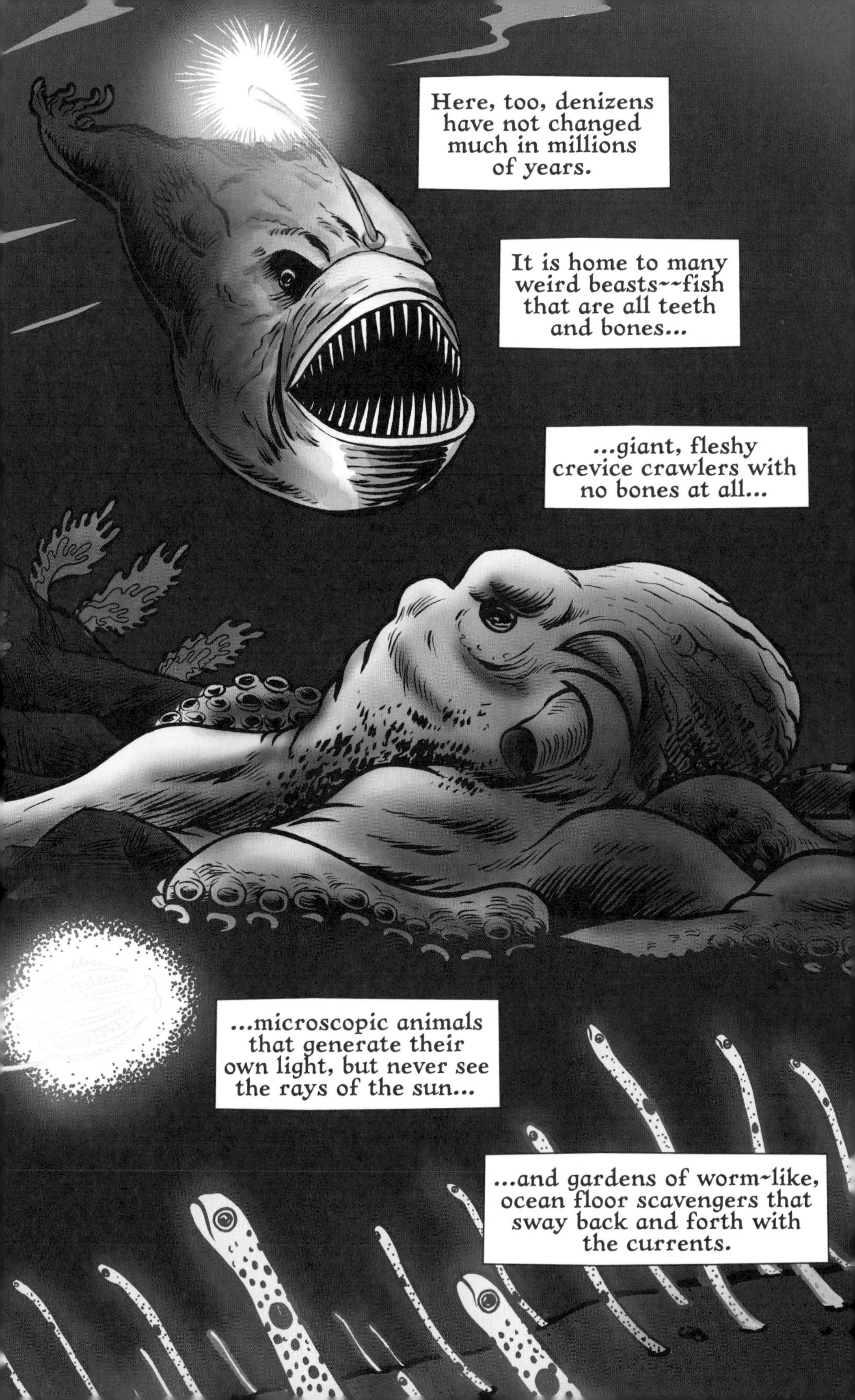
Here, too, denizens have not changed much in millions of years.
It is home to many weird beasts~~fish that are all teeth and bones...
...giant, fleshy crevice crawlers with no bones at all...
...microscopic animals that generate their own light, but never see the rays of the sun...
...and gardens of worm~like, ocean floor scavengers that sway back and forth with the currents.

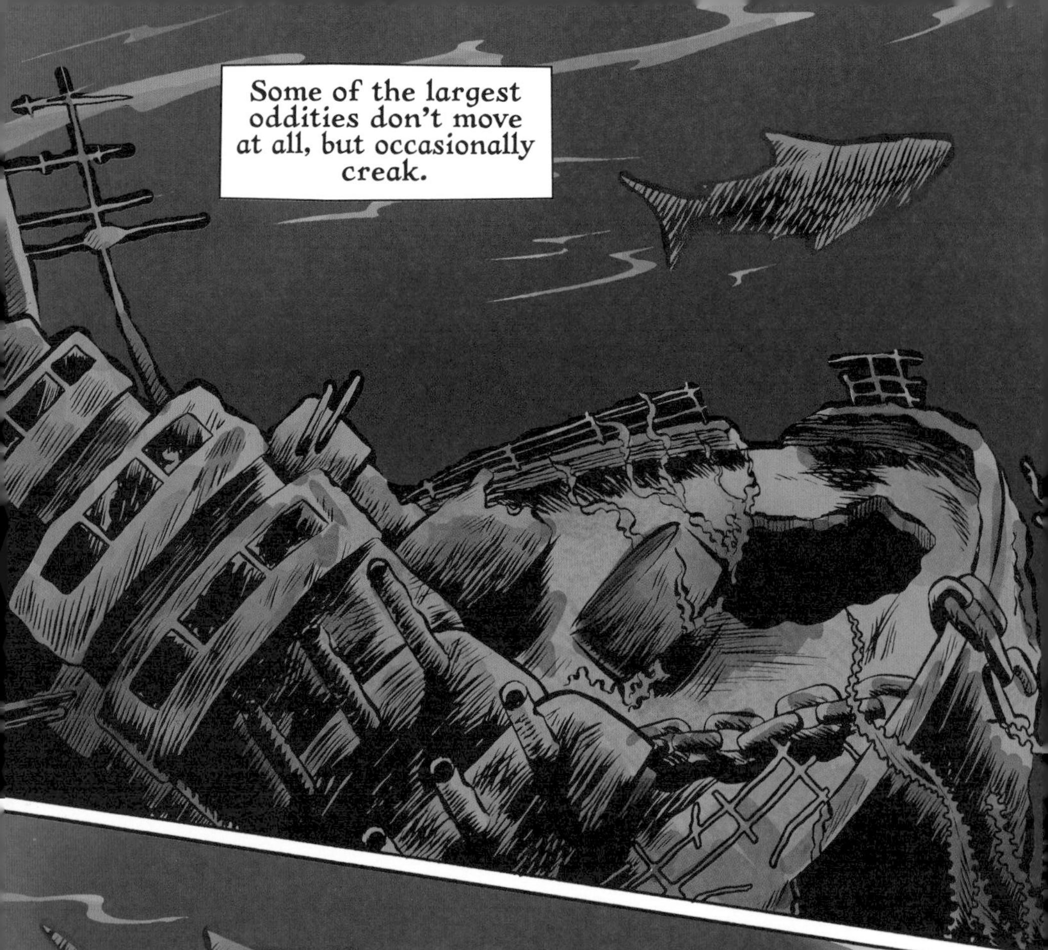
Some of the largest oddities don't move at all, but occasionally creak.

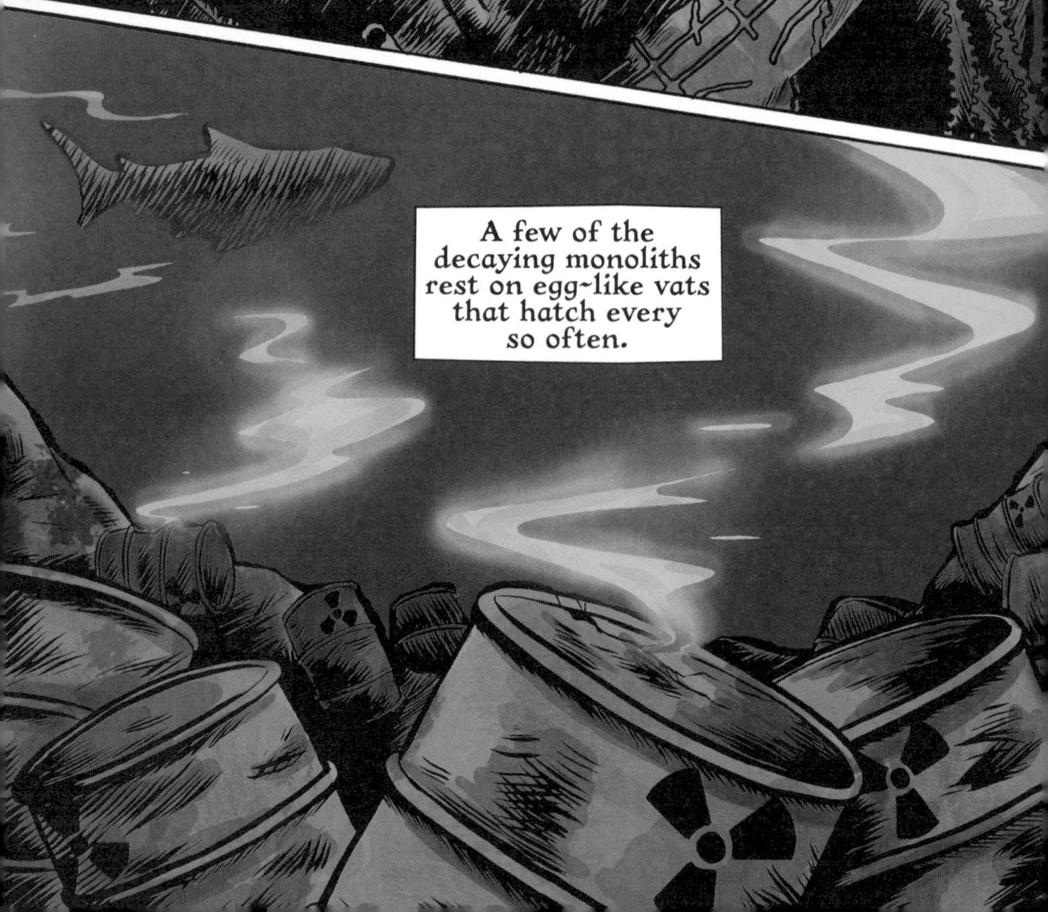
A few of the decaying monoliths rest on egg~like vats that hatch every so often.

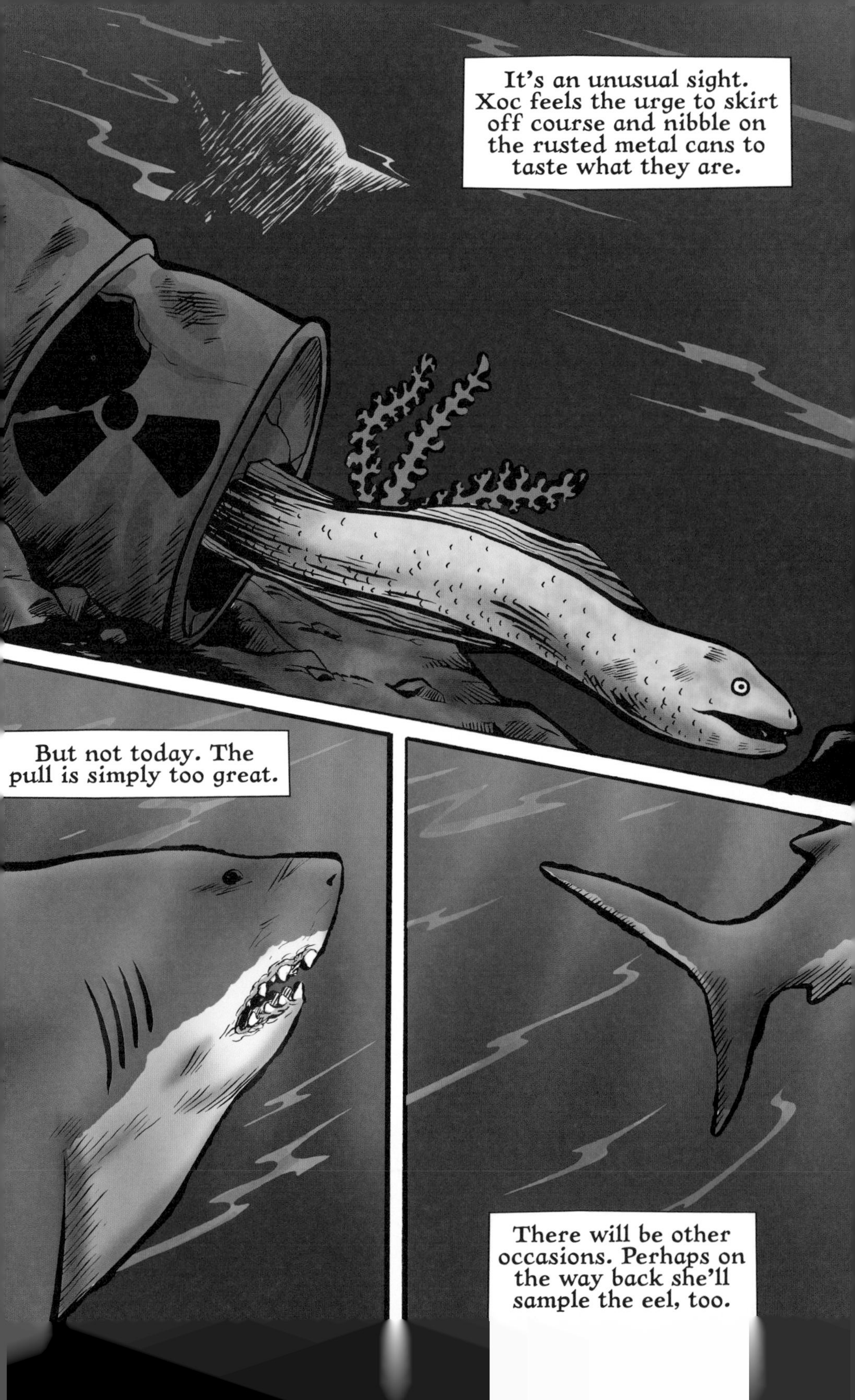
It's an unusual sight. Xoc feels the urge to skirt off course and nibble on the rusted metal cans to taste what they are.
But not today. The pull is simply too great.
There will be other occasions. Perhaps on the way back she'll sample the eel, too.

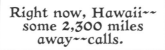

Right now, Hawaii~~
some 2,300 miles
away~~calls.

No one said this
journey would be easy.

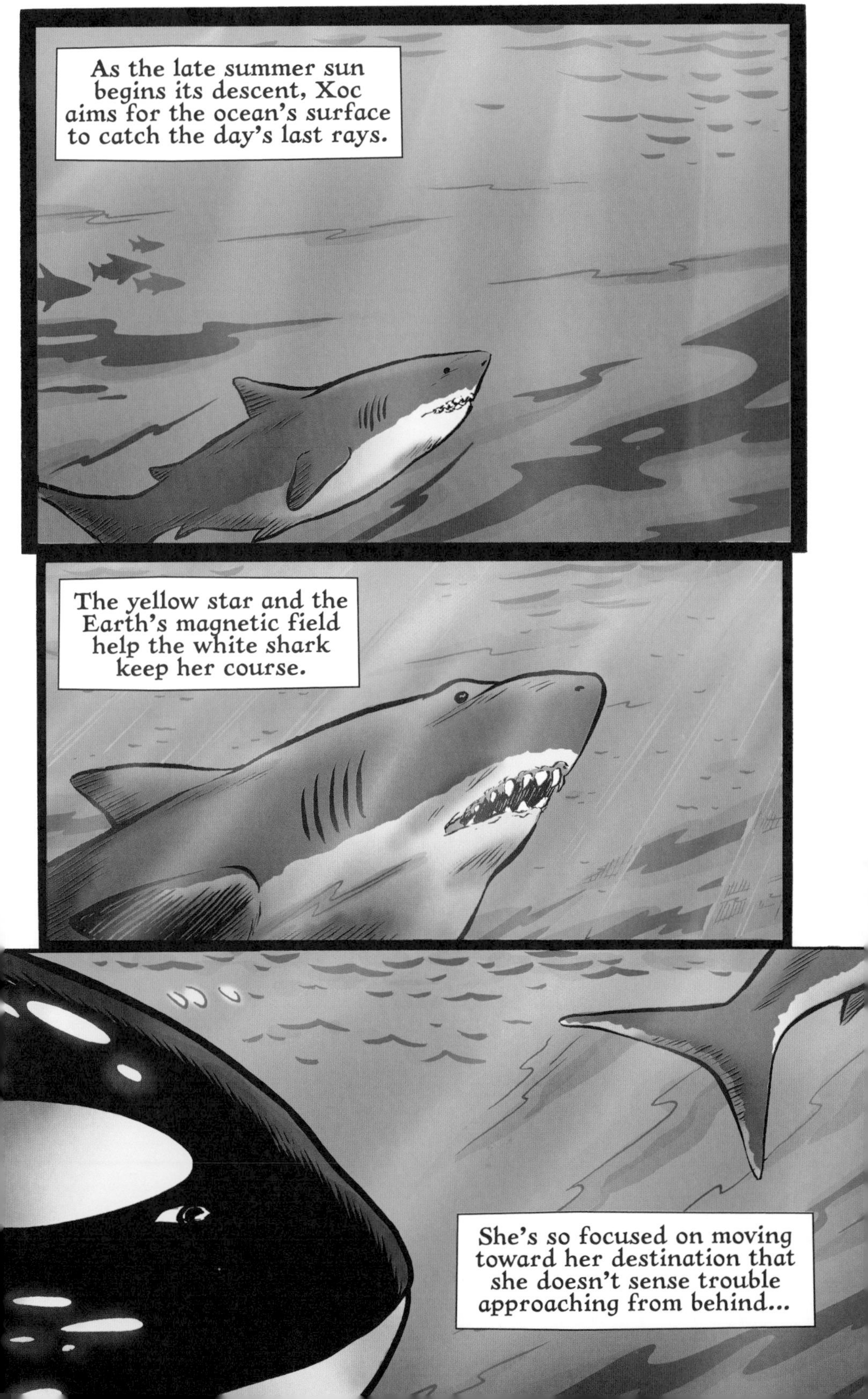
As the late summer sun begins its descent, Xoc aims for the ocean's surface to catch the day's last rays.
The yellow star and the Earth's magnetic field help the white shark keep her course.
She's so focused on moving toward her destination that she doesn't sense trouble approaching from behind...

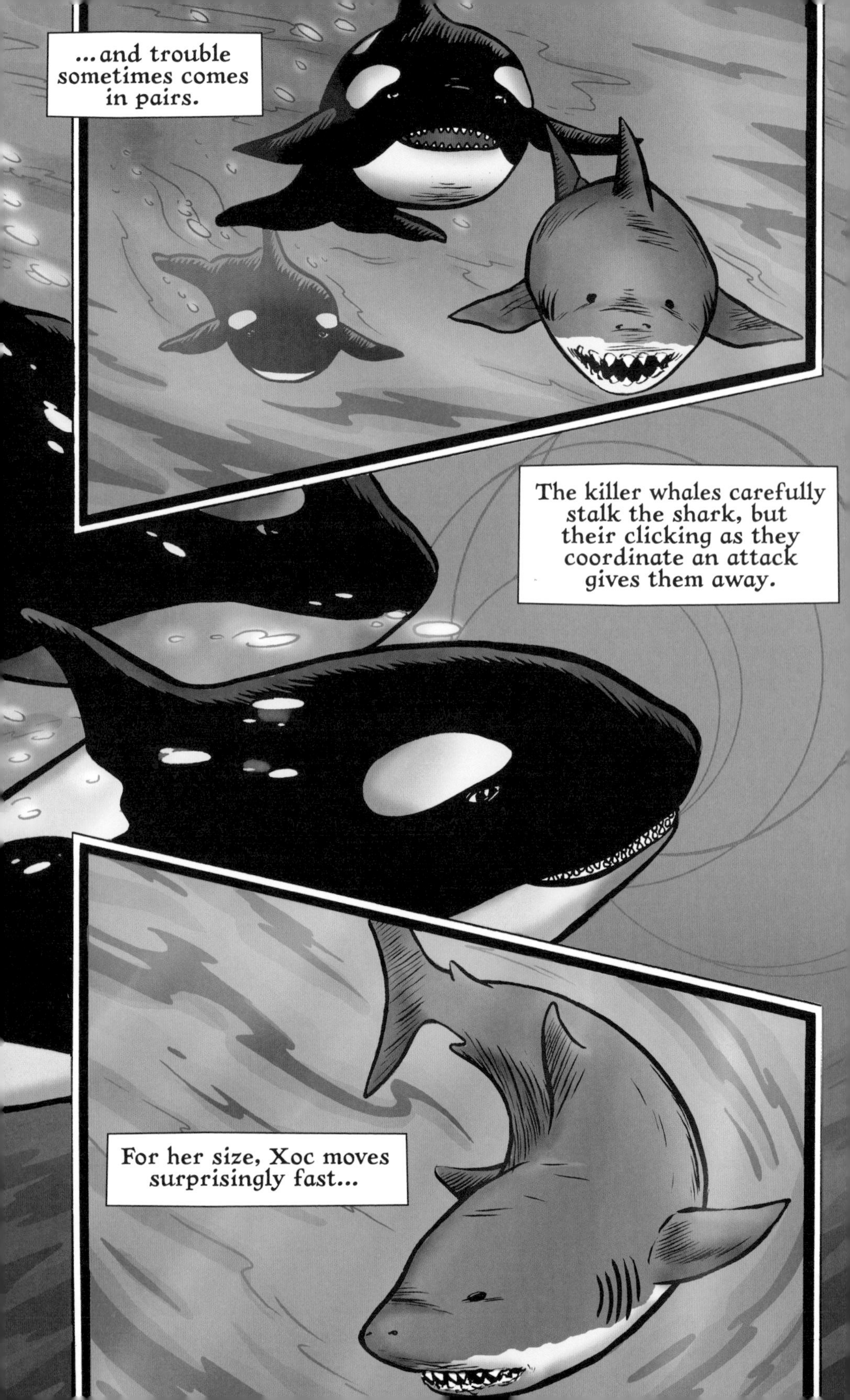
...and trouble sometimes comes in pairs.
The killer whales carefully stalk the shark, but their clicking as they coordinate an attack gives them away.
For her size, Xoc moves surprisingly fast...

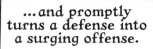

...and promptly turns a defense into a surging offense.

But the orcas are also quick, and they work as a team.

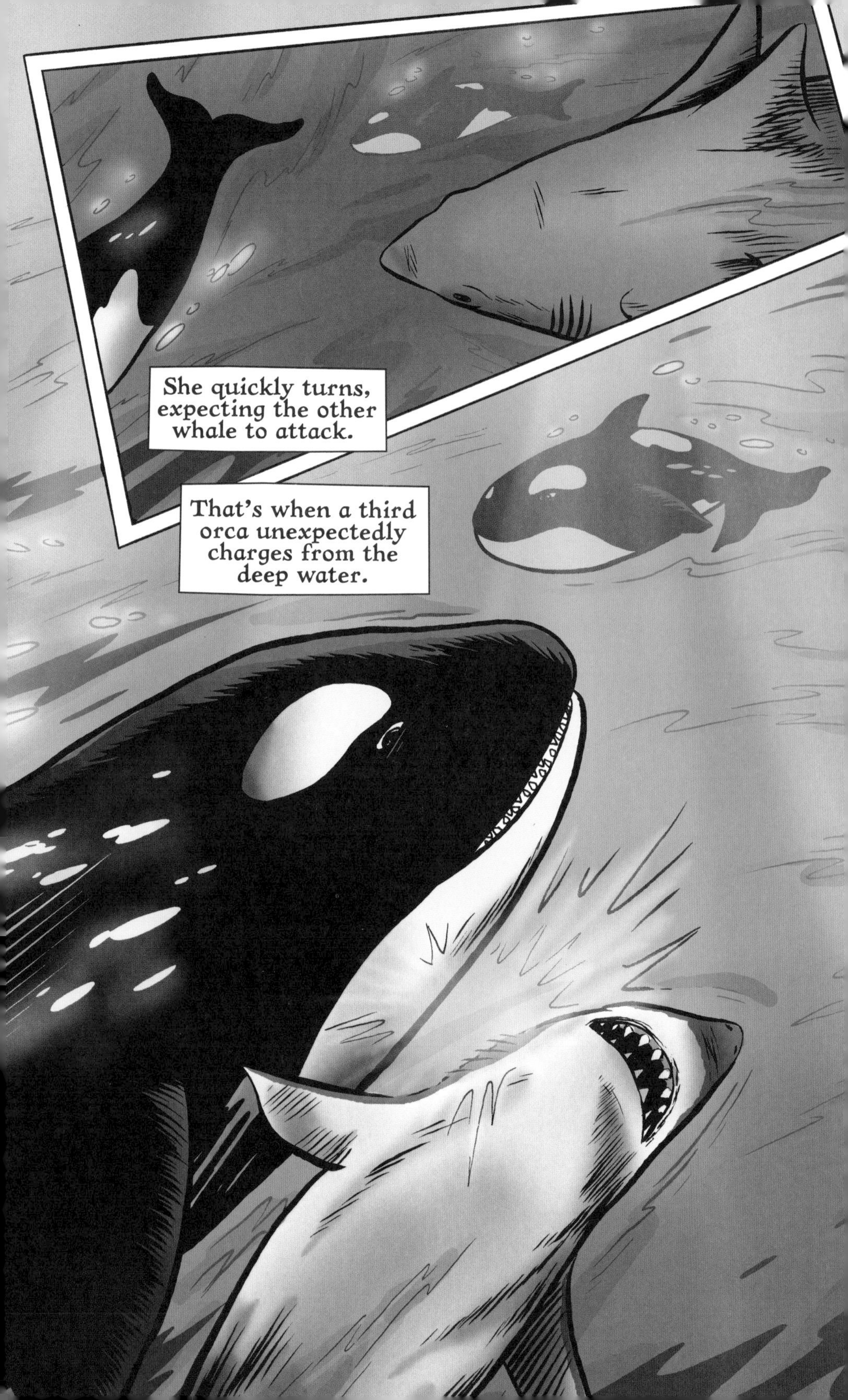
She quickly turns, expecting the other whale to attack.
That's when a third orca unexpectedly charges from the deep water.

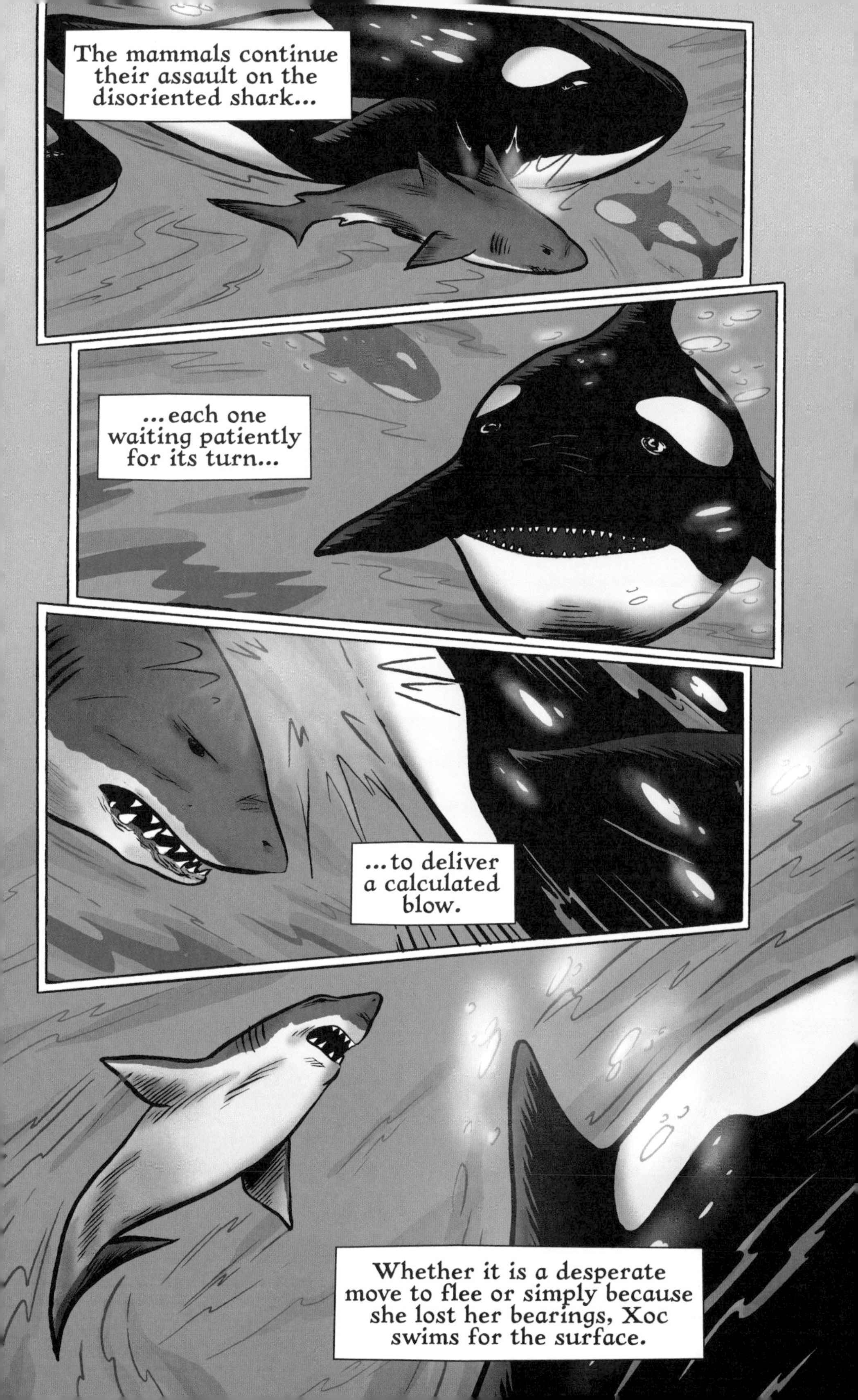
The mammals continue their assault on the disoriented shark...
...each one waiting patiently for its turn...
...to deliver a calculated blow.
Whether it is a desperate move to flee or simply because she lost her bearings, Xoc swims for the surface.

She takes cover in the turmoil spawned by the 20-foot waves just above her.

Seeking to lose her pursuers in the whitecaps, Xoc heads closer to the surface as the a passing storm worsens.

The orcas mill about to see if the great white will dive. It's too risky to venture after her. Even though Xoc is wounded, she's still dangerous.

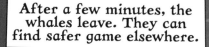

After a few minutes, the whales leave. They can find safer game elsewhere.

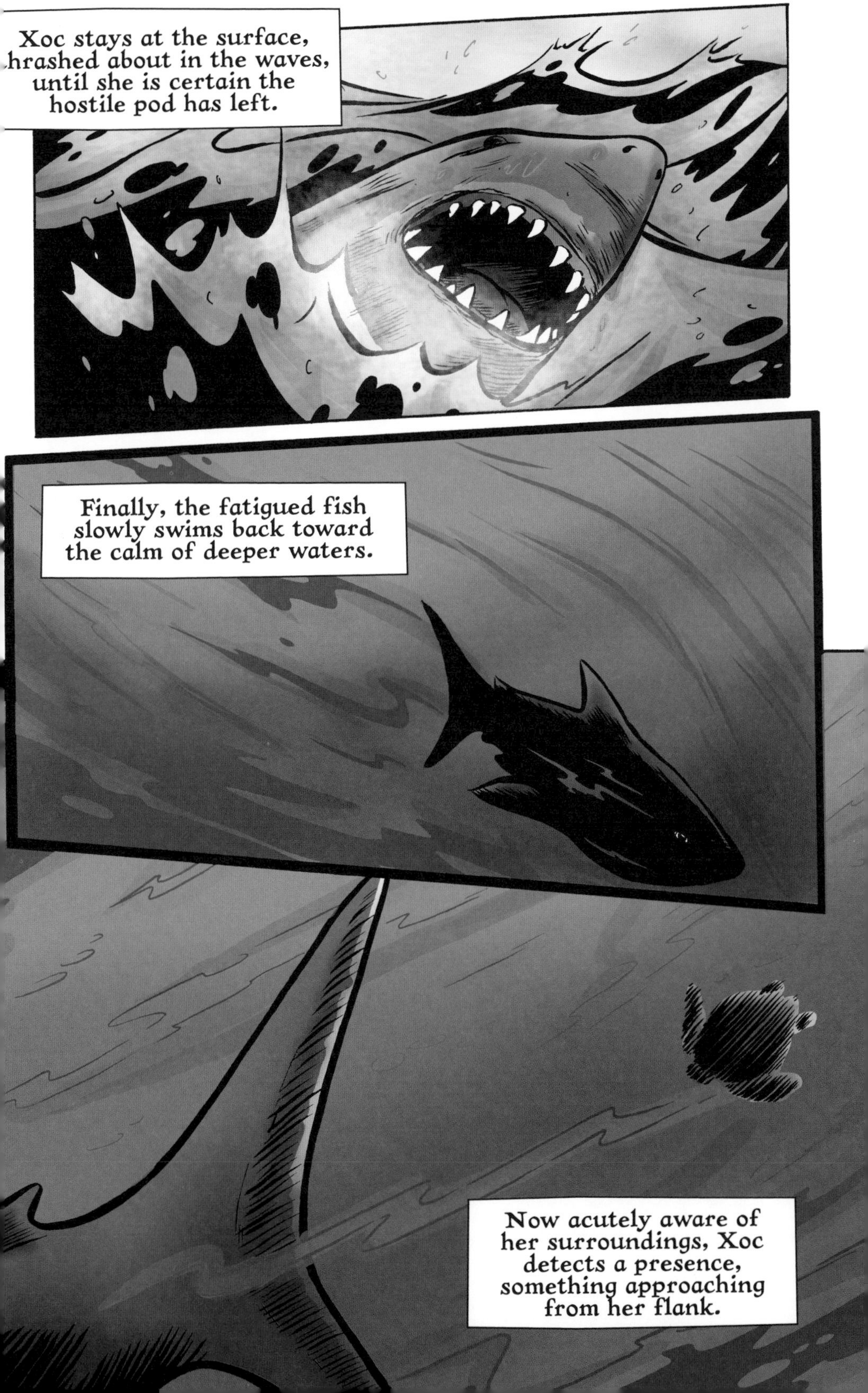
Xoc stays at the surface, hrashed about in the waves, until she is certain the hostile pod has left.
Finally, the fatigued fish slowly swims back toward the calm of deeper waters.
Now acutely aware of her surroundings, Xoc detects a presence, something approaching from her flank.

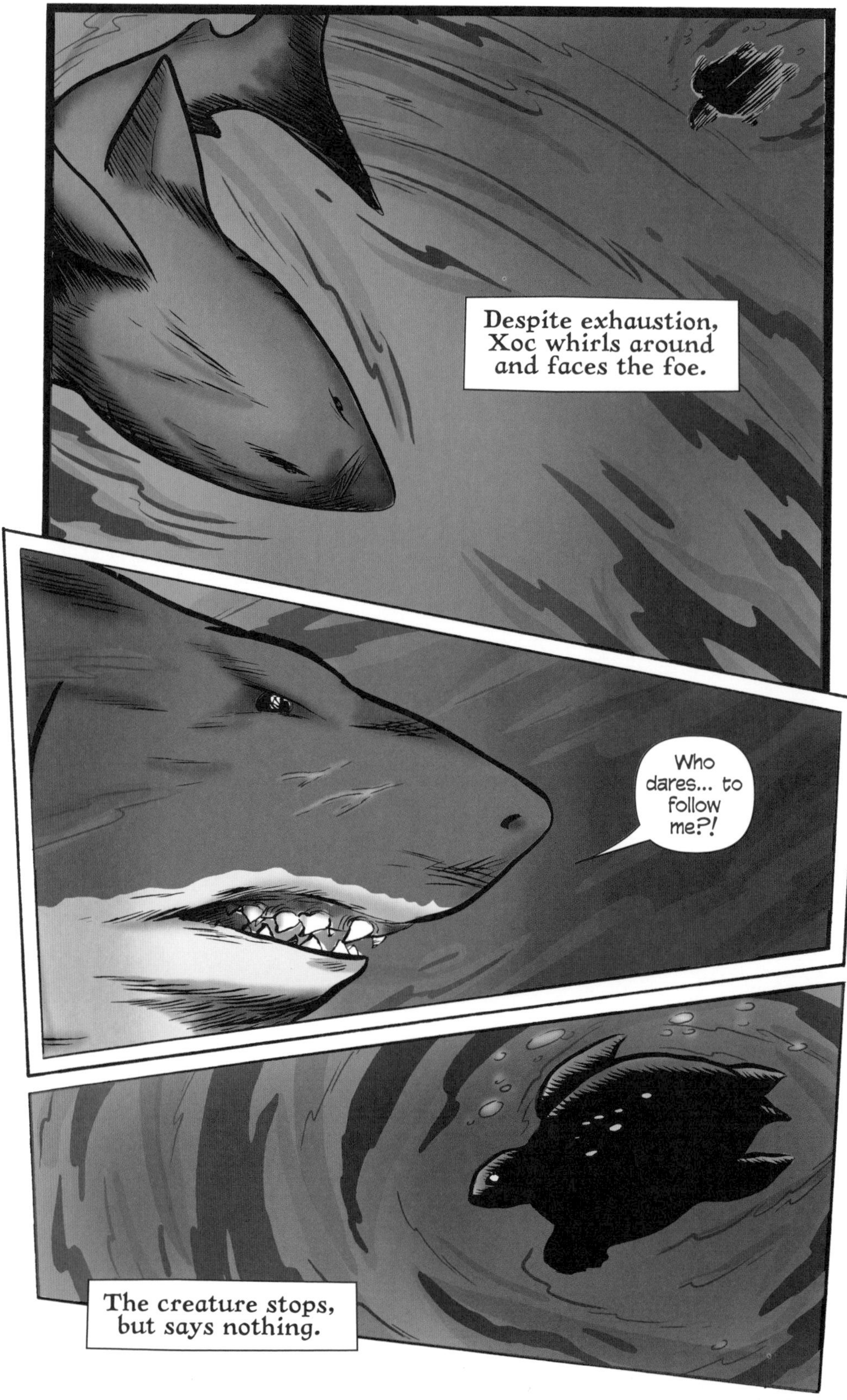
Despite exhaustion, Xoc whirls around and faces the foe.
Who dares... to follow me?!
The creature stops, but says nothing.

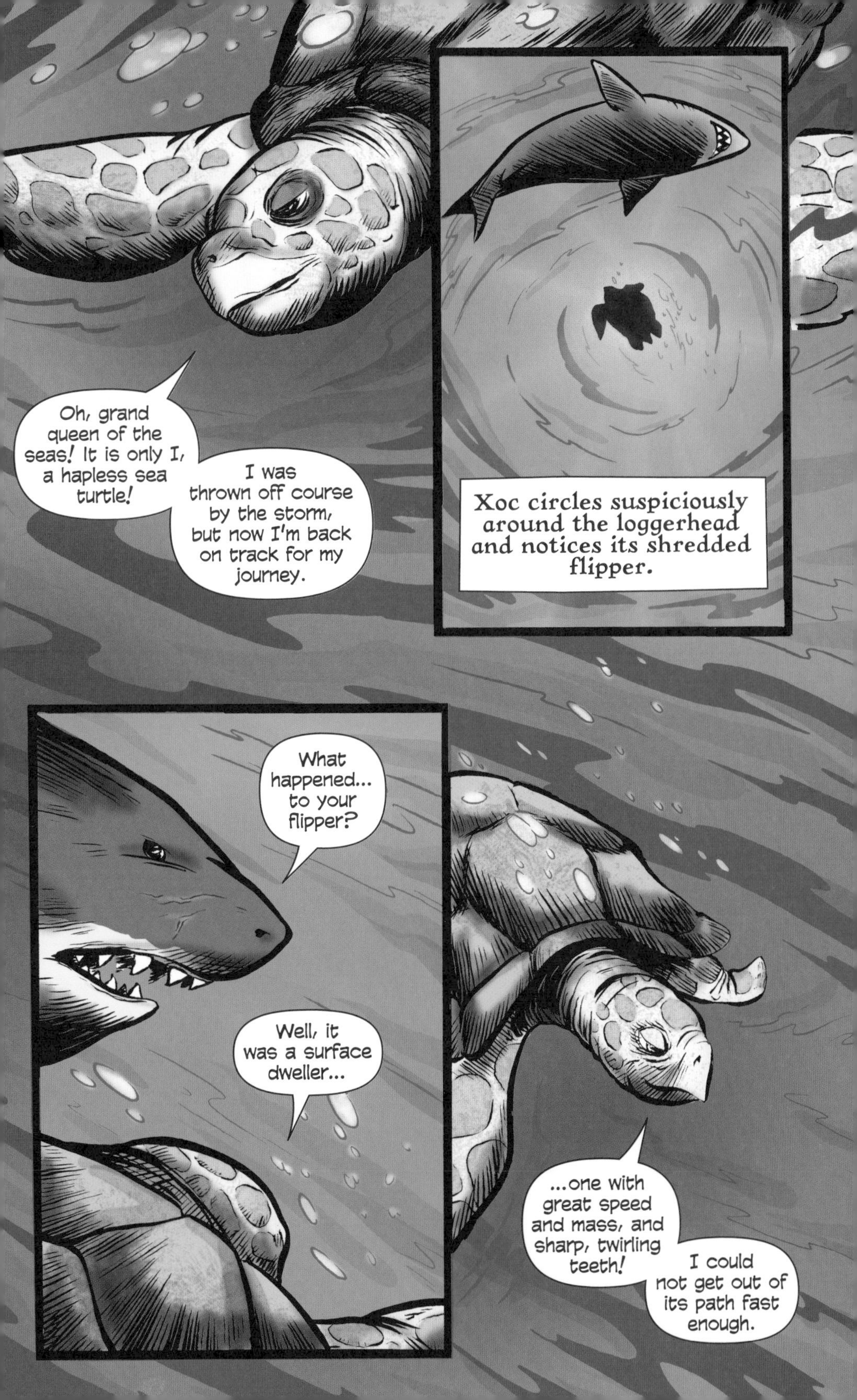
Oh, grand queen of the seas! It is only I, a hapless sea turtle!
I was thrown off course by the storm, but now I'm back on track for my journey.
Xoc circles suspiciously around the loggerhead and notices its shredded flipper.
What happened... to your flipper?
Well, it was a surface dweller...
...one with great speed and mass, and sharp, twirling teeth!
I could not get out of its path fast enough.

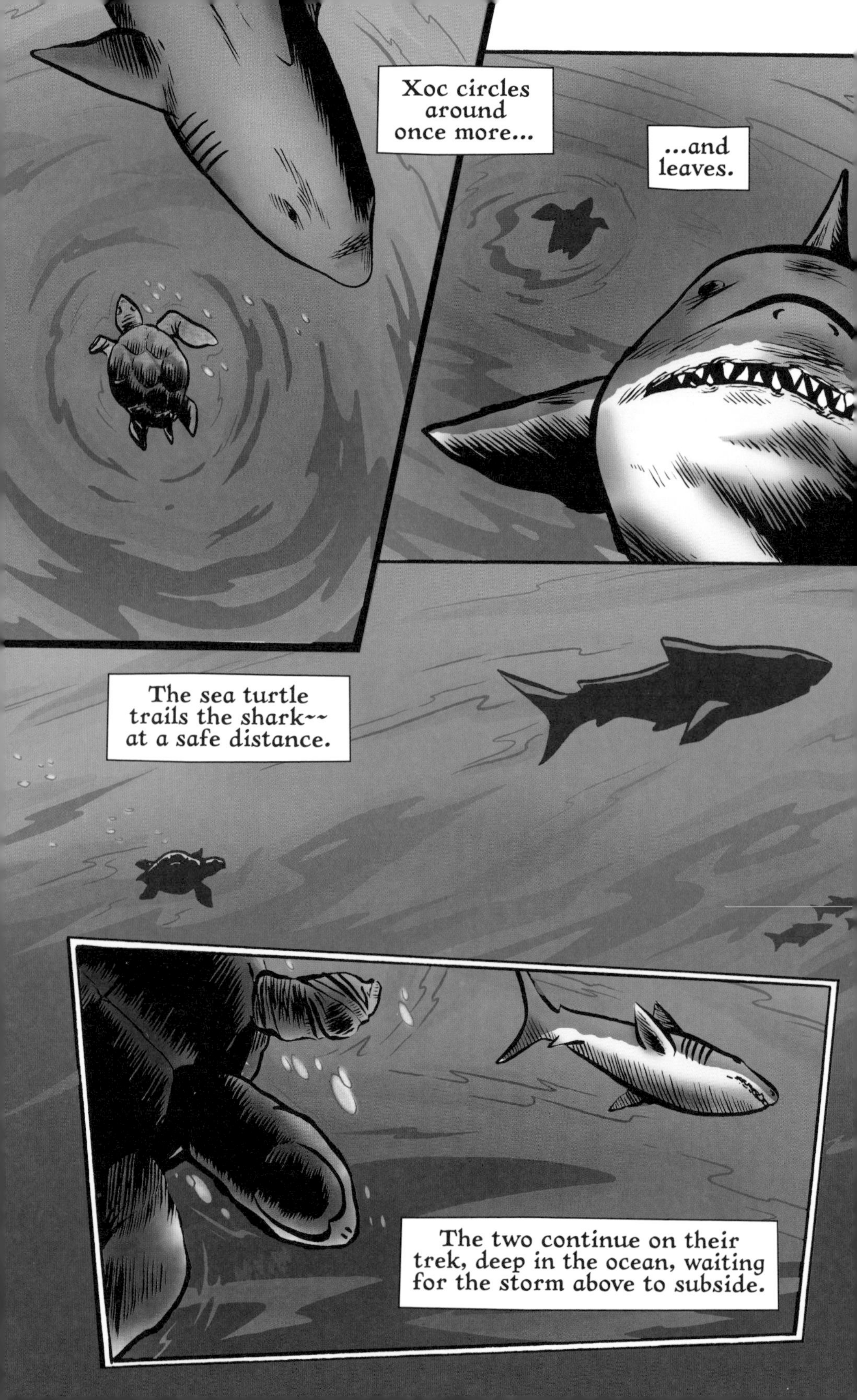
Xoc circles around once more...
...and leaves.
The sea turtle trails the shark-- at a safe distance.
The two continue on their trek, deep in the ocean, waiting for the storm above to subside.

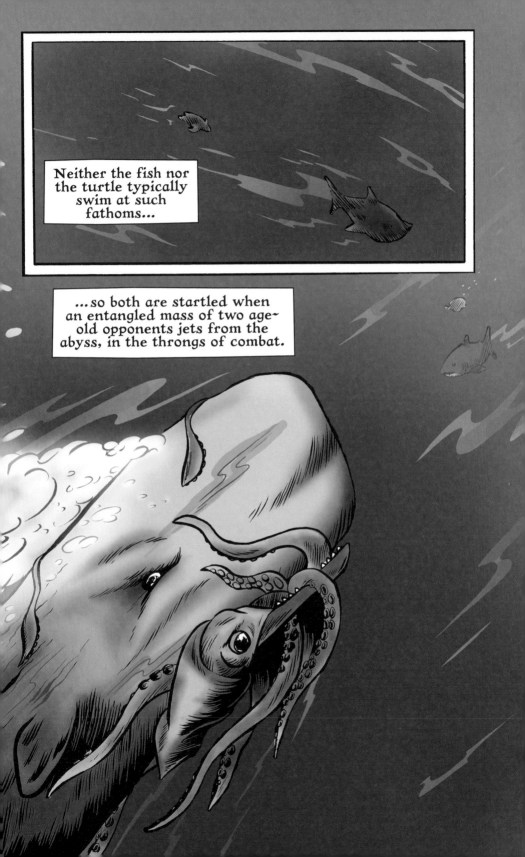

Neither the fish nor the turtle typically swim at such fathoms...

...so both are startled when an entangled mass of two age-old opponents jets from the abyss, in the throngs of combat.

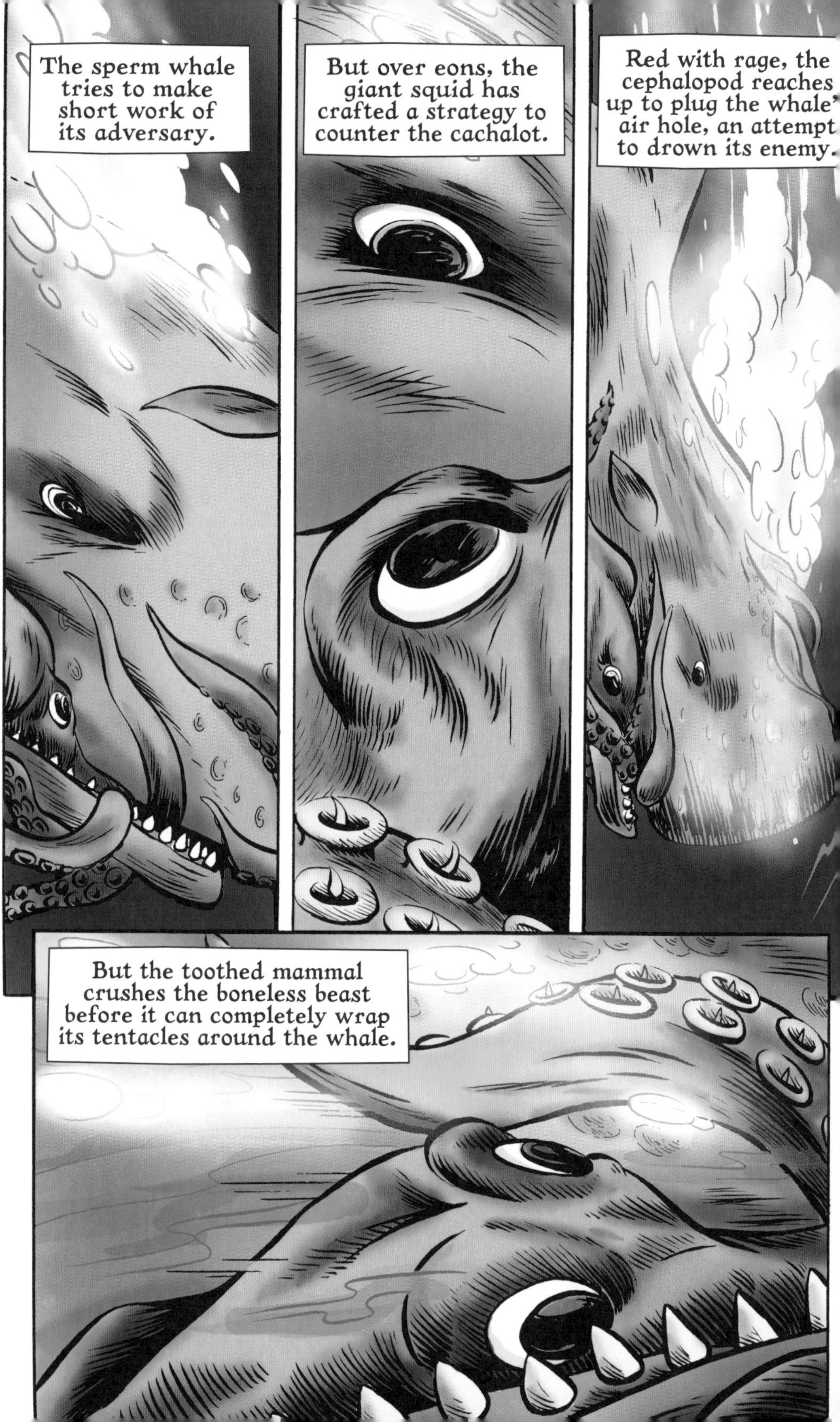
The sperm whale tries to make short work of its adversary.
But over eons, the giant squid has crafted a strategy to counter the cachalot.
Red with rage, the cephalopod reaches up to plug the whale' air hole, an attempt to drown its enemy.
But the toothed mammal crushes the boneless beast before it can completely wrap its tentacles around the whale.

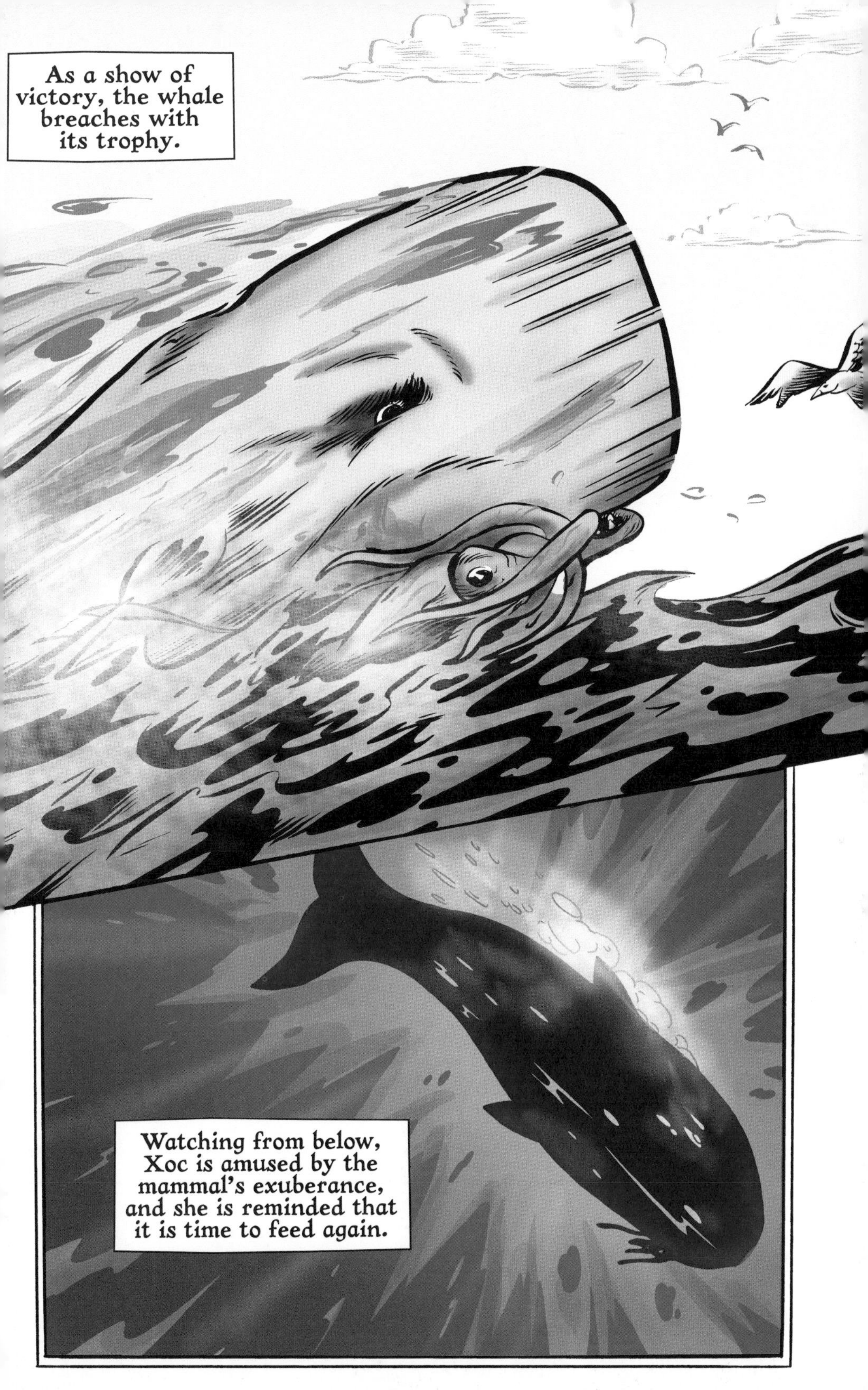
As a show of victory, the whale breaches with its trophy.
Watching from below, Xoc is amused by the mammal's exuberance, and she is reminded that it is time to feed again.

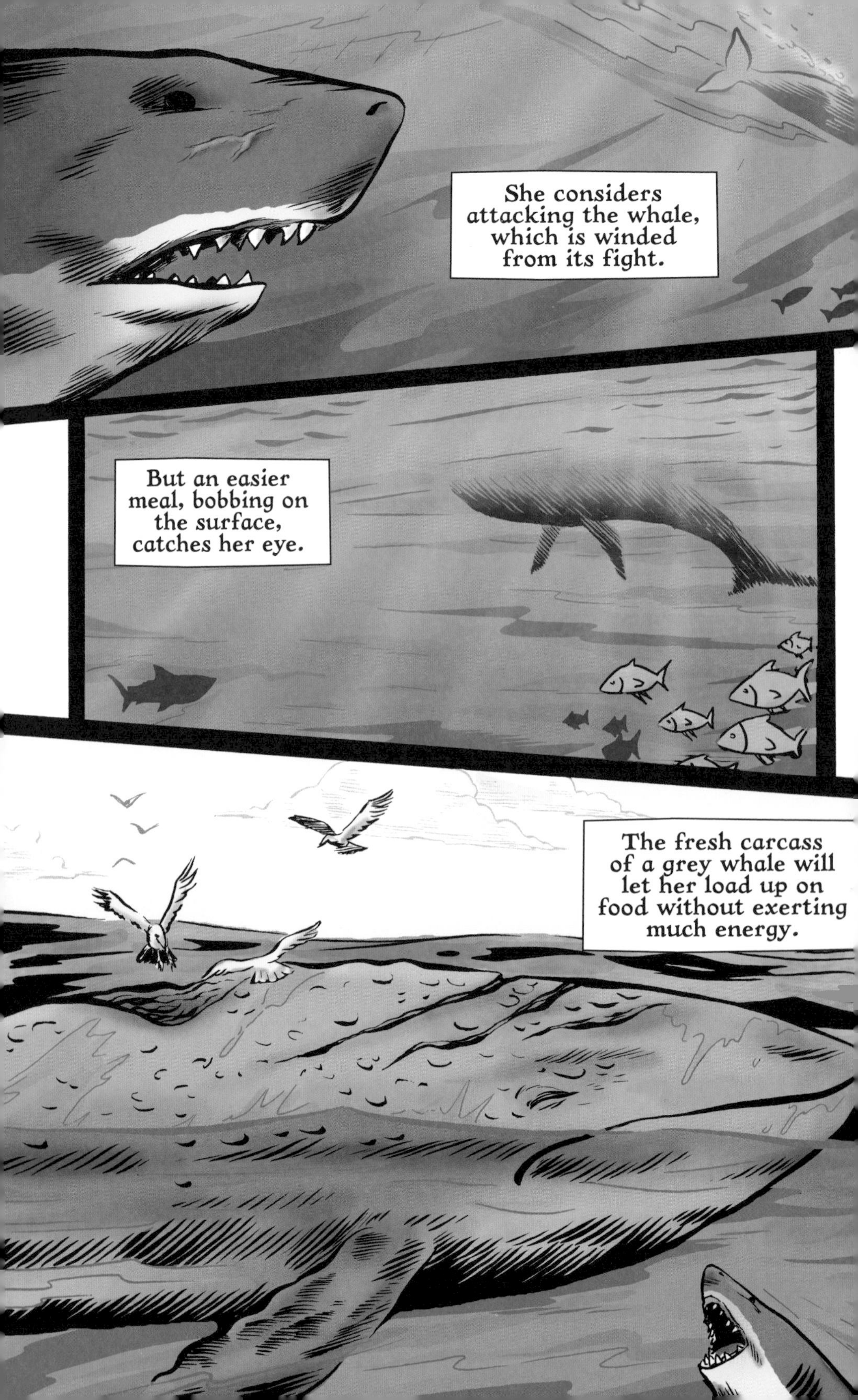
She considers attacking the whale, which is winded from its fight.
But an easier meal, bobbing on the surface, catches her eye.
The fresh carcass of a grey whale will let her load up on food without exerting much energy.

Xoc rips off chunks of flesh and circles back several times until she is full, reaching euphoria.

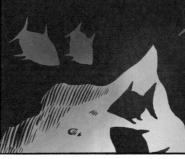

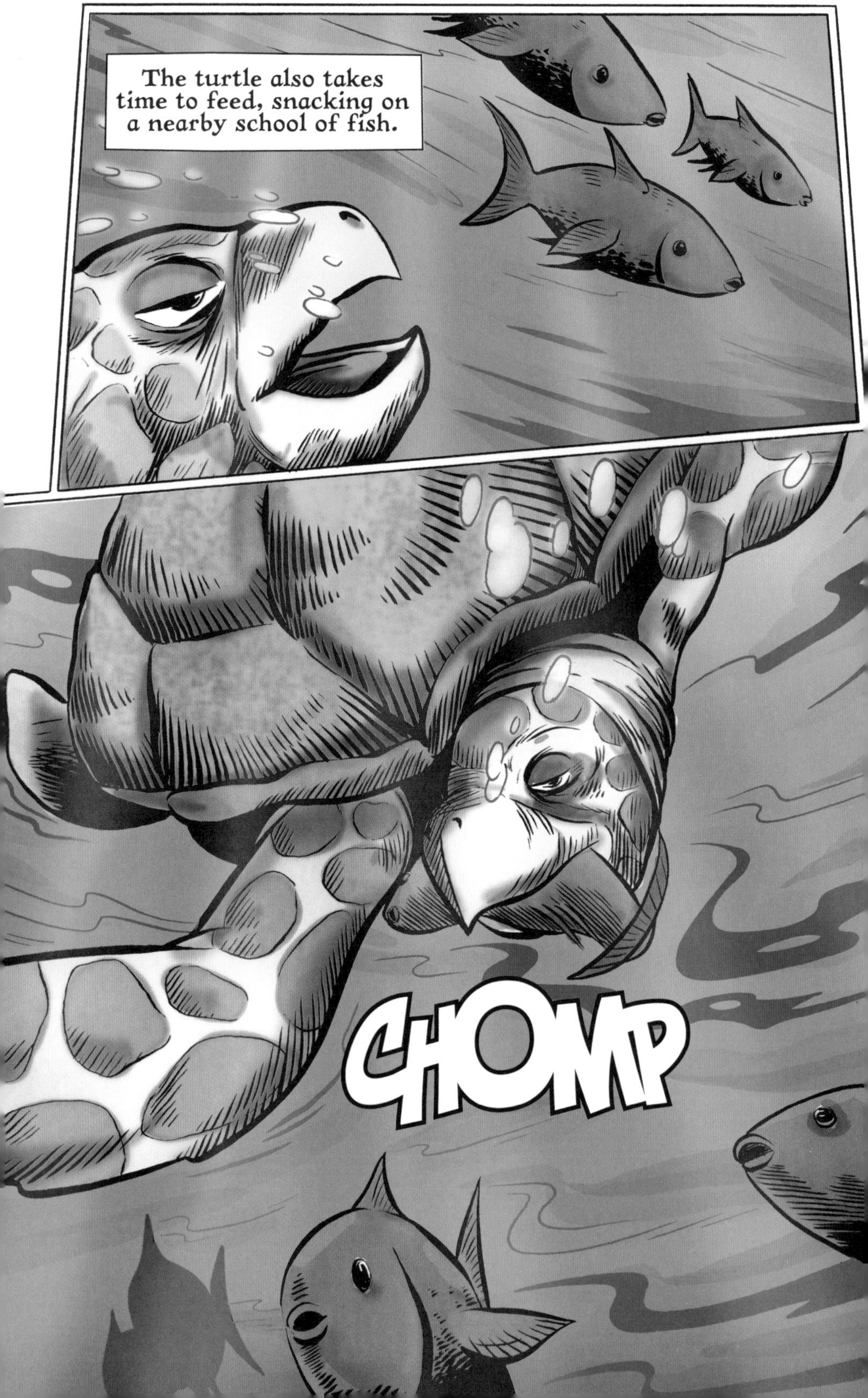
The turtle also takes time to feed, snacking on a nearby school of fish.
CHOMP

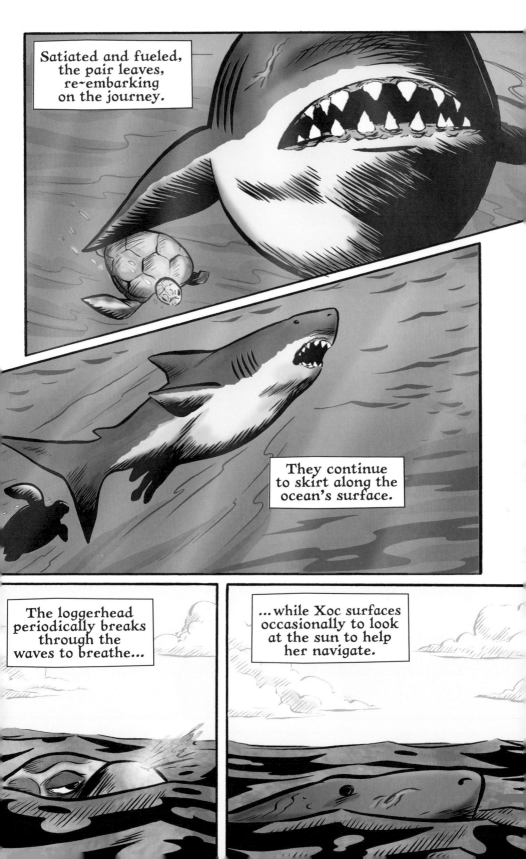

Satiated and fueled,
the pair leaves,
re~embarking
on the journey.

They continue
to skirt along the
ocean's surface.

The loggerhead
periodically breaks
through the
waves to breathe...

...while Xoc surfaces
occasionally to look
at the sun to help
her navigate.

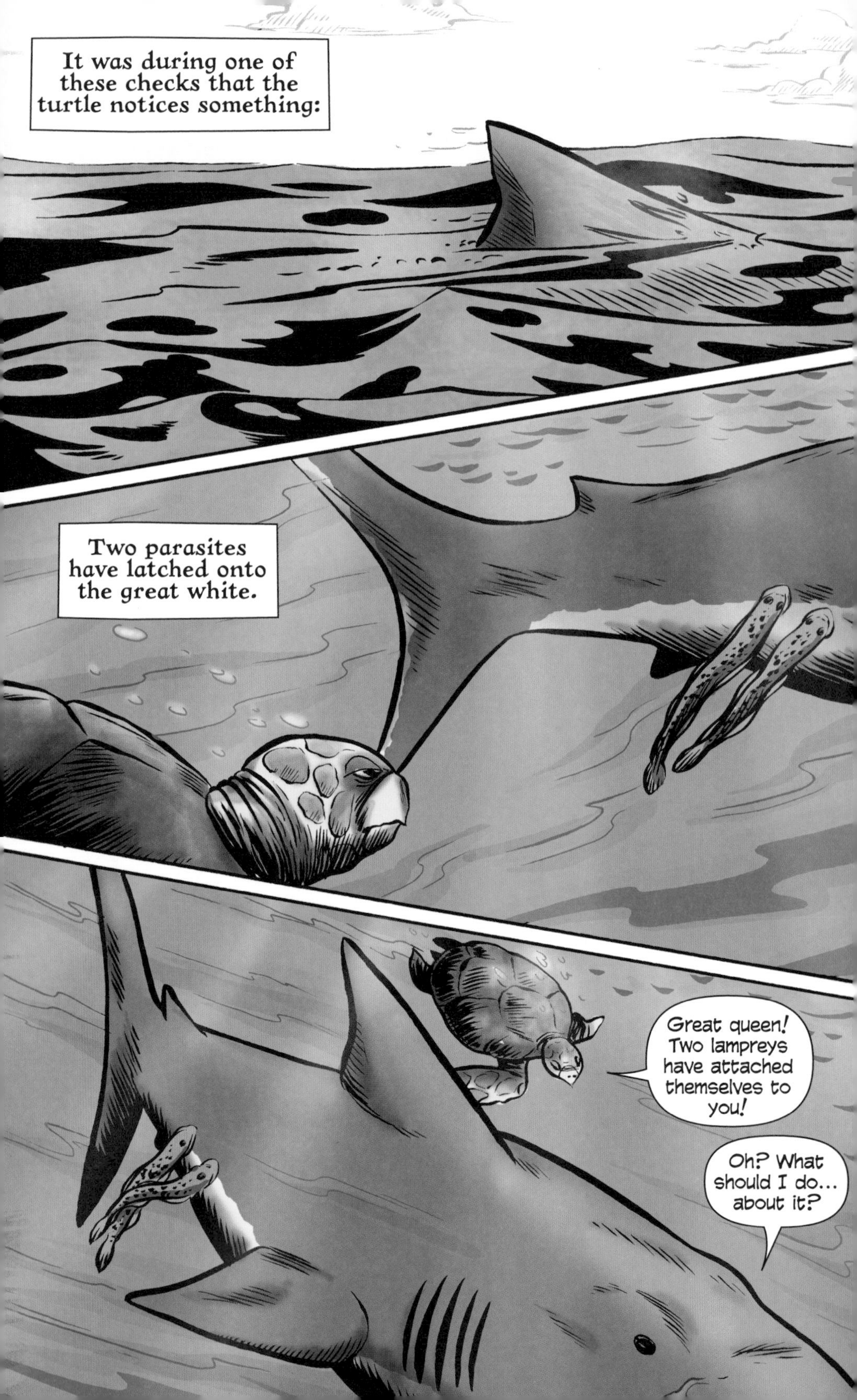
It was during one of these checks that the turtle notices something:
Two parasites have latched onto the great white.
Great queen! Two lampreys have attached themselves to you!
Oh? What should I do... about it?

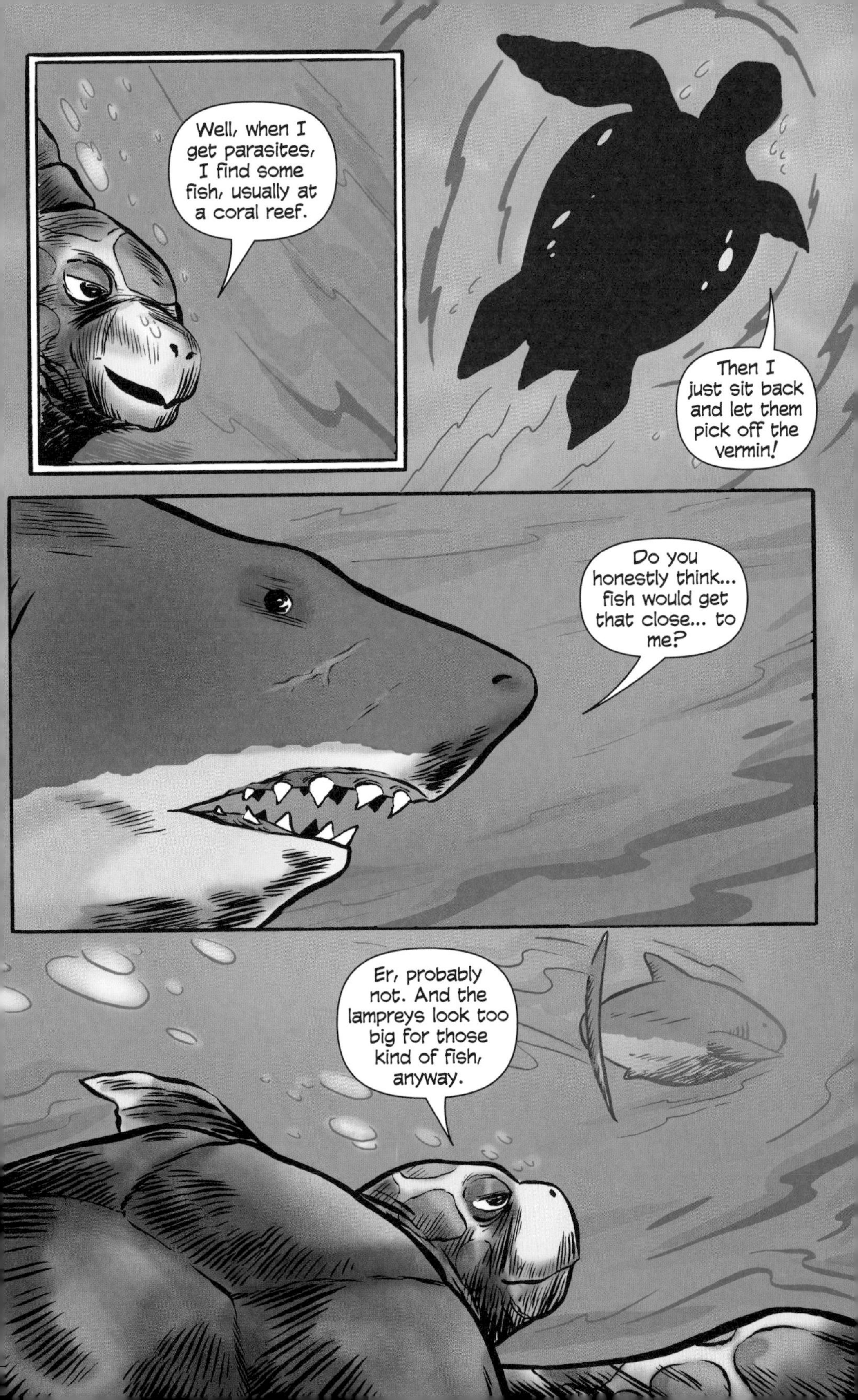
Well, when I get parasites, I find some fish, usually at a coral reef.
Then I just sit back and let them pick off the vermin!
Do you honestly think... fish would get that close... to me?
Er, probably not. And the lampreys look too big for those kind of fish, anyway.

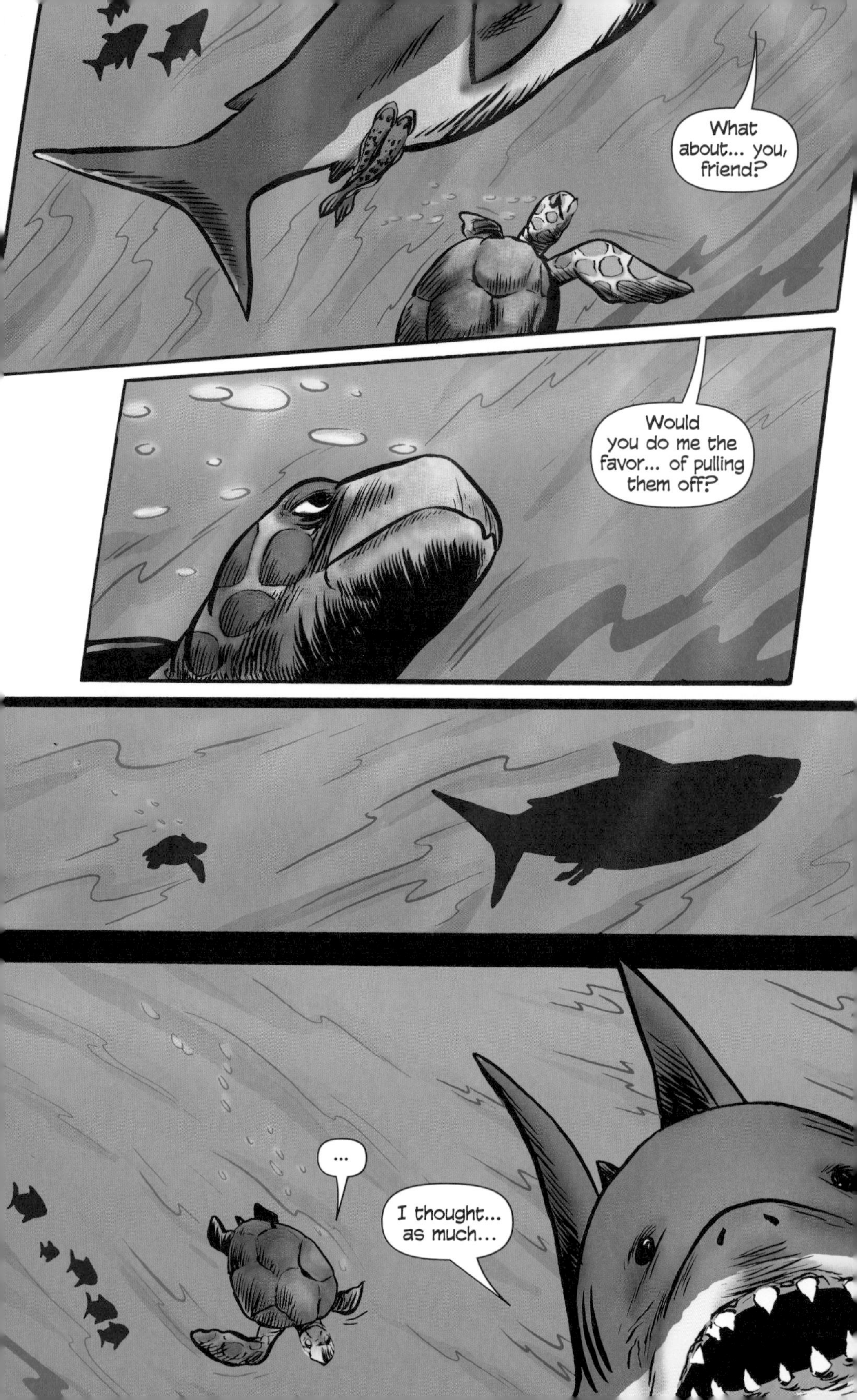

What about... you, friend?
Would you do me the favor... of pulling them off?
...
I thought... as much...

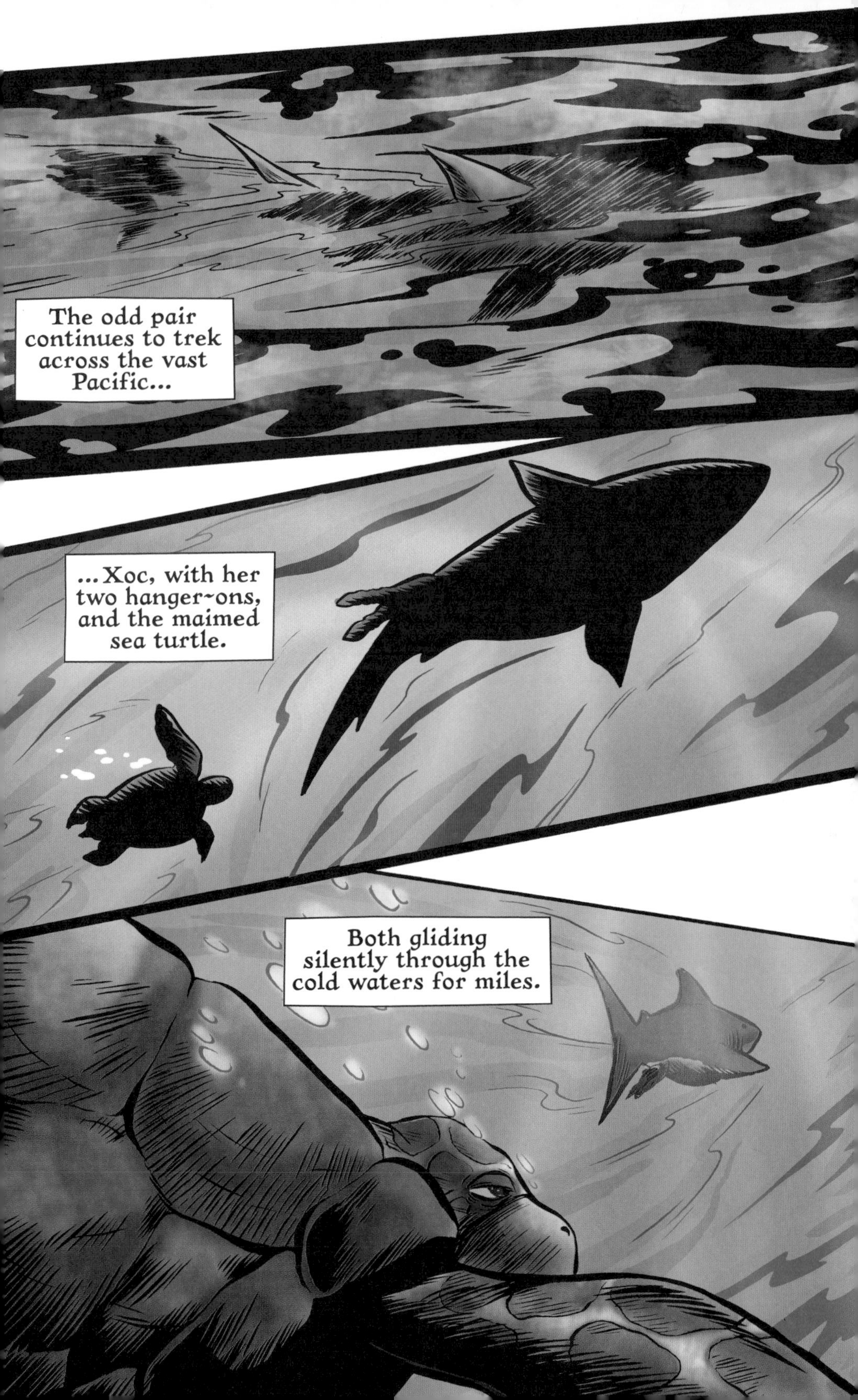
The odd pair continues to trek across the vast Pacific...
...Xoc, with her two hanger~ons, and the maimed sea turtle.
Both gliding silently through the cold waters for miles.

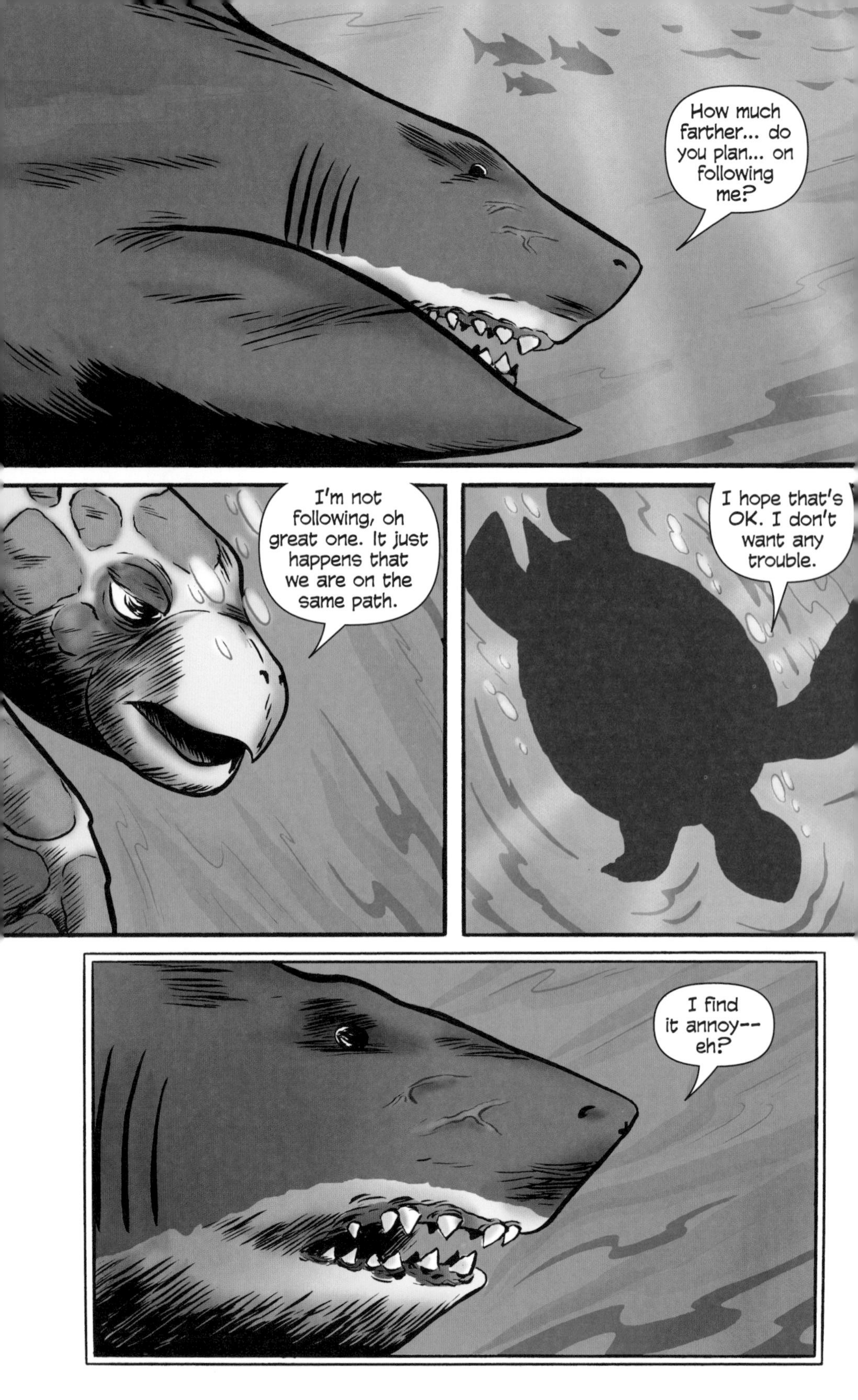
How much farther... do you plan... on following me?
I'm not following, oh great one. It just happens that we are on the same path.
I hope that's OK. I don't want any trouble.
I find it annoy-- eh?

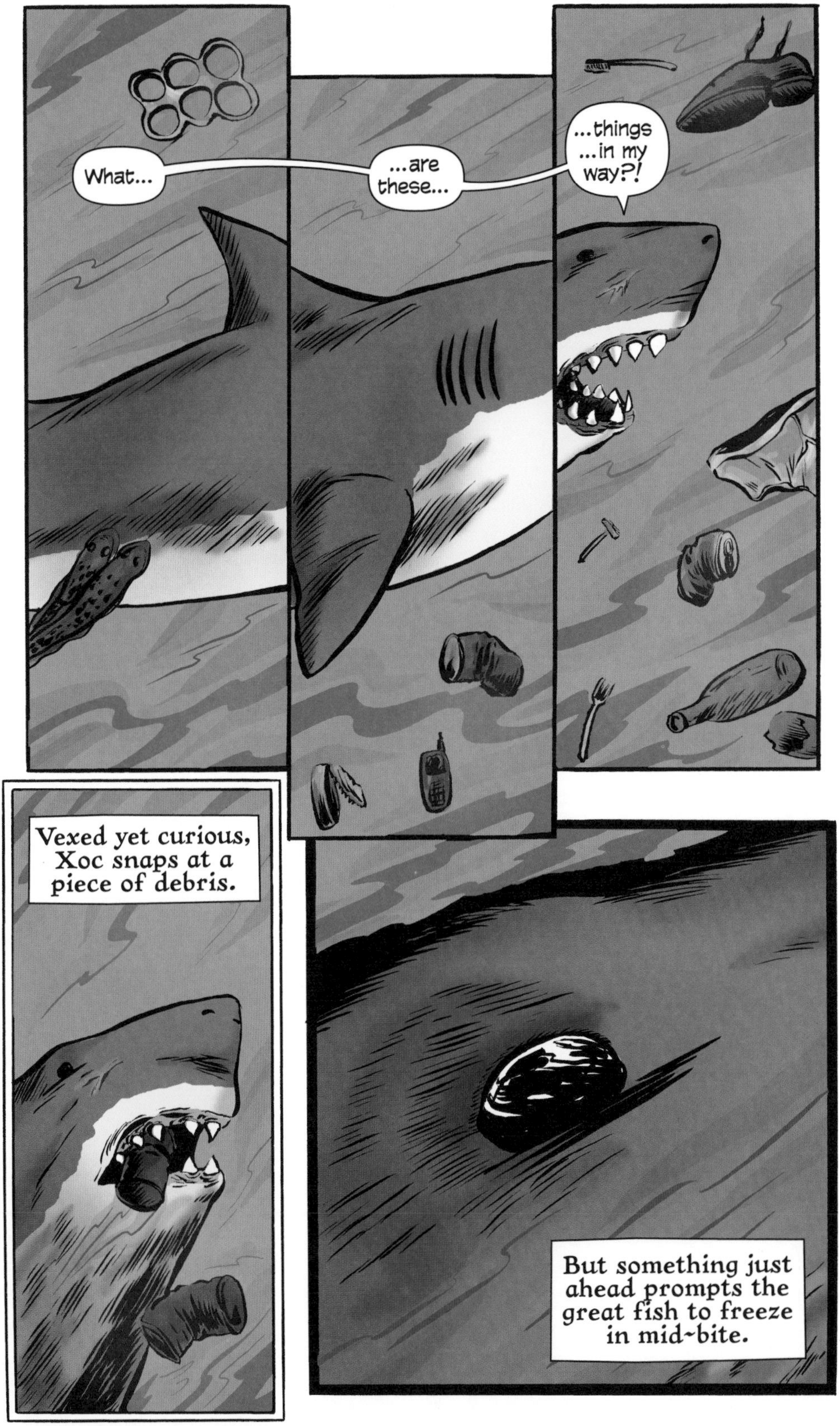
What...
...are these...
...things ...in my way?!
Vexed yet curious, Xoc snaps at a piece of debris.
But something just ahead prompts the great fish to freeze in mid-bite.

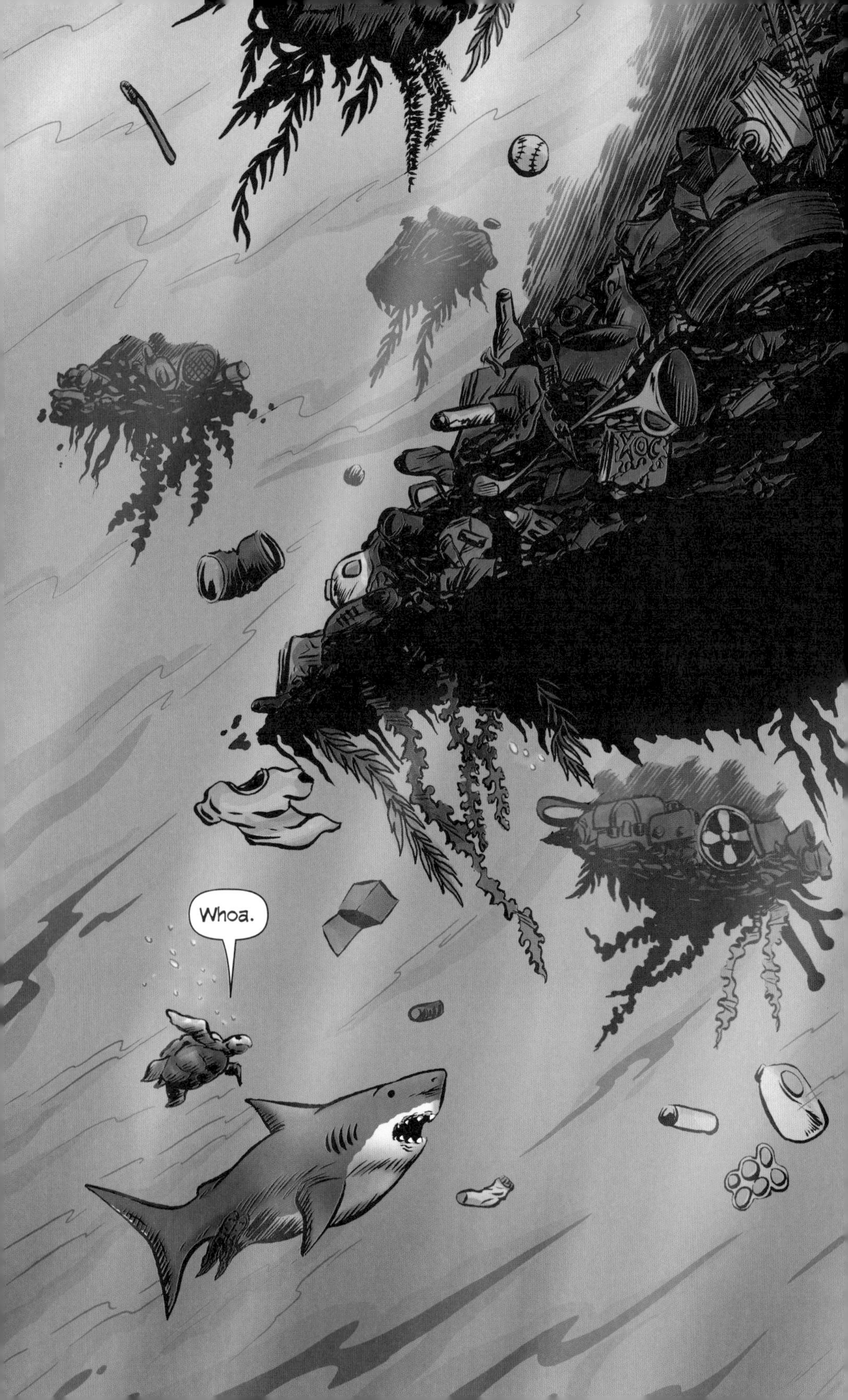
Whoa.

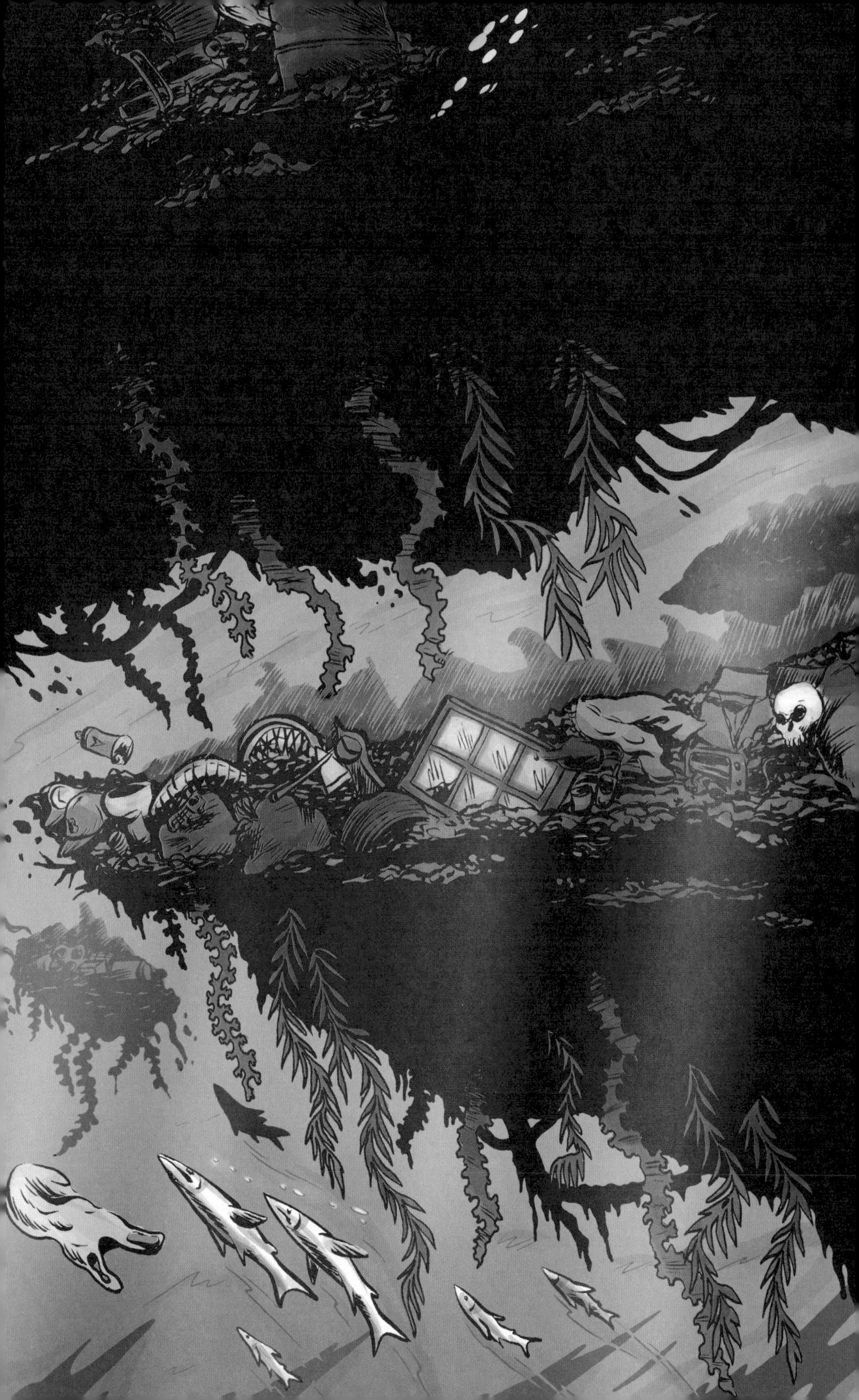

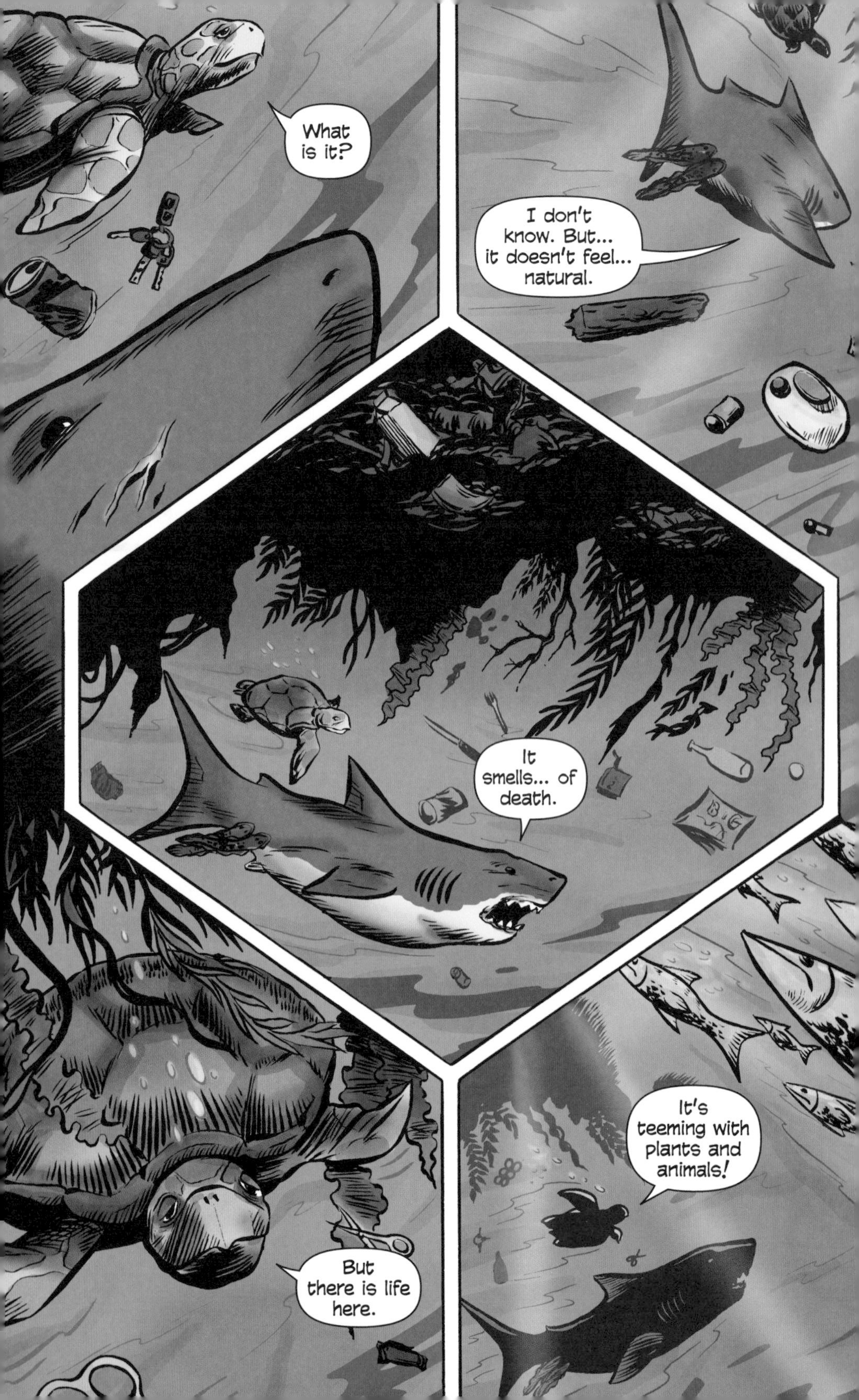
What is it?
I don't know. But... it doesn't feel... natural.
It smells... of death.
But there is life here.
It's teeming with plants and animals!

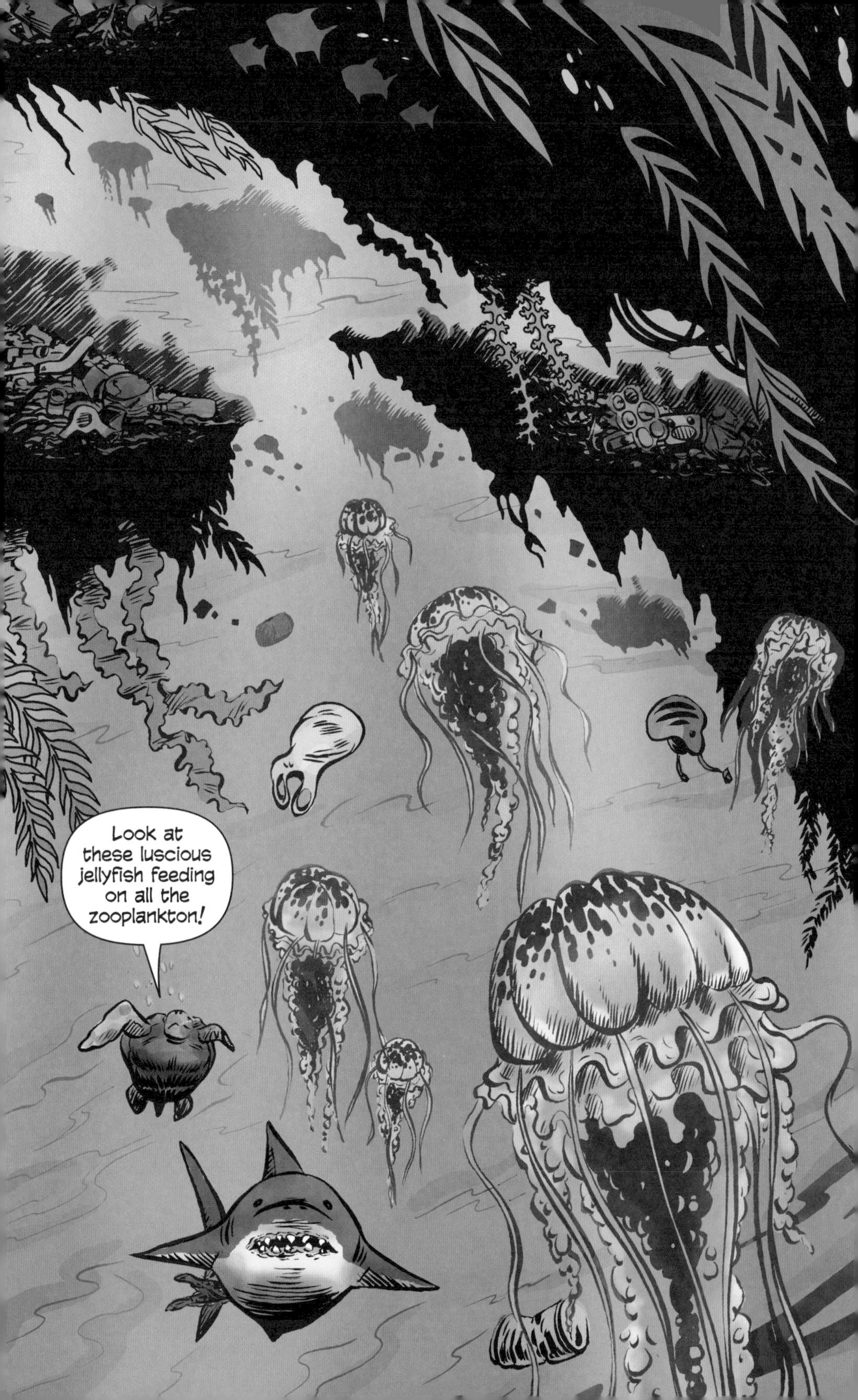
Look at these luscious jellyfish feeding on all the zooplankton!

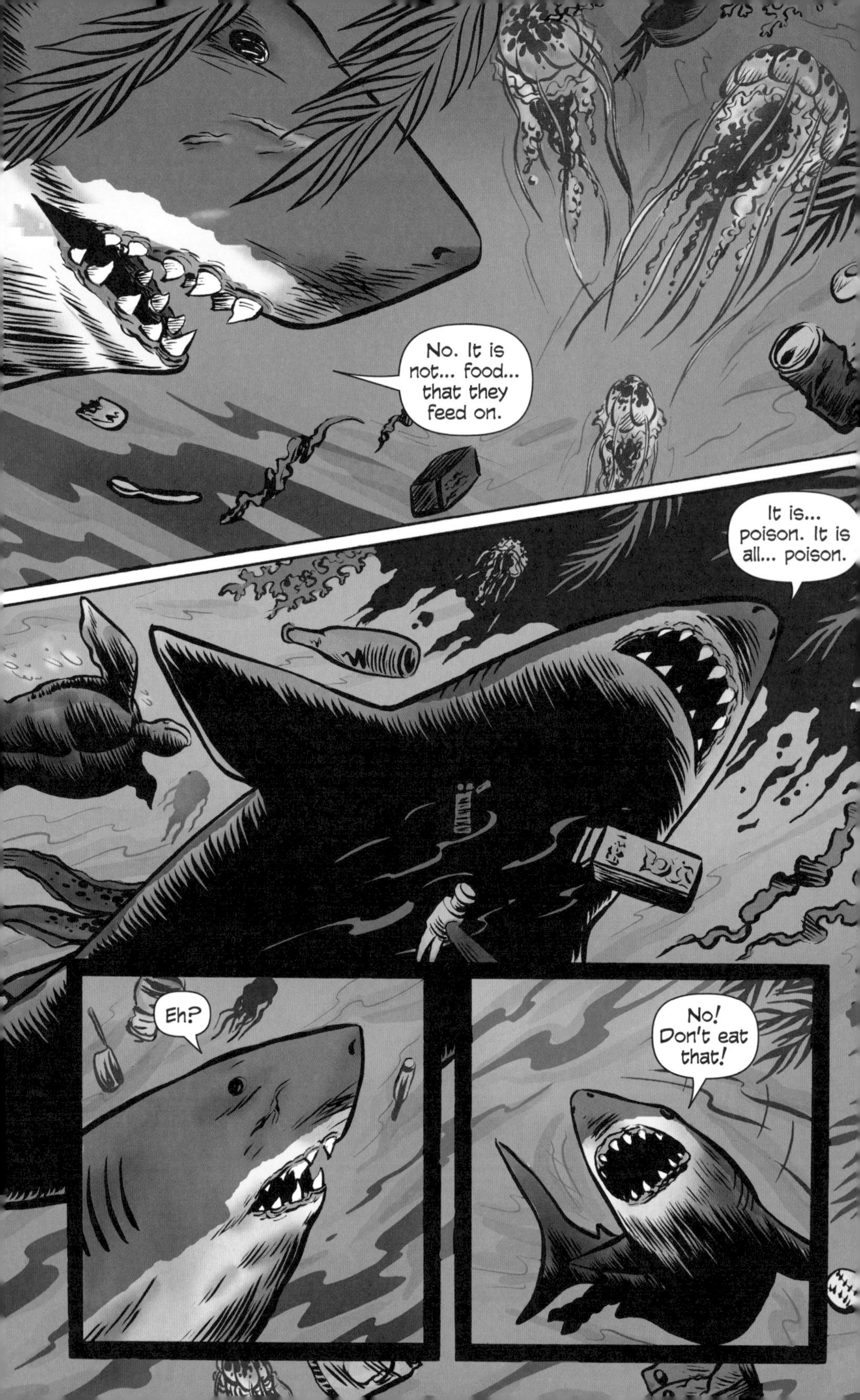
No. It is not... food... that they feed on.
It is... poison. It is all... poison.
Eh?
No! Don't eat that!

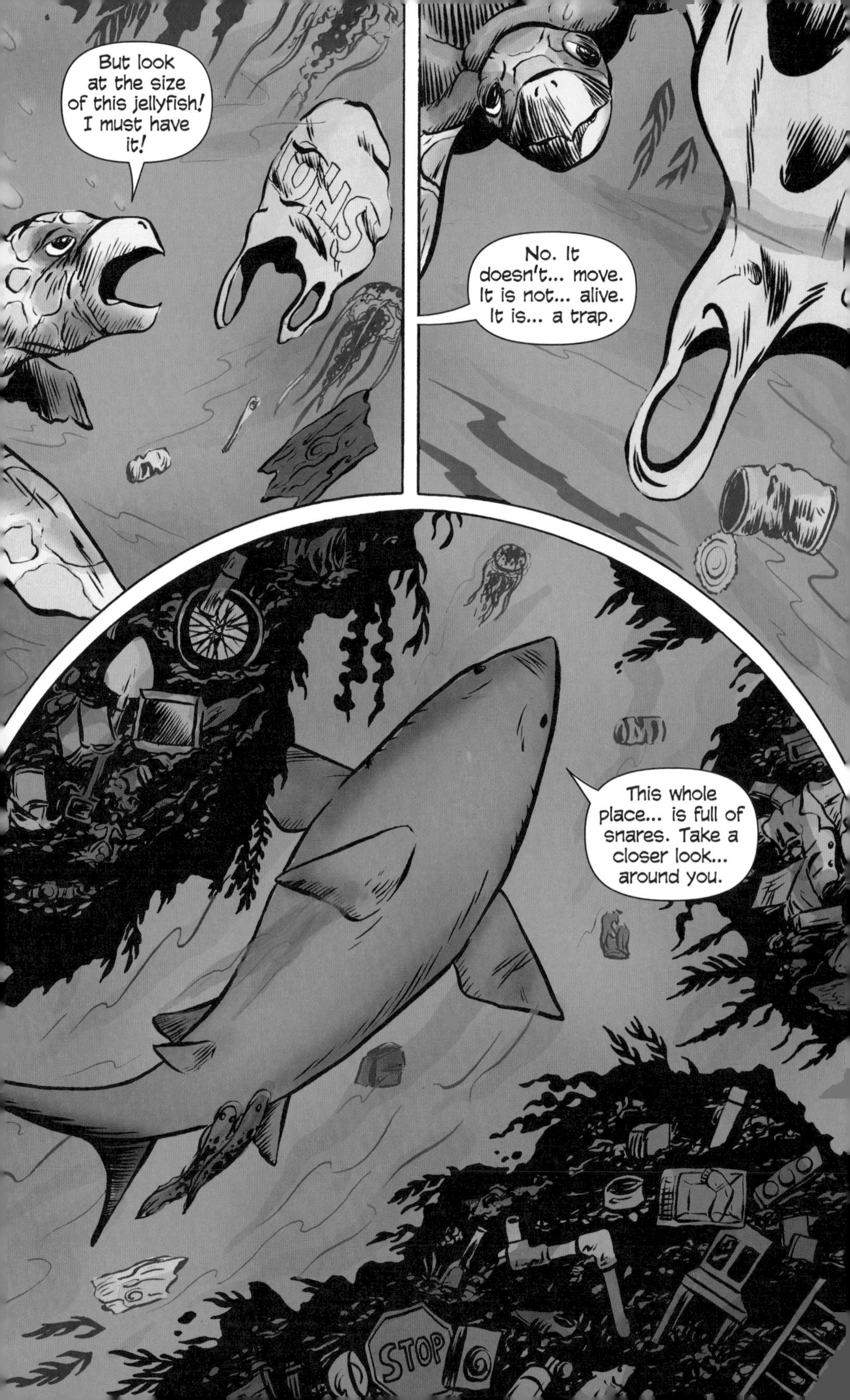
But look at the size of this jellyfish! I must have it!
No. It doesn't... move. It is not... alive. It is... a trap.
This whole place... is full of snares. Take a closer look... around you.
STOP

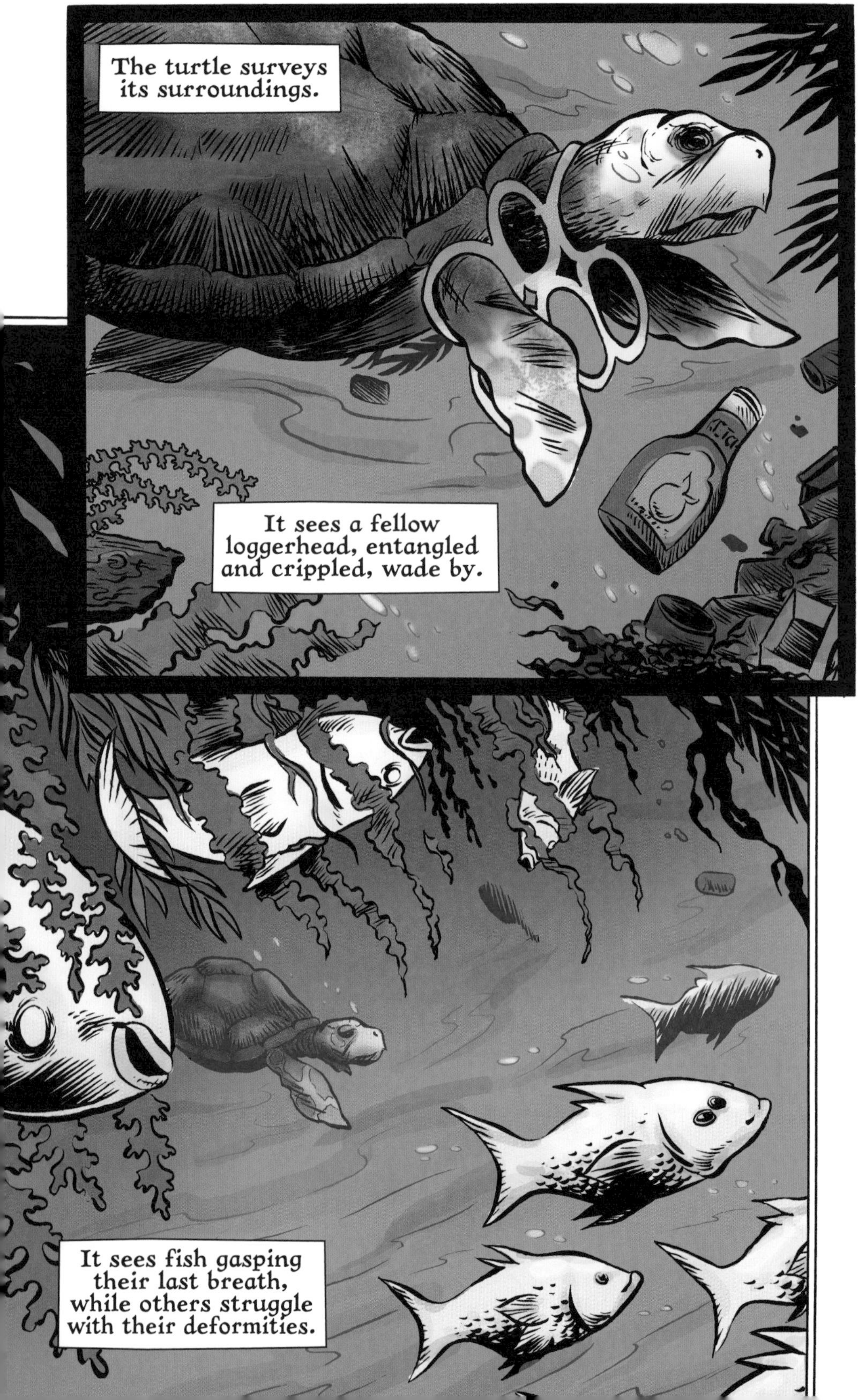
The turtle surveys its surroundings.
It sees a fellow loggerhead, entangled and crippled, wade by.
It sees fish gasping their last breath, while others struggle with their deformities.

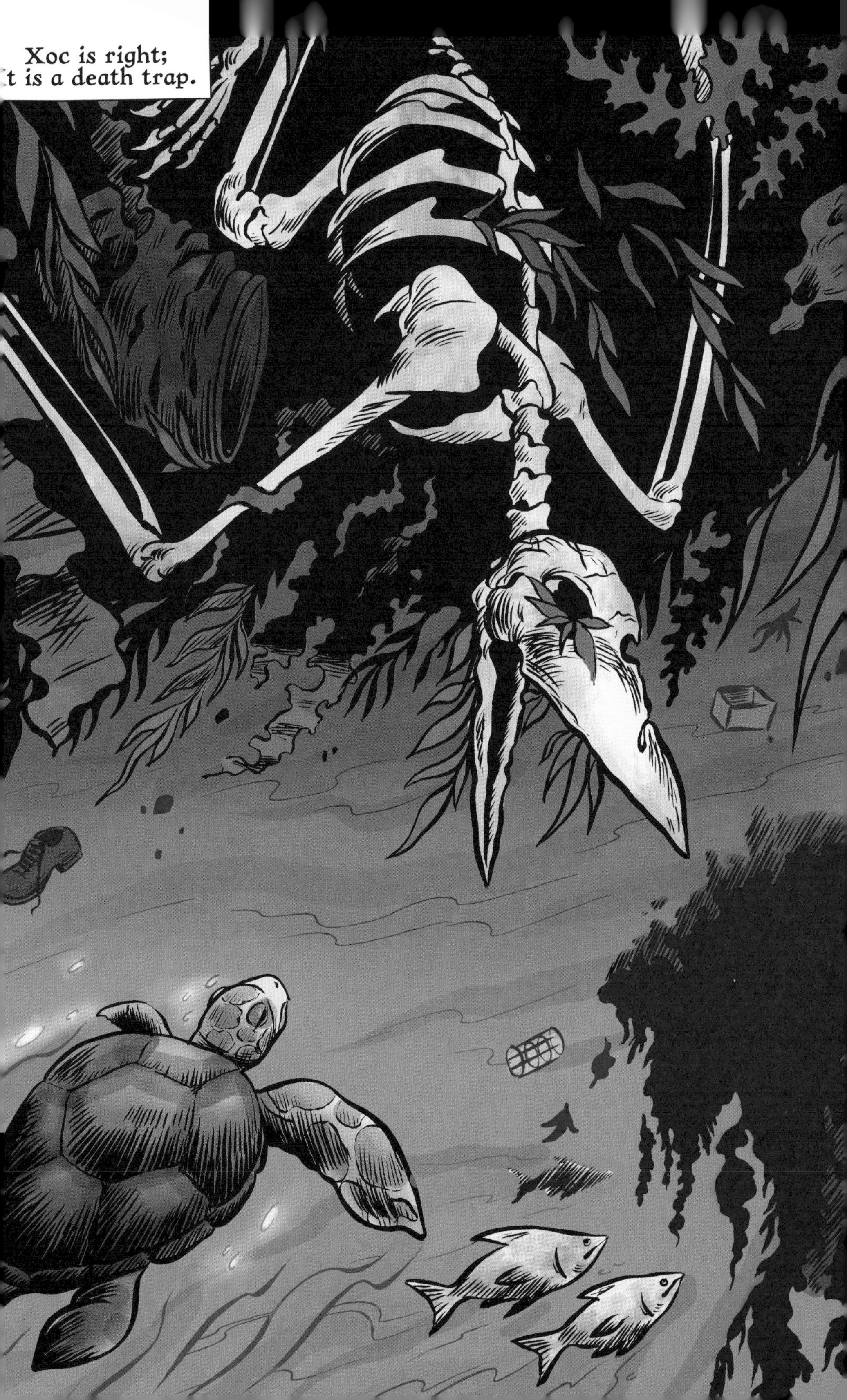
Xoc is right;
't is a death trap.

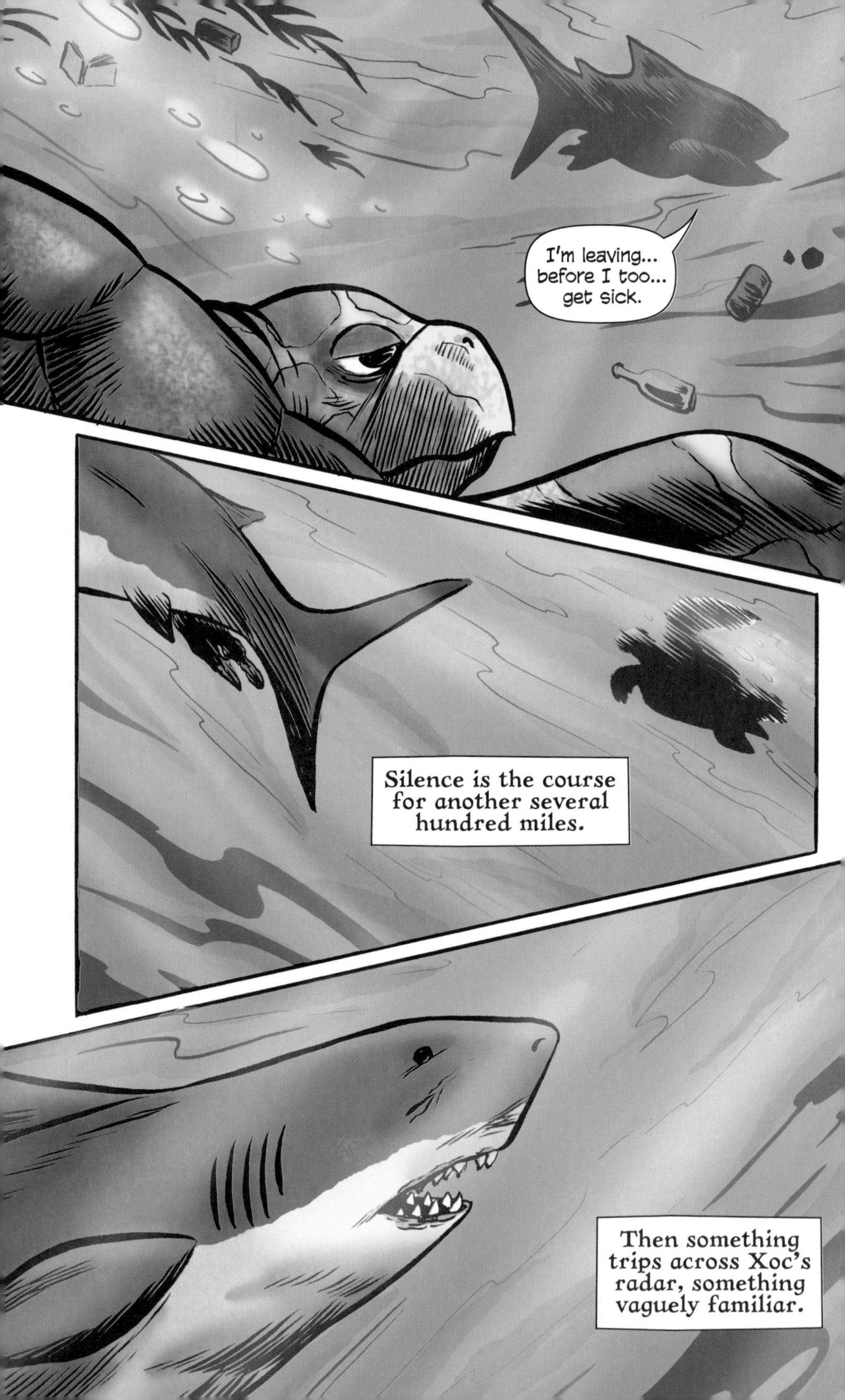
I'm leaving... before I too... get sick.
Silence is the course for another several hundred miles.
Then something trips across Xoc's radar, something vaguely familiar.

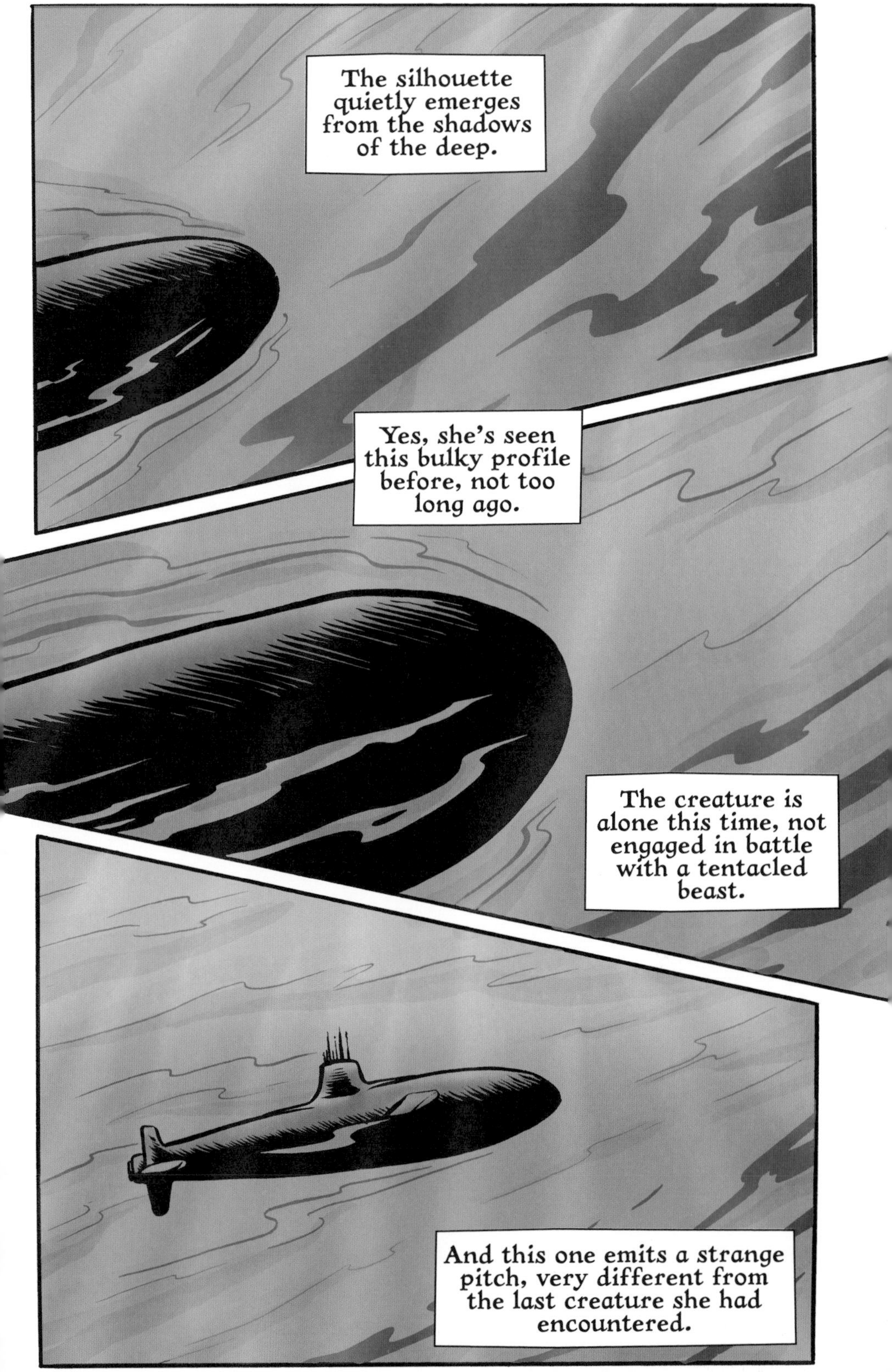
The silhouette quietly emerges from the shadows of the deep.
Yes, she's seen this bulky profile before, not too long ago.
The creature is alone this time, not engaged in battle with a tentacled beast.
And this one emits a strange pitch, very different from the last creature she had encountered.

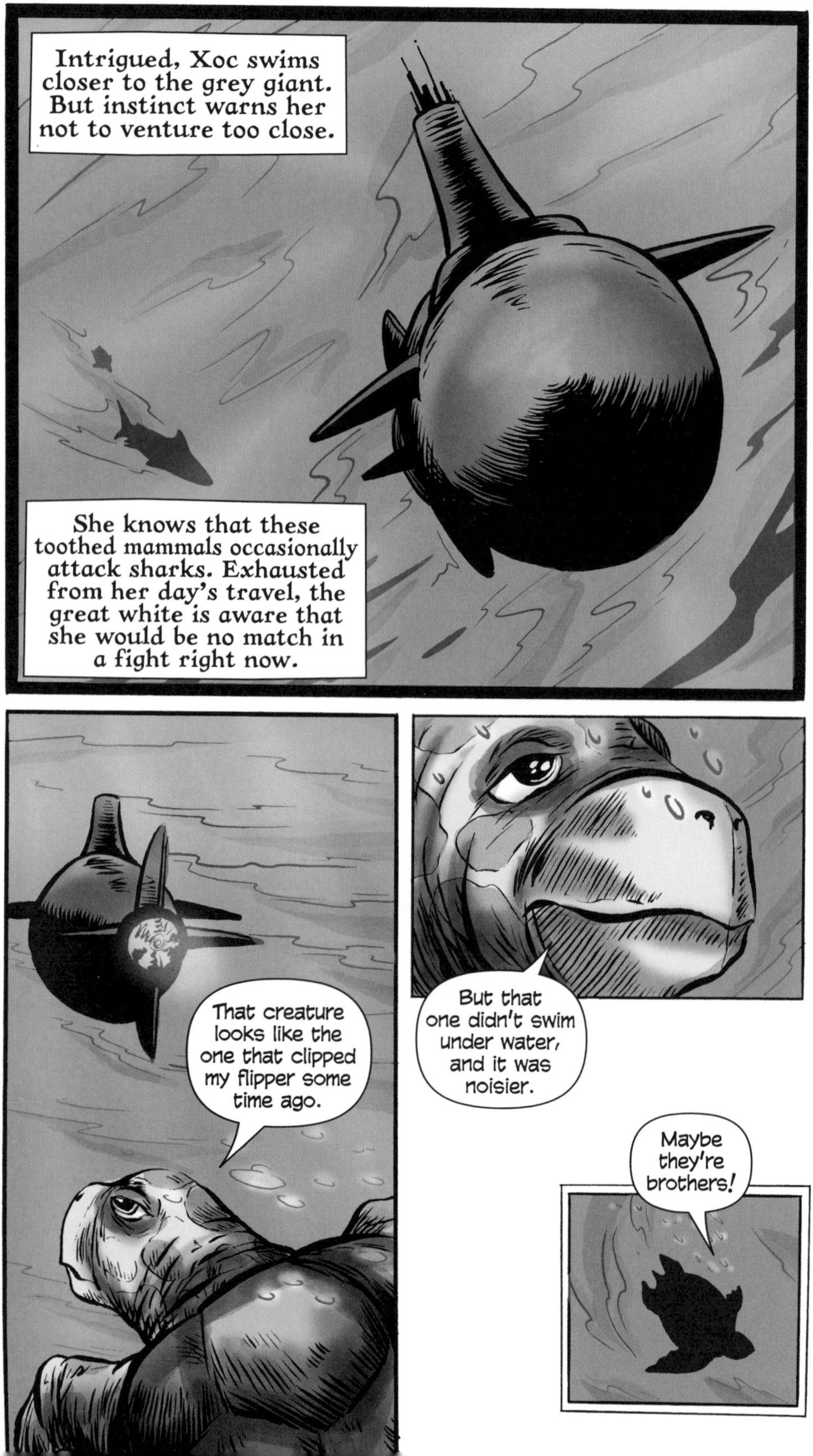
Intrigued, Xoc swims closer to the grey giant. But instinct warns her not to venture too close.
She knows that these toothed mammals occasionally attack sharks. Exhausted from her day's travel, the great white is aware that she would be no match in a fight right now.
That creature looks like the one that clipped my flipper some time ago.
But that one didn't swim under water, and it was noisier.
Maybe they're brothers!

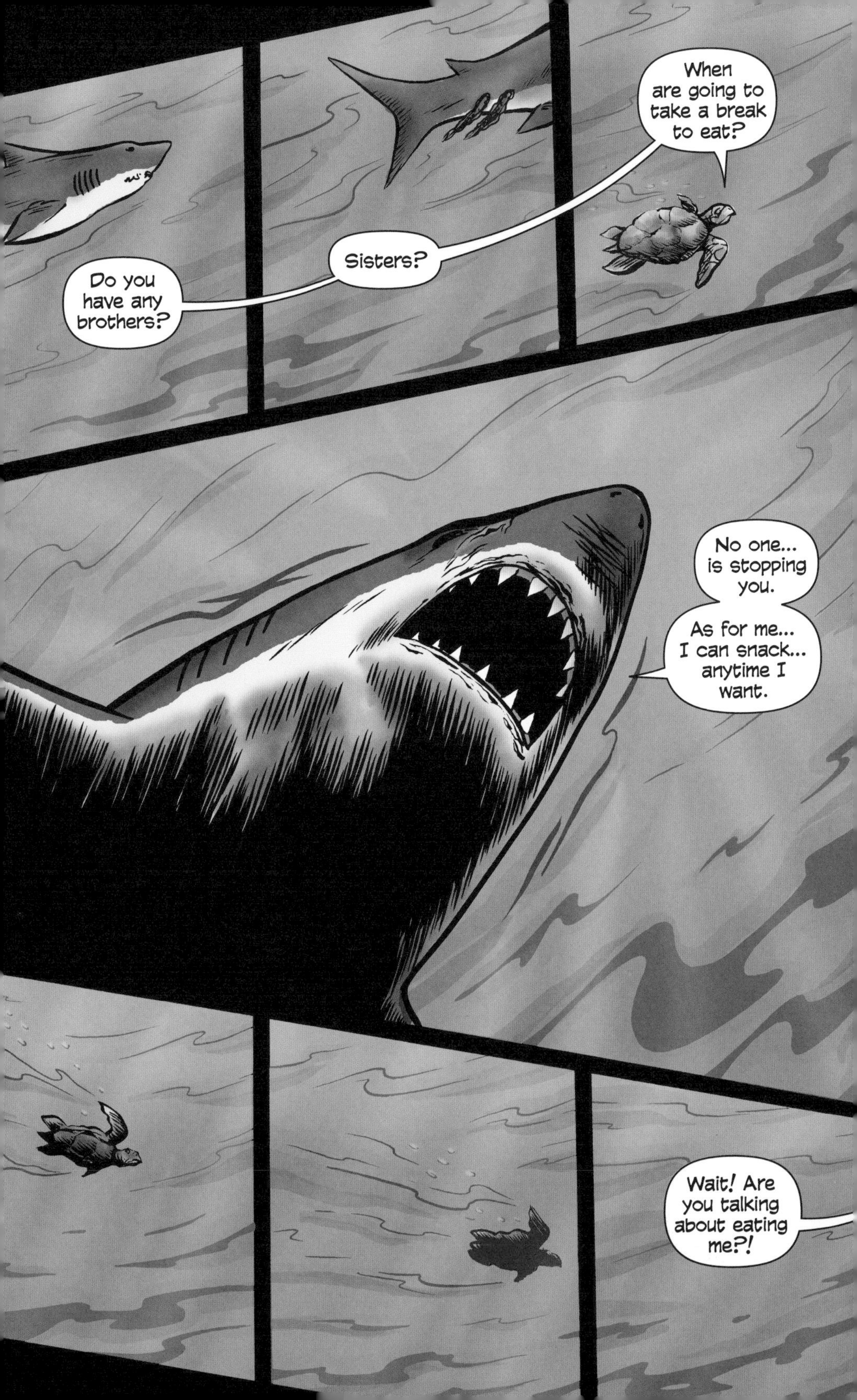
Do you have any brothers?
Sisters?
When are going to take a break to eat?
No one... is stopping you.
As for me... I can snack... anytime I want.
Wait! Are you talking about eating me?!

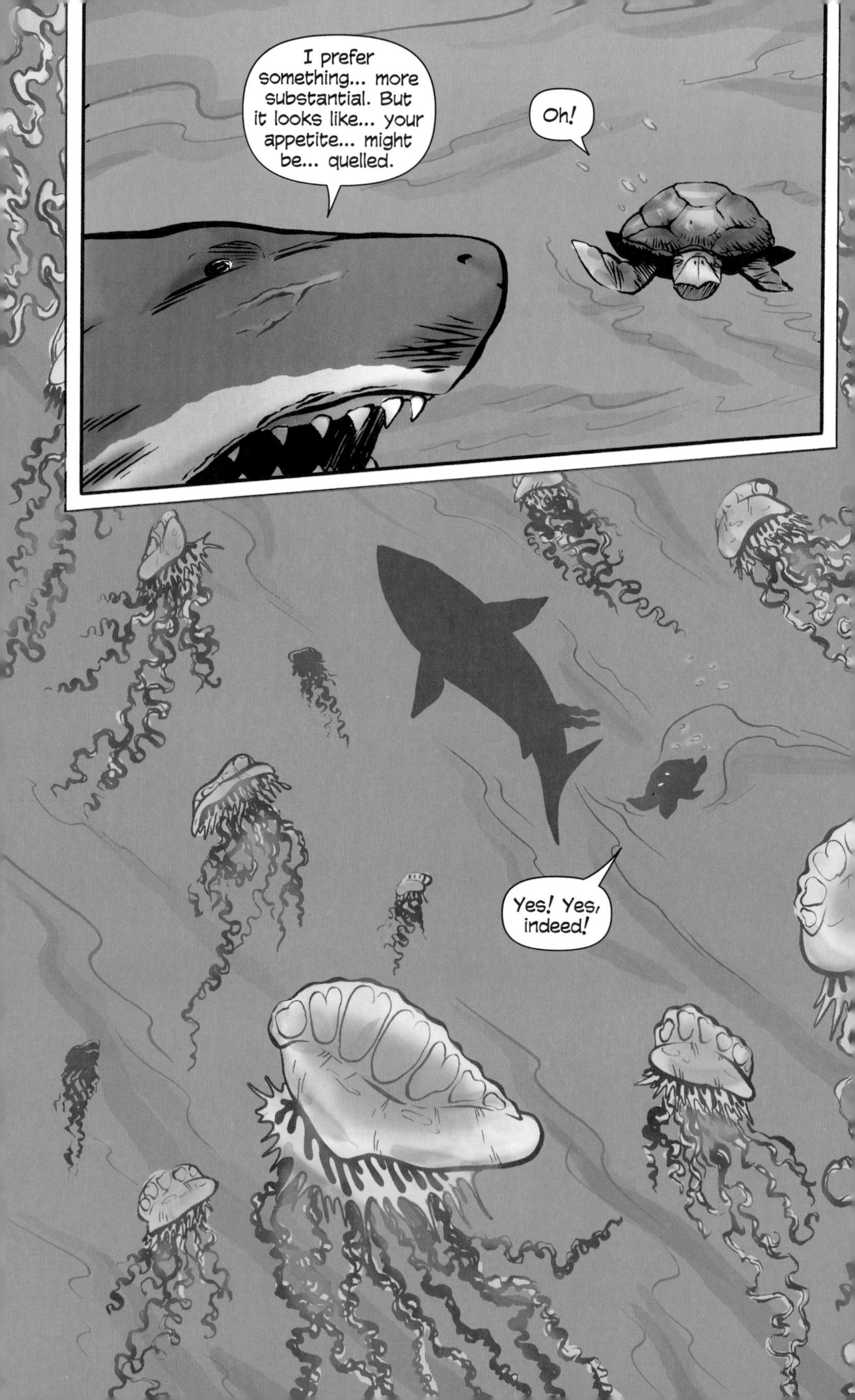
I prefer something... more substantial. But it looks like... your appetite... might be... quelled.
Oh!
Yes! Yes, indeed!

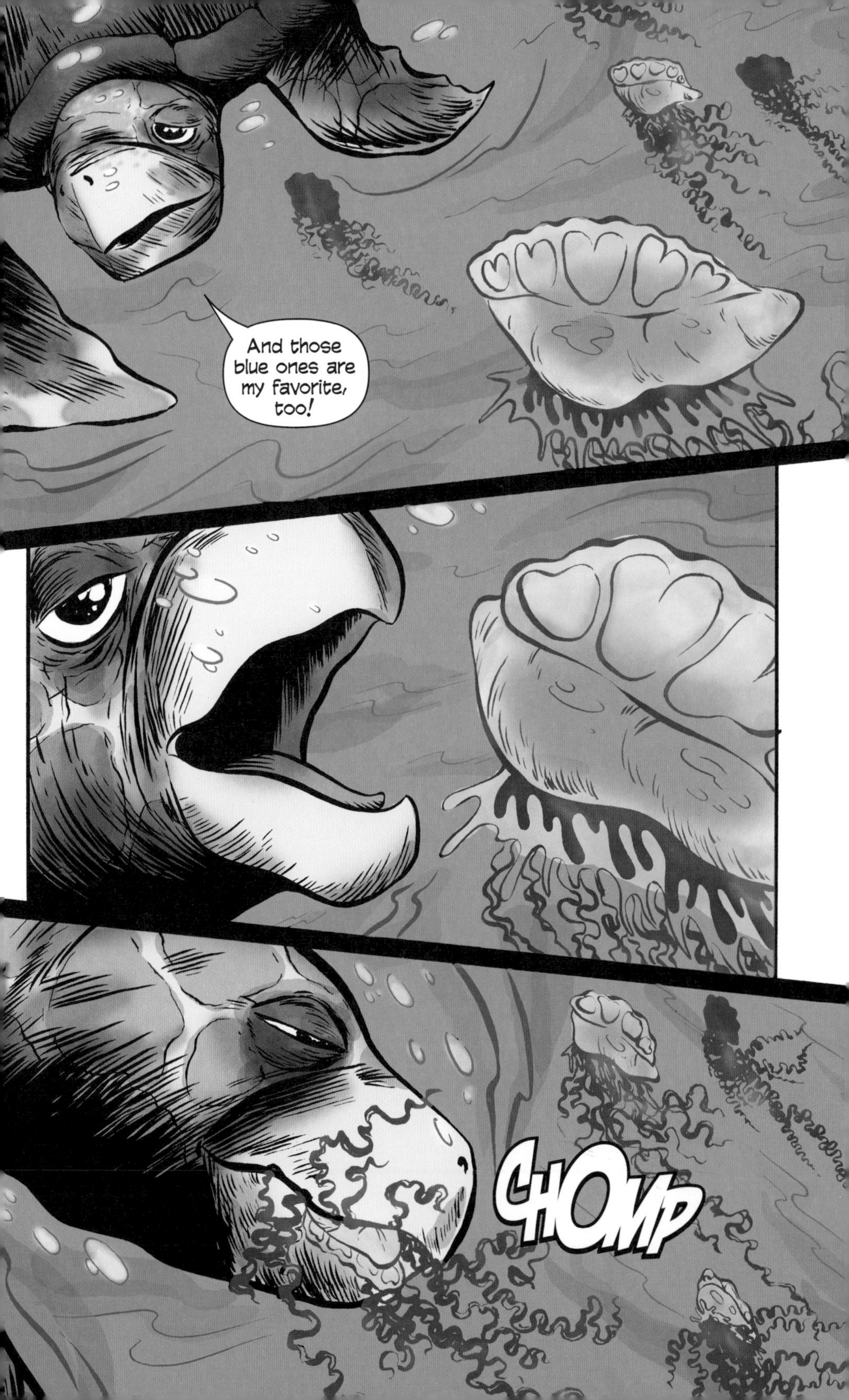
And those blue ones are my favorite, too!
CHOMP

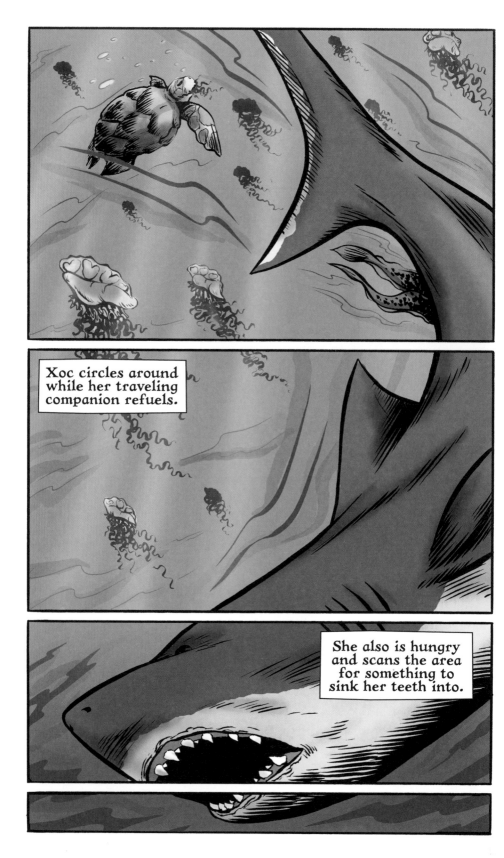

Xoc circles around while her traveling companion refuels.

She also is hungry and scans the area for something to sink her teeth into.

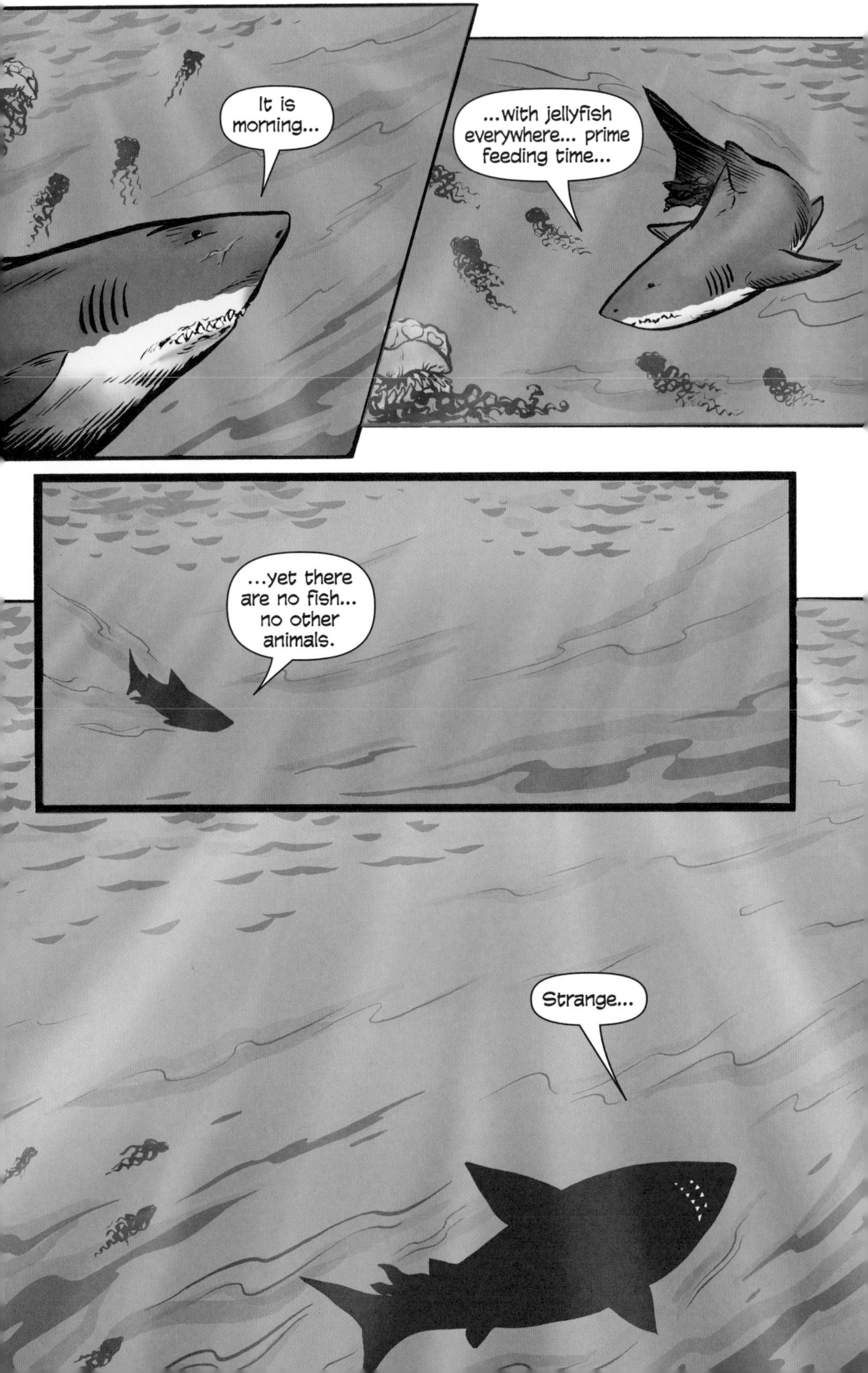
It is morning...
...with jellyfish everywhere... prime feeding time...
...yet there are no fish... no other animals.
Strange...

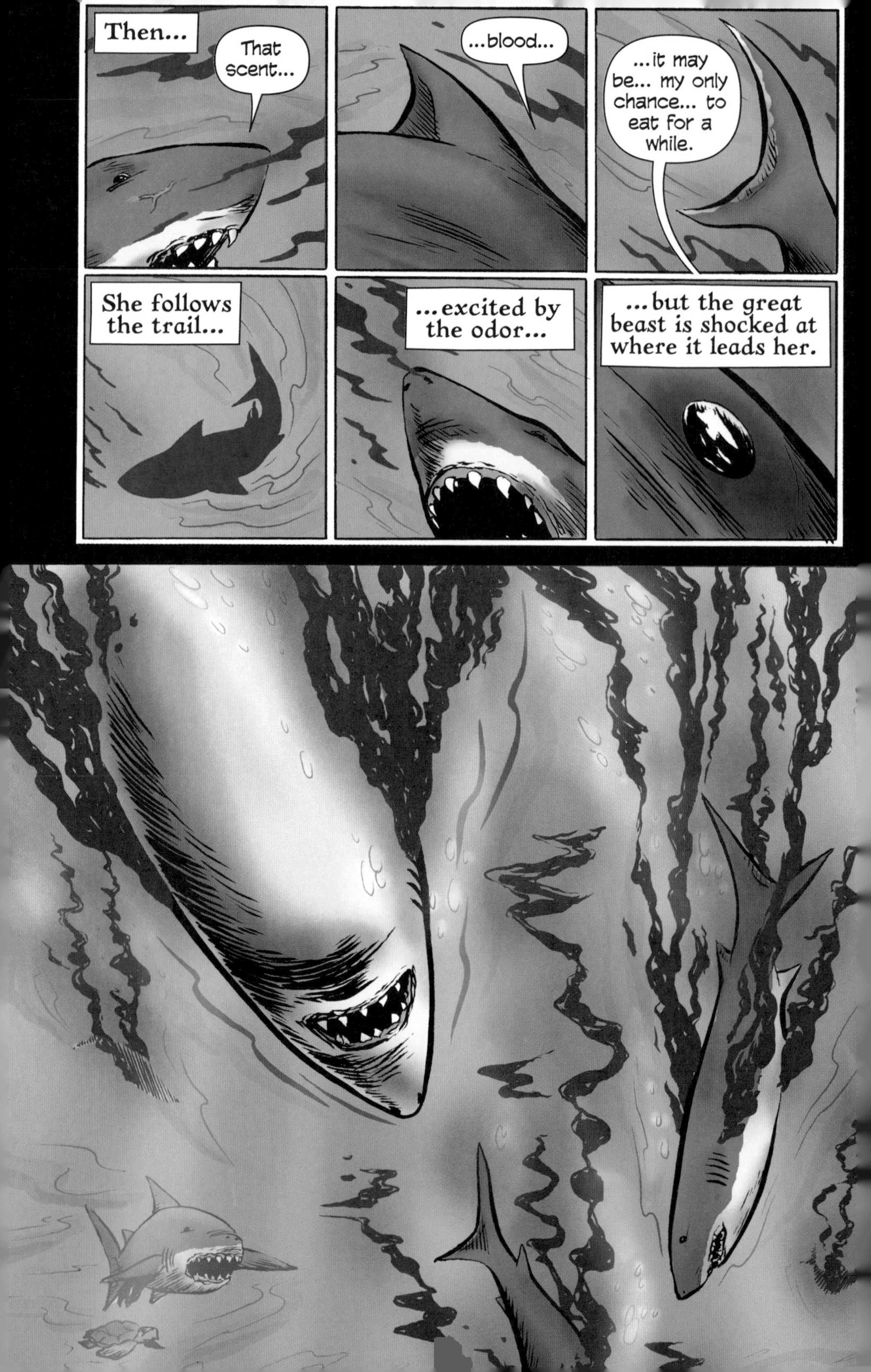
Then...
That scent...
...blood...
...it may be... my only chance... to eat for a while.
She follows the trail...
...excited by the odor...
...but the great beast is shocked at where it leads her.

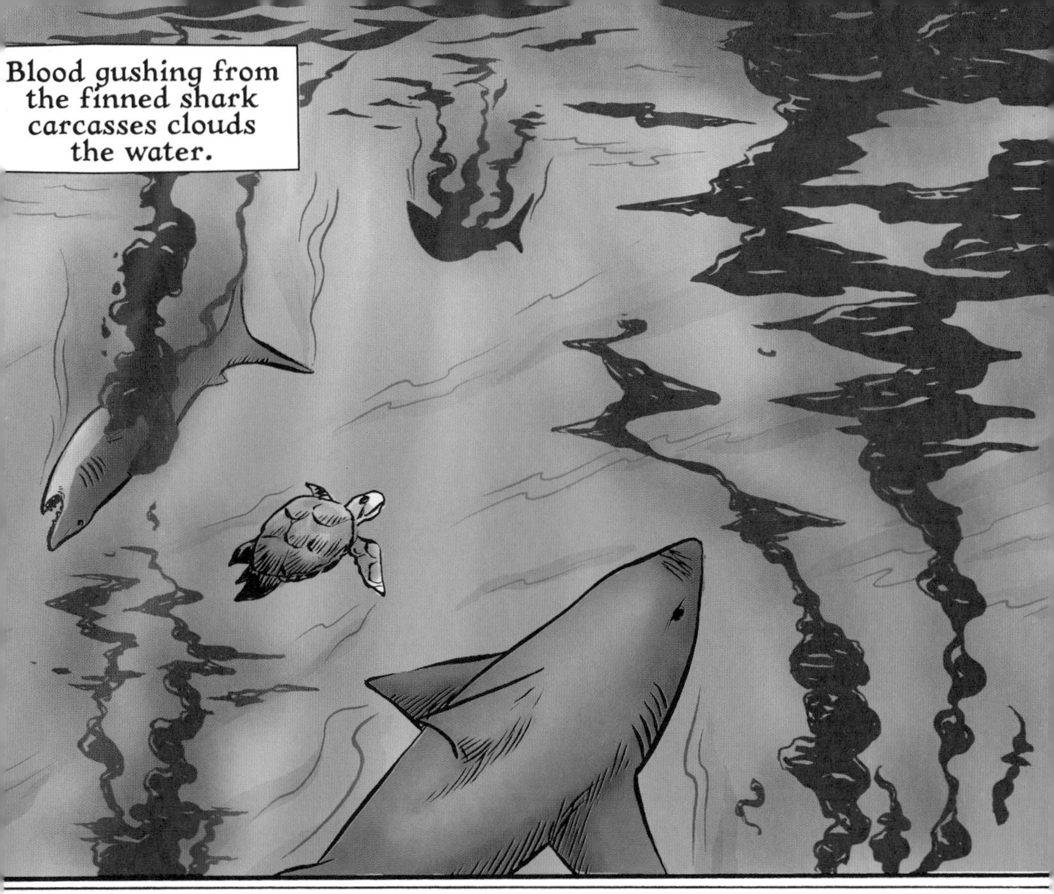
Blood gushing from the finned shark carcasses clouds the water.

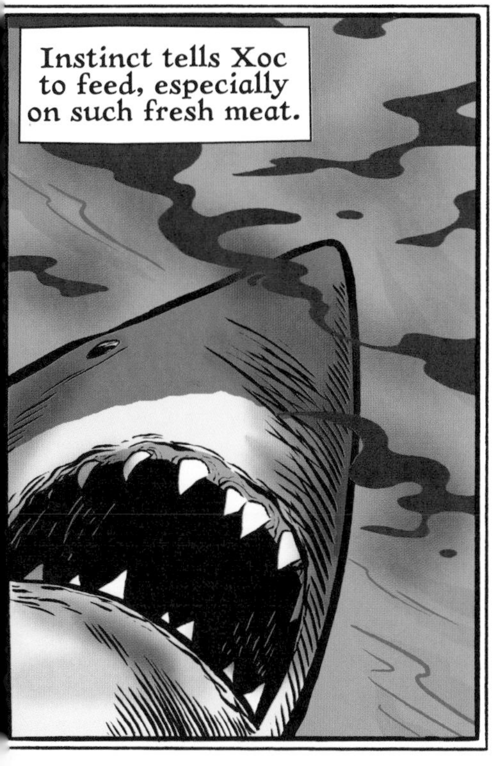
Instinct tells Xoc to feed, especially on such fresh meat.

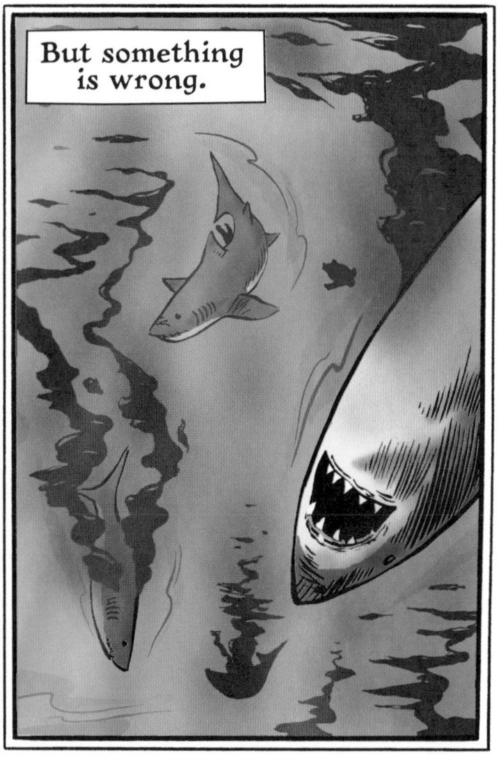
But something is wrong.

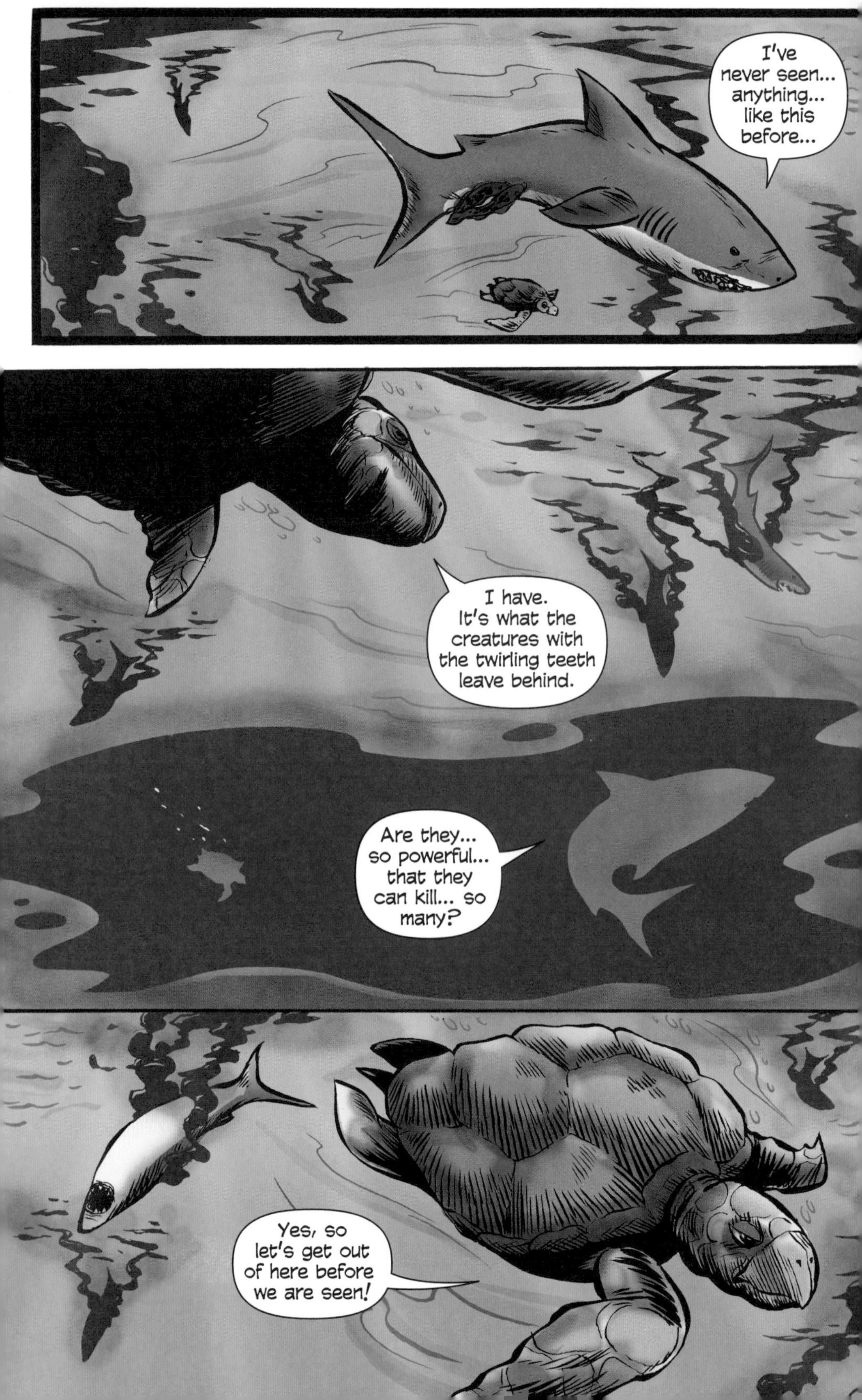
I've never seen... anything... like this before...
I have. It's what the creatures with the twirling teeth leave behind.
Are they... so powerful... that they can kill... so many?
Yes, so let's get out of here before we are seen!

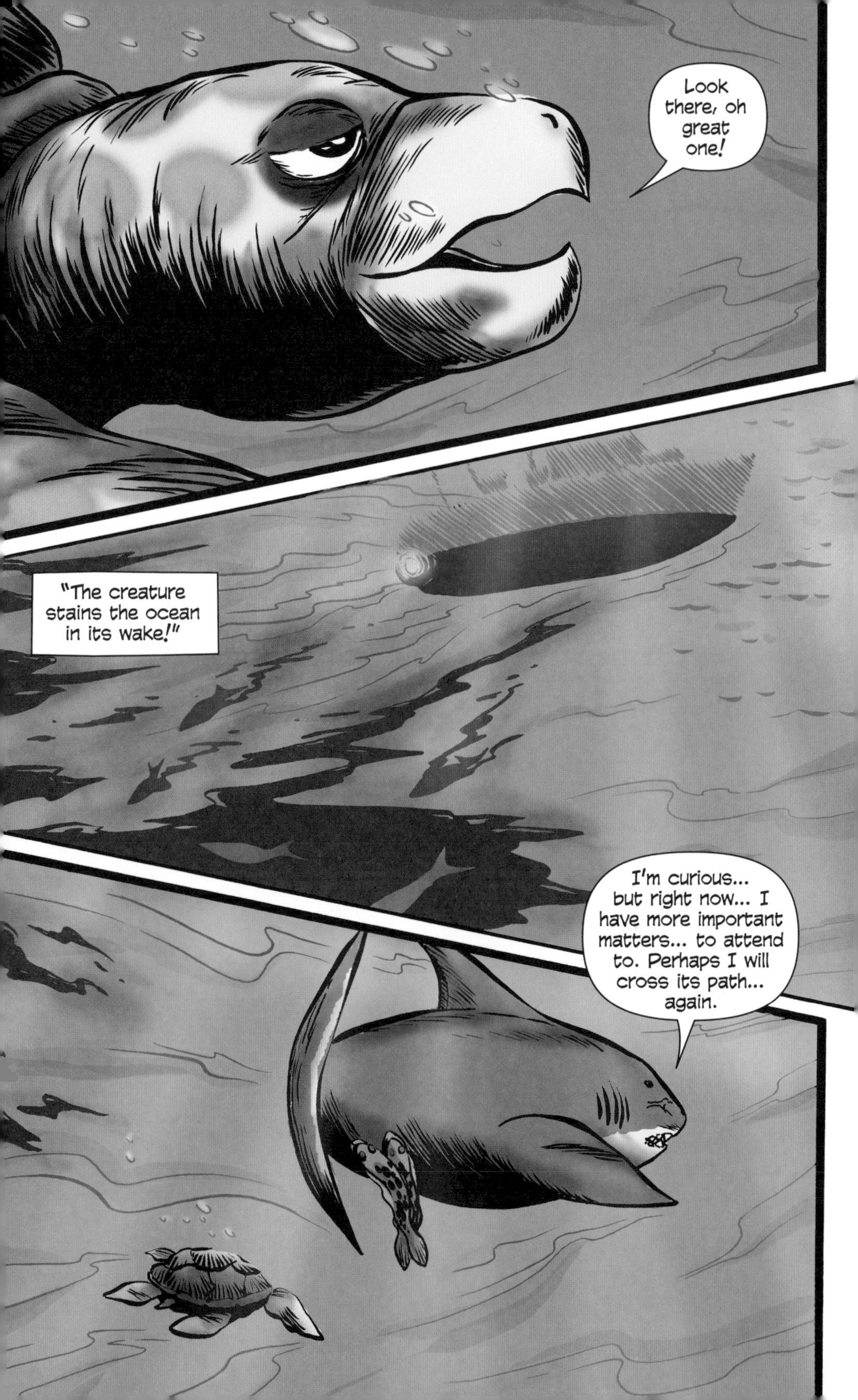
Look there, oh great one!
"The creature stains the ocean in its wake!"
I'm curious... but right now... I have more important matters... to attend to. Perhaps I will cross its path... again.

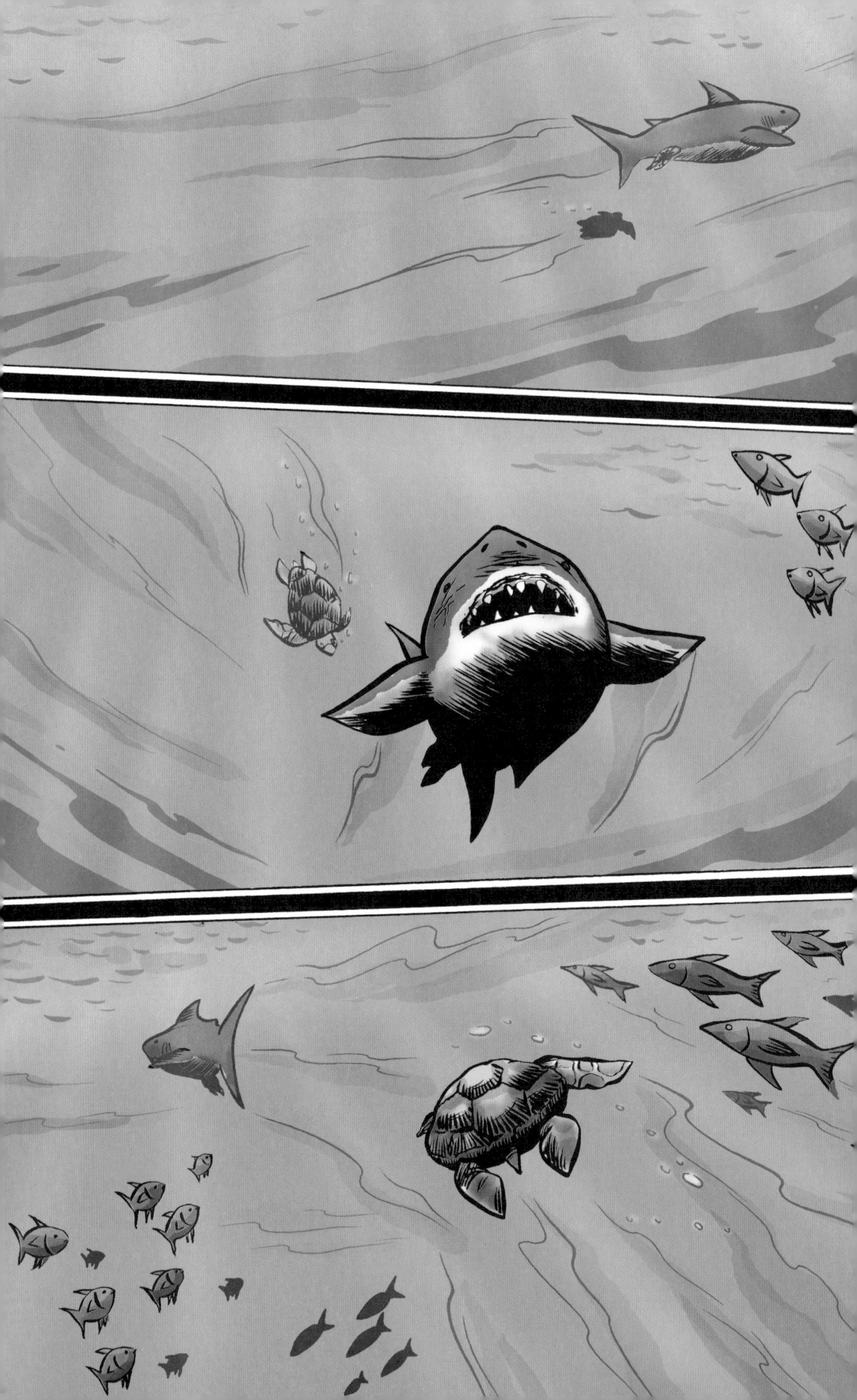

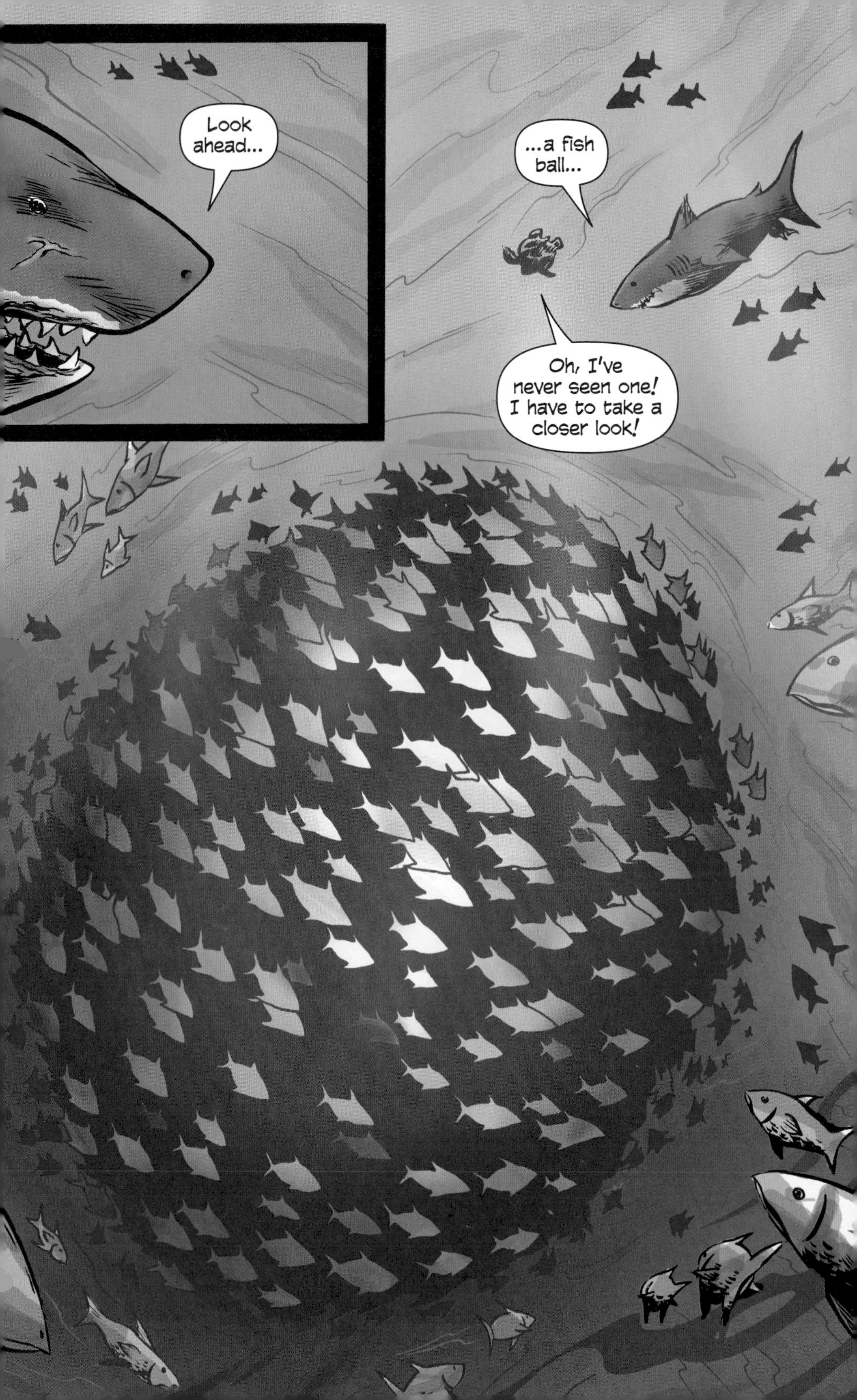
Look ahead...
...a fish ball...
Oh, I've never seen one! I have to take a closer look!

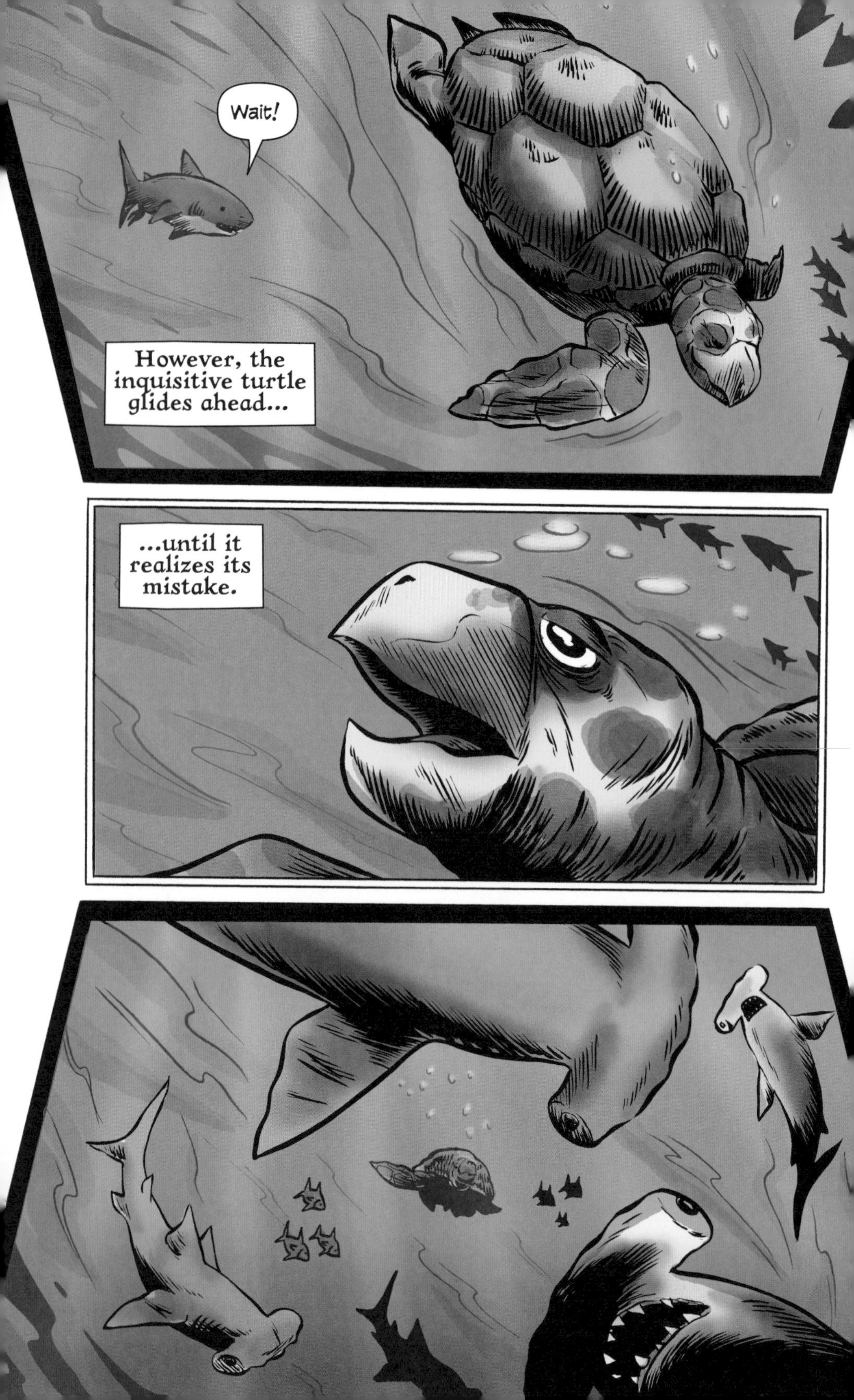
Wait!
However, the inquisitive turtle glides ahead...
...until it realizes its mistake.

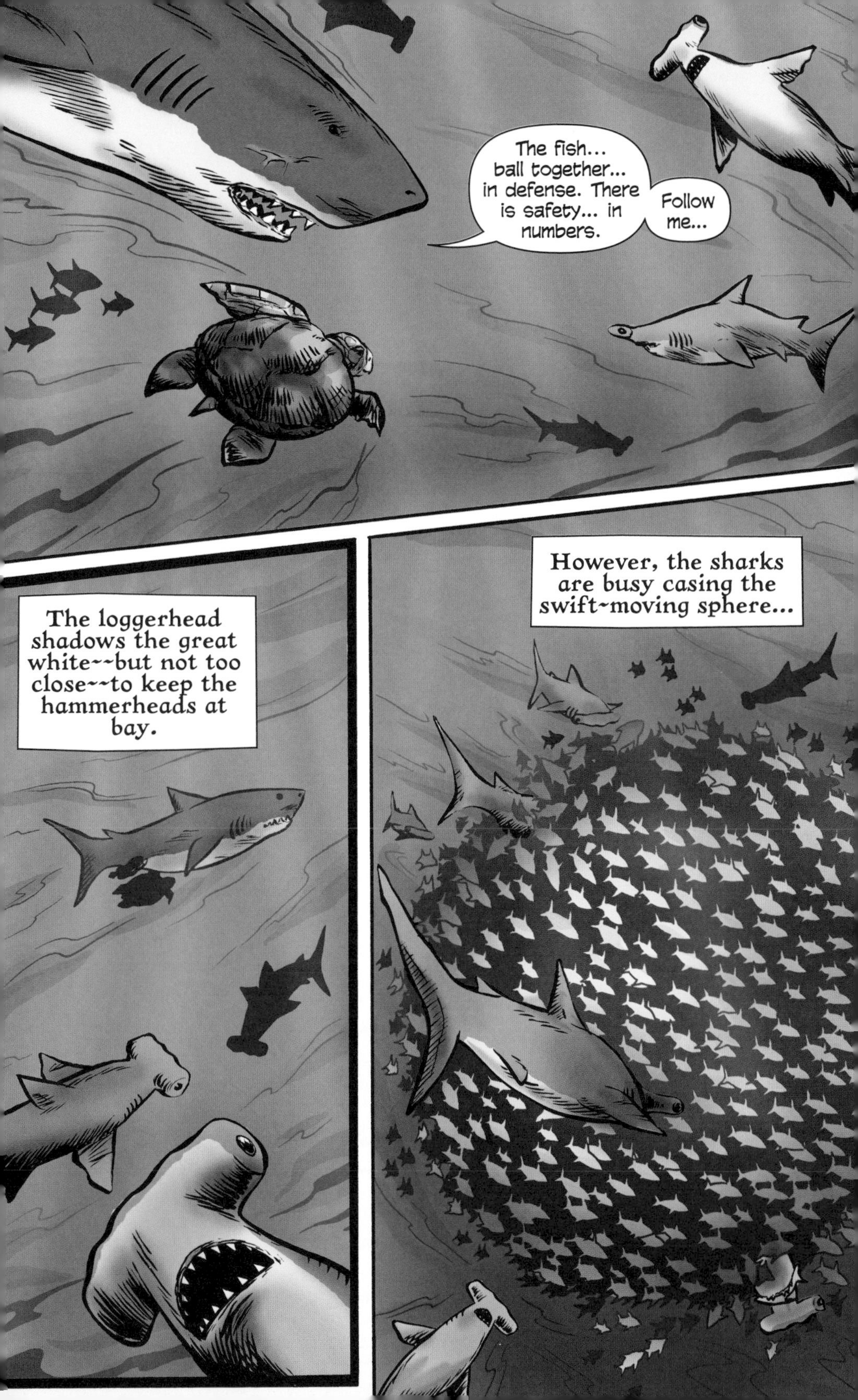
The fish... ball together... in defense. There is safety... in numbers.
Follow me...
The loggerhead shadows the great white--but not too close--to keep the hammerheads at bay.
However, the sharks are busy casing the swift-moving sphere...

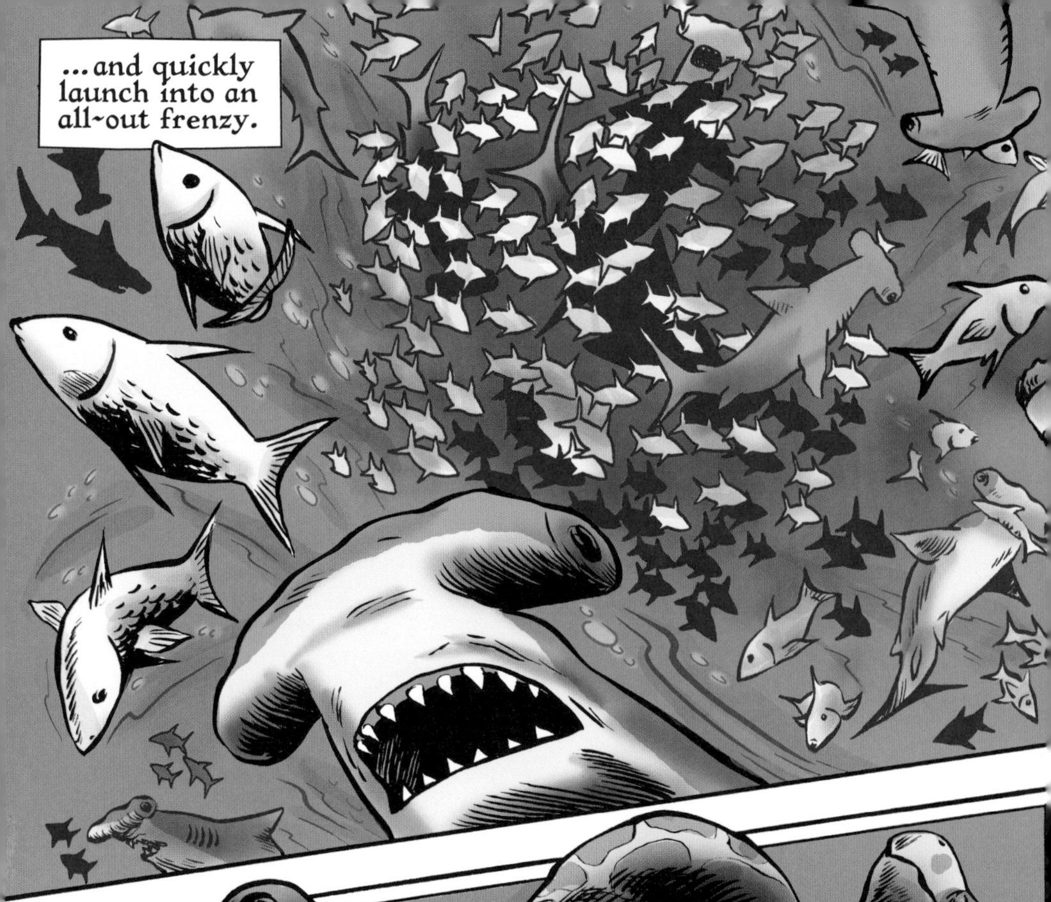
...and quickly launch into an all-out frenzy.

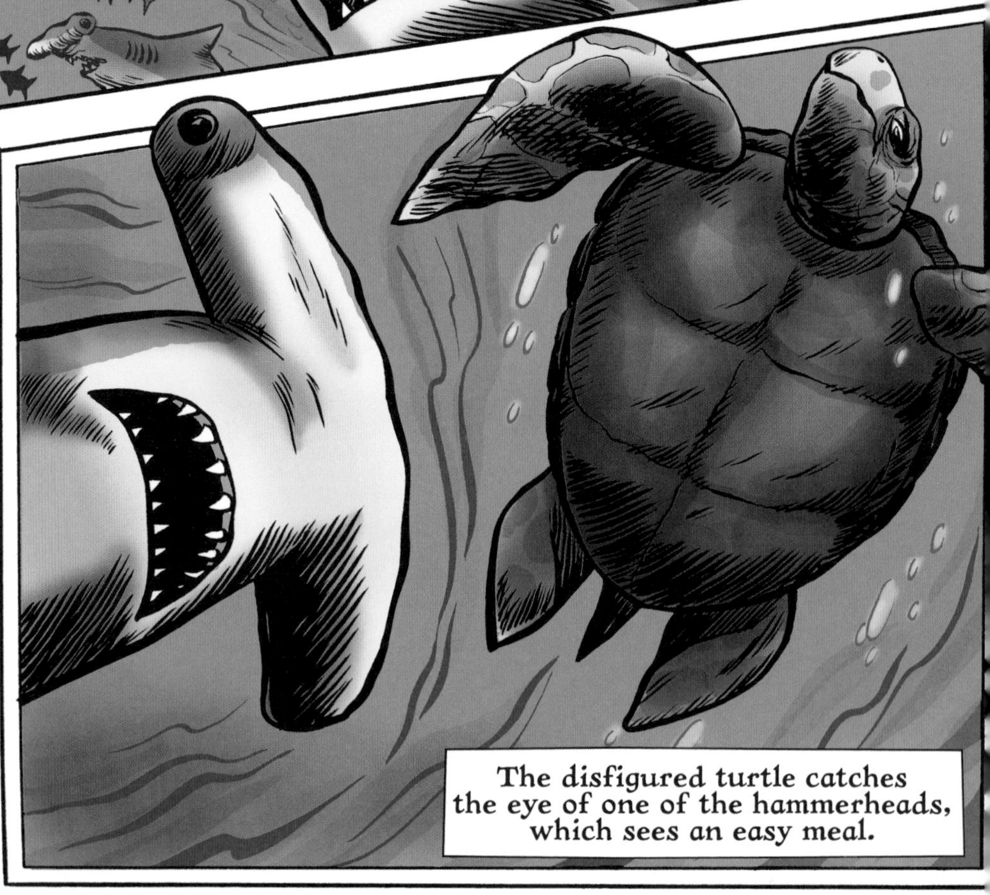
The disfigured turtle catches the eye of one of the hammerheads, which sees an easy meal.

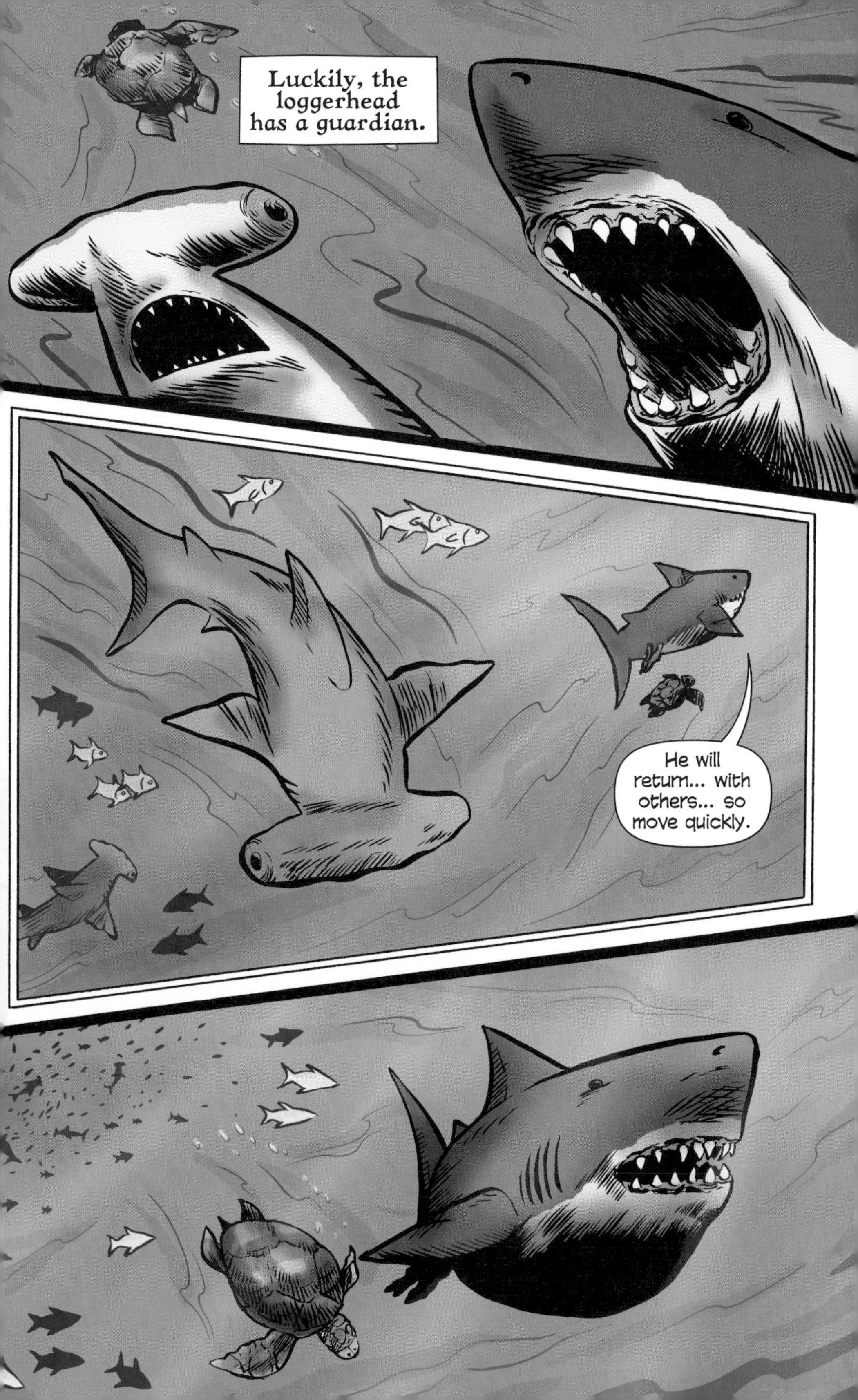
Luckily, the loggerhead has a guardian.
He will return... with others... so move quickly.

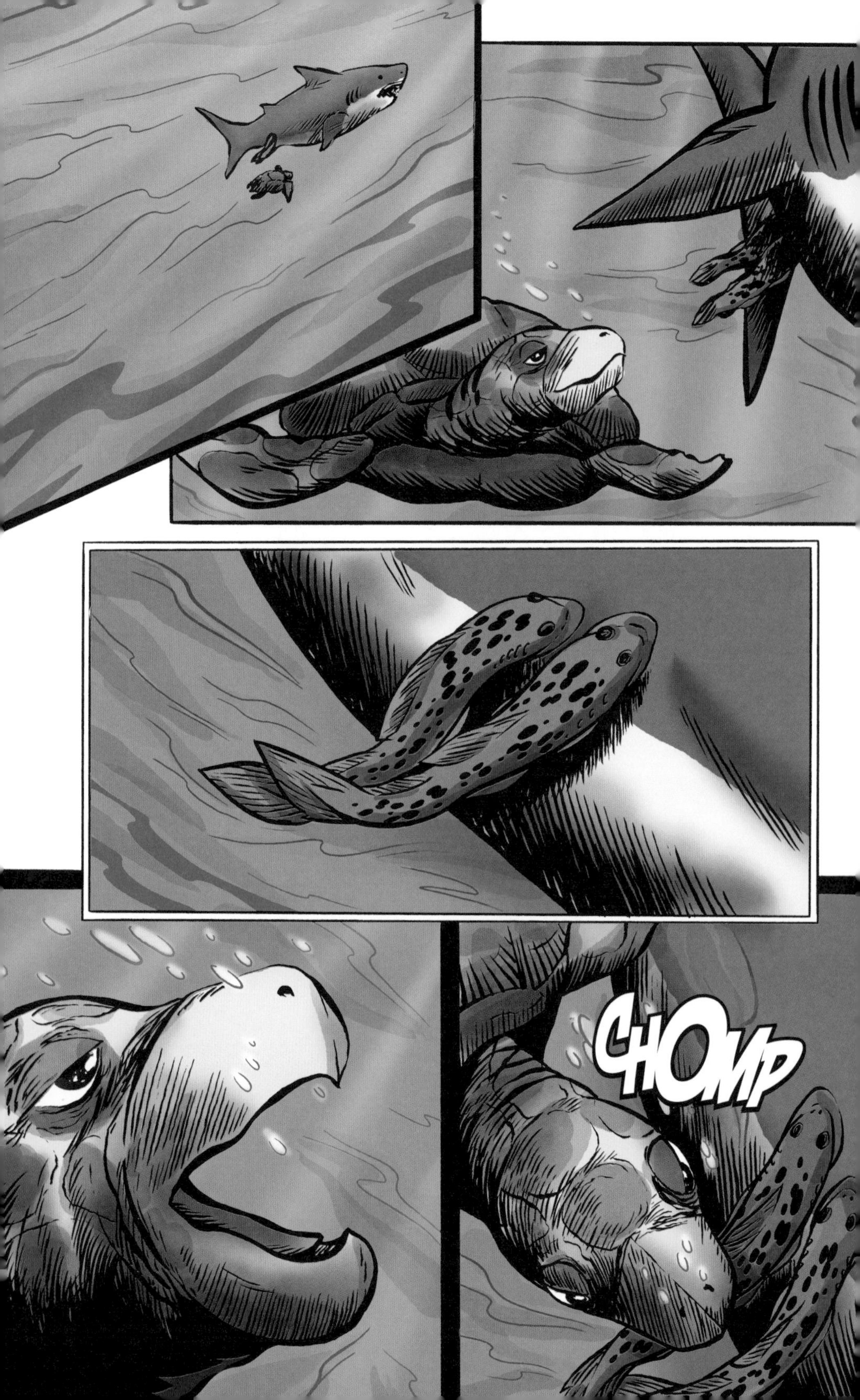
CHOMP

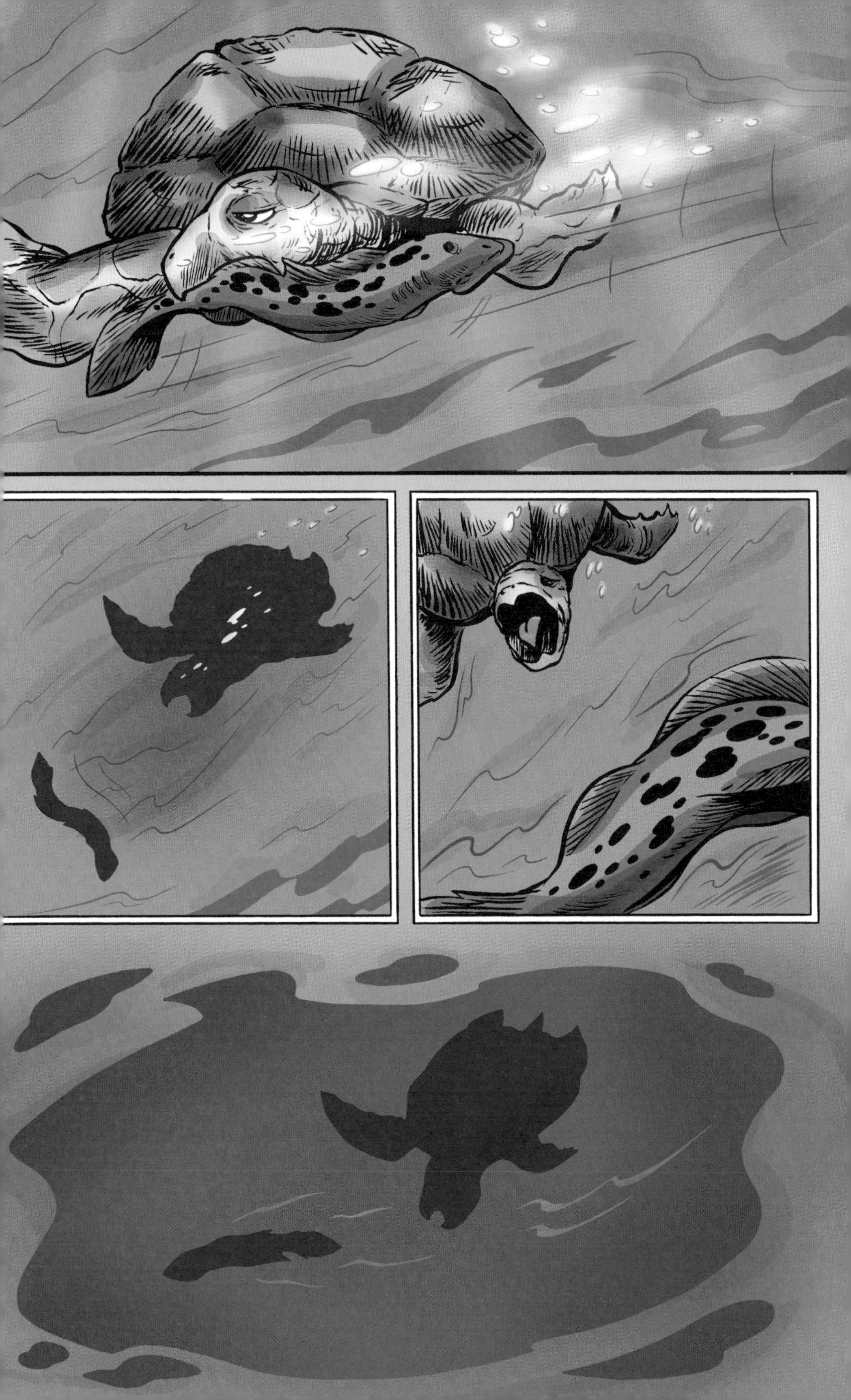

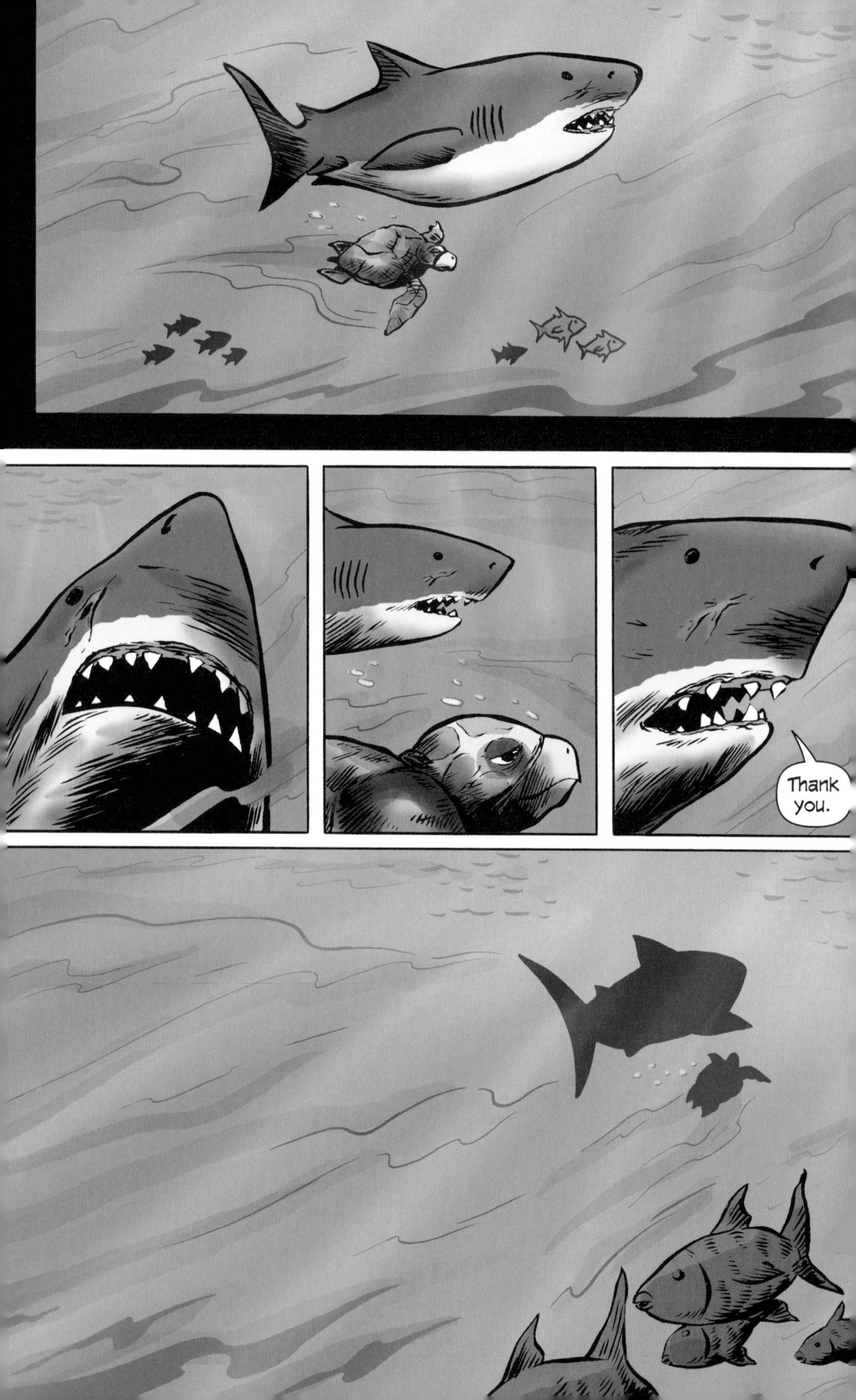
Thank you.

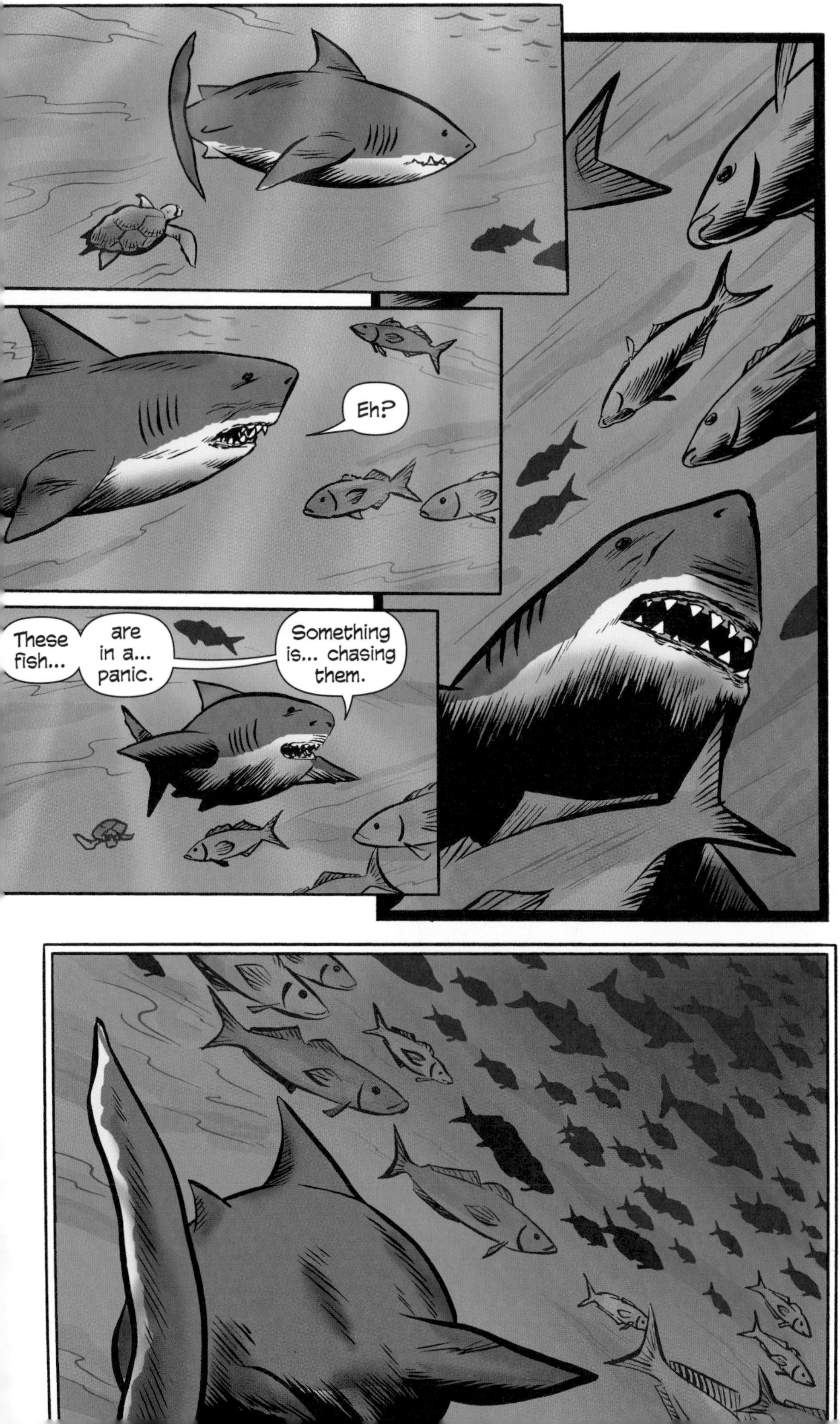
Eh?
These fish...
are in a... panic.
Something is... chasing them.

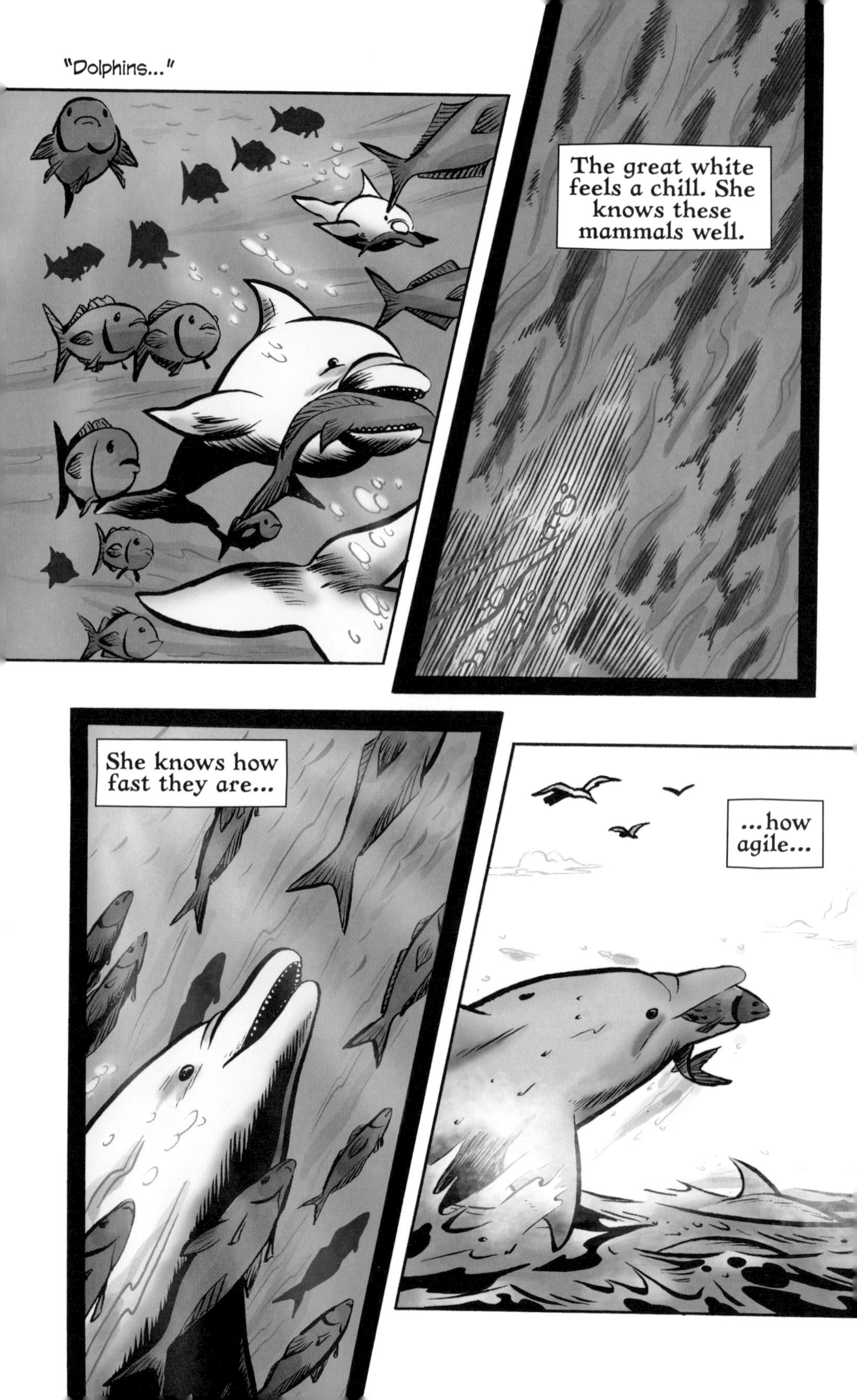
"Dolphins..."
The great white feels a chill. She knows these mammals well.
She knows how fast they are...
...how agile...

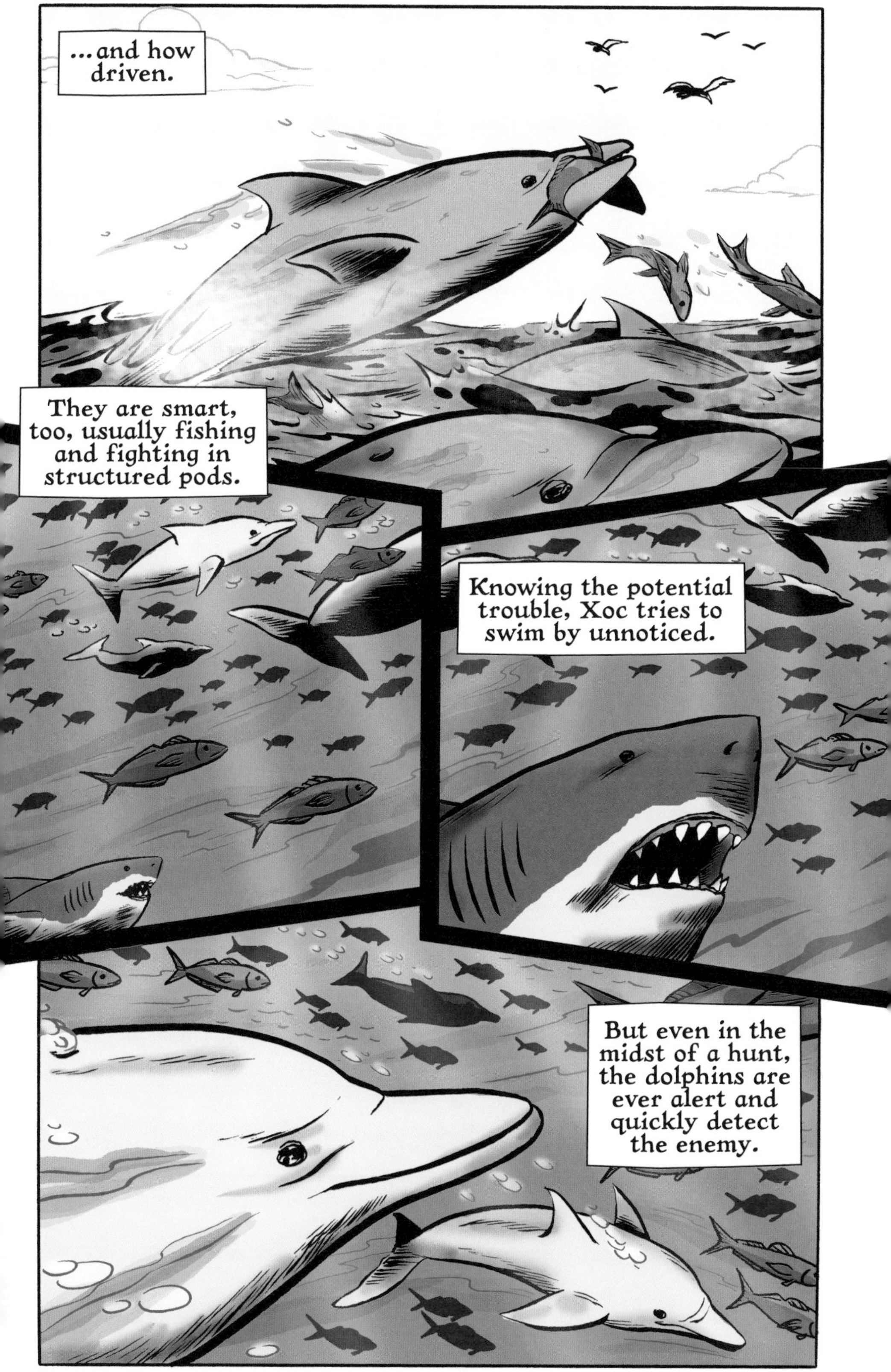
...and how driven.
They are smart, too, usually fishing and fighting in structured pods.
Knowing the potential trouble, Xoc tries to swim by unnoticed.
But even in the midst of a hunt, the dolphins are ever alert and quickly detect the enemy.

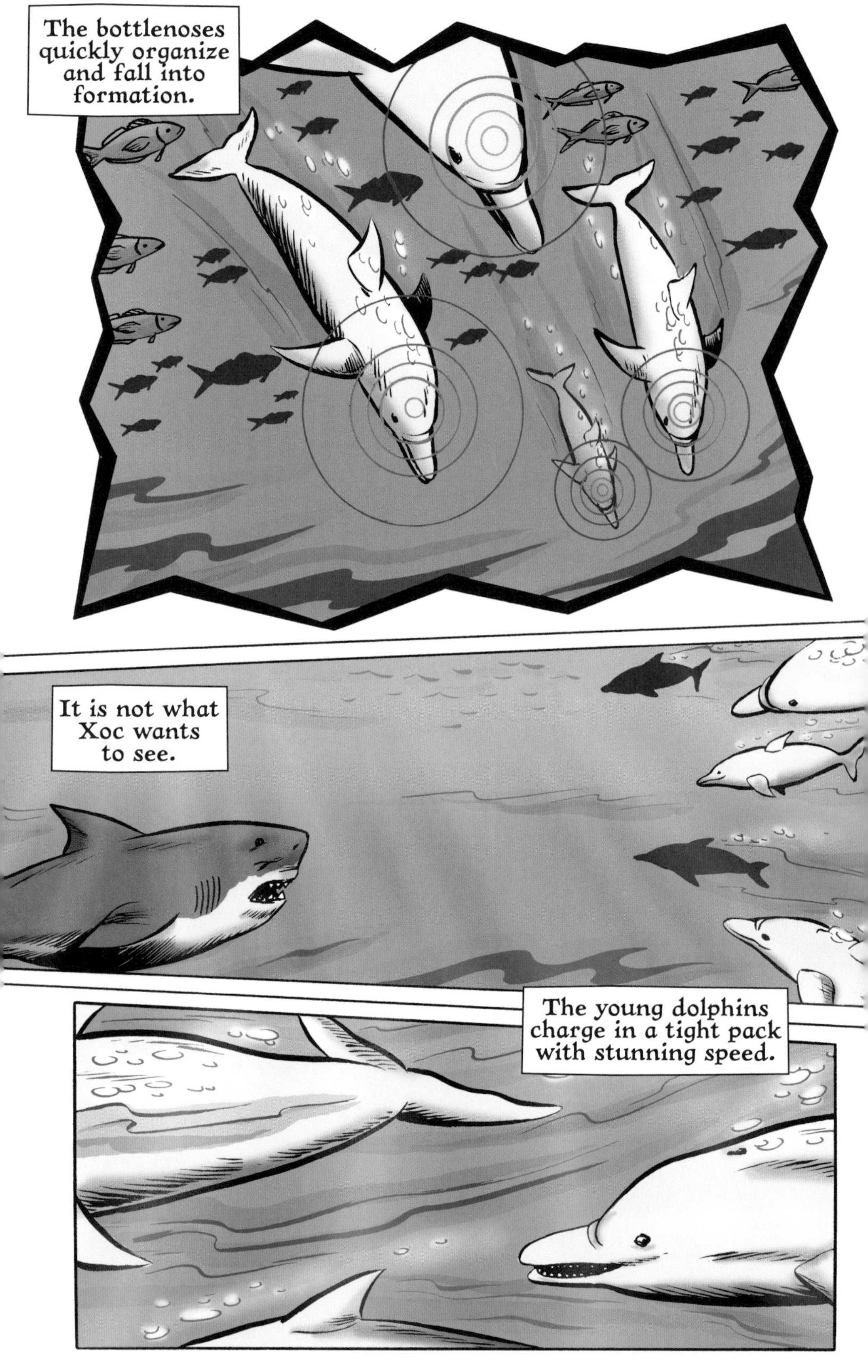
The bottlenoses quickly organize and fall into formation.
It is not what Xoc wants to see.
The young dolphins charge in a tight pack with stunning speed.

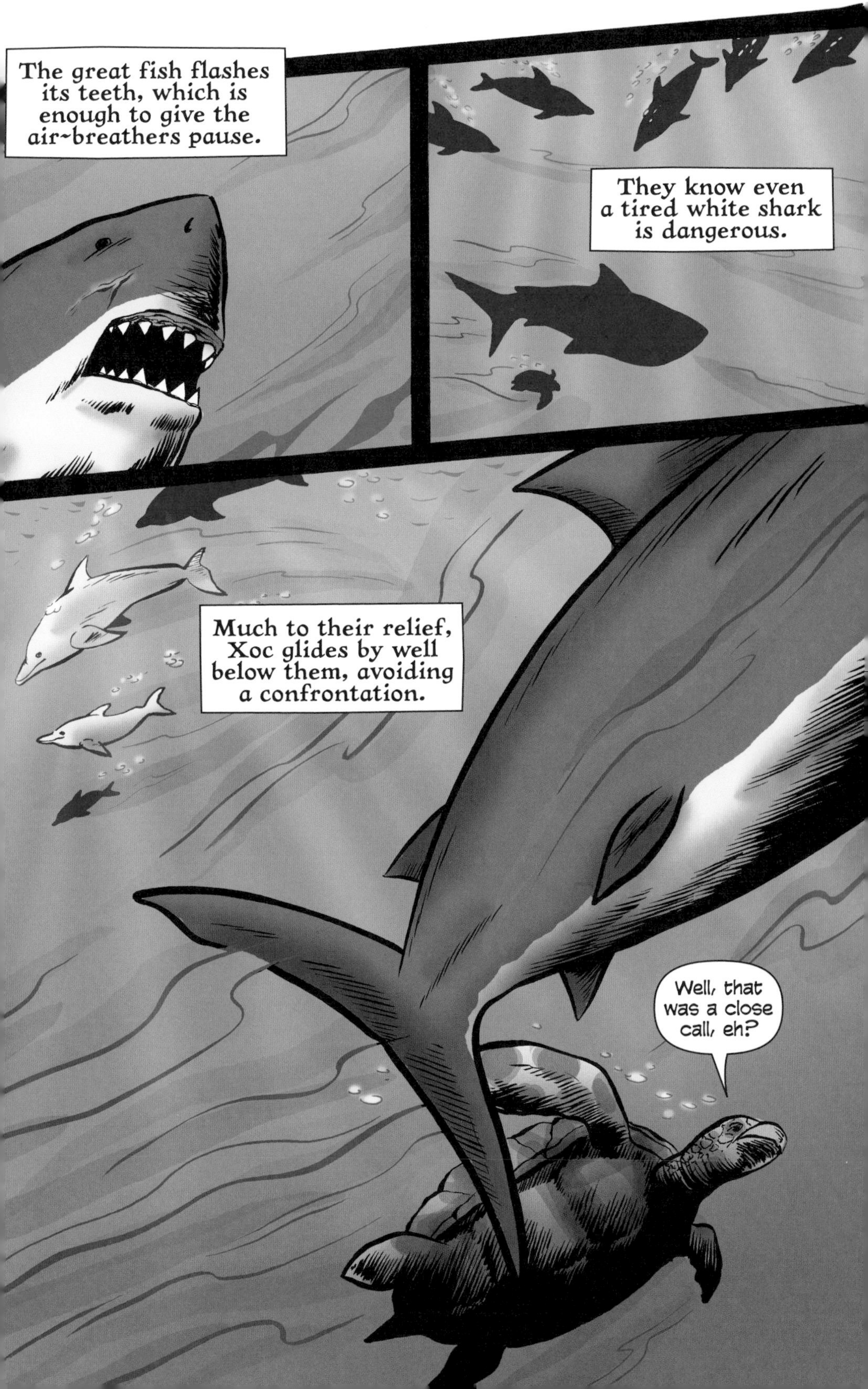

The great fish flashes its teeth, which is enough to give the air~breathers pause.
They know even a tired white shark is dangerous.
Much to their relief, Xoc glides by well below them, avoiding a confrontation.
Well, that was a close call, eh?

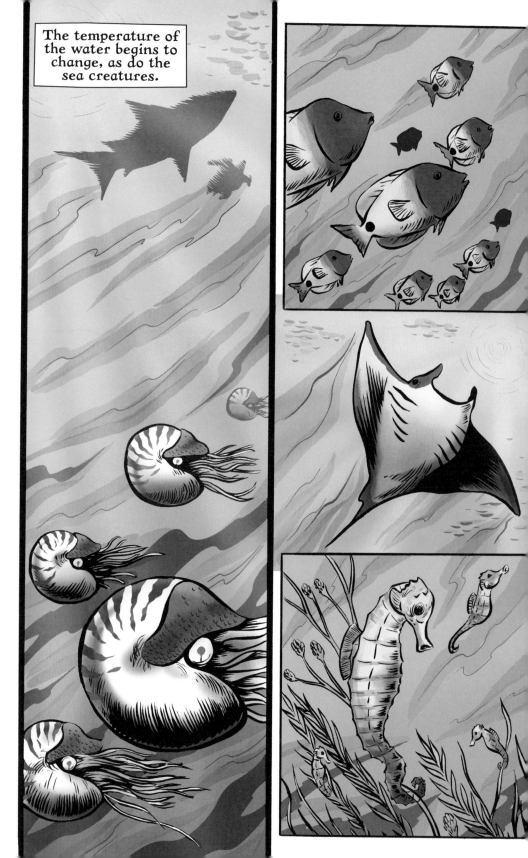

The temperature of the water begins to change, as do the sea creatures.

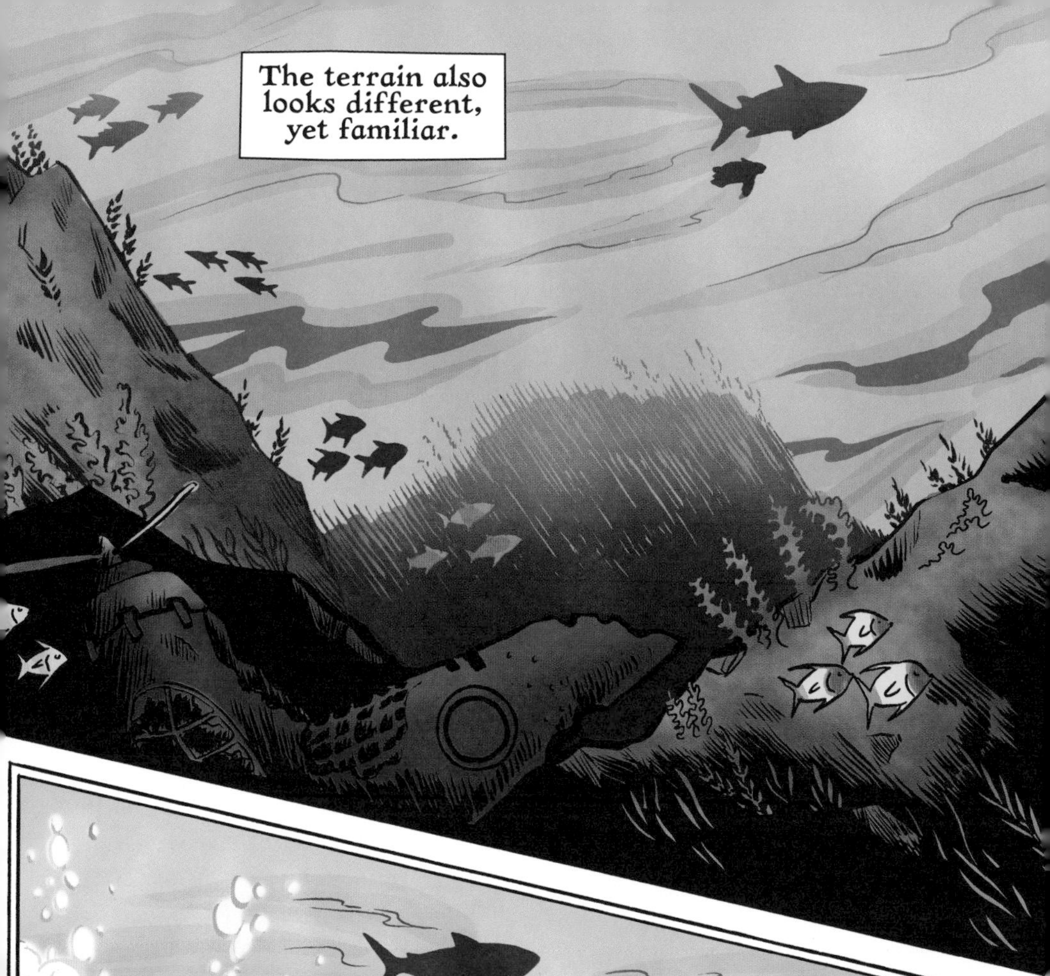
The terrain also looks different, yet familiar.

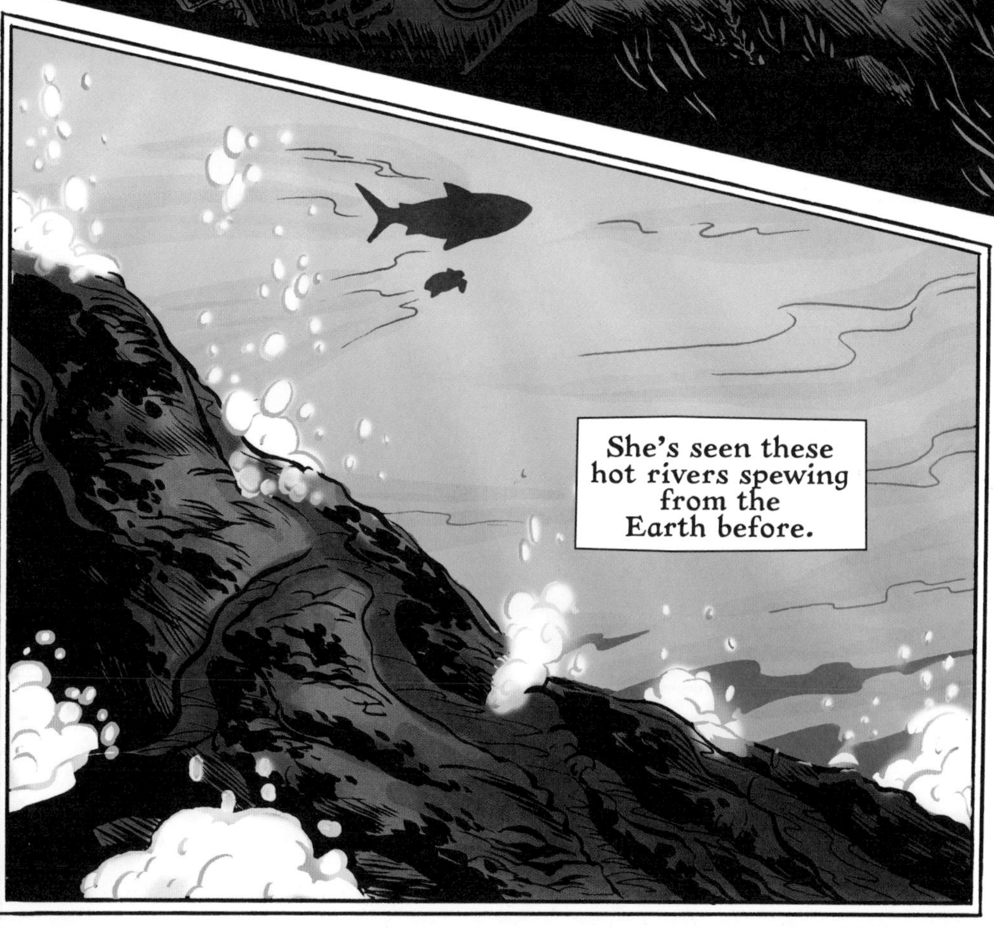
She's seen these hot rivers spewing from the Earth before.

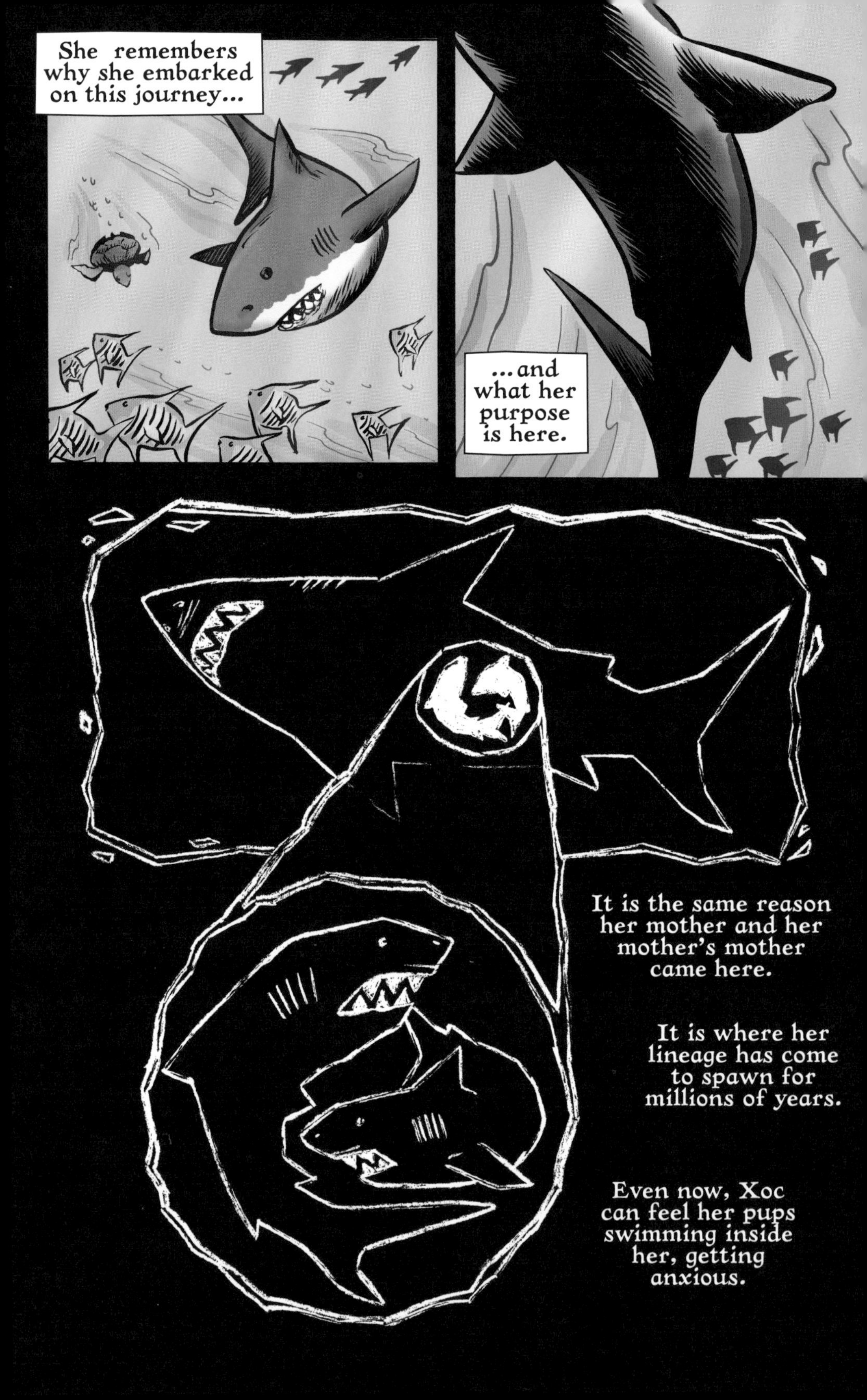
She remembers why she embarked on this journey...
...and what her purpose is here.
It is the same reason her mother and her mother's mother came here.
It is where her lineage has come to spawn for millions of years.
Even now, Xoc can feel her pups swimming inside her, getting anxious.

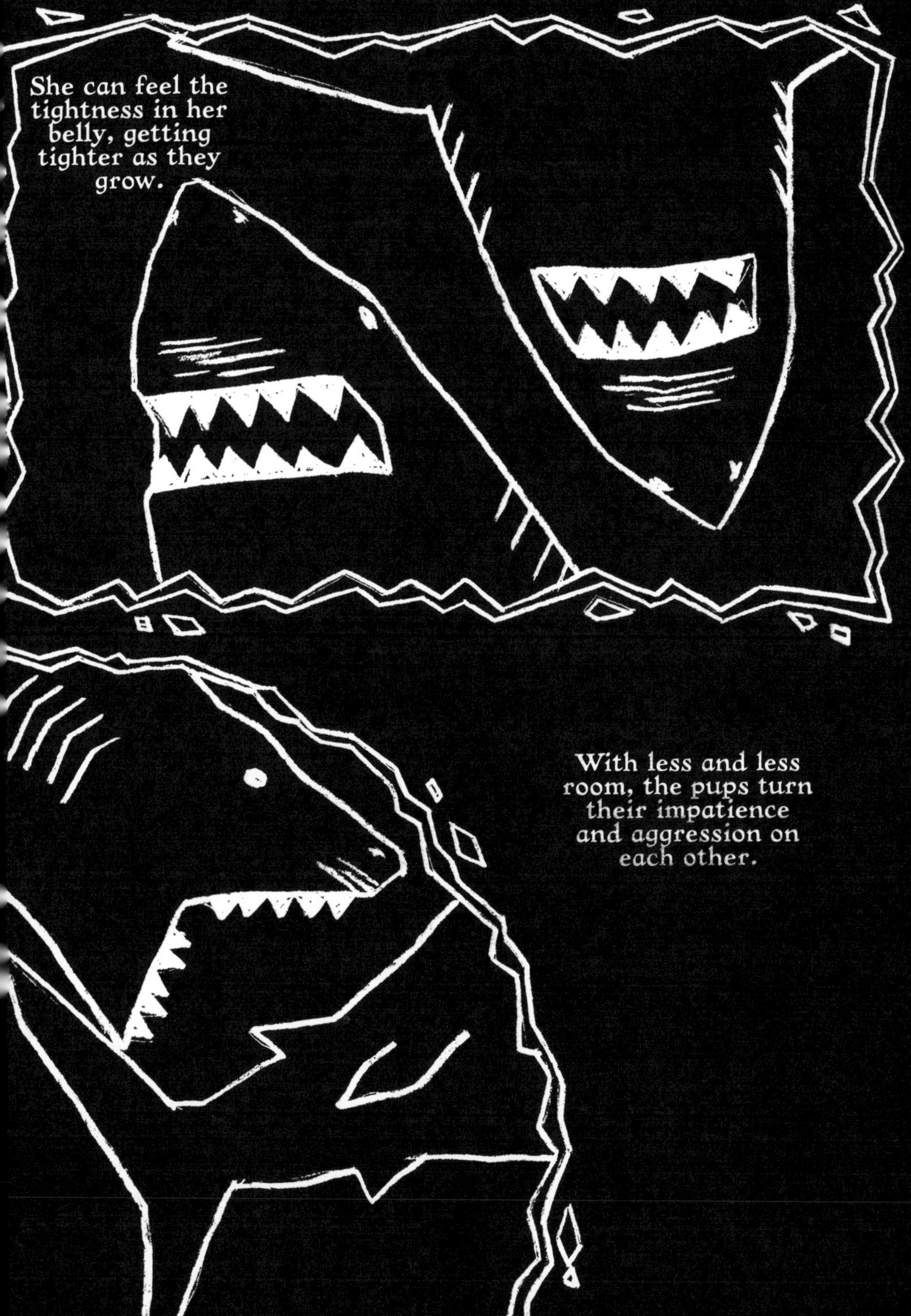
She can feel the tightness in her belly, getting tighter as they grow.
With less and less room, the pups turn their impatience and aggression on each other.

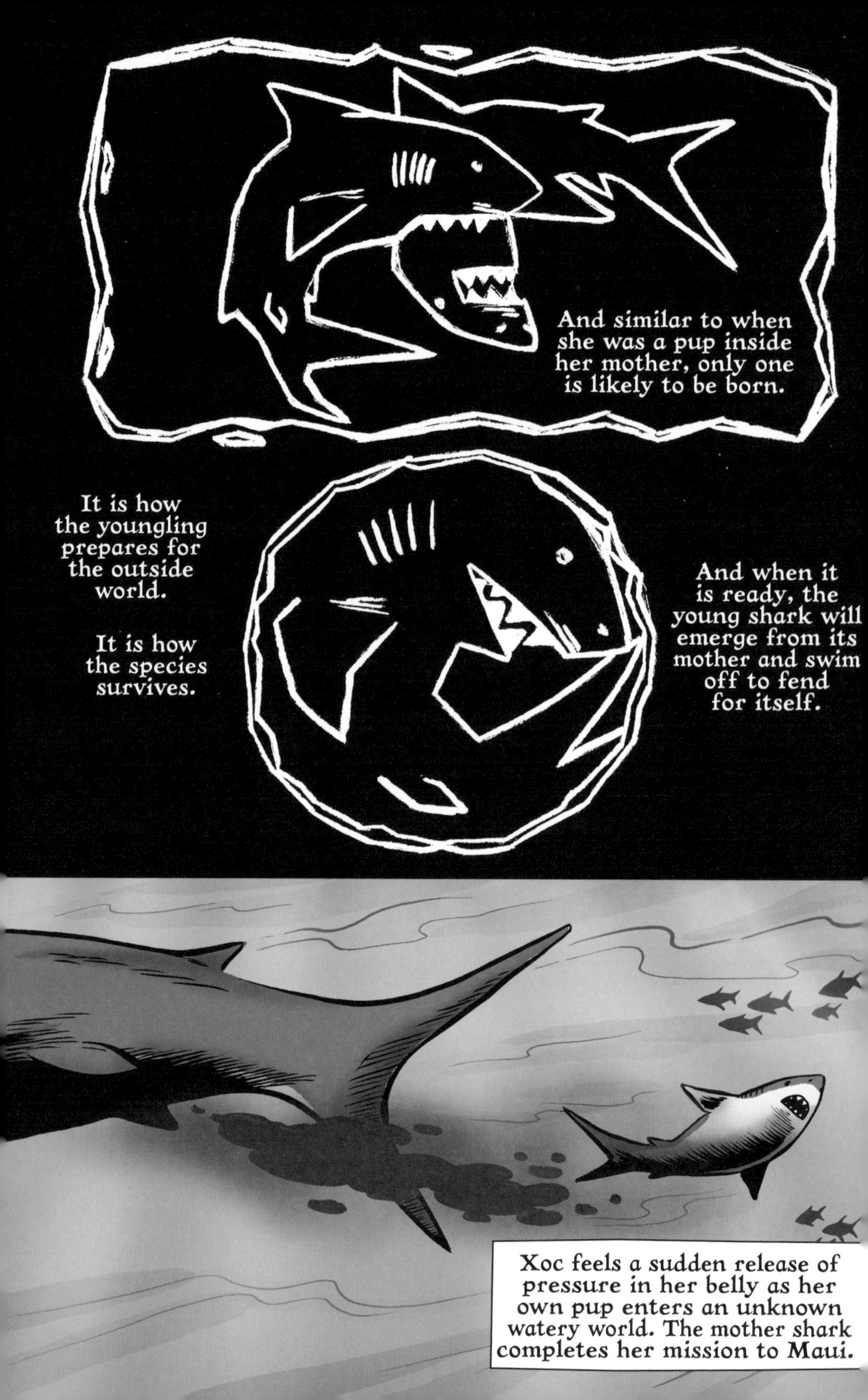

And similar to when she was a pup inside her mother, only one is likely to be born.
It is how the youngling prepares for the outside world.
It is how the species survives.
And when it is ready, the young shark will emerge from its mother and swim off to fend for itself.
Xoc feels a sudden release of pressure in her belly as her own pup enters an unknown watery world. The mother shark completes her mission to Maui.

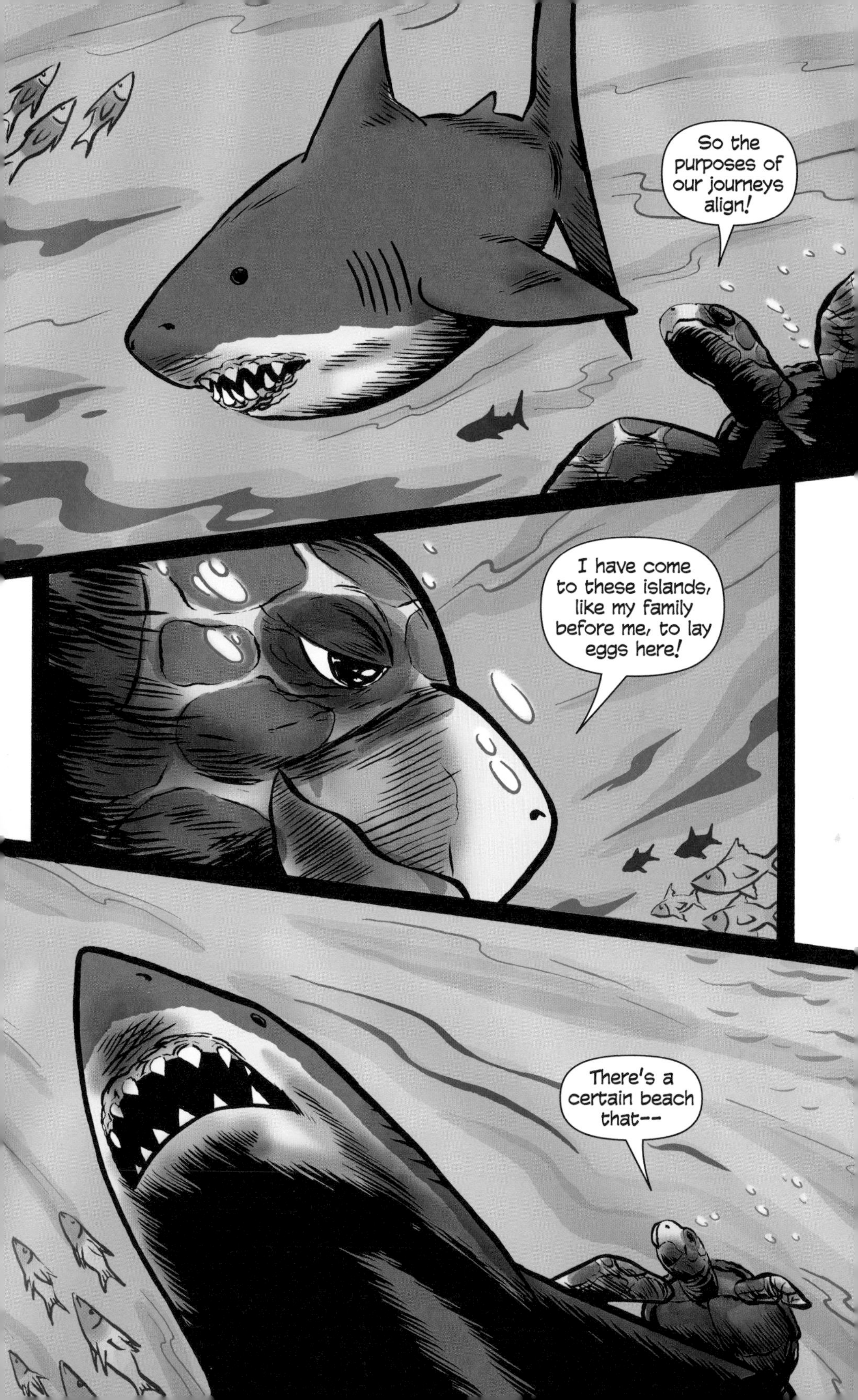
So the purposes of our journeys align!
I have come to these islands, like my family before me, to lay eggs here!
There's a certain beach that--

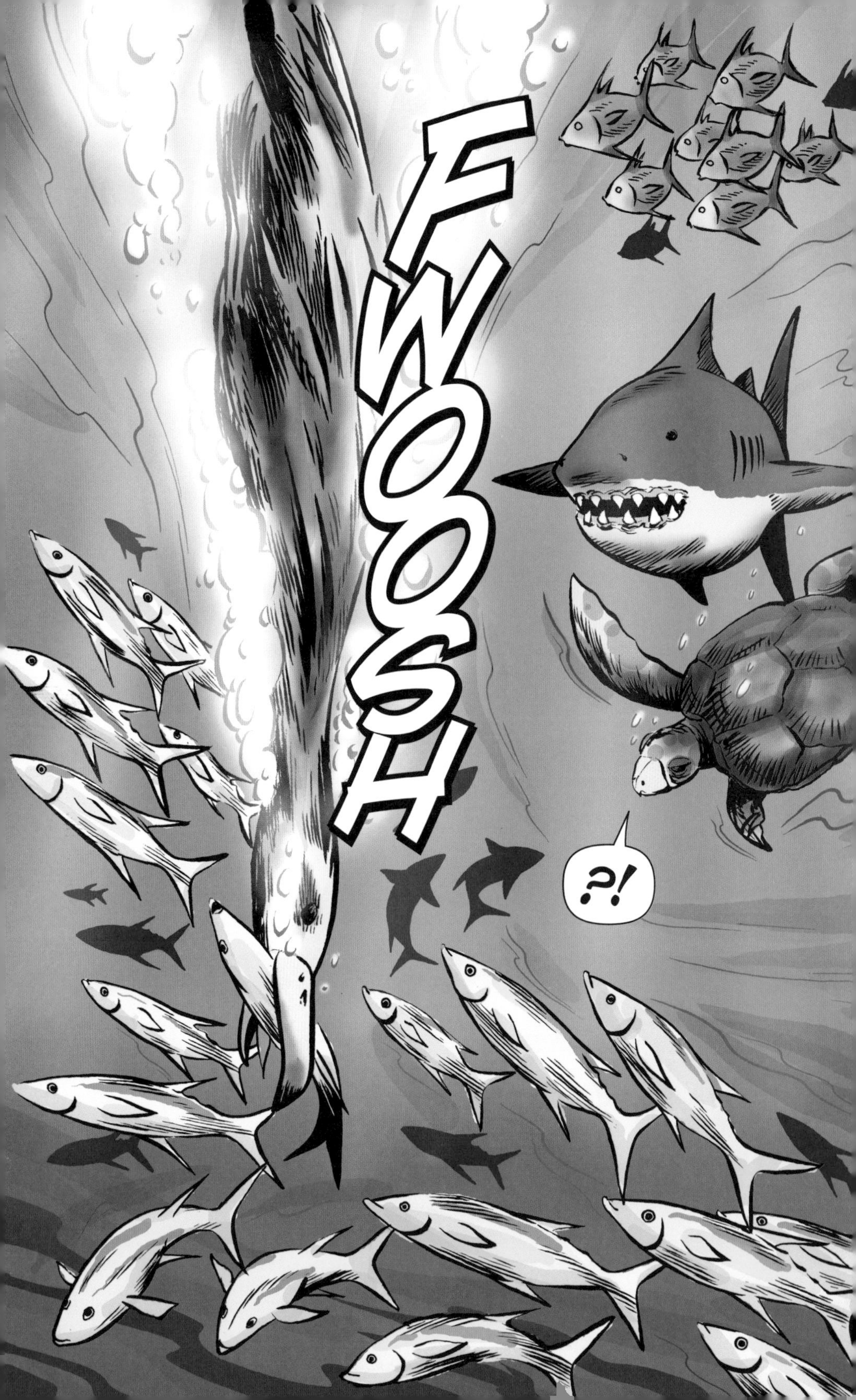
FWOOSH
?!

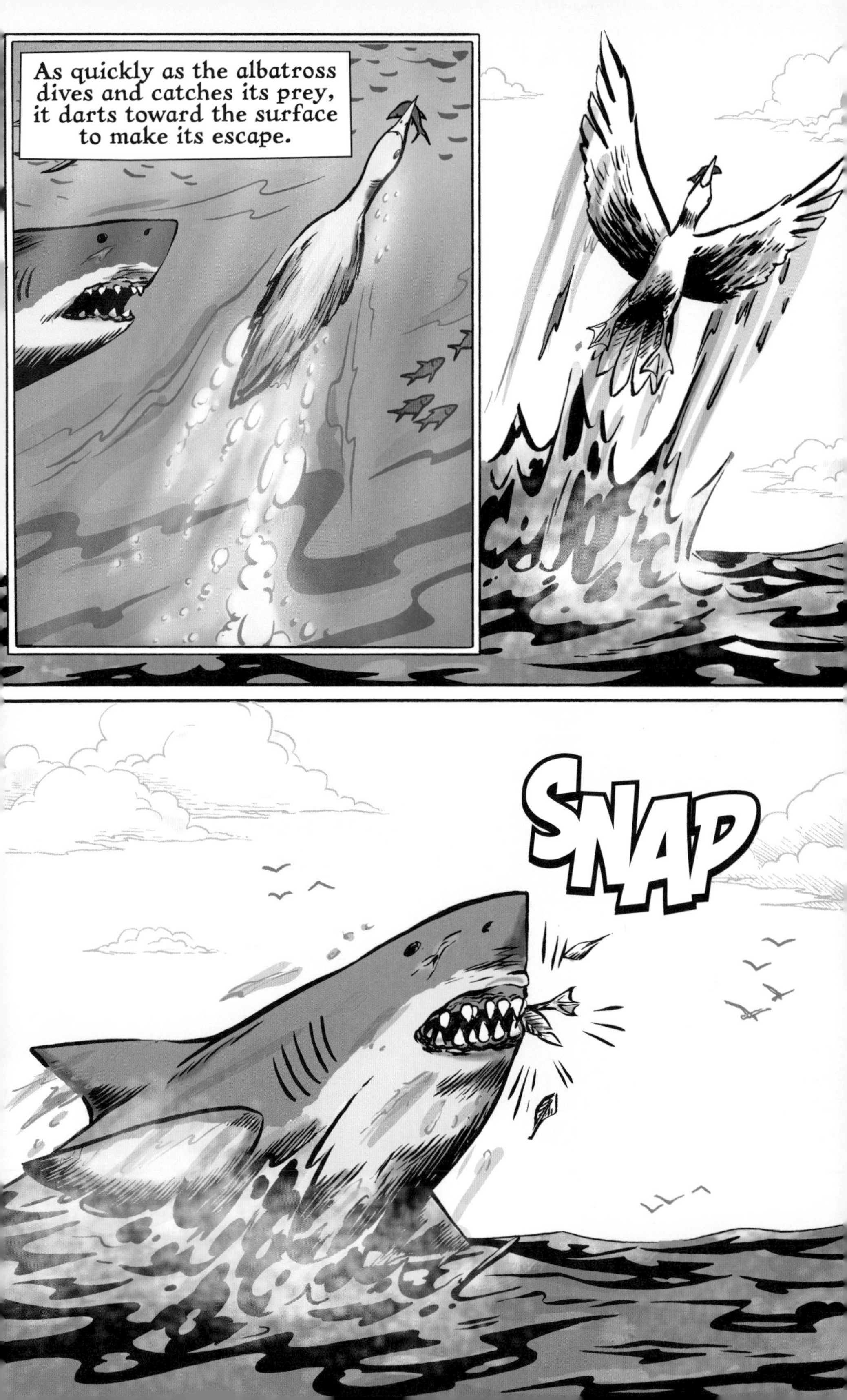
As quickly as the albatross dives and catches its prey, it darts toward the surface to make its escape.
SNAP

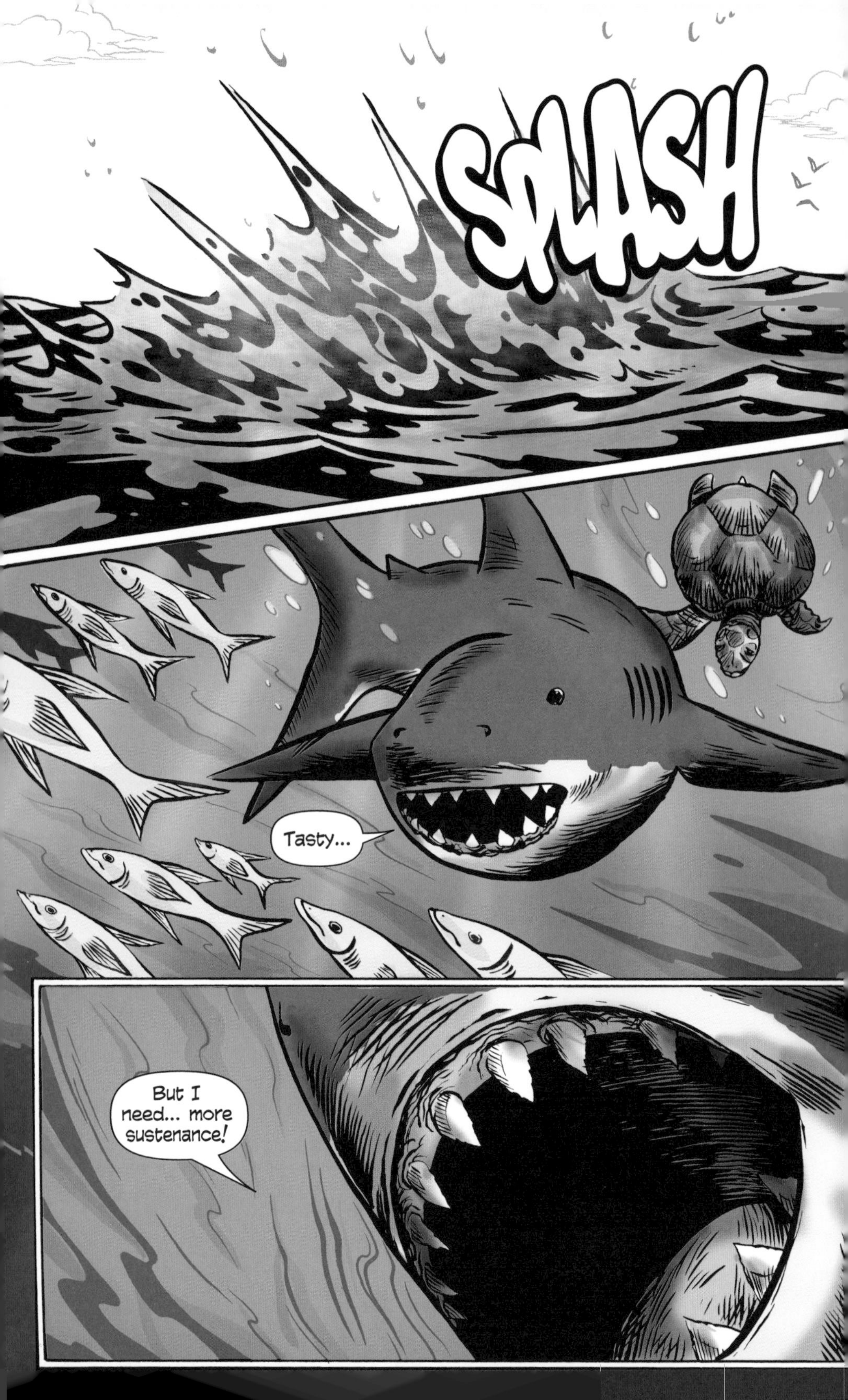
SPLASH
Tasty...
But I need... more sustenance!

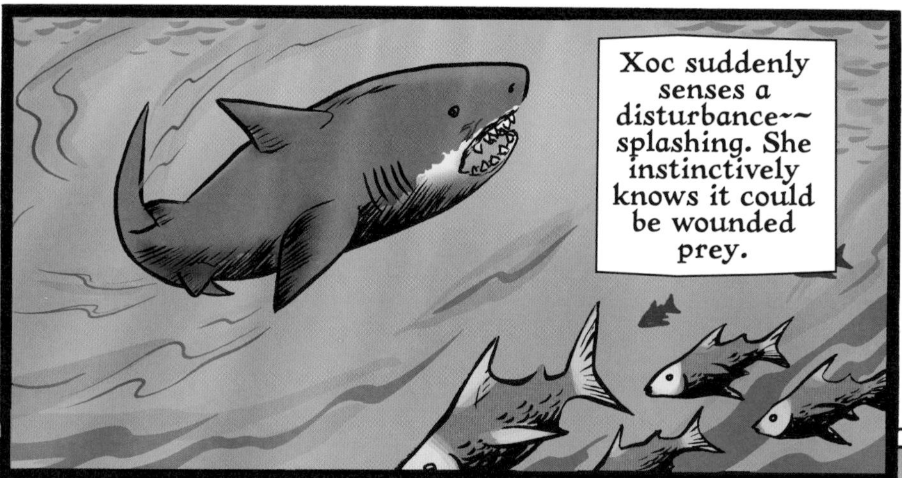
Xoc suddenly senses a disturbance~~splashing. She instinctively knows it could be wounded prey.

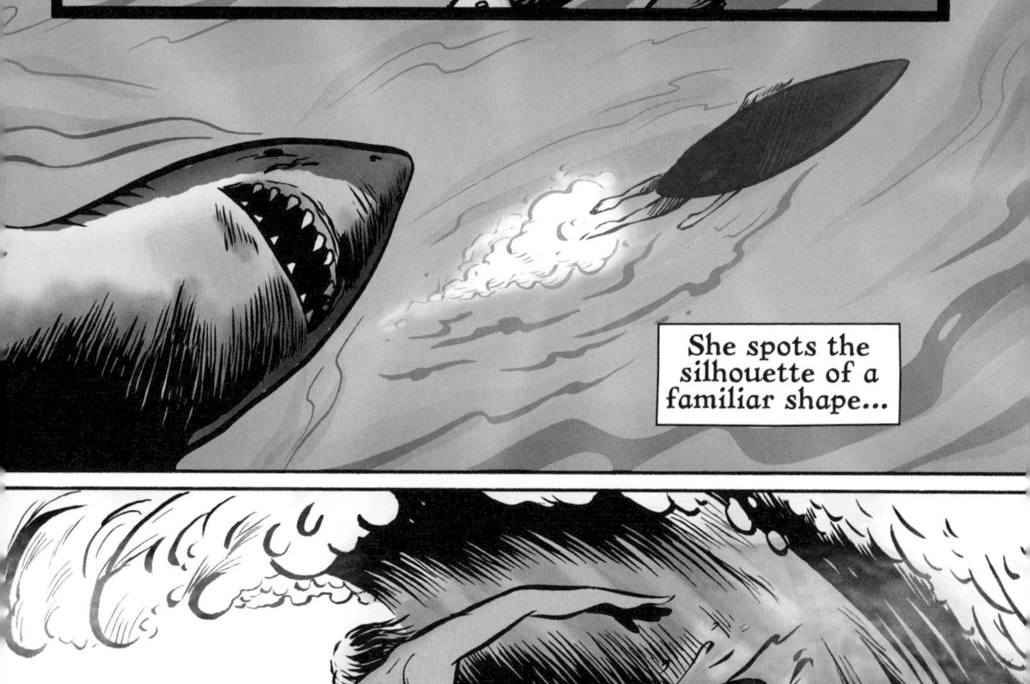
She spots the silhouette of a familiar shape...

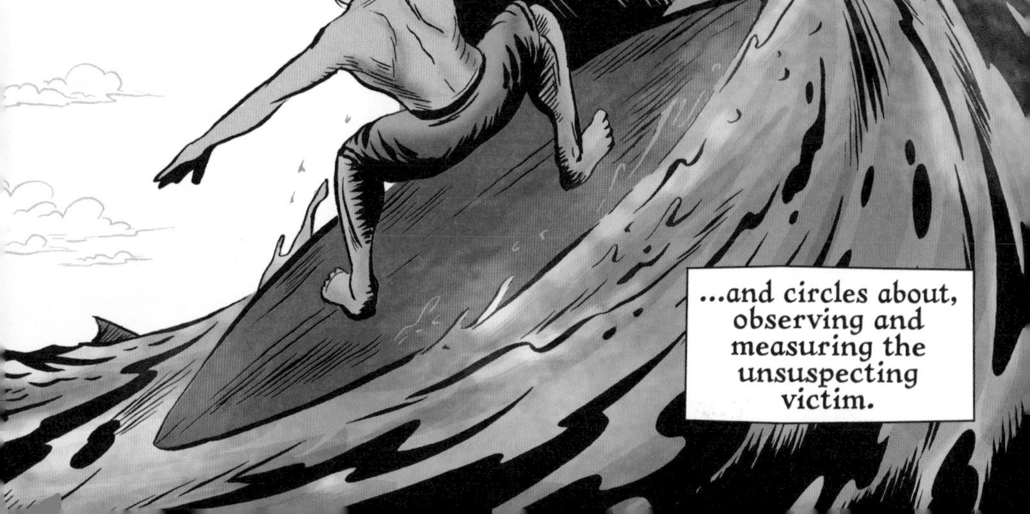
...and circles about, observing and measuring the unsuspecting victim.

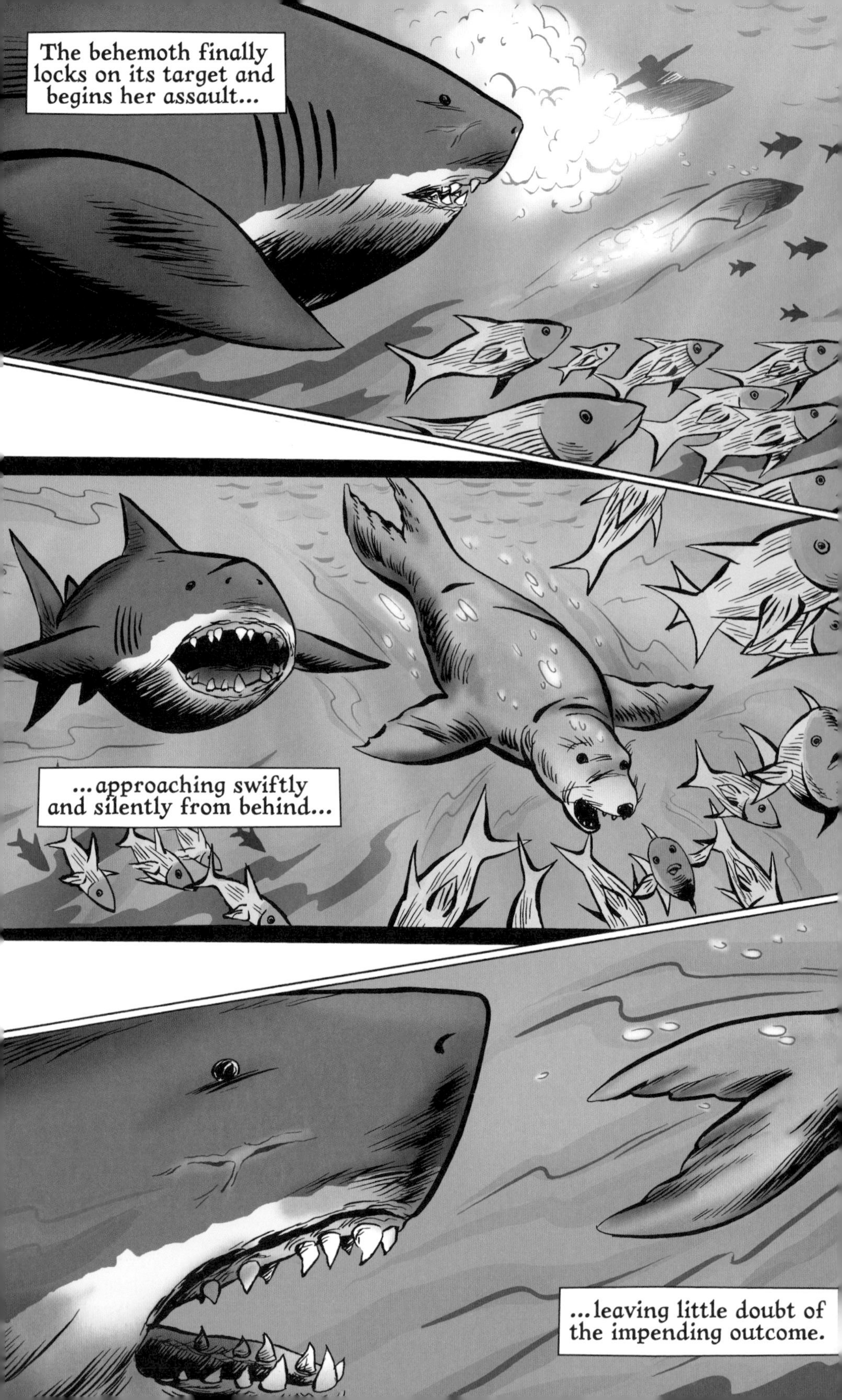
The behemoth finally locks on its target and begins her assault...
...approaching swiftly and silently from behind...
...leaving little doubt of the impending outcome.

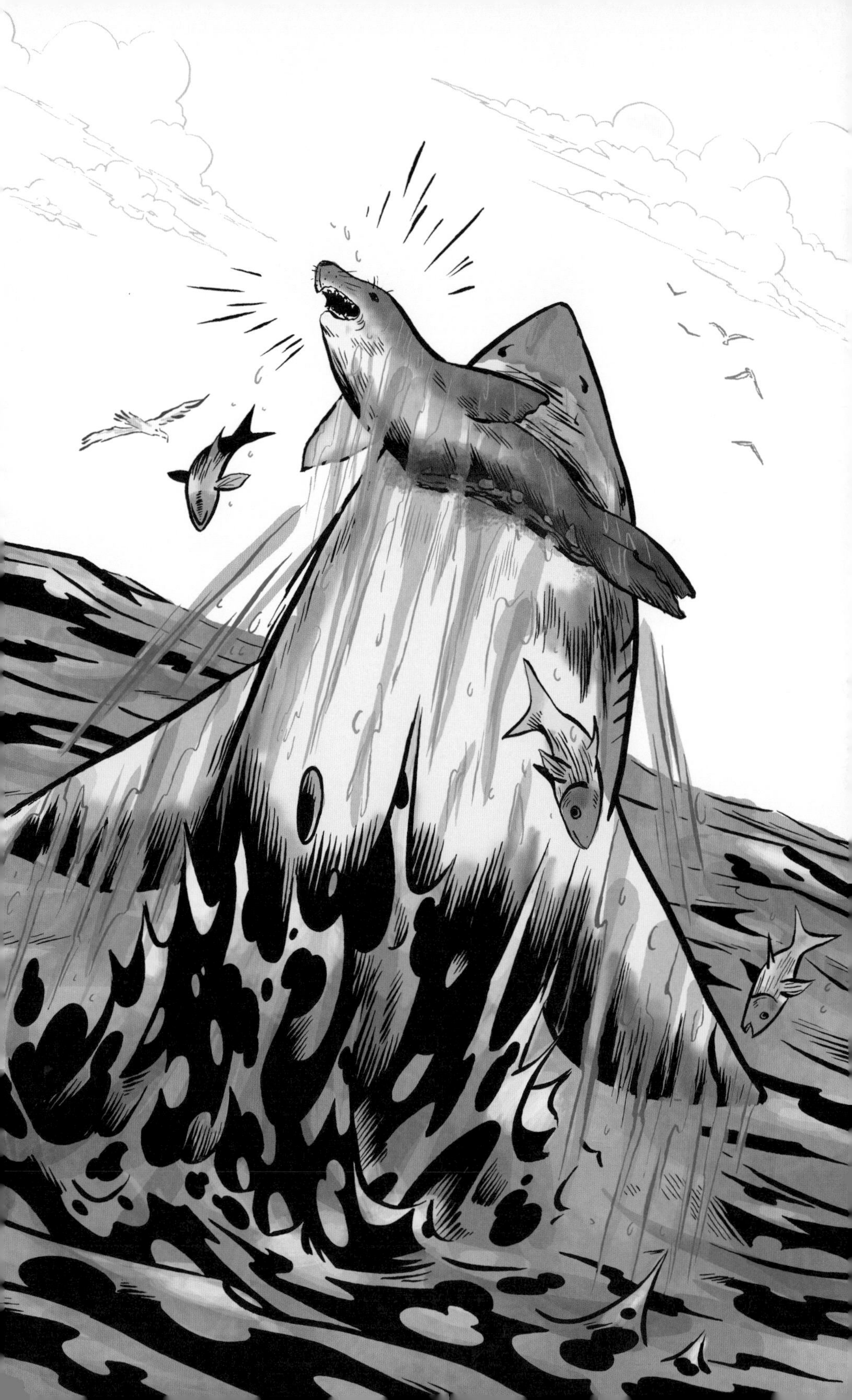

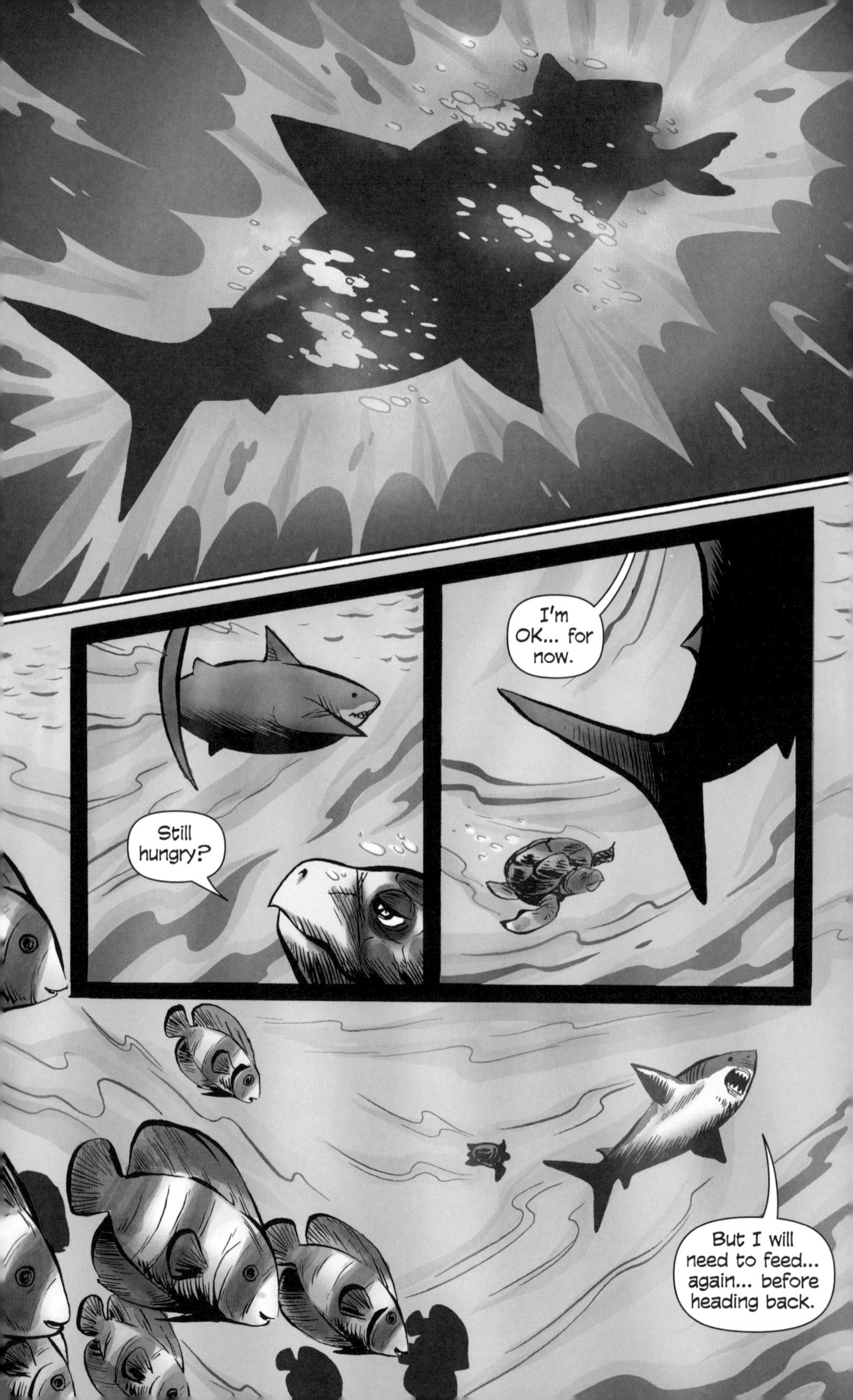
Still hungry?
I'm OK... for now.
But I will need to feed... again... before heading back.

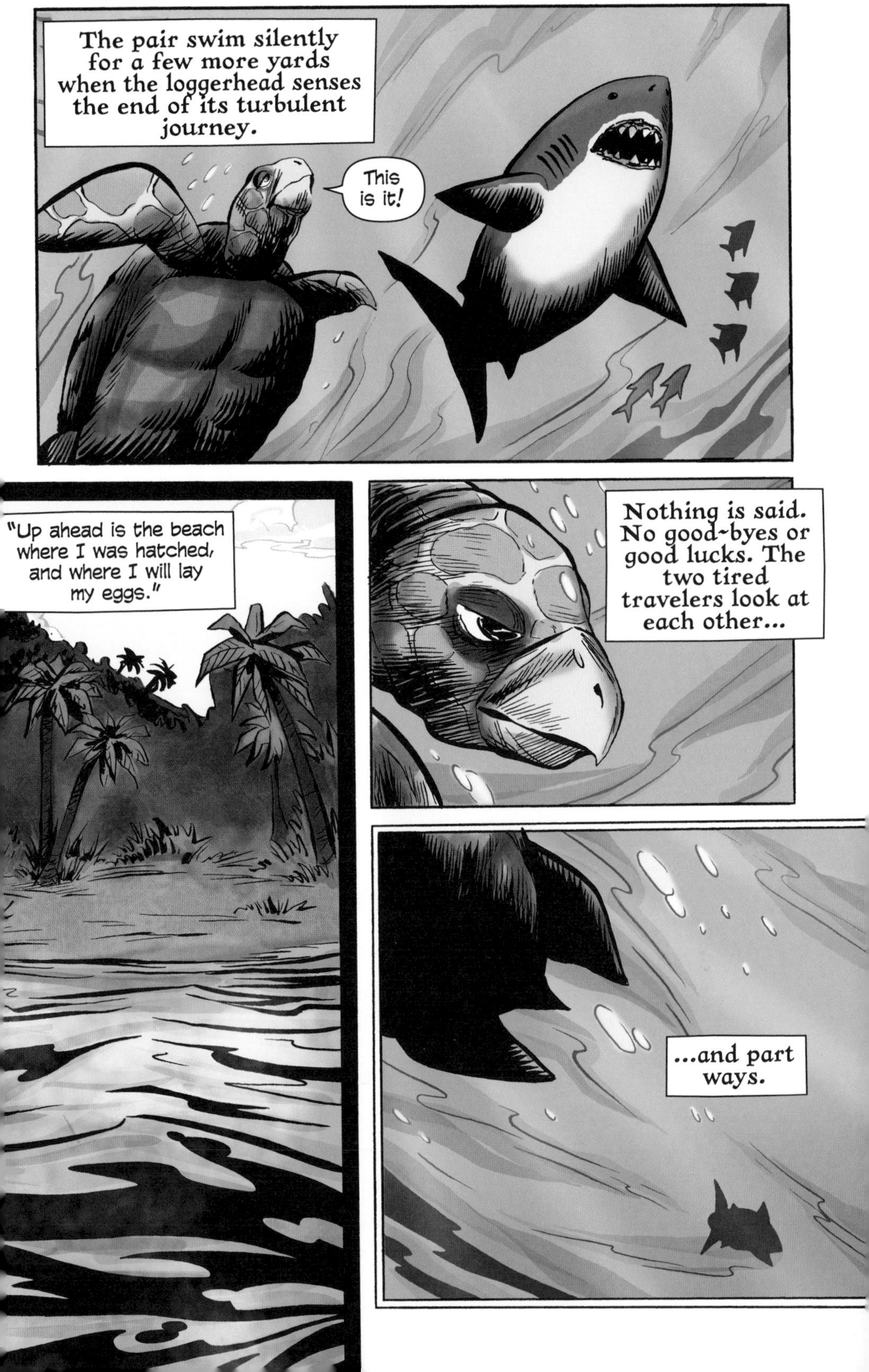
The pair swim silently for a few more yards when the loggerhead senses the end of its turbulent journey.
This is it!
"Up ahead is the beach where I was hatched, and where I will lay my eggs."
Nothing is said. No good-byes or good lucks. The two tired travelers look at each other...
...and part ways.

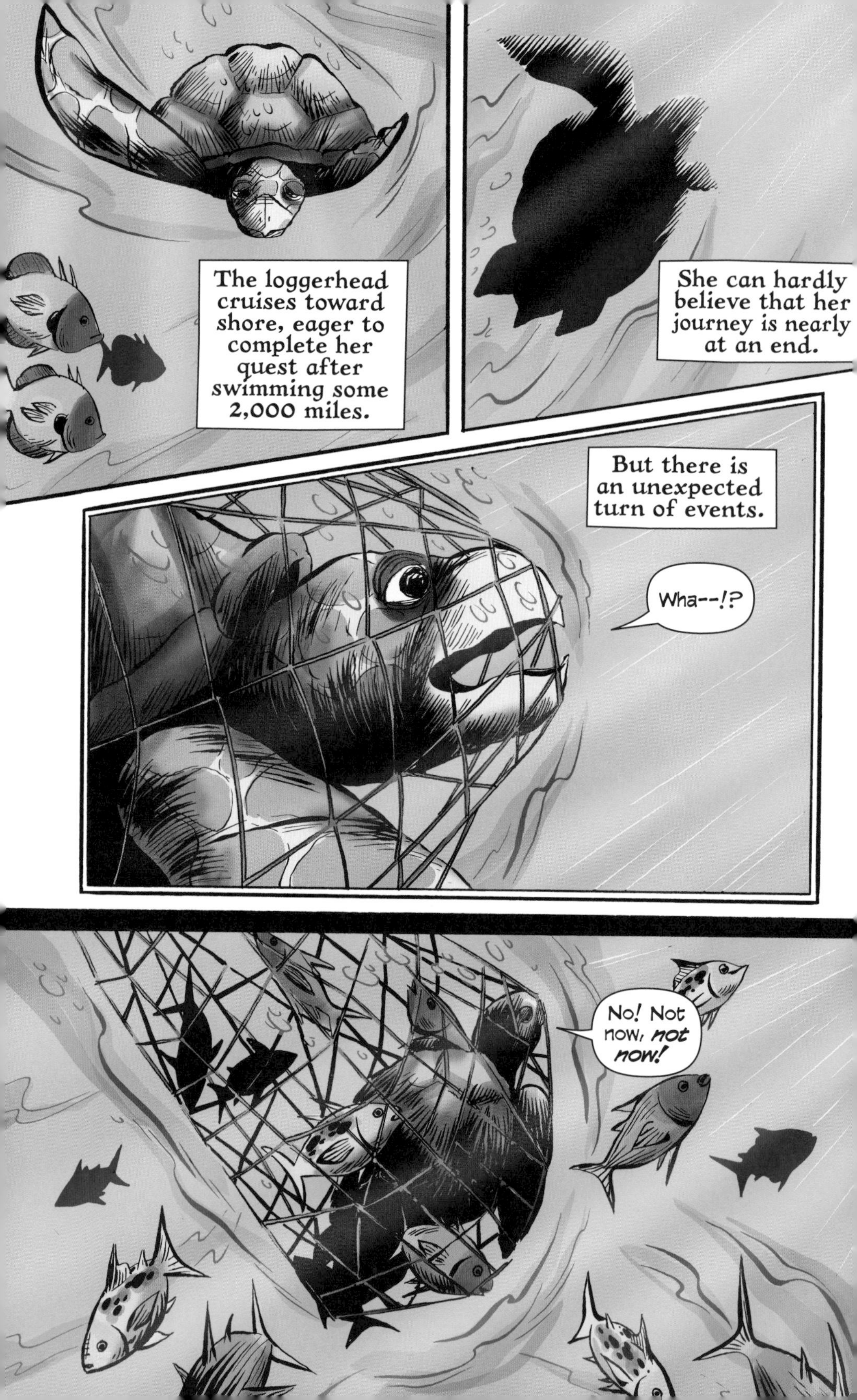
The loggerhead cruises toward shore, eager to complete her quest after swimming some 2,000 miles.
She can hardly believe that her journey is nearly at an end.
But there is an unexpected turn of events.
Wha--!?
No! Not now, *not now!*

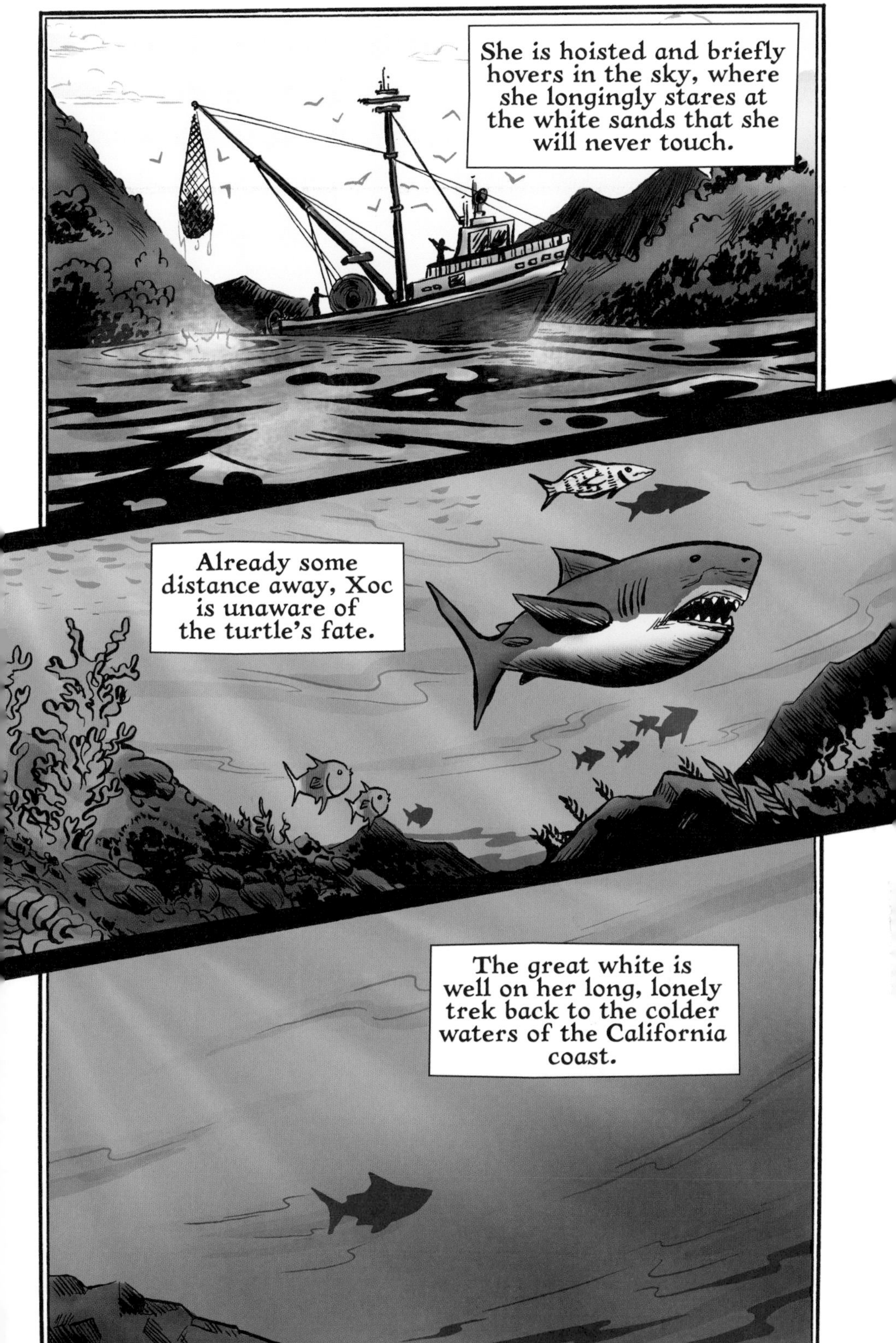
She is hoisted and briefly hovers in the sky, where she longingly stares at the white sands that she will never touch.
Already some distance away, Xoc is unaware of the turtle's fate.
The great white is well on her long, lonely trek back to the colder waters of the California coast.

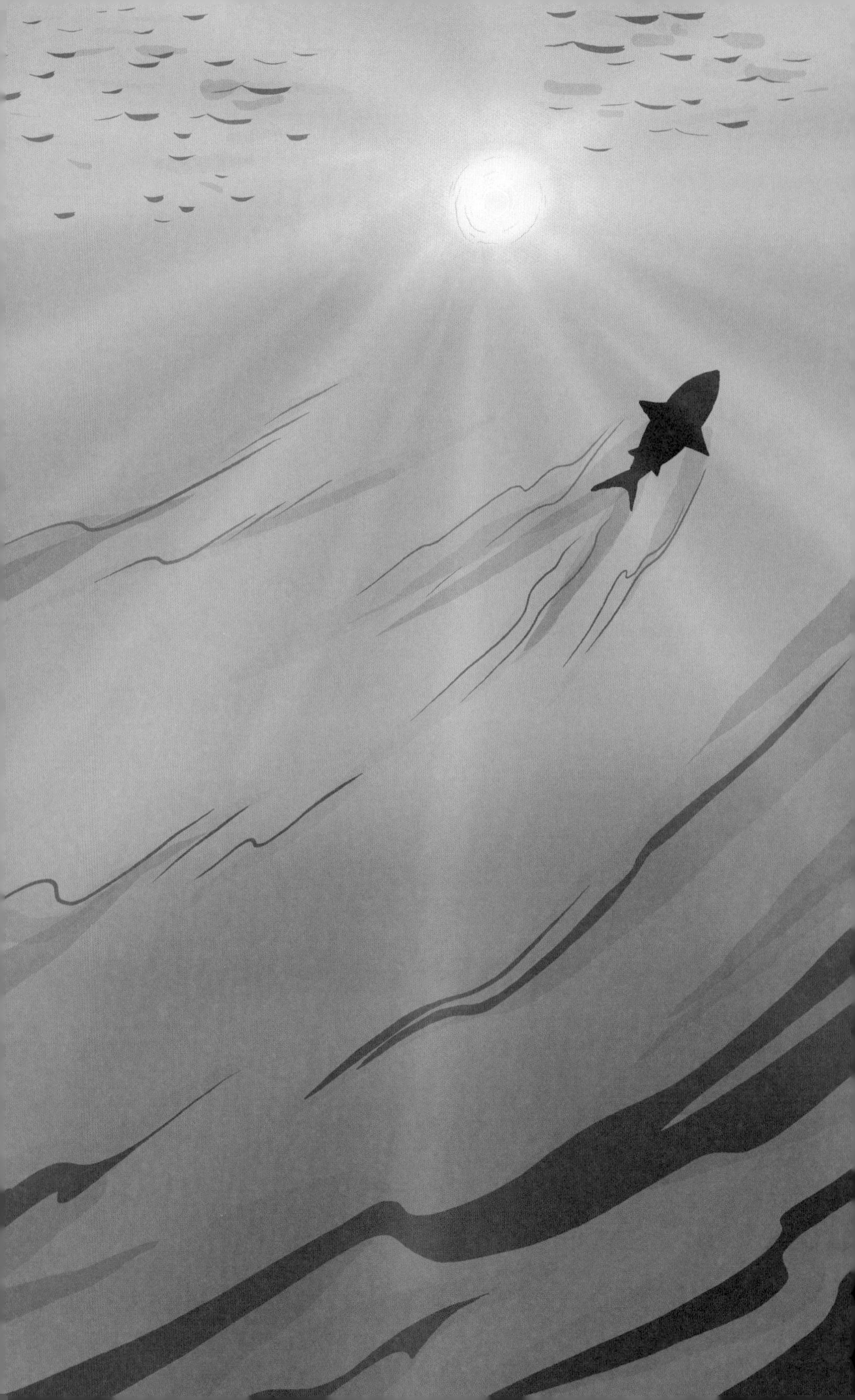

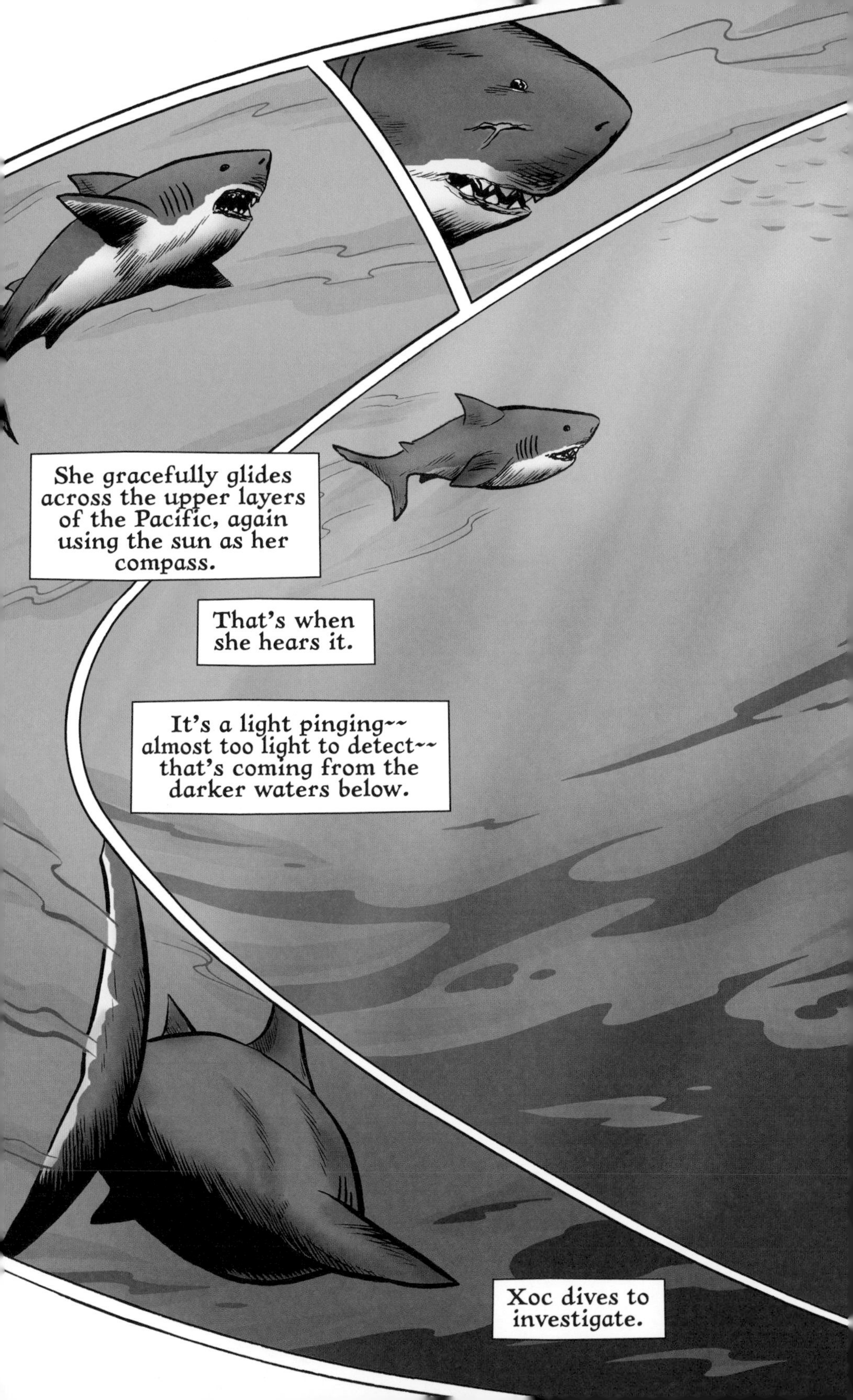
She gracefully glides across the upper layers of the Pacific, again using the sun as her compass.
That's when she hears it.
It's a light pinging-- almost too light to detect-- that's coming from the darker waters below.
Xoc dives to investigate.

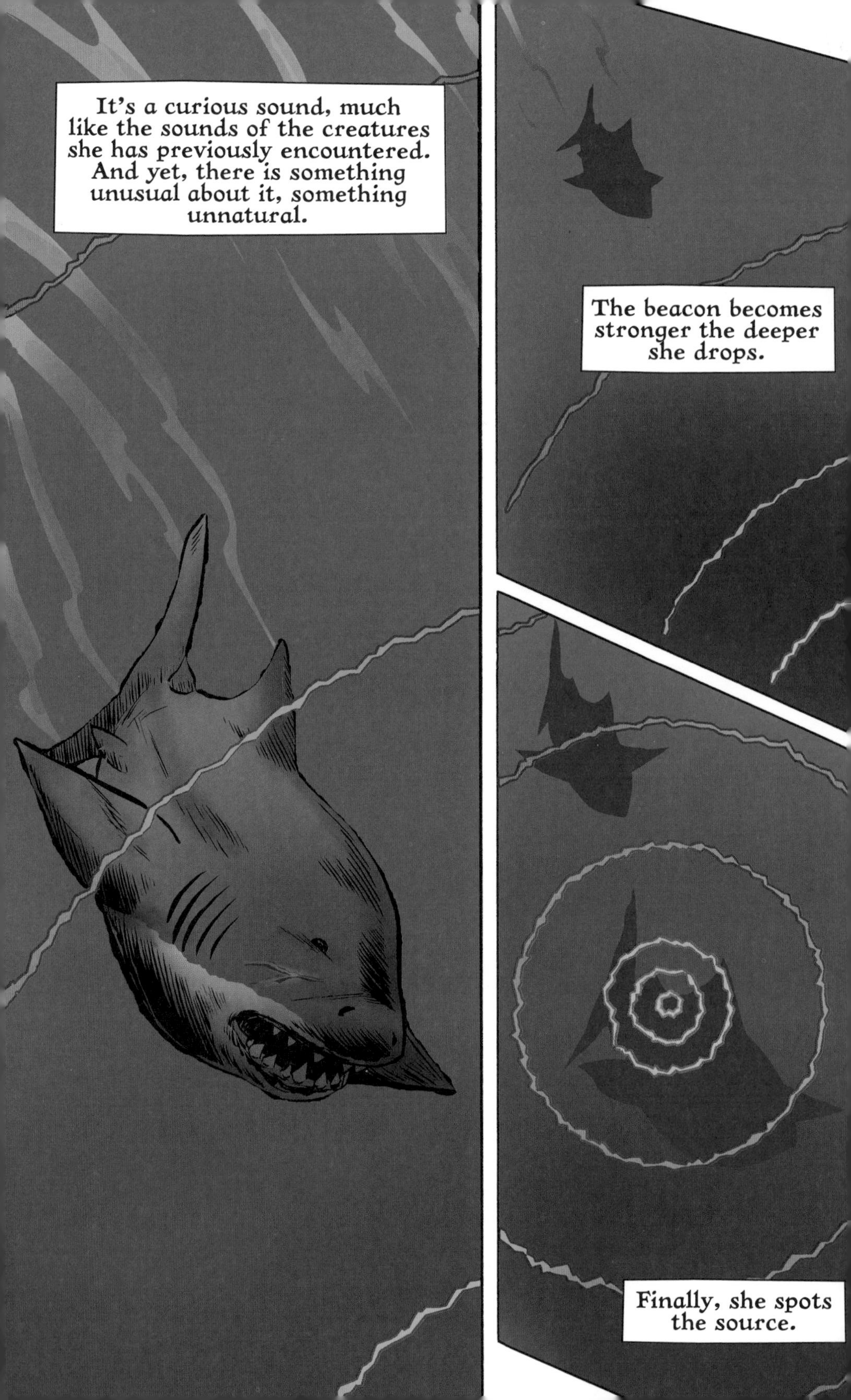
It's a curious sound, much like the sounds of the creatures she has previously encountered. And yet, there is something unusual about it, something unnatural.
The beacon becomes stronger the deeper she drops.
Finally, she spots the source.

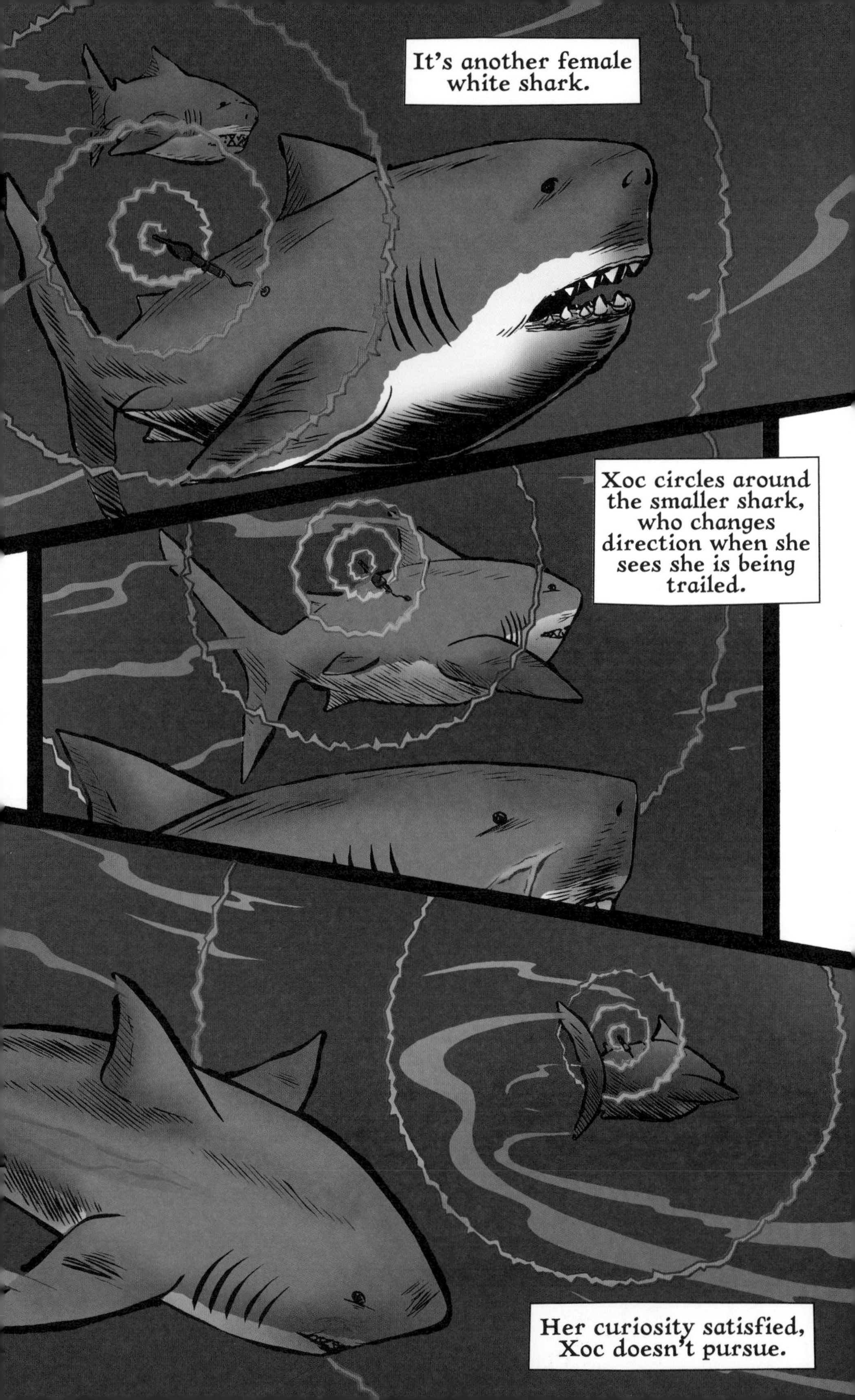
It's another female white shark.
Xoc circles around the smaller shark, who changes direction when she sees she is being trailed.
Her curiosity satisfied, Xoc doesn't pursue.

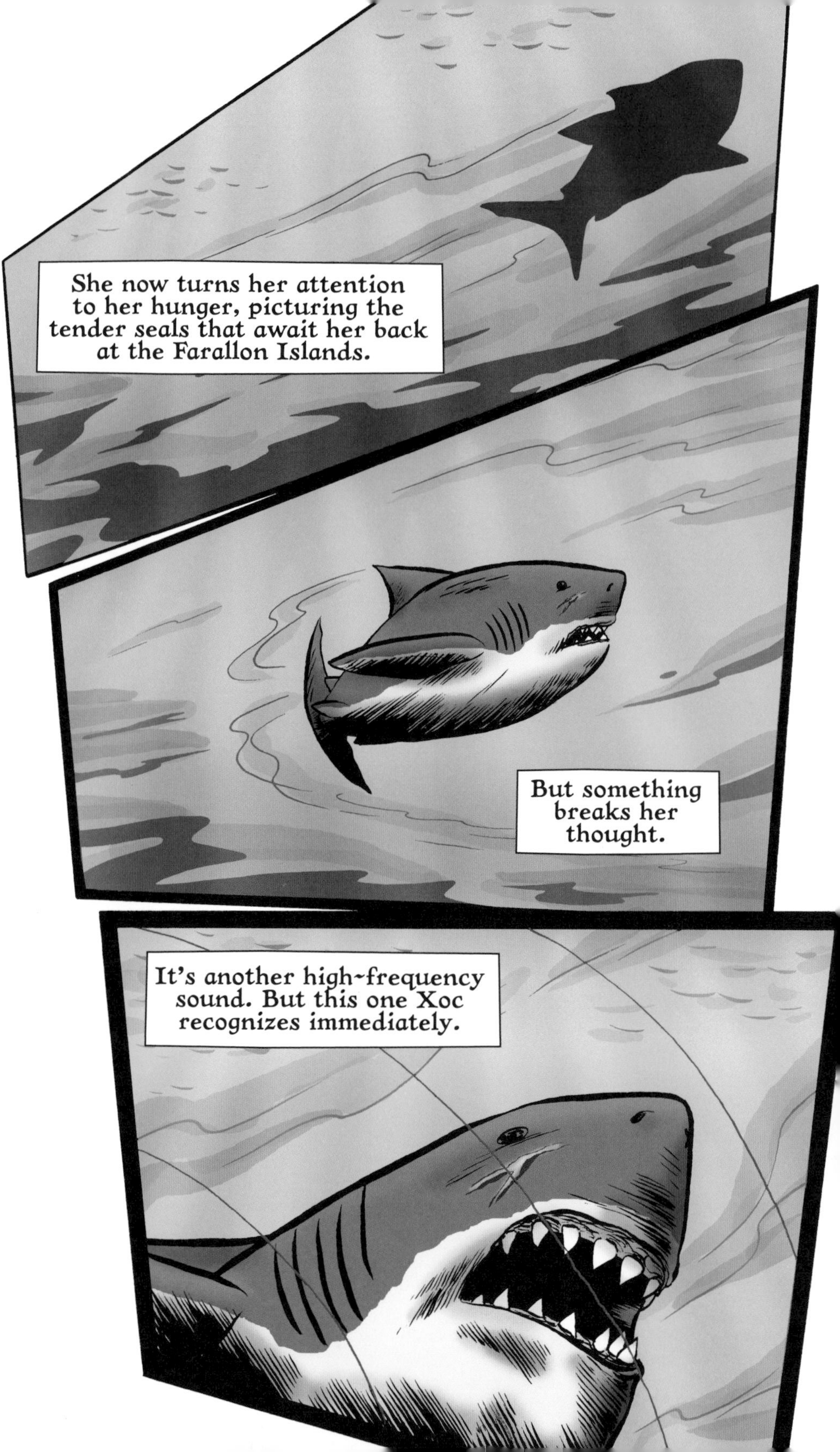
She now turns her attention to her hunger, picturing the tender seals that await her back at the Farallon Islands.
But something breaks her thought.
It's another high-frequency sound. But this one Xoc recognizes immediately.

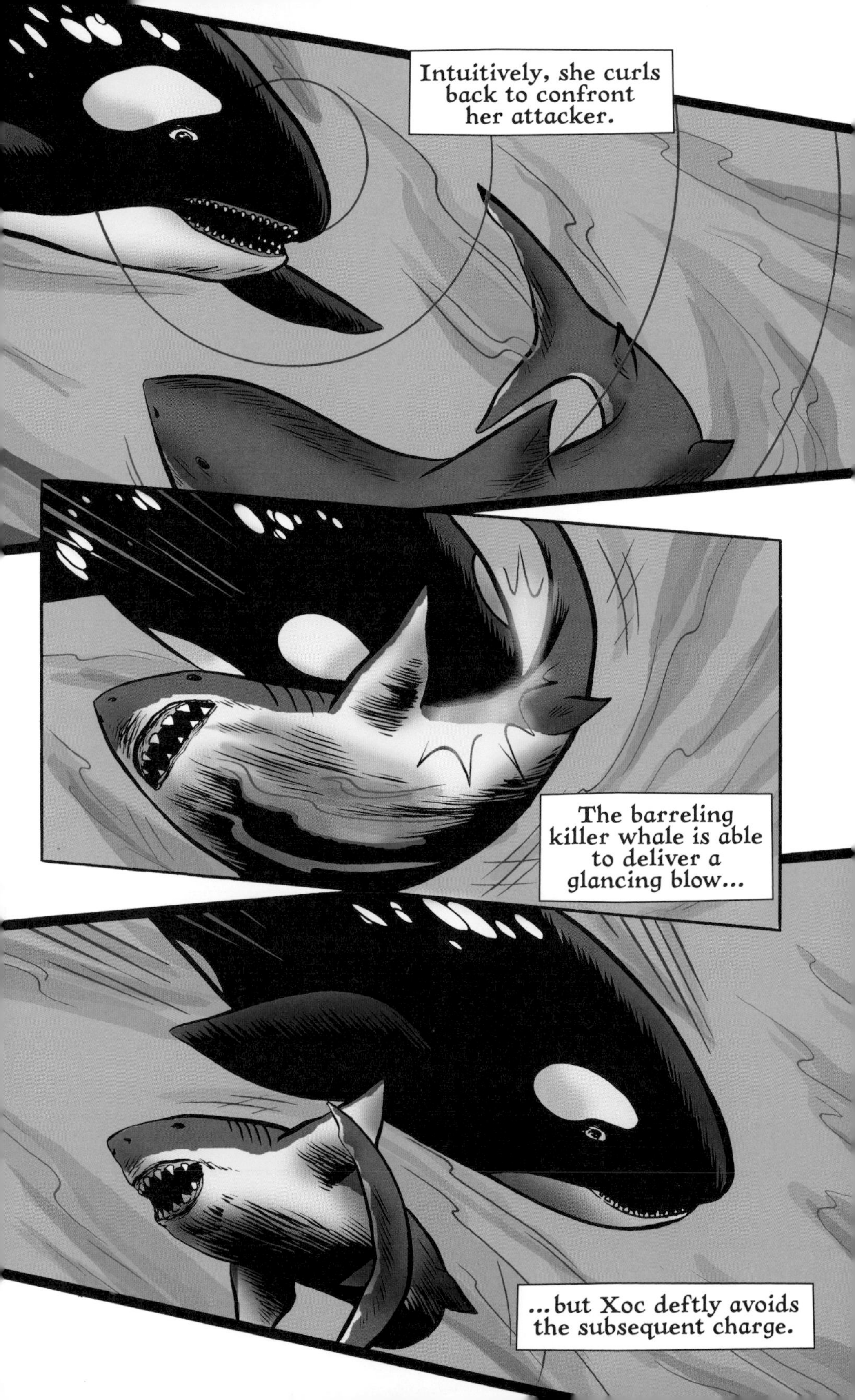
Intuitively, she curls back to confront her attacker.
The barreling killer whale is able to deliver a glancing blow...
...but Xoc deftly avoids the subsequent charge.

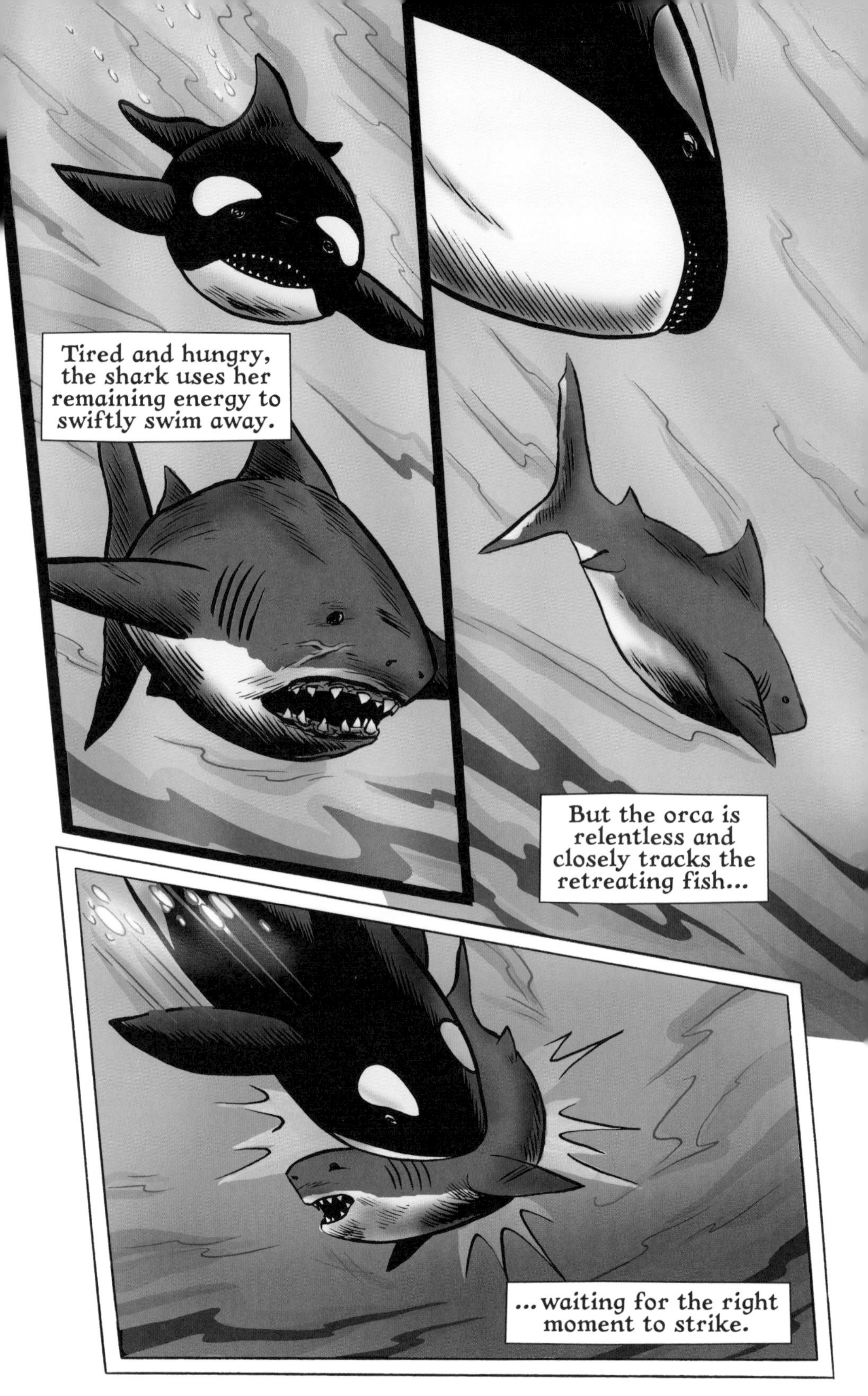
Tired and hungry, the shark uses her remaining energy to swiftly swim away.
But the orca is relentless and closely tracks the retreating fish...
...waiting for the right moment to strike.

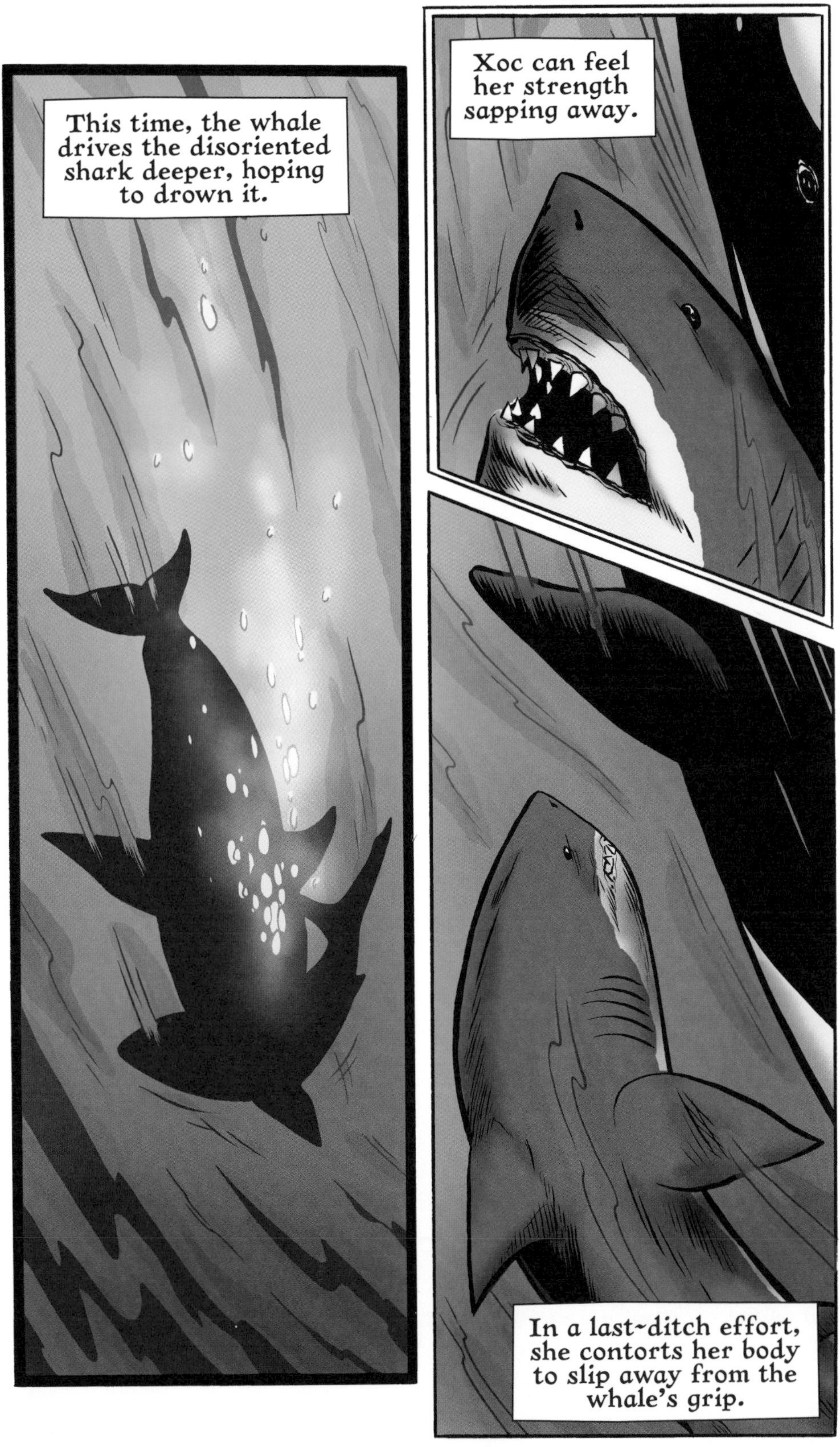
This time, the whale drives the disoriented shark deeper, hoping to drown it.
Xoc can feel her strength sapping away.
In a last-ditch effort, she contorts her body to slip away from the whale's grip.

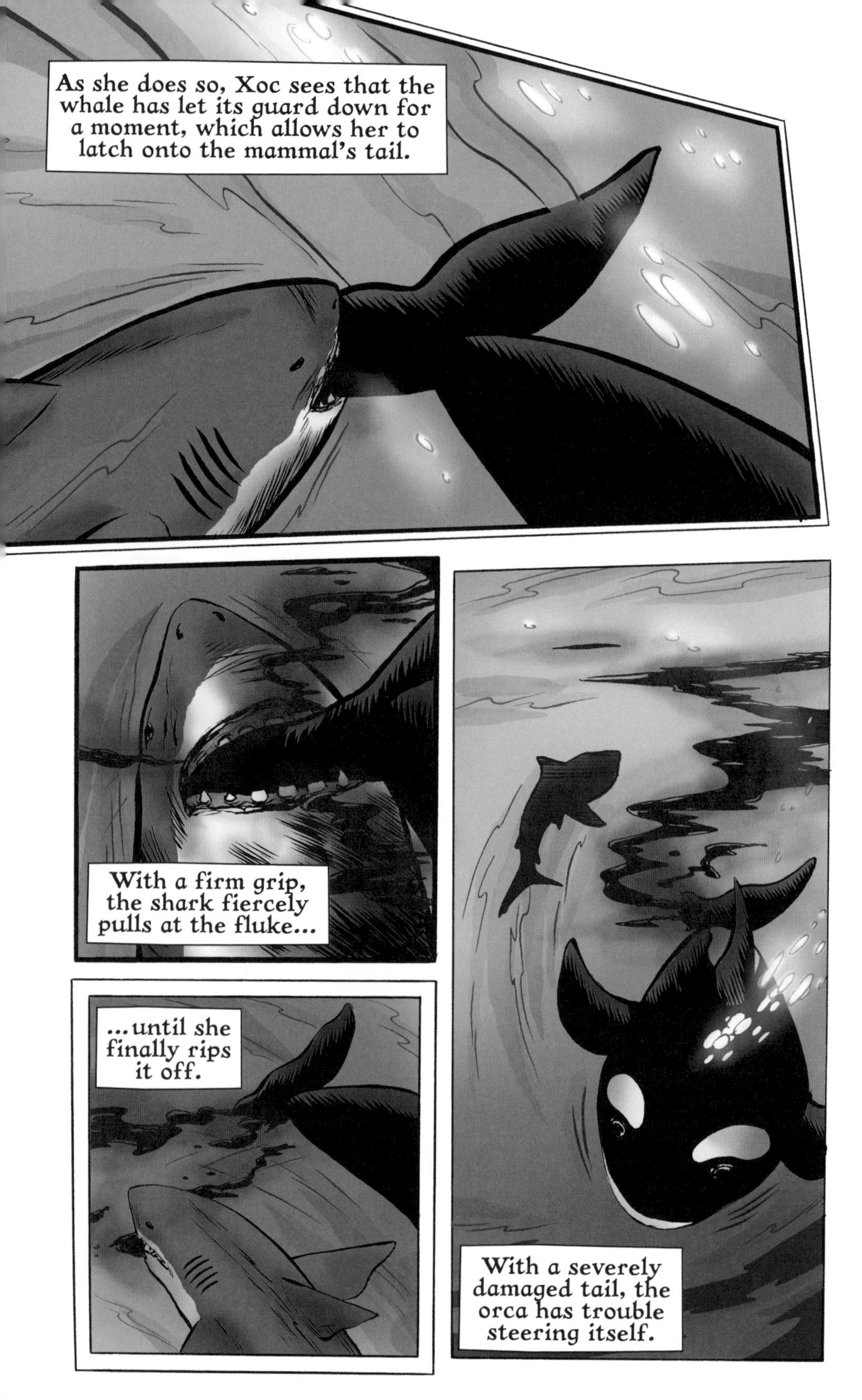
As she does so, Xoc sees that the whale has let its guard down for a moment, which allows her to latch onto the mammal's tail.
With a firm grip, the shark fiercely pulls at the fluke...
...until she finally rips it off.
With a severely damaged tail, the orca has trouble steering itself.

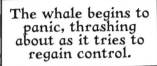

The whale begins to panic, thrashing about as it tries to regain control.

But the wild movements push the mammal deeper into the abyss, until it is swallowed.

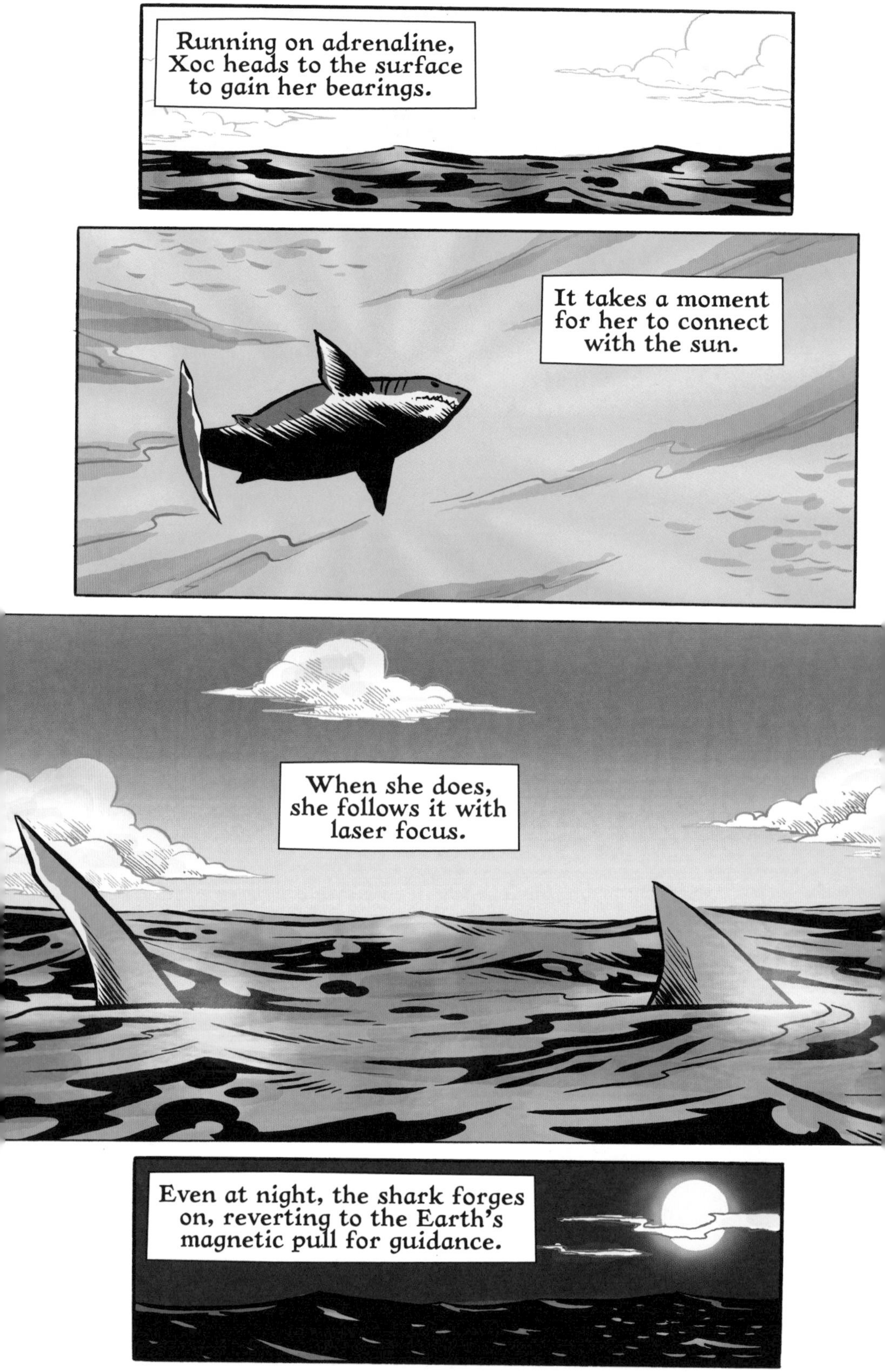
Running on adrenaline, Xoc heads to the surface to gain her bearings.
It takes a moment for her to connect with the sun.
When she does, she follows it with laser focus.
Even at night, the shark forges on, reverting to the Earth's magnetic pull for guidance.

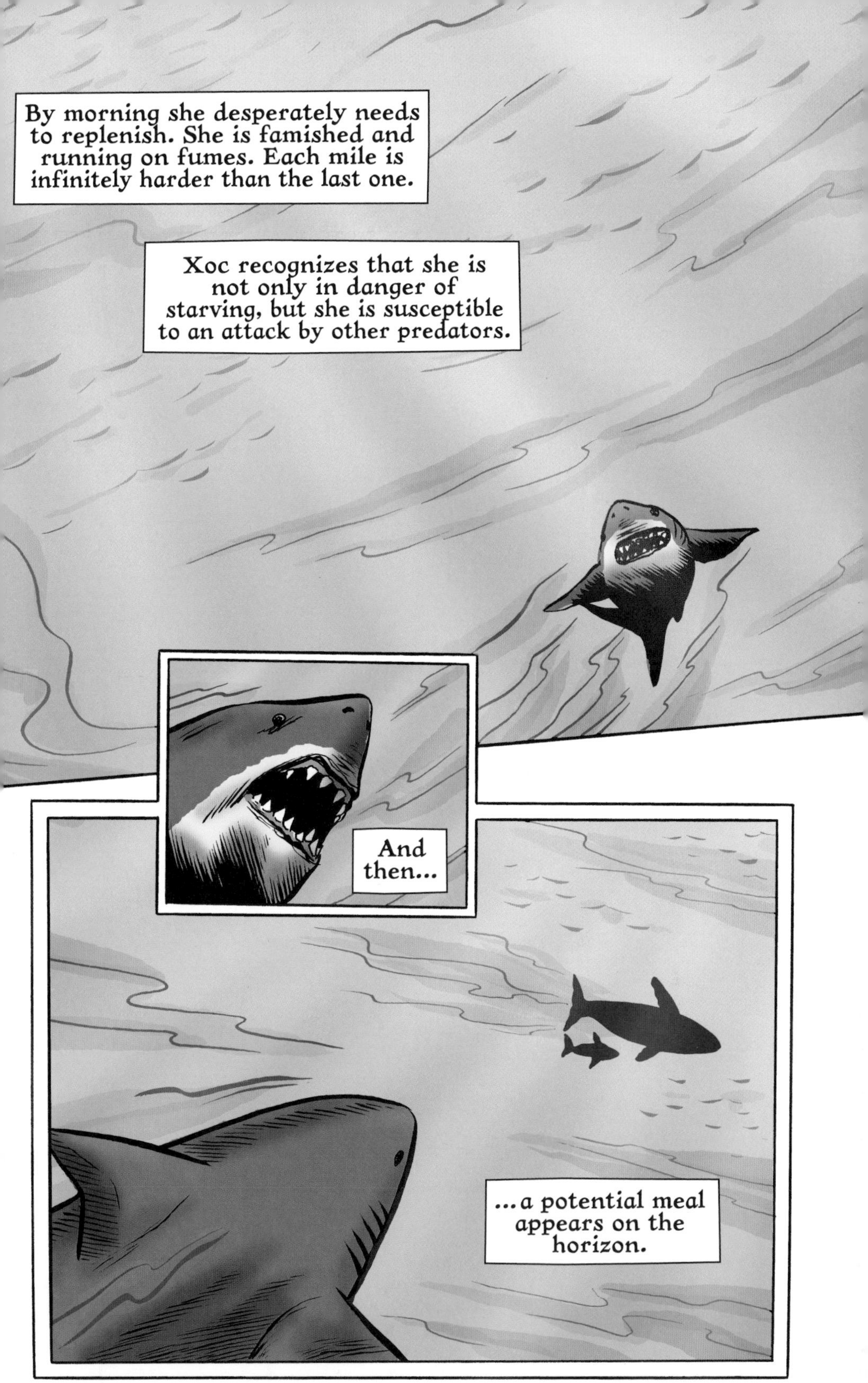
By morning she desperately needs to replenish. She is famished and running on fumes. Each mile is infinitely harder than the last one.
Xoc recognizes that she is not only in danger of starving, but she is susceptible to an attack by other predators.
And then...
...a potential meal appears on the horizon.

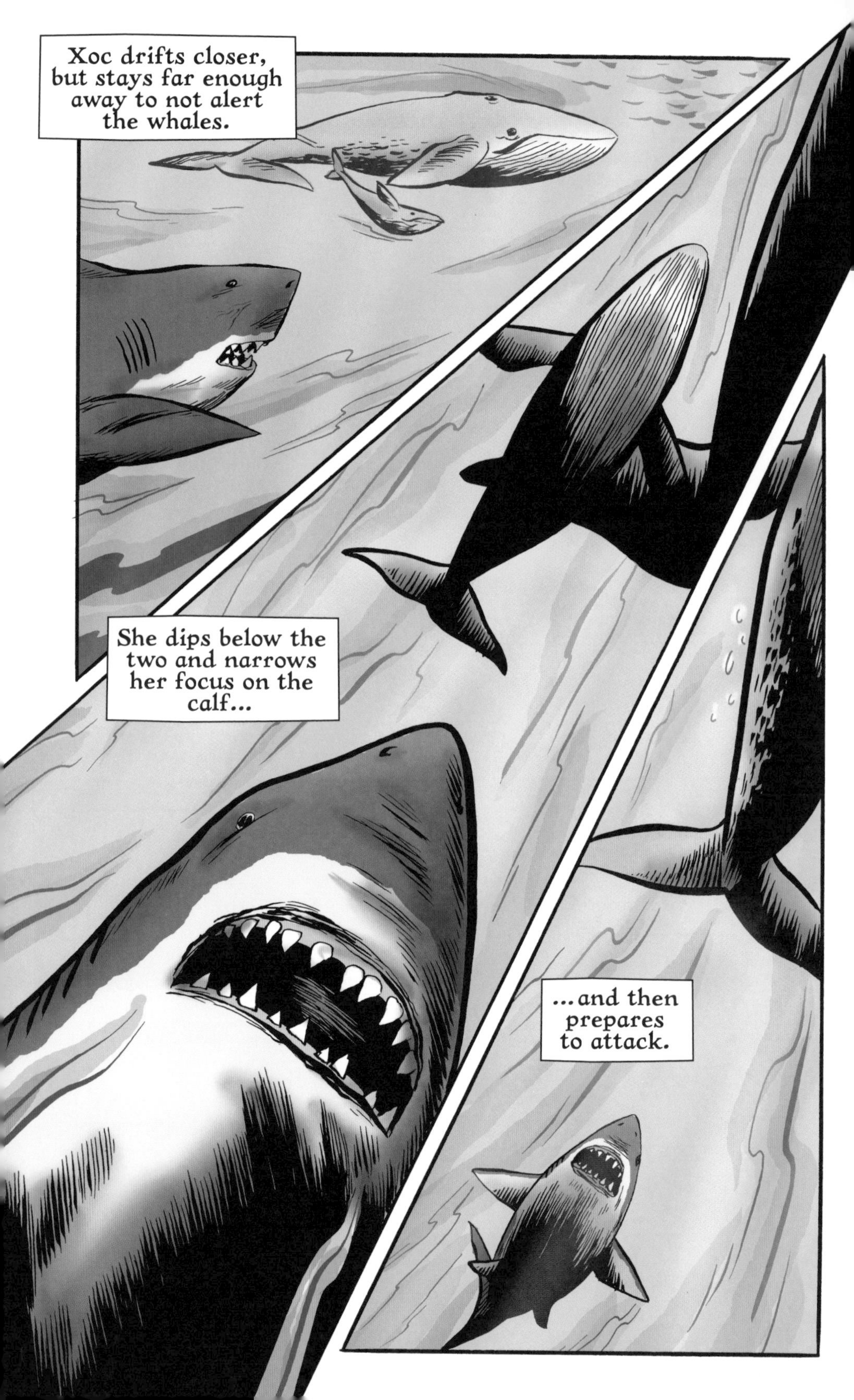
Xoc drifts closer, but stays far enough away to not alert the whales.
She dips below the two and narrows her focus on the calf...
...and then prepares to attack.

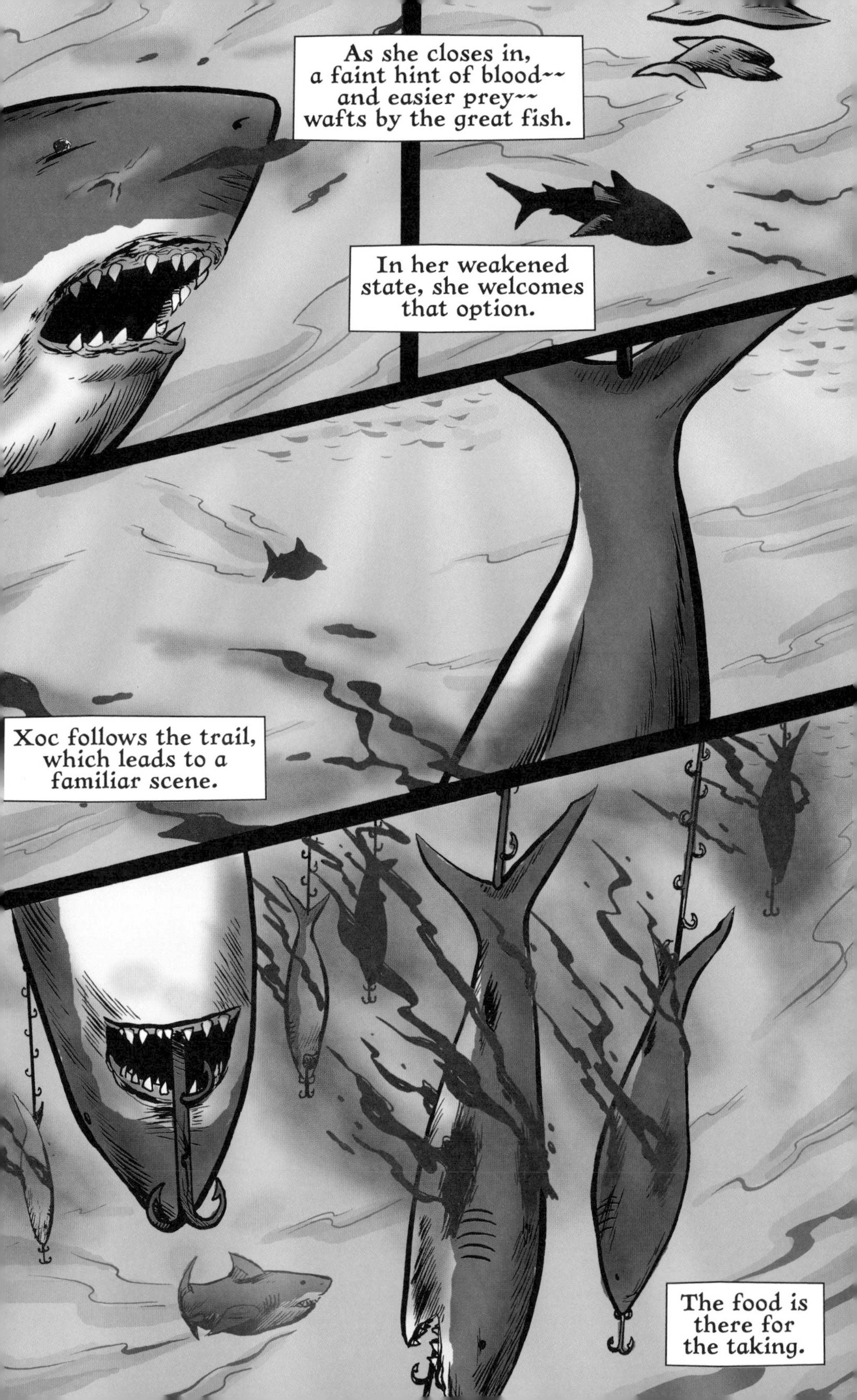
As she closes in, a faint hint of blood-- and easier prey-- wafts by the great fish.
In her weakened state, she welcomes that option.
Xoc follows the trail, which leads to a familiar scene.
The food is there for the taking.

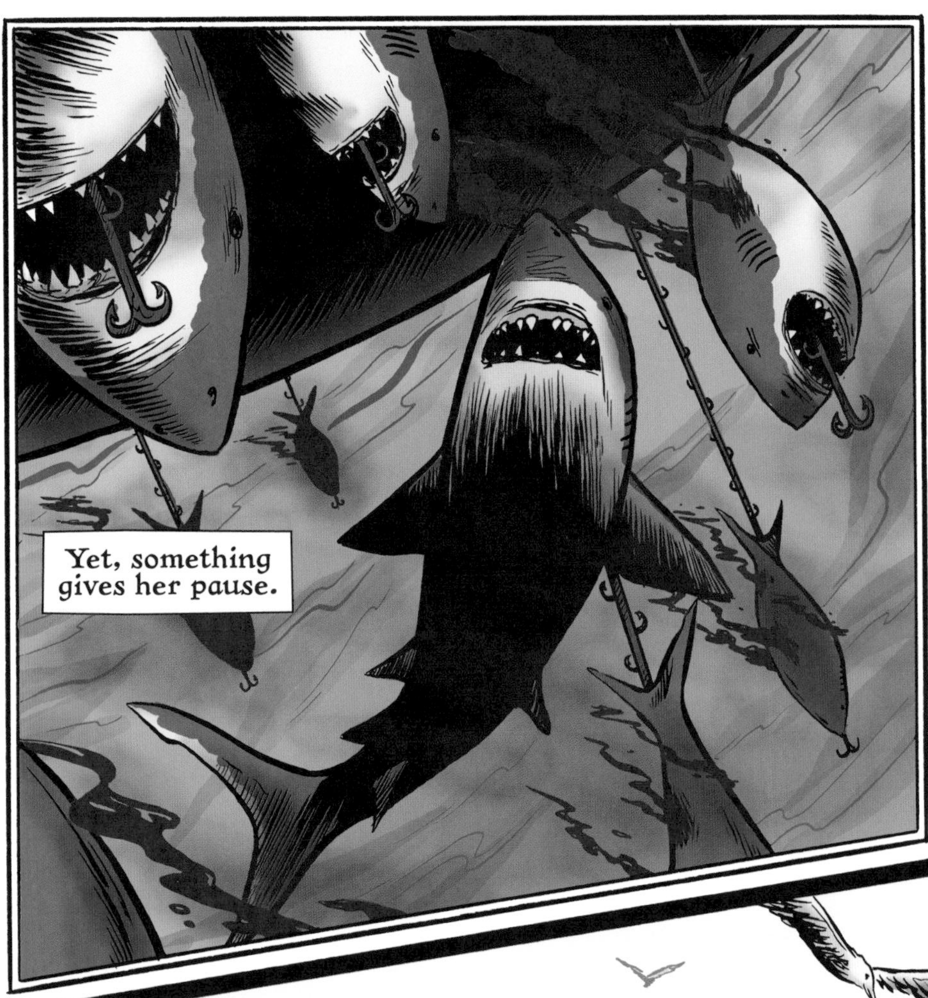
Yet, something
gives her pause.

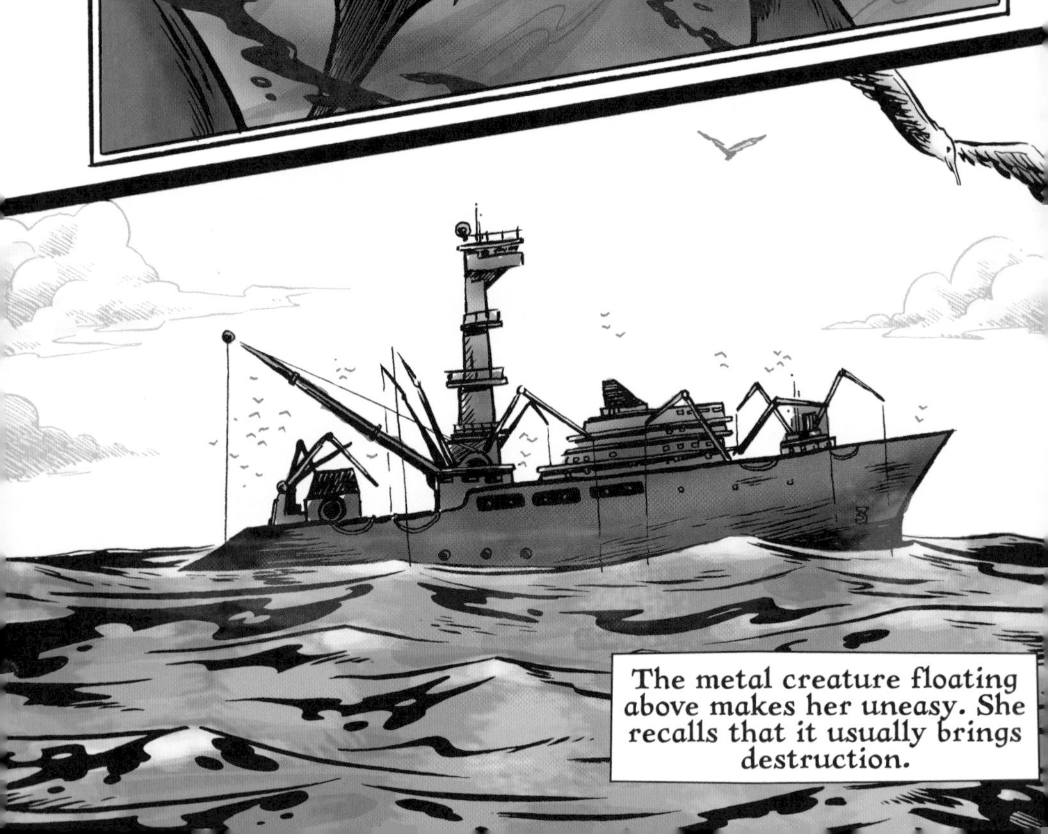
The metal creature floating
above makes her uneasy. She
recalls that it usually brings
destruction.

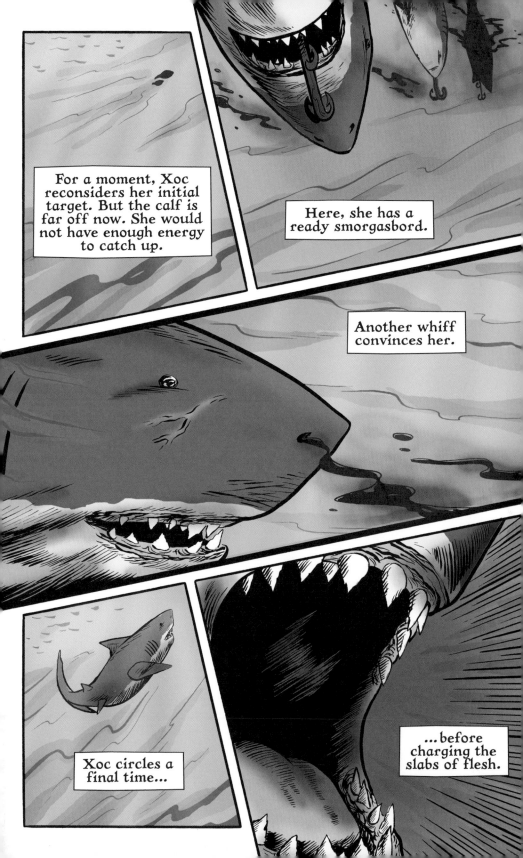

For a moment, Xoc reconsiders her initial target. But the calf is far off now. She would not have enough energy to catch up.

Here, she has a ready smorgasbord.

Another whiff convinces her.

Xoc circles a final time...

...before charging the slabs of flesh.

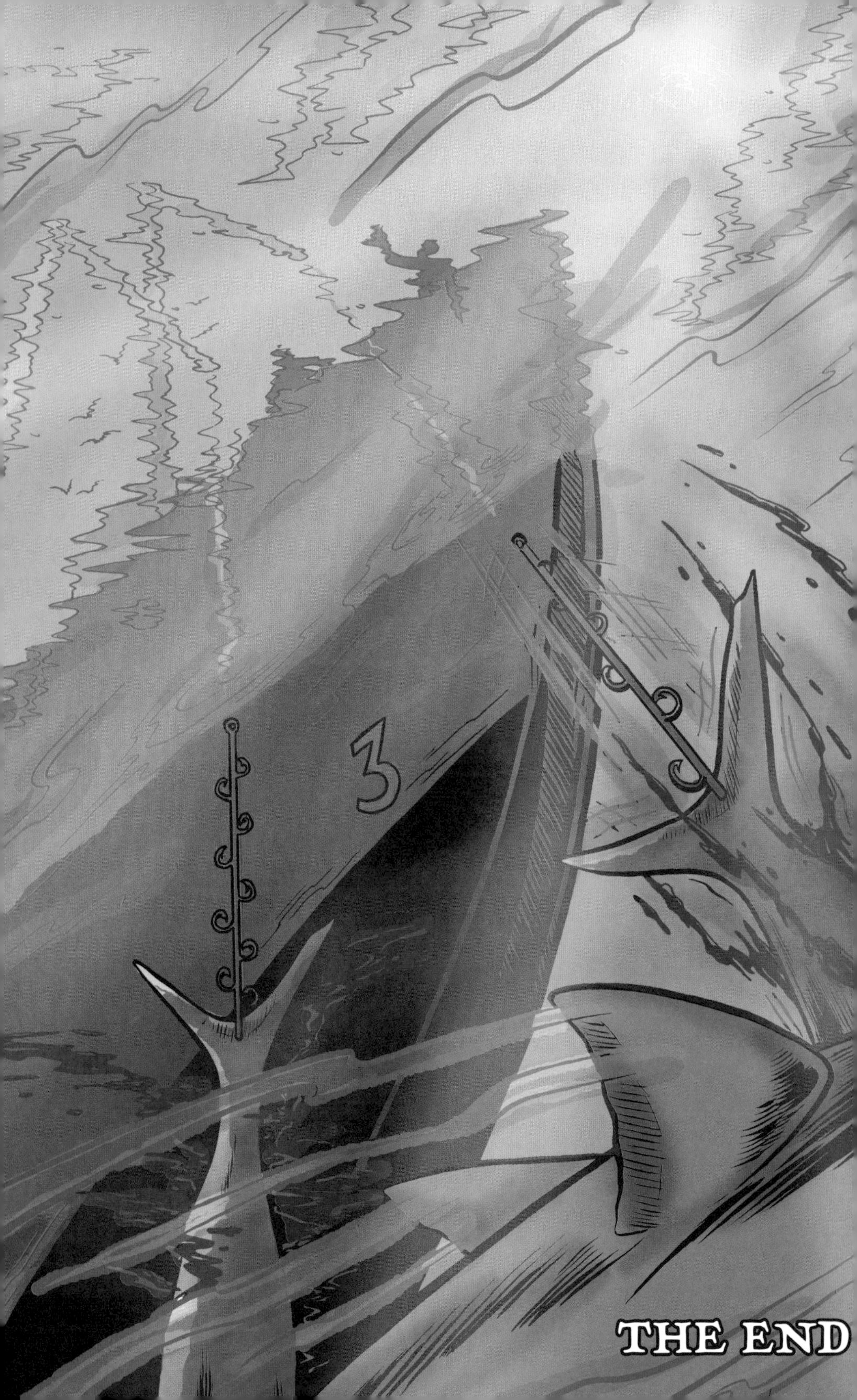
3
THE END

For more information about this book, and to read a short story about Xoc's pup, please visit http://xocing.blogspot.com/.

AUTHOR'S NOTE

Remember the floating islands of trash featured in the book? They exist. The largest one is called the "Great Pacific Garbage Patch." It's sprawling; scientists are uncertain of its exact size, but they estimate that it's twice the size of Hawaii or perhaps as large as Texas. This mass of waste is having a detrimental impact on the wildlife. The necks of turtles get caught in six-pack plastic rings, birds gobble up floating plastic pellets, and fish develop ulcers from leached chemicals.

Yet pollution isn't the only thing threatening the ocean's ecosystem. There's overfishing, illegal poaching, and massive dumping. The wanton destruction is exemplified in the practice of "finning" sharks for a mere bowl of soup. Under this practice, most fishers catch sharks, cut off their fins and then throw them back alive into the ocean, where the sharks drown because they can't swim anymore. It is estimated that 73 million—*million*—sharks are killed this way each year.

If that number is hard to wrap your head around, here are a few quick facts that might put it in perspective. Over the past 30 years, the hammerhead shark population in the Atlantic Ocean has dropped by nearly 93 percent, according to the National Aquarium in Baltimore. And since 1986, nearly all shark populations in the northwestern Atlantic have declined by more than 50 percent.

I encourage you to expand and challenge the research and conclusion for this story. (This book includes endnotes and a brief bibliography used for my research that can serve as a starting point for your own study). I hope it prompts you to become involved in preserving our environment and help find some solutions. Hopefully, there is a budding scientist out there who can find better ways to dispose of trash, or a young lawmaker who is willing to take a stand against an unethical practice, or simply an informed consumer who holds companies liable for their environmental practices, from packaging manufacturers to distributors of food products.

Whether we like it or not, humans are the primary caretakers of this planet, but we have fallen short on our duties to care for our oceans and their denizens. The way we act not only impacts sea life, but it also has cascading effects on us. For instance, in some parts of the country, fewer sharks has meant fewer predators for stingrays. The increase in stingrays has resulted in a significant drop in shellfish populations, which are the main sources of food to stingrays.

Despite the gloomy ending for Xoc, I'm optimistic that we can change things. In 2011, President Obama signed into law the Shark Conservation Act, which closes some loopholes in existing fishing laws, including measures to prohibit removal of any shark fins—including the tail—and discarding the shark carcass at sea. It also encourages the U.S. to seek international shark conservation agreements.

It's good to take a moment and enjoy our accomplishments, but we should continue to strive to do more, which begins with education and advocacy.

—Matt Dembicki

DID YOU KNOW?

- Great white sharks (Carcharodon carcharias) can grow to 6 meters (20 ft) in length, and can weigh more than 2,200 kg (5,000 lb).

- Great whites have a specialized organ (the Ampullae of Lorenzini) that allows them to sense electromagnetic fields. They can "feel" the minute electrical pulse of a heartbeat from several meters away.

- Contrary to popular opinion, great white sharks are not "mindless, eating machines." They are cunning hunters, who stalk and ambush unsuspecting prey from beneath.

- A great white shark may lose more than 1,000 teeth in its lifetime.

- Great whites frequently raise their heads above the surface of the water to get a better view of their prey. Scientists call this practice "spy-hopping."

- While it has proven that great white sharks give birth to live young, virtually nothing is known about their mating habits, and a great white birth has never been observed.

- Great whites are frequently hunted by humans for trophies (jaws, teeth). Their meat is considered a delicacy in some countries.

- Fishing, both sport and commercial, is largely responsible for the massive decline in great white populations over the last 50 years.

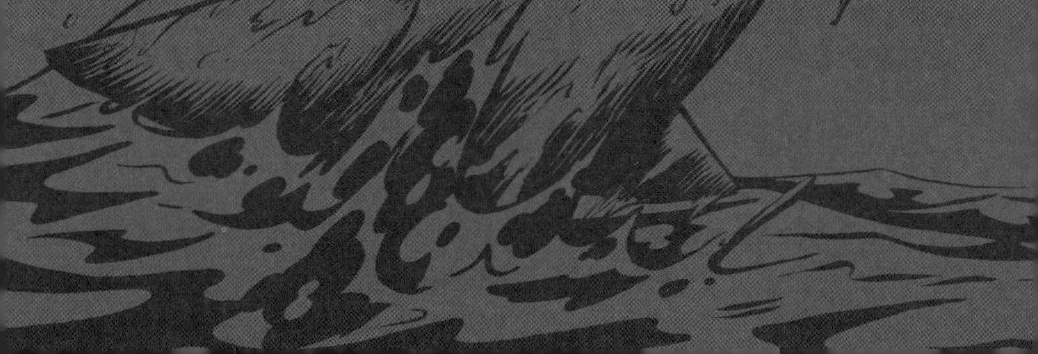

FOR MORE INFORMATION ON SHARKS, PLEASE VISIT ANY OF THE FOLLOWING SITES:

- The National Geographic (NatGeo) site for animal conservation.
  http://animals.nationalgeographic.com/animals/conservation/

- The Florida Museum of Natural History's website has an extensive section covering sharks.
  http://www.flmnh.ufl.edu/fish/Sharks/sharks.htm

- The Marine Conservation Science Institute has a great deal of information about great white sharks, and has also released an app for iPhone or iPad that allows you to track real sharks that have been tagged for research purposes.
  http://www.marinecsi.org/

FOR MORE INFORMATION ON CONSERVATION, PLEASE VISIT ANY OF THE FOLLOWING SITES:

- EarthEcho International is an organization founded by Philippe and Alexandra Cousteau to empower young people in conservation efforts.
  http://www.earthecho.org

- Shark Savers, an organization dedicated to saving sharks, particularly focused on banning finning.
  http://www.sharksavers.org

- Oceana has instituted a campaign to facilitate banning shark finning nation wide.
  http://act.oceana.org/sign/p-scaredforsharks/

- Greenpeace, long known for their conservation efforts, published a report in 2006 on the dangers that non-biodegradable plastics pose for the world's oceans.
  http://www.greenpeace.org/international/en/publications/reports/plastic_ocean_report/

- This is the full text of the 2009 Shark Conservation act, which was signed into law by President Obama on January 4th, 2011.
  http://www.govtrack.us/congress/bill.xpd?bill=h111-81

BIBLIOGRAPHY

Allsopp, Michelle, Paul Johnston, David Santillo, and Adam Walters. "Plastic Debris in the World's Oceans." Greenpeace, November 2, 2006.
http://www.greenpeace.org/international/en/publications/reports/plastic_ocean_report/

Berton, Justin. "Continent-size toxic stew of plastic trash fouling swaths of Pacific Ocean." *San Francisco Chronicle*, Oct. 19, 2007.
http://www.sfgate.com/cgi-bin/article.cgi?f=/c/a/2007/10/18/SS6JS8RH0.DTL

Bonfil, Ramon, Ryan Johnson, Deon Kotze, Michael Meyer, Shannon O'Brien, Herman Oosthuizen, Michael Paterson, Michael Scholl, and Stephen Swanson. "Transoceanic Migration, Spatial Dynamics, and Population Linkages of White Sharks." *Science*, Vol. 310 (Oct. 7, 2005): 100-103.

Casey, Susan. *Devil's Teeth: A True Story and Survival Among America's Great White Sharks.* New York: Owl Books, Henry Holt and Co., 2005.

Cousteau, Jean-Michel and Mose Richards. *Cousteau's Great White Shark.* NewYork: Harry N. Abrams, 1992.

Doubilet, David and Jennifer Hayes. *Face to Face With Sharks.* Washington D.C.: National Geographic Society, 2009.

Jones, Tom. "The Xoc, the Sharke, and the Sea Dogs: An Historical Encounter," *Fifth Palenque Round Table*, 1983, 1985, San Francisco: Pre-Columbian Art Research Institute.
http://www.mesoweb.com/pari/publications/RT07/XocOCR.pdf

Matthiesson, Peter. Blue Meridian: *The Search for the Great White Shark.* New York: Penguin Nature Classics, 1971.

Moore, Charles. "Across the Pacific Ocean, Plastics, Plastics, Everywhere." *Natural History* magazine, Vol. 112, No. 9. (Nov 03) http://www.mindfully.org/Plastic/Ocean/Moore-Trashed-PacificNov03.htm

Pepperell, Julian. *Fishes and the Open Ocean: A Natural History & Illustrated Guide.* Chicago: The University of Chicago Press, 2010.

Raffaele, Paul. "The Brains Behind the Jaws: Why Great White Sharks Are Smarter Than We Think," *Smithsonian* magazine, June 2008. http://www.smithsonianmag.com/science-nature/great-white-sharks.html

Shwartz, Mark. "Great White Sharks Migrate Thousands of Miles Across the Sea, New Study Finds." *Stanford Report*, Jan. 9, 2002. http://news.stanford.edu/news/2002/january9/sharks-19.html

______"Looking into the Mind of a Shark" *Watermarks*, Magazine of the National Aquarium, Summer 2009.

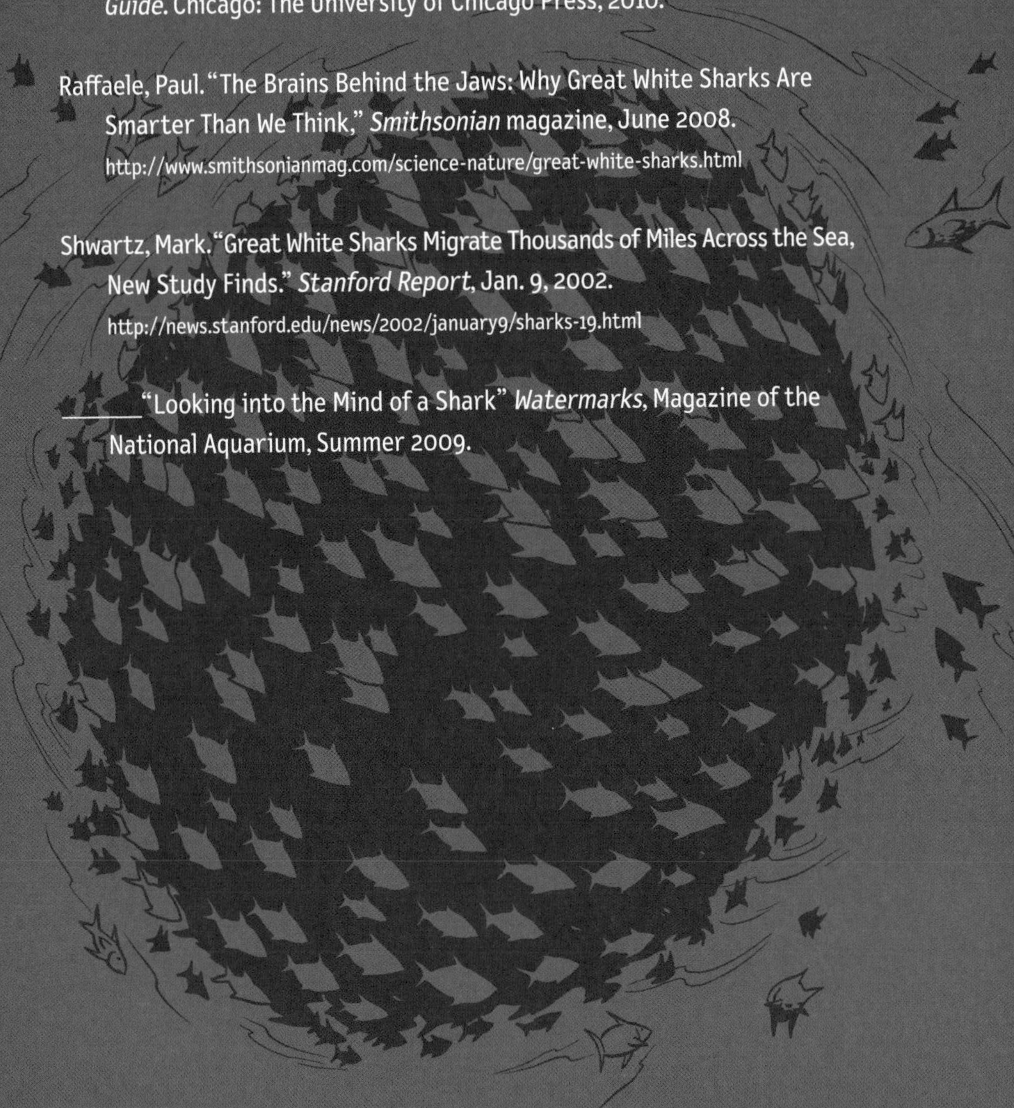

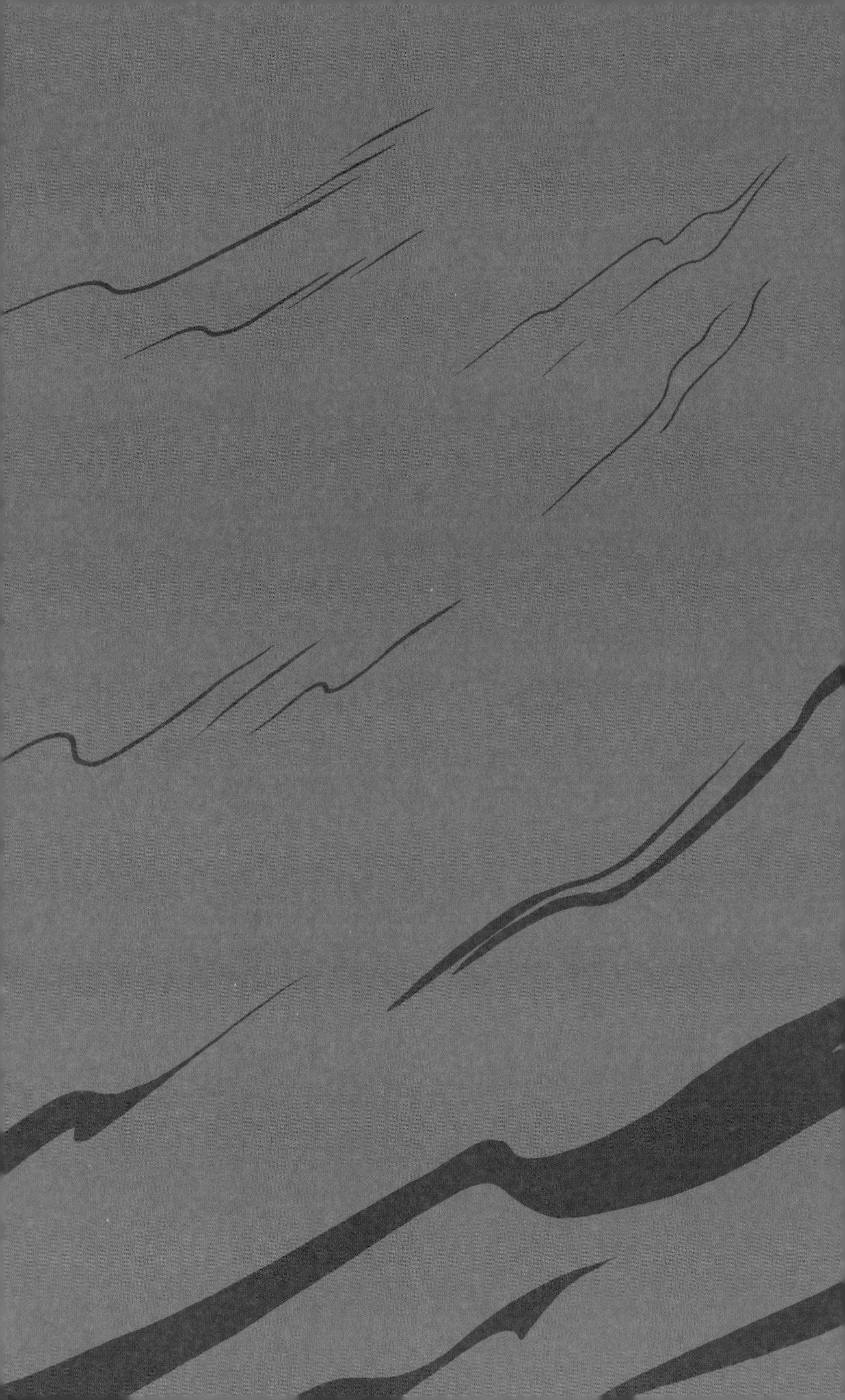

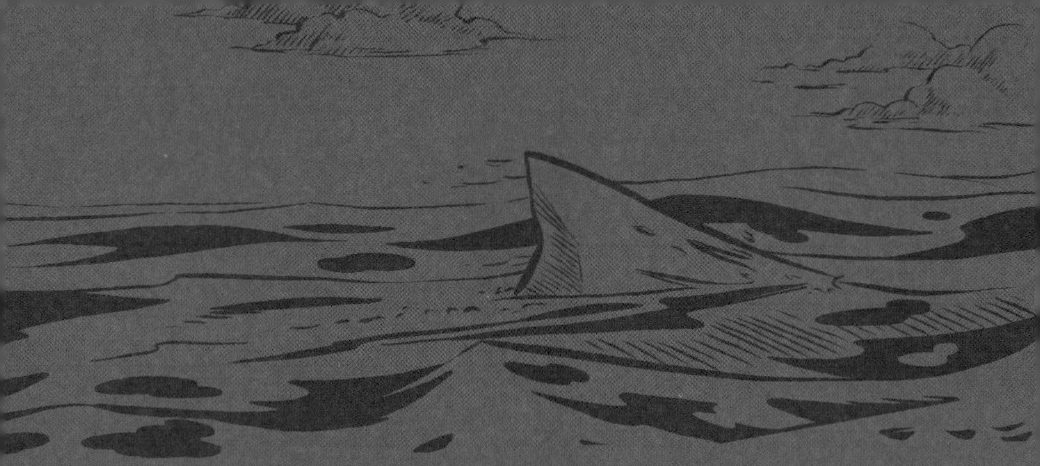

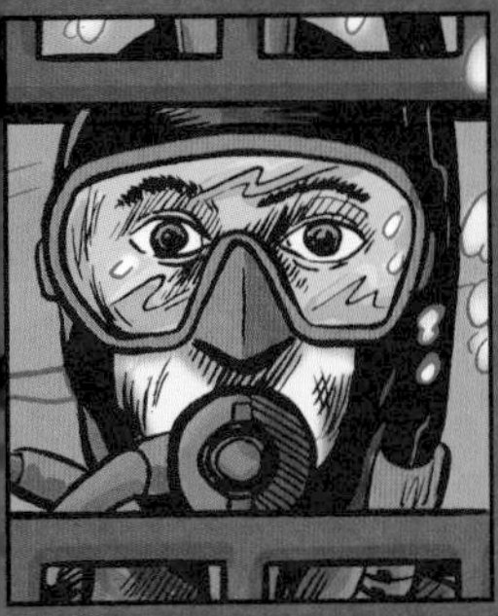

MATT DEMBICKI lives in the Washington, D.C., area with his wife and two boys. He has contributed to numerous anthologies, including Eisner-nominated and Aesop Prize-winning **Trickster: Native American Tales: A Graphic Collection**, which he also edited. His other works include the nature parable **Mr. Big** (which he co-wrote with his wife, Carol), as well as numerous self-published minicomics. He is also a founding member of the D.C. Conspiracy, a comics creators' collective in the nation's capital.

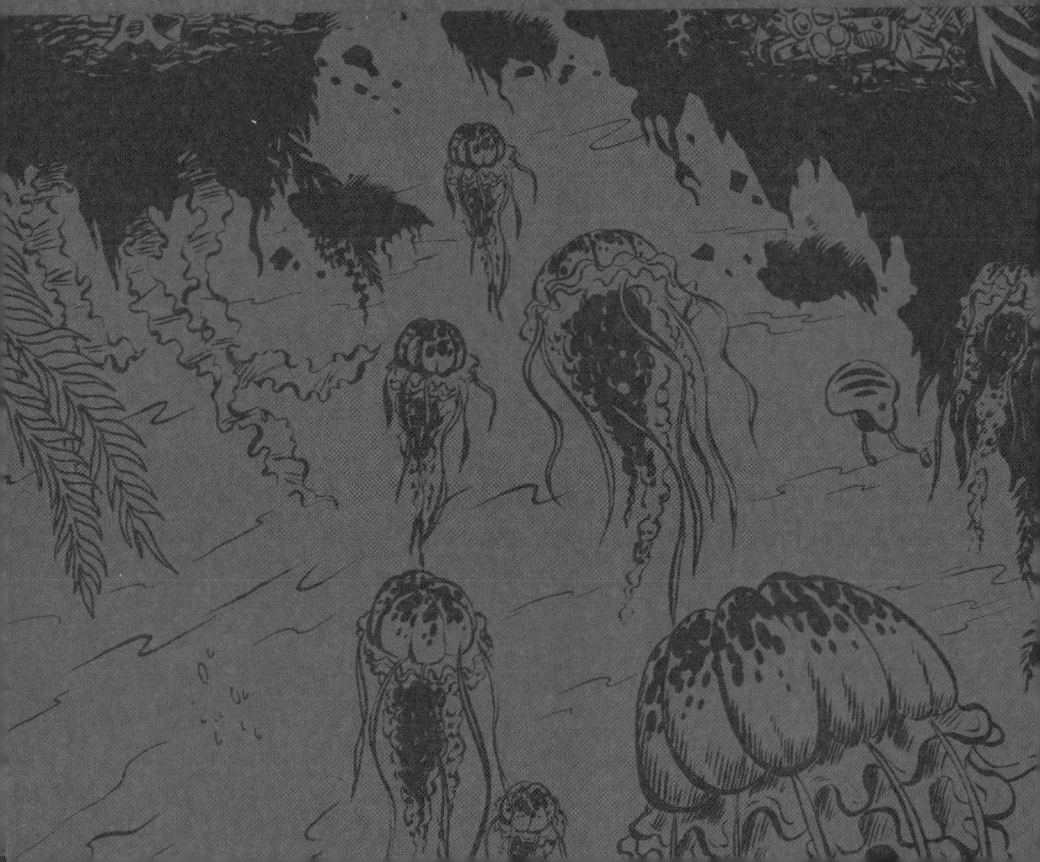

ALSO BY ONI PRESS!

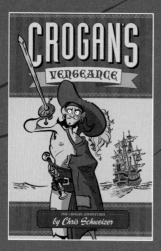

CROGAN'S VENGEANCE
Chris Schweizer
192 pages • 6"x9" • Hardcover
B&W • $14.99 US
ISBN 978-1-932664-35-4

FIRST IN SPACE
James Vining
96 pages • 6"x9" • TPB
B&W • $9.99 US
ISBN 978-1-932664-64-5

LOLA
J. Torres & Elbert Or
106 pages • 6"x9" • TPB
B&W • $14.99 US
ISBN 978-1-934964-33-0

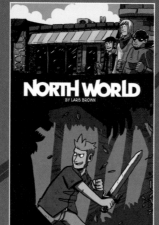

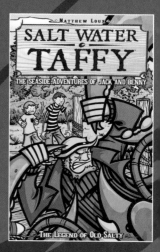

NORTHWEST PASSAGE
Scott Chantler
272 pages • 6"x9" • TPB
B&W • $14.95 US
ISBN 978-1-929998-80-7

NORTH WORLD, VOL. 1:
THE EPIC OF CONRAD
Lars Brown
152 pages • Digest
B&W • $11.95 US
ISBN 978-1-932664-91-1

SALT WATER TAFFY, VOL. 1:
THE LEGEND OF OLD SALTY
Matthew Loux
96 pages • Digest
B&W • $5.99 US
ISBN 978-1-932664-94-2

REVOLUTION**ONI**ZE COMICS
www.onipress.com

For more information on these and other fine Oni Press comic books and graphic novels, visit www.onipress.com.
To find a comic specialty store in your area, call 1-888-COMICBOOK or visit www.comicshops.us.

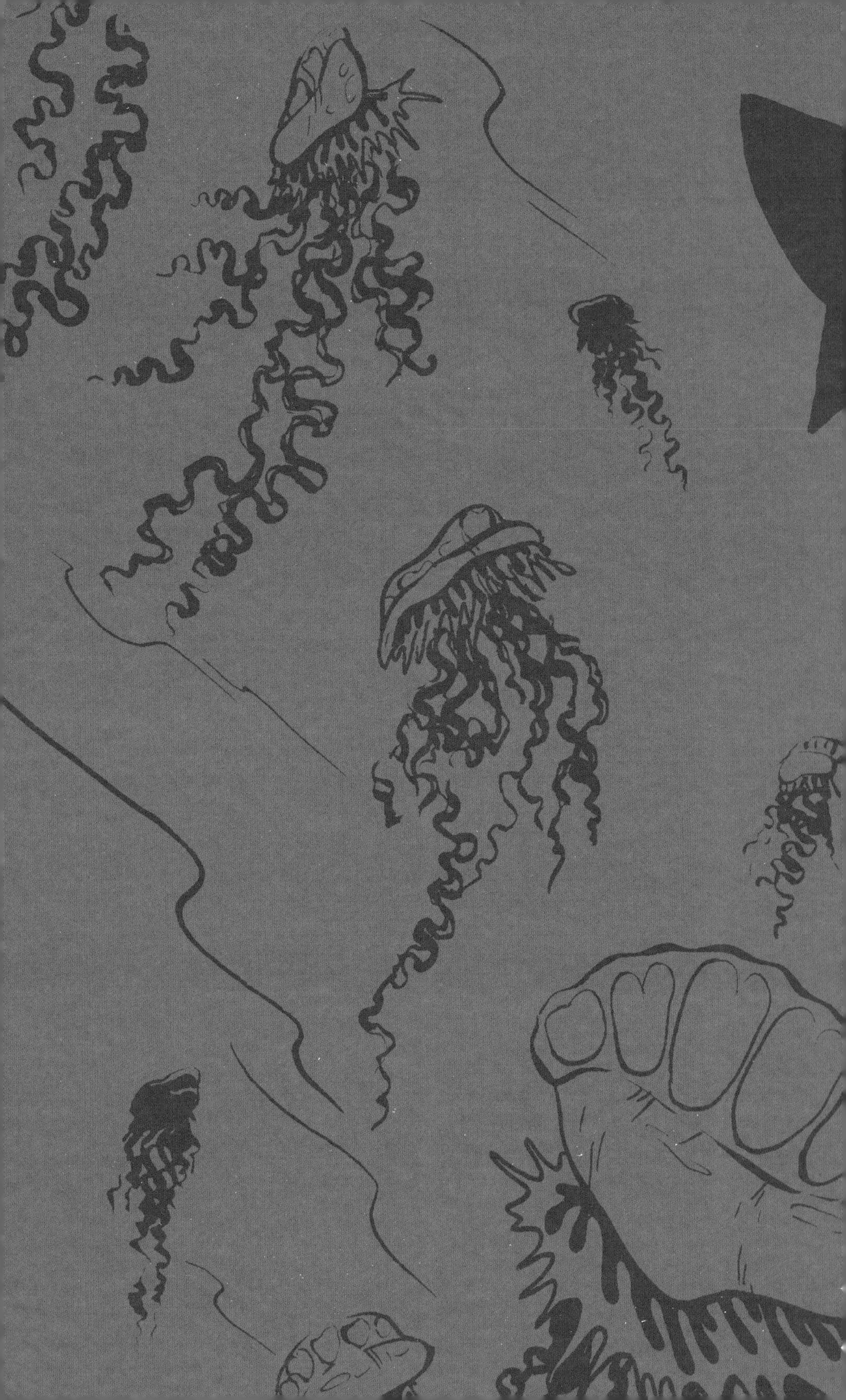